An Intimate Ghost

An Intimate Ghost

ELLEN HART

ST. MARTIN'S MINOTAUR ❧ NEW YORK

www.minotaurbooks.com

Library of Congress Cataloging-in-Publication Data

Hart, Ellen.
    An intimate ghost / Ellen Hart.—1st ed.
      p. cm.
    ISBN 0-312-31747-6
    1. Lawless, Jane (Fictitious character)—Fiction. 2. Women detectives—Minnesota—Minneapolis—Fiction. 3. Caterers and catering—Fiction. 4. Hallucinogenic drugs—Fiction. 5. Minneapolis (Minn.)—Fiction. 6. Weddings—Fiction. 7. Lesbians—Fiction. I. Title.

PS3558.A6775I47 2004
813'.54—dc22

                                                  2003062545

First Edition: March 2004

10   9   8   7   6   5   4   3   2   1

For my two Big Boys, Thomas Gibson
and Friedrich Reeh, with much love.

And welcome to earth, Little Isaac!

Cast of Characters

Jane Lawless—Owner of the Lyme House Restaurant in Minneapolis.

Cordelia Thorn—Creative Director at the Allen Grimby Repertory Theater in St. Paul.

Alden Clifford—High school history teacher. Mary's husband. Nick's father.

Cullen Hegg—Sophomore at Evergreen High School. Burt's son. Steven's brother. Good buddy of Lukas and Wesley.

Mary Clifford—Dramaturge at the Blackburn Playhouse. Alden's wife. Nick's mother.

Lukas Pouli—Junior at Evergreen High School.

Steven Hegg—Sophomore at the University of Minnesota. Cullen's older brother. Burt's son.

Burt Hegg—Cullen and Steven's father.

Gray Donovan—Lawyer. Nick Clifford's best man.

Lauren Bautel Clifford—Real estate agent. Nick's new wife.

Jason Vickner—Prep cook at the Lyme House.

Cecily Finch—Friend of Nick's and Gray's. Aspiring actor.

Kenzie Nelson—Lauren's home health aide.

Wesley Middendorf—Junior at Evergreen High School.

Brittany—Jason's girlfriend.

Tom Moline—Teacher at Evergreen High School.

The truth must dazzle gradually,
Or every man be blind.

—Emily Dickinson

Cottonwood, Kansas

Halloween 1972

Jimmy wasn't in the mood to take his little sister trick-or-treating. For one thing, most of his buddies were waiting for him at the local pizza shop in town. If he didn't show up with the weed, he'd get blamed for spoiling everyone's fun. Jimmy Shore was pissed off and fifteen. He felt like he'd lived his entire life inside an empty box. Nothing happened in Cottonwood. Not unless someone made it happen. And that's what Jimmy was good at. Making stuff happen.

Jimmy couldn't wait to grow up and leave Cottonwood behind, lead his own life somewhere exciting, a place where what he did was nobody's business but his own. In a small town, it was hard to keep a secret, although Jimmy had managed to keep a whopper. The danger he lived with daily made him feel alive in a way nothing else ever had. He wrapped himself around the feeling, plugged himself into it as if he were an electric cord and the danger was his power source.

The entire night had been planned. Mike was supposed to get his hands on some beer. Judd said his dad had some red paint in the garage that they could use on old man Tigen's fence. Sam would bring the toilet paper, and Arty the eggs. The girls would be waiting at the south end of the park. When they were done raising hell, they could raise a different kind of hell with each other. So what if they got in trouble? At least it brought some drama to their lives. Jimmy knew it was all kid stuff—well, except for the drugs. Weed and speed were his major claim to fame. LSD was more of a problem, though Jimmy could get just about anything he wanted these days. He'd become a regular walking pharmacy.

But as Jimmy was headed out the door, the sky fell in. His old man told him th

he'd been called in to work an overtime shift at the plant. Jimmy's mom had the flu. So that left Jimmy as the only one who could take Patsy trick-or-treating.

Jimmy prided himself on being a hard-ass, but he loved his sister. The sight of her standing in front of the mirror in her bedroom, checking out her pink satin fairy costume with the fluffy pink wings, melted his heart. Patsy was only eight. Too young to be interested in the stuff Jimmy was interested in. She hated dolls, but she loved dressing up in silly costumes. He didn't want to see her disappointed. And anyway, it wouldn't take that long to walk her to a few houses. His buddies wouldn't leave without him because he had the weed, so he figured he could let Patsy wander around for an hour or so, then he'd bring her back home, sit her in front of the TV, and tell her to count her booty.

Pushing Patsy out the door, the two of them walked slowly through the blue twilight to the edge of the gravel driveway. Patsy was all squirmy and giggly, so Jimmy decided to calm her down by telling her a ghost story. It was her favorite. He'd made it up one hot summer night while they were lying in the grass looking up at the stars. As they walked along the edge of the road, he could tell when she really started to listen because she took hold of his hand.

There was once a little girl who got lost in the big woods east of town and couldn't find her way out. She looked and she looked and she looked, but everywhere she turned, she just saw more trees. The sun was setting fast and she was starting to get scared. People said ghosts lived in the woods, but they only came out at night. What the little girl didn't know was that the longer she stayed lost, the more likely it was that she'd turn into a ghost herself. And if that happened, she could never go home again, never play with her toys or sleep in her bed or eat ice cream cones from Bellmont's Drugstore.

Patsy was all big-eyed now, listening to Jimmy spin his tale. He figured it was kind of hokey, but Patsy never seemed to mind. He told her that after the little girl had walked around for a long time, she spied a tree with a door in it. She rushed up to it, but couldn't decide if she should open it. Finally, screwing up her courage, she touched the handle. She was immediately sucked into the darkness. Hands poked at her, voices whispered that she was a silly little girl and that she wouldn't ever leave the forest alive. She got down on the floor and crawled back toward the door and finally, after the third push, she tumbled out into the night. She got up and ran away from the tree as fast as she could. She kept running all night and when the sun came up in the morning, she found the road that led her home.

Jimmy could feel Patsy's sigh of relief. She always sighed at that point, even though she knew the ending. He had to finish the story fast because they were

4

coming up to the first house. He told her that when the little girl finally got back to her home, nobody could see or hear her. Her mother and father walked right through her as if she were invisible. Because the little girl had spent the night in a forest crawling with ghosts, she'd become a ghost herself. Only her brother could tell when she was in the room. Sometimes he'd sit out on the front porch at night listening to the crickets, and she'd sit next to him. But it wasn't like before, when she was a real little girl.

"Couldn't her brother save her?" asked Patsy, pressing her hands into the folds of her crinoline wings.

"He wanted to," said Jimmy. "But what could he do? A ghost is a dead person. Dead people don't come back to life."

"He should make some magic," said Patsy, gazing up into her brother's eyes. "Or she should. Maybe ghosts have special powers."

"Yeah, well, maybe they do. Who knows?"

"Can I go knock on the Van Gelders' front door?" She looked over her shoulder at the first farmhouse on the edge of town. Directly across from them was a field.

Jimmy bent down and straightened her fairy wings. "Go for it, sis."

As she scampered off, he stood and watched the door open and an old woman drop several pieces of candy into Patsy's sack. Mrs. Van Gelder was a major talker. Jimmy kicked a stone around while he waited for the conversation to end. Hearing the sound of a car starting, Jimmy glanced to his right and saw a van pull out of a stand of trees. It came to a stop directly across the road from where he was waiting.

Shit, he thought, recognizing the van. He silently cursed his bad luck.

Two men got out and stood next to the back fender.

Jimmy smiled at the tall, thin one. "Hey, Frank. What's up?" He trotted across to them.

"You tell me," said Frank, chewing on a toothpick.

Jimmy spotted the shoulder holster under Frank's leather jacket. He backed up a couple of steps.

Before he could slip too far away, Frank clamped a hand over Jimmy's shoulder. "I want the money, Jim. Hear me? Now."

Jimmy's smile grew strained. "I don't have it with me."

"Okay. Why don't we give you and your sister a ride back to your place? We'll wait outside while you go get it."

"But, see, I don't keep it there."

Frank's eyes turned into tight slits. "Just tell us where to go and we'll take you."

"I, ah . . . I'll meet you tomorrow. Outside Picket's Standard Oil."

"You think I'm retarded? Huh? You already stiffed me once. I gave you an extra two weeks and now I want my money."

"Honest, Frank. If you'll just let me have until tomorrow, I'll meet you at the gas station. Promise."

Frank leaned down and breathed his foul breath into Jimmy's face. "But I want my money tonight, kid. Comprende?"

"I . . . need a couple more days." He couldn't exactly tell him that he'd, well, sort of borrowed some of the money. He figured a little creative finance couldn't hurt. But he'd taken too much. He tried to raise the prices on what he was selling, but he hadn't made the money back yet. He needed more time.

"Now," said Frank.

"I can give you half of it tonight, then . . ."

Patsy skipped across the road. "Look what Mrs. Van Gelder gave me." She held up her sack and tugged on Jimmy's hand.

Jimmy grabbed her and pulled her behind him. "Just be quiet."

"Look, Jim, we made a deal," said Frank. "You knew the rules and you broke them. Maybe you're using the stuff yourself, or you're stealing from me. Either way, it don't work."

"But I can explain." Before he knew what was happening, Frank had spun him around and slammed him against the side of the van. His head cracked against the hard metal as the door handle bit into his back. Frank's hand pressed against his throat. Jimmy could hear Patsy crying.

"We're talking serious cash here, Jim." Frank tightened his grip. "You know what I do with little boys like you when they mess with me?"

"I don't have it," Jimmy gasped. "If you could just give me—"

"I don't give you nothing," said Frank. "You wanna know what I think?"

Jimmy tried to shake his head.

"I think maybe you got the money but you're holding out on me. Playing me for a sucker."

"No, that's not true!"

Frank nodded to his friend. "Get the girl."

"No!" screamed Jimmy, trying to squirm away. "Leave her alone."

"Maybe I take her for a few days, see if you change your mind."

"Let her go. I'll get you the money. I promise."

Frank looked at him hard. He seemed to be thinking about something. Whipping out his gun, he pressed it under Jimmy's chin as the taller man picked Patsy up. He cupped his hand around her mouth to stifle her screams and tossed her into the back of the van.

"Your time's up, asshole," whispered Frank, pushing the gun harder into Jimmy's soft flesh.

Jimmy was trembling so hard he could hardly stand up. "What are you going to do?"

"If I can't get my money one way, I'll get it another."

May 2003
Evergreen High School
Evergreen, Minnesota

Alden Clifford stood at the head of the class, about to begin his lecture on the Cuban missile crisis, when Cullen Hegg entered the classroom through the rear door. Cullen was rarely late for fourth period, so Alden was a little surprised to see him sneak in. He wore a long black raincoat over his black T-shirt and jeans. Instead of sitting down, he slumped against a filing cabinet at the rear of the room, chewing on the inside of his cheek. Alden could tell by the spacey look in his eyes that he was high on something.

"Cullen, why don't you take your seat?" Alden kept his voice calm. His instincts told him to tread carefully.

Cullen's eyes darted around the room. Everyone in the class was looking at him. With every passing second, his expression grew darker, more moody.

"You tie one on last night, Hegg?" asked Brandon Alquist. He snickered. The other students laughed—and kept on laughing.

"Shut up," muttered Cullen. "All of you, just shut the fuck up."

A small shiver of dread rolled through Alden's chest. "Cullen, I'd like to talk to you out in the hall." He came around his desk and stood next to the door at the front of the classroom.

Cullen didn't move.

Alden nodded to a girl in one of the front seats. "Leah, I need you to run down to the office and get—"

"No!" shouted Cullen. "Nobody leaves." He pulled a gun from the pocket of his jacket. It was a casual movement, but Alden could see Cullen's hand shake.

A gasp went up from the students. One girl screamed.

"It's a toy," said Brandon Alquist, his voice full of disdain.

Cullen fired a shot. Plaster exploded from the ceiling. "That sound like a toy, asshole?"

Alden caught the turned-on, almost self-congratulatory look in Cullen's eyes, a look that frightened him almost more than the gun.

A ringing silence descended on the room.

Outside in the hall, people were running, shouting, trying to figure out what was happening, where the shot and the scream had come from. The assistant principal appeared at the door and looked in. Alden gave his head a stiff shake, hoping the guy would get the message and back off.

"Cullen, give me the gun," said Alden, returning his gaze to the young man at the back of the room. "Come on. Don't screw with your life like this."

"Like you're so pure. Like you've got the right to tell me what to do," he muttered.

"*Think* about this, Cullen."

"I am. I *have*."

"Then let your classmates leave, okay? You and me . . . we can talk about whatever's bothering you."

"The way we did the other night?"

All the kids in the classroom turned to stare at Alden now. He felt their terror, and a kind of confused accusation.

"It's all your fault," shouted Cullen. "I wouldn't be in this mess if it weren't for you."

Alden tried to clear his head and think. He had to act to diffuse the situation, but how? Every kid in the room was in danger as long as Cullen had the gun. Alden had been a teacher for almost twenty years. Of course he'd seen all the reports on TV about school shootings, but he never expected a kid with a gun to show up in his classroom. "Listen to me. If your beef is with me—"

Cullen glared at him.

"—then let your classmates go."

"I hate you all," shouted Cullen, looking around without actually focusing on anyone in particular.

Two girls next to the wall started to get up.

"Sit down," he ordered, pointing the gun at them.

The school alarm bell went off. Through the window in the door, Alden saw security guards gathering. Kids rushed past the room in the growing pandemonium.

Inside the classroom, it was deathly quiet.

Taking a few steps toward the back of the room, Alden said, "Look, Cullen—"

"Sit down and shut up. I have to think." He ran a hand over his short brown hair, adjusted his glasses. "Sit the fuck down!"

Alden backed up to his desk and perched on the edge. "Tell me what you want! Tell me what I can do!"

Cullen edged over to the door and looked out. Ducking down and pivoting, he said, "Alquist, go out there and tell those guys that I've got a gun. Anybody tries to get in here, they're dead." He turned to another kid. "Sperling, find some paper and tape and cover the door windows. Do it fast, man, or you're my first casualty."

Boyd Sperling got up slowly, looking at Alden for permission.

Alden nodded.

Several of the students started to whimper.

"Shut up," demanded Cullen. He slumped against the filing cabinet again, staring sullenly at the tip of the gun. "I don't want to hear a word out of any of you, got it? No noise. No talking."

The students' attention returned to Alden, their eyes pleading with him to *do* something.

An hour later they were still there, still at an impasse. Cullen had rebuffed all of Alden's efforts to get him to open up and talk. After yanking the classroom phone out of the wall, Cullen had moved to the windows overlooking the football field and that's where he'd stayed.

From his position at the desk, Alden could see what Cullen saw. The field crawled with cops and press. Cameramen with handheld video recorders focused on the building. Onlookers had been cordoned off behind the far bleachers. A helicopter had been flying overhead for the past half hour.

Half a dozen of the kids had cell phones with them. As they went off, Cullen confiscated them and when they rang again, he seemed to take great pleasure in stomping on them with the heel of his black work boot.

Through a loudspeaker, the police tried to open up a dialogue, but Cullen refused to communicate. Alden could tell he'd been thinking hard about something, though with whatever was in his system, he couldn't be processing clearly. Cullen wasn't a thug, even though he was behaving like one. He was a troubled kid. But sometimes one person's troubles leaked into other people's lives with terrible results.

At exactly two-thirty Cullen stood up. "Get out. Everyone. Just get the hell out."

The students were too scared to move.

"Did you hear me? I said *leave*."

"Go," urged Alden. He rose from his desk.

"Sit down, Clifford." Cullen pointed the nine-millimeter at Alden's chest. "You're staying."

In less than a minute, the room had cleared.

As the kids burst out the side door of the school, a roar went up from the football field.

From his position at the back of the room, Cullen said, "It's just you and me now." He sat down on the floor and pulled his knees up to his chest.

"What are you going to do?" asked Alden. Adrenaline drilled through his body like a jackhammer.

"I haven't decided."

"Why did you bring the gun?"

"Why do you think?"

"To scare people. To scare *me*."

"Wrong." His face was a sullen fist of anger.

"You're so young, Cullen. Don't do this. Listen to me. *Please*. Let's just talk about it."

"Why do you care so fucking much?"

"You know why."

"Do you love me, Clifford? Really love me?"

That stopped him.

"I'm so sick of feeling alone. Nobody cares, not really. Nobody's ever going to care."

"You're depressed, Cullen. You can get help for that. We've talked about it."

"I'm *not* depressed, I'm fucking sick and tired of being galactically stupid! If anybody ever finds out what I've done . . . God, I couldn't stand it." He mashed a hand against his right eye, tears starting to form. "I feel like my brain's rotted clear through."

Carefully, Alden got up. "I can help."

"Right. Like you've already helped."

"I can get you out of here, make sure nothing happens to you. You're a juvenile. You haven't hurt anyone."

"Like you'll keep my secret."

"Will you keep mine?"

Cullen looked up at him.

"What do you want from me?" asked Alden. "Just tell me what I can do."

"Nothing."

"Then give me the gun. Let's stop this right now."

"Stay there. Don't come any closer."

"Why did you bring the gun, Cullen? Really."

"You already asked me that."

"But you didn't answer." Alden thought he knew the answer, and it sickened him.

"I went home for lunch. My dad was there, so I waited until he'd left for work and then I took it from his closet. I thought . . . hell, I don't know what I thought. I just wanted to look at it. Feel it in my hand. And then, it was time to get to class."

Alden kept moving toward the back of the room. Slowly. One step at a time. "You came here for a reason. What was it?"

Cullen shrugged. "Putting off the inevitable, I guess."

"I do care about you, Cullen. I care about you more than you know."

The young man's smile was almost wistful. "You taught me a lot. I guess . . . maybe I do think you care. That's why I came. I thought maybe you could stop me. But you can't. I see that now. Nobody can." Lifting the gun from his lap, he looked up at Alden.

"Give it to me."

"Sorry."

"Cullen, don't do it. There's another way."

Alden lunged at him but he was too far away. Before he got halfway across the room, Cullen had racked the slide, shoved the gun in his mouth.

And pulled the trigger.

Six Months Later
Late October
Evergreen, Minnesota

2

The hour before sunup was the worst. Alden lay in bed, his wife sleeping peacefully beside him. At this time of day, he nearly always found himself struggling to make sense of what had happened. Ever since the day Cullen Hegg died, people had called Alden a hero, said he'd saved the life of every kid in that classroom. He'd kept his cool and hadn't acted rashly, hadn't provoked a seriously disturbed young man to further violence. His actions had helped to avert an even greater tragedy.

Seconds after Alden had walked out the front door of Evergreen High, the press had descended like a thunderstorm, strobes flashing, newsmen and -women shoving microphones in his face, cameramen vying for better angles. All he could remember from those first few moments was that he'd covered his face, bent down, and forced his way through the crowd until the police caught him and stopped him. They'd led him to one of the classrooms on the first floor to begin their interrogation. It wasn't really an interrogation, he supposed, it was more on the order of a debriefing. Every cop he talked to was polite, even respectful. But it had gone on for hours.

Once he'd done his civic duty, once he'd explained the afternoon's events in minute detail, he'd finally been allowed to leave. He'd made his way through the crowd one more time. Friendly faces—parents or other teachers—patted him on the back, tried to shake his hand. Everybody seemed to want a piece of him.

From that day on, Alden had refused all interviews. Every time he saw his face on CNN or discovered a picture of himself in the newspaper, he cringed. Ted Koppel had even called him personally to ask him to come on his show as part of a panel discussion on violence in the schools, but Alden politely declined the invitation. He wasn't a hero. He thought people threw the term around way too easily. When people called him heroic, it made him sick inside. He knew the truth, even if nobody else did.

Even now, six months after Cullen's death, the press continued to hound him. His reticence only fueled their interest. They chased his son, Nick, around for comments, called his wife, Mary, hoping to get her to open up about her hero husband. Mary couldn't understand why Alden didn't just go with the flow. After all, he'd behaved admirably. Why not enjoy his five minutes of fame?

What he couldn't tell her, or anyone else for that matter, was that he was scared to death. Pandora's box had finally been opened. It was only a matter of time before the ghouls came tumbling out.

The early-morning light was beginning to bleed through the window shades. Alden turned and pressed himself close to Mary, breathing in her warmth as if her body gave off certainty. If he stuck close to her and kept his head down, maybe everything could still be okay.

Closing his eyes, his thoughts drifted back to the first day of class in September. Alden had taken a young man aside, a kid named Lukas Pouli. Lukas had been a friend of Cullen's. He was a junior this year in Alden's third-period American History class. Alden carefully explained that anything Lukas wanted to tell him would be held in the strictest confidence— that Lukas could trust him. Alden wanted him to know that *if* he had some of the same problems that Cullen had been dealing with before his death, Alden was there for him. He only wanted to help.

Lukas was one of those strange chameleon types, a kid who could adopt whatever form his audience demanded. Alden had never liked him, though that wasn't the issue. Alden had hoped that Lukas would open up to him, but instead, Lukas told him that he wasn't sure what Alden was getting at, but that everything in his life was just fine and dandy. And that was a mistake. No adolescent boy was ever fine and dandy. It was possible Alden had misinterpreted what he'd seen, but he doubted it. Alden could usually spot a kid who was in trouble.

Mary stirred in bed next to him, but didn't wake. Once again, Alden tried to shut his eyes and go back to sleep, but it was no use. His stomach felt raw, like he'd eaten industrial corrosive for dinner last night instead of spaghetti. Sitting up in bed, he grabbed his robe, pushed his feet into his slippers, and headed into the bathroom. After downing several gulps of Maalox and then giving his teeth a good brush, he went downstairs to start the coffee brewing.

In the late fall, the old farmhouse turned cold and drafty. Pools of chilly air drifted across his bare ankles, making him wish he'd put on a pair of socks before leaving the bedroom. The winter wood delivery had come yesterday, so maybe he'd start a fire in the woodstove in the sunroom. Take the chill off the place.

On his way through the front hall, he glanced out the frosted oval window in the front door to see if the bird feeder was empty. Coming to a full stop, his body froze at the sight of a motorcycle parked on the dirt road leading up to the yard. Leaning against the cycle was a man dressed entirely in black—black leather jacket, motorcycle chaps over black jeans, black leather gloves, thick boots—arms folded across his chest as he gazed at the house. The sleek, modern lines of the full-face helmet made the stranger look like a character in a Schwarzenegger movie. Dangerous. Not quite human. His identity hidden behind the tinted visor. Who the hell was he? thought Alden. And what was he doing out there?

Alden kept an old .38 in a box on the shelf in the front closet. He and Mary were well past the kid stage, so the box wasn't locked. Opening the closet door, he reached up, checked quickly to see that the clip was full, then pressed it into the pocket of his robe and opened the front door.

When he stepped out onto the porch, he figured the biker might take off, but he just sat there, the morning sun glinting off his visor and hitting Alden square in the eyes.

"This is private property," called Alden, shading his eyes from the reflection.

The biker didn't move.

"Tell me what you want or get the hell out of here." He planted his feet firmly on the porch floor. Alden was a big man—six feet two, 190 pounds stripped. He'd used his size to intimidate more than one person in his past. The biker was thin, slight. He could be a kid or a small man.

"Who are you?" demanded Alden.

The biker's casual stance suggested a total lack of concern.

Alden stepped off the porch and walked a few yards into the hoar-frosted grass. He breathed in deeply, feeling the raw bite of dying vegetation fill his nostrils. "You want to leave quietly or do I call the police?"

"Honey," called Mary from the porch. "What's going on? Is that a friend of yours?"

He turned to look at her. She was so beautiful with her long copper-colored hair dangling around her shoulders, still flushed and warm from their bed. "Get back inside. I'll handle this."

"But, honey—"

"Do what I say. Shut the door and lock it." He didn't know what the biker represented, but whatever it was, he wanted Mary safe and out of the way.

She hesitated, but finally disappeared inside.

There were a good twenty yards between the biker and him. Alden figured he had maybe sixty pounds on the guy, but since he couldn't see the face, the age difference might make up for it. Of course, Alden had the .38.

"It's just you and me," said Alden. He waited this time, trying to stare the guy down, sensing that behind the tinted plastic, the eyes were as cold and blank as the visor.

Suddenly the biker's hand dipped into his jacket.

Alden pulled his gun and trained it on the man's chest. "Careful, pal," he said, moving a few feet closer. With a weapon in his hand, he felt more sure of himself. "Take off the helmet."

The biker lifted his hands into the air.

"Did you hear me, asshole? I said take it off."

Very slowly, keeping one hand in the air, the biker reached into his jacket again. He pulled out what looked like a piece of jewelry on a chain. He tossed it into the dirt. Moving carefully and deliberately, the man swung a leg over the seat and kick-started the engine. Touching a hand to his helmet, he turned the cycle around and roared off down the drive.

Alden walked over and crouched down to look at what he'd left behind. It appeared to be a cheap gold locket, nothing he recognized.

When he opened it and saw the picture inside, his heart fluttered and nearly stopped. After a full minute of staring into the familiar face, he dropped to his knees.

Looking up at the cloud of dust, all that was left of the biker, he screamed, "Get the hell back here and show me your goddamn face!"

Two Weeks Later
Friday Night
Twin Cities

3

Something had gone wrong. As Jane rocketed across town to the home where her catering crew was working an evening wedding, all she knew was that a call had come for her at the restaurant. It took half an hour before one of her staff had finally delivered it. The message asked her to get over to the Donovan mansion on the double.

It was a busy Friday night at the Lyme House. Jane was jumping from hot spot to hot spot, expediting orders in the kitchen, greeting guests in the second-floor dining room, restocking the pub downstairs, stepping in and working the line while one of her chefs had a momentary meltdown.

The wedding in Wayzata was a small event, not more than fifty people were expected to attend. The bride and groom had asked for a buffet instead of a formal dinner, which made the prep and presentation even easier. Jane couldn't imagine what had gone wrong. No, that wasn't entirely true. She could imagine a million things that could go wrong, but her crew had worked hundreds of catering jobs over the years. She had confidence in their ability to handle anything that came up. So why the S.O.S.?

As she sped out highway 394 in her new Mini Cooper, the car a nostalgic sop to her years growing up in England, she called her catering manager for the third time, but he still wasn't answering. Instead of panicking, she took a moment to recall the details of the affair.

Alden and Mary Clifford had come to her in late August to ask if the restaurant would cater their son's wedding in early November. Jane had known the Cliffords for years, partly because they always celebrated their wedding anniversary at the Lyme House, but also because Mary Clifford worked periodically as a guest dramaturge at the Allen Grimby Repertory Theater in St. Paul. Jane's best friend, Cordelia Thorn, was the creative director at the theater.

Jane had been delighted to put Nick Clifford's wedding banquet on the schedule. She liked the Cliffords enormously. Nick was in his late twenties, the manager of an athletic club in Burnsville. His best buddy, Gray Donovan, was the son of Earl Donovan, president of Donovan Industries—hence the use of the Donovan mansion in Wayzata for the wedding.

Shortly after eight, Jane rolled her Mini into the circular drive. Cars were parked two and three abreast, but no valet seemed to be on duty. As she got out, she could hear the sound of a lone trumpet playing an agonizingly slow, heartbreakingly sad rendition of "American Pie." Not exactly dinner music. The wedding was to take place at five, cocktails and hors d'oeuvres at six, and dinner to follow shortly thereafter.

The house, a modern wood and steel structure that looked like a series of blocks stacked haphazardly to form an L, was perched atop a hill facing Lake Minnetonka. The lawn swept down to a private dock. In the back, near the tip of the L, was the pool. Jane had been given a tour of the place in September when she'd driven out with her catering manager to look at the facilities. But that was during the day. At night, the house looked even more impressive. The tallest flank of the building was covered by a bold pink and blue neon sculpture, one that was meant to look like a sailboat, but in reality looked more like an upside-down ice cream cone with arthritic elbows. The house glowed, every window ablaze with light.

Snaking her way through the jumble of cars to the steps that led up to the front door, Jane was surprised and a bit baffled to find three of the guests lying in the frozen grass, gazing up at the stars. She knew they were guests because they were all wearing tuxedos. She was about to say something when she heard a moan, and then a woman cry out. Whirling to her left she found a man and woman, stripped to their underwear, going at it like, well, like rabbits. She grinned and shook her head. Not your typical Minnesota wedding.

The front door was open, so she walked in, nearly tripping over a woman sitting, or more accurately cowering, on the floor in the center of the entrance hall.

"Is something wrong?" asked Jane.

The woman cringed. "Are you . . . *her?*"

Jane cocked her head. "I don't know. Maybe."

"If you were *her,* you'd know."

"Well then, I guess I'm not."

The woman squeezed her eyes shut and looked away.

Jane was beginning to get an idea of why her crew manager had called. On her way to the great room, she noticed two men standing by a hanging fern, picking off the leaves one by one and watching them float to the oriental carpet.

"Hi," said Jane. "Can one of you tell me where I can find Nick Clifford?"

They ignored her.

"Alden Clifford, then. Or Mary."

"I think Nick's taking a dip in the pool," said one of the men, his voice so soft Jane wasn't sure she'd heard him correctly.

"Ah . . . I doubt that," she said, pushing her hands into the back pockets of her jeans. "It's November. The pool's been drained."

"You don't know that for *sure,*" said the other man indignantly.

Following a burst of laughter into the kitchen, Jane finally found the female contingent of her crew. Two were sitting on the floor in the dark, their backs against the counters. The other was dancing around the center of the room—or doing Yoga exercises. It was hard to tell.

"What's going on?" demanded Jane. She could see the buffet table through the double doors. The food was pretty much gone.

Emily, the woman closest to the door, looked up at her with a serene smile. "There's a funny smell in this room, Jane."

"What happened here? Where's Otis?" Otis Wells was Jane's catering manager.

"I'm a *nutritional* snack," said the woman next to Emily. She scrutinized the ash end of her cigarette as if it contained the secret of eternal youth.

Jane didn't know whether to laugh, get angry, or be scared.

Determining that these women were too far gone to give her the information she needed, she entered the great room. With the exception of two men in tuxedos stacking champagne glasses on top of each other at a far table, the room was empty. But not for long. Two cops strode through the open double doors.

"Jesus," said the shorter officer, a woman with short-cropped blond hair. "What the hell happened here?"

The other officer, a burly middle-aged guy with a thick mustache, zeroed in on Jane. "Are you straight?"

He didn't realize it, but for Jane, it was a loaded question. "Yes," she said. "More or less."

"What happened?"

"I don't know. I just got here."

"Whose wedding is it?" he asked, looking around at the dregs of the dinner meal.

Jane had no idea where the guests had gone, but from what little she'd seen, she figured they were probably scattered throughout the house, exploring the wonders of each other's navels. "Nick and Lauren Clifford's."

"Where's—" The woman officer slipped a pad out of her pocket and flipped it open. "Earl Donovan, the owner of the house?"

"I think he's vacationing in the Florida Keys," said Jane. "His son, Gray, is the groom's best man."

The male cop pushed his hat back on his forehead, scratched his brown stubble. "I'm runnin' back to the squad car. I gotta call this one in, see what they want us to do."

The woman nodded. As he walked off, she studied Jane for a moment. "You a friend of the family?"

"Something like that."

"Our dispatcher got a call from some guy who said the food had been spiked with hallucinogenics. You're lucky you didn't get here for dinner. Otherwise you might be doing the nasty out on the front lawn with the family dog." Hooking her thumbs around her belt, she turned to the buffet table. "I'd hate to be the owner of the company who catered this affair."

Jane's throat felt like sawdust. "Yeah, me too."

As the woman cop ambled over to examine the guy crooning his sad memorial to the death of rock and roll on his silver trumpet, Jane decided to check the pool area. On the off chance that the man denuding the fern had been right, maybe she'd find the bride and groom out there.

30

Passing a woman enraptured by the miraculous workings of a light switch, Jane stepped onto the back patio. All the chairs and chaise lounges had been covered with tarps in preparation for winter. There were fewer windows on this side of the building, so she had to squint into the darkness to get her bearings.

Jane recalled that the pool was recessed into the hill about fifty feet or so down from the side of the house. It was open toward the lake, but enclosed on two sides by a concrete retaining wall. As she approached, she saw that Lauren was standing knee-deep in dried leaves in the deeper section of the pool, moonlight slicing across the shallow end.

Lauren caressed the nosegay of white roses in her hand. She was humming softly, moving through the leaves as if she was in a trance.

Jane paused by the pool steps.

"I feel like I'm flying," called Lauren.

"Lauren, it's Jane Lawless. I think you should come in the house. You must be cold." But just like the other members of the wedding party, the bride seemed to be in a world of her own.

Stretching out her arms, Lauren began to twirl. "Come on in, honey. The water's fabulous. Better than fabulous."

Jane turned just as Nick Clifford stepped out of the shadows and walked out to the end of the diving board.

"No!" screamed Jane. "Stop! Nick, stop!"

Nick's feet were already together. Raising his arms above his head, he did a perfect swan dive, plunging headfirst into the pool.

4

For the next few hours, Jane felt as if she were swirling in the midst of a cyclone. Paramedics arrived to take Nick to the hospital. As he was being lifted from the pool, Lauren became hysterical. The EMTs wanted to sedate her, but because they didn't know what drugs she'd taken, all they could do was talk to her and try to calm her down.

While waiting for the paramedics to arrive, Jane had searched every room in the mansion looking for Nick's parents. They didn't deserve to hear news like this from a stranger. But to her dismay, Alden and Mary were nowhere to be found. Neither was Jane's catering manager. Of the fifty people invited to the affair, only a couple dozen still remained in the house.

Jane stood on the patio and watched Nick being wheeled away. Her eyes burned with tears as she absorbed the shock of seeing him in a body brace, blood streaming from a gash near his left eye. He was alive, but until the doctors got a look at him, nobody would know how badly he was injured.

Just as the back doors on the ambulance were closing, a police detail arrived to comb the neighborhood for missing guests. Inside, another detail was already securing the kitchen area. Until matters could be sorted out, the cops were treating the house as a crime scene.

Jane headed out to her Mini as soon as the ambulance left. She wanted to follow Nick to the hospital, try to find out some information about his condition. Just as she was about to get into the front seat, a light-colored SUV roared past her, nearly taking the Mini's door off.

"Hey!" she screamed, wrenching her body backward to get out of its way. She squinted hard at the license plate, but all she could make out before the car disappeared into the night were the first three letters: M-E-E. The driver was probably high as a kite. If he'd been three inches closer, she could have ended up plastered like a stain to the rear fender. Unsticking her heart from her throat, Jane slid into the front seat and started the engine. She looked up at the moon for a few seconds, then put the car in gear and headed off for North Memorial.

The full horror of the situation was just beginning to sink in. She would certainly be sued. She had no facts, no hard evidence to prove that her catering company hadn't spiked the food. Surely Alden and Mary wouldn't think she had anything to do with it, and yet someone had to pay. If Nick lived, the medical bills could be astronomical.

Breathe, she told herself. Just breathe.

Grabbing her cell phone, Jane punched the number for her dad. Raymond Lawless had been a criminal defense attorney in St. Paul for almost thirty years. Although he'd recently retired, he still kept a hand in at his firm. When his voice mail picked up, Jane gave him a quick snapshot of what had happened and asked him to call her as soon as he got the message. Next, she called Cordelia, remembering as soon as the line started to ring that Cordelia was at the governor's mansion tonight. She'd attended the wedding, but had to leave before dinner to make it to the "gala at the gov's" as she'd been calling it. Thank God, thought Jane. At least she was safe.

Jane arrived at the hospital just after ten. Before she went inside, she checked her look in the visor mirror, scraping the tear marks away from her cheeks. She took a second to repin her long chestnut hair back into a smooth bun. She'd cut it short a while back, but found that it was more trouble short than it was long. Wondering why the hell she was thinking about her freaking hair at a time like this, she stared into her eyes, deciding if she looked as scared as she felt.

The emergency-room lights blazed as she passed the waiting room and headed to the main desk. Clearing her throat, Jane knocked on the glass to get the receptionist's attention. She introduced herself, explaining what had happened at the wedding reception, adding that she was the owner of the company that had catered the affair.

The woman looked at her with undisguised pity. "Mr. Clifford has been admitted."

"I assumed that. But do you have any further information? Is he going to be all right?"

"He's being prepped for surgery. That's all I can tell you."

"What about the wedding guests? Some of them were brought here as well."

"They're being looked at, Ms. Lawless. Sorry I can't give you more specific information. It's against hospital policy. You could speak to the head of the ER, but he's pretty busy right now. I'm sure you understand."

In other words, *get lost*.

Jane thanked the woman. As she passed by the waiting room on the way back to her car, she glanced in to see if she recognized anyone. There, seated in one of the back chairs, was Otis Wells. His head was tilted back against the wall, eyes closed.

Jane couldn't believe her good luck. She slipped quickly into the chair next to him. "Otis?"

He opened his eyes, turning his head to look at her. "Oh, God," he said, running a heavy hand over his face.

"Are you okay?"

He blinked a couple of times. "Did anyone tell you about the Cliffords' wedding dinner?"

"Yes, I know."

"Jane, you gotta believe me. I had nothing to do with it. Swear to God."

"I believe you."

"I mean, what the hell happened?"

"You ingested some kind of hallucinogen."

"No shit."

Otis Wells was in his late forties, a burly guy with a badly pockmarked face. He was an ex-hippie who still wore his hair in a long ponytail. He'd worked for Jane for nearly eight years. She'd trained him personally. Otis liked to work hard and play hard and he didn't deal well with nine-to-five routine. That's why catering suited him.

"How did you get here?" she asked.

"I drove," he said, leaning forward and resting his elbows on his knees. He rubbed the back of his neck, then shook his head, as if he were trying to clear the cobwebs from his brain. He was still wearing his catering uniform—black slacks, white shirt, tweed vest, and red bow tie.

"Are you sure you're okay?"

"Yeah, but that stuff was *intense*. It was like, one minute we were serving dinner and the next, everything just started to shimmer. Somewhere in there I heard a woman shout to call 911. That's when I called the Lyme House. But, like, the room was filled with rainbows, Jane. I got so psyched. And then I must have wandered off. I don't know." He rubbed his neck again. "The colors were so amazing. Everything was just so freaking *meaningful*, like, I could see the walls *breathing*."

"Do you have any idea what it was?"

He shrugged. "LSD?"

"Have you ever tried LSD before?"

"Sure. Once or twice."

"Was this like being on LSD?"

He thought about it. "Similar, but different. Don't ask me how. I'm in no condition to explain it."

"What was it like at the house? Did people freak out?"

"Not when I was there. But then, I think I left pretty quick. I remember walking down the street with this guy in a tux. Can't remember what we talked about. Then I sat by the lake for a while. Nearly froze. That's why I climbed a tree. Heat rises."

"Not think-tank logic, Otis."

He shrugged as he examined the bloody gash on the inside of his arm. "That's how I got this. I thought somebody should look at it."

"Ouch."

"I imagine it would hurt a lot more if I wasn't still sort of high." He gave a disgusted grunt. "Trees and me never did get along."

Jane sat back in her chair and looked around. "So, let me get this straight. The wedding took place at five, as planned."

"Yeah."

"You'd served the hors d'oeuvres and champagne at six."

"Right. I assigned four people. The rest of us prepped the buffet table for the dinner following."

"Nobody was acting weird until . . . when?"

"Well, it was toward the end of dinner, when the bride and groom were cutting the cake. I started to notice that people were getting up from the tables and just kind of drifting out of the room. Walking zombies, you know? Then more and more. That's when I started to lose it."

"Did you eat any of the hors d'oeuvres?"

"Sure. I imagine everybody did."

"How about when you were making the food? You ate it then, too, right?"

"Yeah."

"But it didn't affect any of you?"

"Not that I know of."

"So, maybe you ate more of it tonight?"

"Oh, for sure. You know how it goes. When we're prepping it, we just take small bites to make sure it's seasoned right. When we're at the affair, we usually each have a plate of food, whenever we can squeeze it in."

"So you ate larger quantities."

"Yeah. Absolutely."

Jane had one last question. The most important. "Do you have any reason to believe someone on the crew tampered with the food?"

He shook his head. "No way. Not my people."

"Excuse me," said a voice from behind Jane.

She turned to find a blond man in blue scrubs standing over her.

"Are you Jane Lawless, the owner of the catering company?"

Rising from her chair, she said, "Yes?"

"I'm Dr. Chandler, chief of ER. I was hoping we could talk for a few minutes." Glancing at Otis, he added, "Privately."

Jane cracked open a beer and leaned against the counter in Cordelia's kitchen. It was going on midnight.

Cordelia stood by the wall of windows in her fifth-floor loft, looking down on the electrified anthill that was downtown Minneapolis. She was still dressed in her favorite black evening gown, the one with the plunging neckline and sequins from shoulder to ankle. "Ms. Va-voom!" as one local newspaper reporter had recently called her. Cordelia was six feet tall, well over two hundred pounds, and had an energetic, plus-sized persona that she could use like a laser beam. Think Sappho meets Danielle Steel, Jane once told someone, and you got the picture.

Cordelia was clearly stunned by the news Jane had brought with her. "You mean, Nick just jumped right into the empty pool?"

"Like it was a summer day. He was still in surgery when I left the hospital. If the leaves hadn't broken his fall, he'd already be dead."

"In surgery for what—specifically?"

"They wouldn't tell me."

"God in heaven, poor Mary and Alden. You never found them?"

Jane shook her head.

"And you have no idea who mixed the joy dust into the food?"

"If that's what really happened, no. No idea." She took several swallows of beer, then held out the hand holding the can. It was shaking so hard, the beer was in imminent danger of going flat. "I reached the pool just seconds before Nick jumped. It all happened so fast."

Cordelia adjusted the sound on the stereo, then draped her Rubenesque form dramatically across the couch. The muted voice of Ella Fitzgerald pumped out the blues in the background. "Far be it from me to make this all about *moi,* but boy am I glad I missed dinner. I realize those words rarely pass my lips, but in this case——"

"I hear you," said Jane.

"I mean, usually, your food is so good."

"Cordelia!"

"I didn't mean that the way it came out. I just meant——"

"You said what everyone is probably thinking. That some freak on my catering crew decided to get his jollies by adding a few funny mushrooms to the rice pilaf. Except, I know all those people. They've worked for me for years. None of them would do something that idiotic. Even so, I'm not looking forward to facing Nick's family. Or the police."

"Want me to talk to Mary? I do, after all, employ her occasionally."

"What are you suggesting? You think you can order her not to sue me for every penny I'm worth?"

"It's a thought."

"I'm not going to hide, Cordelia. It wasn't my fault." Jane downed several more gulps of beer. "I mean, maybe I'm catastrophizing here, but this is serious, not just for Nick and his family, but for me too. Not only does this put my catering company in jeopardy, but my restaurant as well."

"Because of potential lawsuits."

"Exactly."

"But you carry tons of insurance. You have to, right?"

"Yes, but there were fifty people at that wedding. How far will it go if they all come after me?"

"Earth to Jane. Come in, Jane! That's not going to happen."

"Easy for you to say. And what if the worst happens? What if Nick dies? There's a chance his death could be ruled a homicide. If the police think I'm responsible for serving him the drug that led to his death, I could be arrested—charged with murder!"

"Manslaughter," said Cordelia, adjusting the neck on her sequined gown. "Unless they can prove intent. Of course, there's always 'depraved indifference.'"

"Gee, thanks for that clarification. I feel so much better now."

"But you know, Janey. You really shouldn't jump to conclusions. Nick may turn out to be just fine. Just a broken leg or something. Even if it's more serious, doctors do amazing things today. And maybe the rest of the wedding party all had good trips."

"From your mouth to God's ears."

"Yes, that's frequently the way it works." Cordelia shot Jane her best "buck up" look.

Before leaving the hospital, Jane had talked with Dr. Chandler, the head of ER. She was anxious to get an update on Nick's condition—as well as the rest of the wedding party—but he proved to be as tight-lipped as the receptionist. Instead of providing information, he wanted to know if Jane had access to the wedding guest list, and if so, could she fax it to him asap. Jane recalled that Mary had included a sheet of paper that might have been a tentative guest list with an early note about food choices. Jane offered to run back to her restaurant and see if she could find it. Chandler seemed pleased and a little surprised that she was willing to be so cooperative. And that told her loads about where he placed the blame for the wedding dinner fiasco.

Sitting down on a fake velvet bench in Cordelia's living room, a "borrowed" prop from one of the Allen Grimby's many productions, Jane finished her beer. She was just beginning to realize how exhausted she was.

"Janey, stay put, okay?" said Cordelia, rising from the couch. "Don't think I'm not still listening or that I'm not appalled, but I've got to do a little cleaning up while we talk. My Mildred Pierce Cell is meeting tomorrow night." She began to bustle around her apartment, organizing books and scripts into neat piles, tossing cat toys into a basket, picking up discarded clothes, jewelry, wigs, shoes, a feather boa here, a fringed shawl there.

The cell meeting she referred to was a group of theater pals who had initially been drawn together by their joint adoration for the old movie *Mildred Pierce,* starring Joan Crawford. They eventually formed a group that met once a month, ate lots of great food, and then watched an old black-and-white flick from the forties on Cordelia's humongous TV.

Jane found the sight of Cordelia hustling around the loft oddly soothing. It was an anchor of normalcy in an otherwise insane evening. She grabbed another beer from the fridge, then sat back down on the bench. The interior of the loft had been changed since her last visit. Gone was the Egyptian faux. In its place Cordelia had installed a kind of Bloomsbury-bourgeois faux. Velvet and terra-cotta, uncomfortable Victorian furniture, and even more plants than normal. Cordelia's massive book collection along with various stacks of scripts only added to the bohemian image. Virtually anything could fit into the loft's thirty-two hundred square feet.

"You could hide a 747 in here," said Jane.

Cordelia was at the far end of the room, flinging more junk into a different box.

"What? You want to hide in a 747?"

Jane repeated the comment again, only this time she shouted.

"Well, not quite. But if the carousel at the fairgrounds ever goes missing, you'll know where to look. Don't stop talking, Janey. My hearing is as acute as Roderick Usher's. Is that allusion too esoteric for you?"

"I've read as much American literature as you have. He was the central character in Poe's 'The Fall of the House of Usher.' But . . . wasn't his hearing acute because he was insane?"

"In pain?" repeated Cordelia. "Of course he was in pain. The dead people around him wouldn't stay dead."

Jane decided to wait until Cordelia returned to the part of the loft she'd recently begun referring to as "the drawing room." This wasn't a conversation, it was the verbal equivalent of the Keystone Kops.

Cordelia was a true theater rat. The dead of night was her time to boogie. Mornings were another matter. As she so often pointed out, she didn't *do* mornings. With all due homage to Stephen Sondheim, she considered herself the personal embodiment of "the music of the night."

"What am I going to do?" asked Jane, sounding as glum as she felt.

"Get sued," said Cordelia, returning to the drawing room carrying the heavy box. She set it on the couch, then turned around, hands on her hips.

"Thanks for the vote of confidence."

"That's what insurance policies and lawyers are for. Call your lawyer in the morning. Let her handle it. And wipe that guilty look off your face. If you act like you were responsible, people will assume you are."

"That's the whole point, Cordelia. To stop feeling guilty, to rescue my catering company and my restaurant from malicious slander and myself from total bankruptcy, I've got to figure out what really happened."

"Then find a good PI. Here, I'll get you the yellow pages."

40

"Forget it, Cordelia. I need to do it myself."

She groaned. "Did anyone ever tell you that you're your own worst enemy?"

"I'm sure you have once or twice."

"Well, it's true. You see the potential to become involved in some new sticky situation and it's like . . . *sign* . . . *me* . . . *up!*"

"Look, nobody is going to be as interested in getting to the bottom of this mess as I am. Ergo——"

Cordelia bugged out her eyes. "Don't 'ergo' me."

"When this hits the news, just think what it will do to business. People will stop eating at the restaurant because they'll be afraid they'll get poisoned."

"Or," said Cordelia, holding up her pointer finger, "an entirely new class of people might start showing up. Wigged-out druggies hoping they'll get a little free blow in their Yorkshire pudding. It could actually turn out to be a financial boon."

"Cordelia!"

"Chill *out!*"

"I can't."

She stared at Jane for a moment, then flung her arms in the air and returned to her cleaning frenzy. She was down on her hands and knees now, removing dusty magazines and empty cereal boxes from under her favorite chair. "This place is a pit. Life is sure a mixture, isn't it? One minute I'm at the governor's mansion being wined and dined and the next I'm the charwoman."

"Hey, how did the dinner go?"

"What can I say? The gov digs me big time." She sniffed, then sneezed. "He wants me to head a new state arts council."

"Great. Will you do it?"

"As long as it doesn't interfere with my vacation. The next month is mine, Janey, all mine. I haven't had any significant time off in years. Marion and I already have our tickets to Italy."

Marion Vinsetto, a published poet and the owner of Marion's Muffler Shop in Northeast Minneapolis, was Cordelia's newest girlfriend.

"We leave in two weeks. We'll rent a car and drive down the Amalfi coast. I shall be in hog heaven, dearheart, eating pasta in out-of-the-way little trattorias, sipping Nocino, adding to my collection of majolica."

"I'll write you from prison."

"And you think *I'm* a drama queen?"

"Just work with me here, Cordelia. Help me analyze this for a second. Then I promise, we can talk about Italy."

"Oh, all right," said Cordelia, fishing more junk out from under her chair. "I'm listening. But I think you're blowing this all out of proportion. The police will figure out what happened and you'll be off the hook. End of story."

"If only it could be that easy." Jane took a moment to pull her thoughts together. "I figure that whoever slipped the hallucinogen into the food was trying to disrupt the wedding. Our mystery man—"

"Or woman."

"Our mystery *person* must not have cared if someone got hurt. I mean, most of the people I saw were just giggly, doing things that were relatively harmless. So, the drug, whatever it was, wasn't a chemical that caused people to totally freak out. On the other hand, when you're dealing with a substance that plays with your mind and your perception of reality, anything can happen. So, again, the only conclusion I can come to is that whoever planted the drugs must not have cared. And in my mind, that makes that person dangerous."

"Or stupid." Cordelia whipped off her shoe and began pounding the floor with the heel. "God, I hate it when wildlife sneaks into my apartment."

Jane cocked her head. "Wildlife?"

"A spider."

"Spiders aren't *wildlife*."

"Of course they are."

Jane jumped at the sound of a knock on Cordelia's front door.

"Who on earth is that?" grumbled Cordelia, heaving herself to a standing position.

"If it's Marion," said Jane, taking a last swallow of beer, "I'll make myself scarce."

"Stay put," said Cordelia, brushing the dust off her glitzy gown as she marched across the room. Flinging open the door, her jaw dropped when she saw who'd come to visit.

"Octavia," said Jane, rising from the bench. It was Cordelia's sister. Her sister who lived in *Connecticut*.

"What are you doing here?" demanded Cordelia.

Octavia, wearing Jackie O sunglasses and a floor-length fur, turned to her right and waved. An older woman carrying a sleepy toddler in her arms appeared.

"What's going on?" said Cordelia, eyeing her sister suspiciously.

"Is that any way to greet weary travelers? We've come for a visit," she announced with a triumphant smile, lifting the child from the arms of her nanny. Taking in Cordelia's sequined evening gown, she added, "Are you about to leave or just getting home?"

"Would it matter?" Cordelia glanced at all the luggage stacked behind them in the hall. "I hope you brought a staff of twelve to bring all that stuff in here."

Octavia's smile was like the Mona Lisa—pregnant with secrets.

Jane hadn't seen Octavia in over two years. She didn't seem to have changed much. She was still a fashionista, still as beautiful as ever—and as unpredictable.

"I thought it was about time you met your little niece," said Octavia. "Cordelia, this is Hattie Thorn Lester. Hattie, meet your auntie Cordelia."

The little girl took one look at Cordelia, covered her face with her hands, and burst out crying.

6

Hattie's nanny, a slight but imposing older woman named Valenka Ivanova, whisked her off to a guest bedroom at the rear of the loft. After an assortment of tired cries and muffled sobs, Hattie quieted down, and so did Valenka. Jane assumed that the two of them had settled in for the night.

Cordelia had chosen to keep the loft entirely open, closing individual spaces off with standing screens that she could rearrange whenever the spirit moved her. The loft was more of a theater set than a place of real human habitation, although Cordelia had made it a comfortable space, when the odd piece of prop furniture didn't fall apart. The trick was to know which furniture was real and which was just for show. For Jane, it was a running battle.

Because the ceilings were fifteen feet high, the only room that was walled off was a loft bedroom, one that had been built onto a six-foot-high platform. It all worked remarkably well for a space that had once been part of a rug factory.

Jane watched Cordelia and Octavia move around the room, sizing each other up like two prizefighters about to beat each other bloody. Both Jane and Cordelia were in their early forties. Cordelia was seven years Octavia's senior. They'd never been close, but two Christmases ago they'd achieved a certain rapprochement. From the looks of things, it hadn't lasted. Jane had known both Thorn sisters since she was sixteen. Octavia's main complaint was that she felt constantly criticized by her older sister. In Cordelia's defense, Octavia had made some bad decisions over the years. She always tried to make amends, but it was often a case of too little, too late. Cordelia's position was that whenever Octavia showed up, it was because she wanted something. Neither trusted the other, no matter how hard they tried to make nice. Paranoia seemed to be a part of their genetic makeup.

Jane had to agree with Cordelia this time. It *was* strange for Octavia to just arrive completely uninvited, especially this late at night and with a small child in tow. But that was Octavia. She was almost as impulsive as Cordelia. The sisters insisted they were nothing alike, but Jane thought they were two peas in a very weird pod.

Octavia had been the toast of the New York stage for many years, starring in hit after hit and winning two Tony Awards. Quite suddenly two years ago, she married Roland Lester, the famous director from Hollywood's Golden Age. Lester had been eighty-three at the time. Little Hattie was Lester's child, though he'd died before she was born.

Doing her best Joan Fontaine imitation, Octavia affected a familiar pose: a brave smile that hinted at dire secrets. She exuded a sort of tragic stoicism as she glided about the room in her Prada pumps, cashmere cardigan and slacks, dripping in Cartier. "So, Cordelia . . . Jane . . . how are you? You both look wonderful. Jane, how's that restaurant of yours?"

"You picked the wrong day to ask."

"I did? Well, I'm sure you just had a busy evening. But that's good—good for business. What about your leg?"

"It's much better, thanks."

"And your . . . how did that policeman friend of yours refer to your mental state?"

"Post traumatic stress," said Jane, folding her arms over her chest. "I've been seeing a therapist."

"Is it helping?"

"I think so."

"Are you taking medication?"

"That too."

"Good. Good." Passing a mirror, Octavia stopped to check her hair and makeup. She was, as always, flawlessly turned out. Jane didn't know if the blond hair was natural anymore. As a child, Octavia's hair had been platinum, almost white. And her skin had the creamy golden glow of clover honey. Cordelia, on the other hand, took after their father. Her hair was auburn—curly—and her skin color was tinged with olive.

"Cut to the chase," grumbled Cordelia. She had retreated to the drinks cart and was preparing a martini shaker with ice, gin, and vermouth.

"What chase?" replied Octavia, looking wounded.

"Just get it over with. Tell me why you're here."

"Isn't it enough that I wanted you to meet your little niece? Correct me if I'm wrong, Cordelia, but you don't have any other nieces out there, do you? This child is likely to be the only one you'll ever have, so I would think she'd be special, even for someone who's notoriously *not* fond of children. Given time, Hattie will learn to love you, just as I do."

Cordelia snorted. "*That's* what I have to look forward to?"

Octavia picked Blanche up off a chair and cuddled her in her arms. Cordelia's oldest cat was a pushover for affection. Blanche had little in the way of feline aloofness, which Cordelia always saw in the blackest of terms. She'd been named for Blanche DuBois in *A Streetcar Named Desire.* As far as Cordelia was concerned, she took after her namesake, relying entirely too much on the kindness of strangers.

"Hattie will be rested in the morning," continued Octavia, running a perfectly manicured hand down Blanche's back. "It will be a different story then. You'll see. Say, I forgot to tell you. I just bought the most beautiful place overlooking Central Park. You'll have to come visit sometime soon."

Cordelia eyed the stack of expensive luggage piled in the middle of the drawing-room floor. Surrounding it were shopping bags from Bergdorf Goodman, Tiffany & Co., Saks, and Lord & Taylor. It looked as if someone had belched Fifth Avenue. "Okay. We'll make this simple. We'll take it one step at a time. Creep up on it, so to speak. Now, if you would kindly cast your thoughts to tomorrow evening, would you perhaps still be here?"

"Why, yes," said Octavia, sitting down at a stool next to the cart.

"And the following night? When I come home from . . . wherever, will I find you here again?"

"I should think so."

"Ah ha!" cried Cordelia, picking up the martini shaker and thrashing it wildly. "You're hedging."

"Hedging?"

"Just tell me the bad news up front. You can't need money so it has to be something else."

"You make me sound totally manipulative."

Cordelia narrowed her eyes. "Don't play with me, sweet pea, otherwise I'll toss you, the rug rat, and the Russian dowager *out*."

Octavia held up both hands. "I'm just here for family solidarity. Honestly. I simply thought it was time you met Hattie. I have some time off right now. You mentioned on the phone the other night that you did too. I hoped we could spend a little of it with you. That's it, Cordelia. If you don't want us to stay, I'll call my travel agent in the morning and arrange for a flight back to New York. I don't know how I'll explain it to my daughter. She's been looking forward to meeting you for *such* a long time."

Cordelia was about to strain the liquor into the glasses, but stopped. "Correct me if I'm wrong, but the kid's only a year old."

"A year and eight months. And she's very precocious. She can already pick your photo out of the family album I made for her. She calls you 'Deeya.'"

Cordelia stretched her mouth into a smile. "How precious." She flashed her eyes at Jane. "Isn't that precious?"

"Precious," said Jane.

"Yes, I thought so, too," said Octavia, rummaging through a bowl of salted nuts on the cart until she came across a pecan.

"There you have it," said Cordelia. "We all agree. But what do you *want*, Octavia?"

"A martini and an intimate heart-to-heart with my dear sister and her best friend. I don't think that's setting our sights too high. Do you?" She turned to Jane. "You'll stay for a while, won't you?"

"Well, I—"

"Good," said Octavia, returning her gaze to Cordelia. "Is this great or what? All of us together again. Just like old times."

7

Steven Hegg felt like a jerk for not calling his dad. As he raced down Fulbright Avenue behind the wheel of his rusted '84 Corvette, he berated himself for his selfishness.

Not that his father would ever blame him. Steven could see the pathetic scene in his mind's eye. He would walk in the front door. His dad would be sitting in the living room watching some stupid TV show. The sound would be switched off. The house would be silent. His father would have a drink in his hand, warming himself by the glow from the TV screen as if he were sitting in front of a roaring fire. He would look up, smile at Steven, never mentioning that Steven had failed to show up for dinner as promised. Oh, his dad might say something like, "There's a cold casserole in the fridge, Steven. Help yourself." No guilt would be attached, just the fact that the food was there. His dad took everything on the chin these days, like he expected the world to hurt him.

Steven was sick of hearing his father tell him that he shouldn't worry about his old man, that he should get on with his life. Have a good time. Enjoy being a young college guy. What kind of a heartless bastard would he be if he enjoyed himself while his dad rotted away alone in an empty house? This had been the single worst year of Steven's life, and yet he knew that he would survive it. His father was a different matter.

Burt Hegg was drowning. Everyone could see it. He would never recover from Cullen's death because he blamed himself for it. Oh, he didn't say those exact words out loud, but Steven knew. Steven's mother had died when he was nine, Cullen was six. From that point on, his father had tried to be both mother and father to his boys. He'd worked himself silly at his crummy middle management job so that he could have his evenings and weekends free. Taking care of business and raising his sons had been Burt Hegg's whole life. He'd given it his best shot, but ever since Cullen's suicide, he'd apparently decided that his best wasn't good enough.

Steven slammed his fist into the steering wheel. He turned up the volume on the rap station he'd been listening to because he needed something loud and raw to blow the static out of his brain. The whole situation at home drove him nuts. His father was the last person on earth who should blame himself for Cullen's suicide. If anyone was to blame it was Steven. *He* should have seen it coming. He knew his brother was depressed, but he thought Cullen would work through it in time. Cullen had always been too sensitive for his own damn good. Not monitoring his brother more closely had been Steven's mistake. Sometimes his guilt was so intense, it was all he could do to just hold himself together. Cullen would never have confided in their dad, but he would have talked to Steven—*if* Steven had been around more. "Too freakin' busy being 'The Big Man on Campus,'" he muttered, feeling the bitterness inside him well up hot and sour in his throat. He might have let Cullen down, but he wasn't going to make the same mistake with his dad.

Steven took a quick right onto Bendix Lane, then pulled into the driveway behind his father's Ford Explorer. Since his brother's death last spring, Steven had spent at least two weekends a month at home. He was in his second year at the University of Minnesota, but hadn't declared a major yet. Lately, he'd been thinking that if he could keep his grades up, he might try to get into med school. He liked helping people. Actually, he felt he had a natural gift for it.

Scraping his boots on the mat outside the front door, Steven entered the silent house and walked into the living room. The scene he'd imagined had been dead-on. His father sat in the old brown La-Z-Boy at the far end of the room, a bottle of Bud in his hand, the TV across from him turned on with the sound on mute. His father hated ads. He'd turn the sound off, then get lost in thought and forget to turn the show back on.

"Hey, son," he said, holding up his beer and smiling, "glad you could make it."

Steven could tell by the slight slur in his dad's voice that he was tight. He'd been drinking too much lately, though Steven was the last person to preach.

"If you're hungry, Stevey, you'll find a meat loaf in the fridge. I did a big one so we could make sandwiches tomorrow. It's your mom's recipe."

Steven removed his coat and tossed it over a chair. "Thanks, but I'm not hungry."

"No, well, then help yourself to a beer." His eyes dropped to the cordless phone resting next to him on a TV tray.

Steven sat down on the couch. "I'm sorry I'm late, Dad. I—"

"No excuses necessary. You're a busy man these days. I understand. How are your classes going?"

"Fine."

"You still like your professors okay?"

"For the most part."

He nodded. "Good. That's good."

"And how's work?" asked Steven, mostly to keep the conversation going. He and his dad didn't always have a lot to say to each other.

"Ugh," he said, smoothing the back of his thinning brown hair. "The same as usual."

After Cullen's death, his dad had taken a leave of absence from his company. He'd stayed away so long that his boss had finally threatened to hire someone else to do the work unless Burt returned immediately. Steven had been at the house the night his father's supervisor had stopped by. The man was a prick. Steven didn't even try to be friendly. The supervisor started by saying that he felt sorry for Burt. He understood that it had been a hard time for him and his family. But business was business. And life goes on. Without Burt at the office doing his job, his department was falling behind. It was time he either came back or quit.

Since Steven's father didn't have any other means of support, he had no choice but to return, even though he'd lost all interest in his job, as well as most everything else in his life.

As a kid, Steven often pictured his dad as sort of a Viking warrior. He was always two heads taller than any other dad. With his wild hair, his reddish face, and his massive shoulders, you couldn't miss him in a crowd. He was athletic, liked to swim and sail, and he was a dad who could fix anything. He whipped off square roots at the speed of light, and he knew lots of neat stuff, like how many feet in a mile, where to find the best fish in Cross Lake, and how to make maple candy by pouring strings of syrup in the snow. The only bad thing Steven saw from his father's can-do approach to life was that it allowed him to think he could fit more stuff into a day than he really could—which often left two disappointed boys to deal with failed promises.

But that was kid stuff. The man with the Viking strength seemed dead and gone now, just as surely as Cullen was dead. In just six months, his father had withered into an old man, with old man movements and old man smells. He'd even begun to walk with a stoop. Steven was ashamed at how repelled he was by his dad's weakness. He needed him to get back on his feet, get involved in life again. Be a man. Be strong. His dad was fifty-one years old. Okay, that was old, but not elderly.

"Look, Dad, I got a couple tickets to the Vikings game in a few weeks. I thought maybe you and me, we could go. They're playing Green Bay. Should be a great game."

His father sipped his beer, glancing down at the cordless phone again. "You sure you wouldn't rather take one of your buddies—or a date?"

"Nah. I figure we'd make a day of it. Either go out to eat first, or after it's over. My treat."

"Stevey—"

"Call me Steven, okay? Remember?"

"Sorry. I meant to say Steven. You don't have that kind of money, son. I don't want you skimping on something important just to take your old man out."

"Not a problem. A friend gave me the tickets. And we don't have to go to the Ritz for dinner. Just grab a burger somewhere. What do you say?"

His father continued to stare at the cordless.

"Dad? Are you listening to me?"

"What? Sure. I'd love to go. You got a deal."

"Great." Steven watched his father. "Hey, uh, what's with the phone? You expecting an important call or something?"

"You remember Doris French? She goes to our church."

Steven nodded.

"She works at the County Sheriff's Office."

"Yeah?"

"I was talking to her last Sunday. Did you know the day Cullen died, the police taped his conversation with that teacher, Alden Clifford."

Steven sat up straight. "You're kidding. How'd they do that?"

"Somebody crawled up and pushed a mike under the door. It was after Cullen threw everyone out—everyone except Clifford."

"Why didn't the police tell us about it?"

"Damn good question. I don't know."

"So, have you heard it?"

His father took a slug of beer, then shook his head. "But Doris thinks she can get me a copy. I'm not sure it's legal, but what the hell do I care? Doris said I could get myself a lawyer and he could probably get me a copy legally, but if she's willing—" His voice drifted off. After a few seconds, he continued. "If I could just hear my son's last words, maybe I'd understand why he did what he did." He picked up the phone and held it in his hand. He looked as if he were willing it to ring. "I never liked that teacher, you know? And I'm not alone." Glancing over at Steven, he asked, "Were you ever in any of Clifford's classes?"

"No."

"What did you think of him?"

Steven shrugged. "No opinion, really. He had a reputation as sort of a maverick. Had some unconventional opinions about American history. Some of my friends thought he was pretty cool."

"*Radical* is how I've heard him described. A few years back a group of parents tried to get him fired. Did you know that? He was given a slap on the wrist, but that's as far as it went."

"How come? What did he do?"

"It's what he was teaching. Saying stuff like Helen Keller was a communist. Woodrow Wilson was a racist. What kind of un-American crap is that?"

"Were you one of the parents who tried to get him fired?"

"No, but if they'd needed my support, they would have gotten it." He set the phone down, but kept his eyes on it. "Cullen talked about him every now and then."

"Yeah?"

"I got the impression he liked him—respected him."

"So?"

"Why did my son choose to end his life in Alden Clifford's classroom?"

Steven shrugged.

"There's a reason."

Steven watched him take another swig of beer. "What are you saying? You think Clifford had something to do with Cullen's death?"

"Maybe." Setting the beer bottle on the TV tray, he threaded his fingers across his stomach. "Doris thought she might stop by with that tape tonight. She said she'd call first. But . . . I suppose it's too late now." When he sighed, the blankness returned to his eyes.

"Look, I think I should be here with you when you play it."

His dad had already zoned him out.

"Dad?"

"Hmm?"

"Did you hear me? When you listen to the tape, I want to be here."

"Oh, sure. You need to hear it too." He gazed at the silent TV screen for a minute. "I put clean sheets on your bed. And the towels in the bathroom are all clean too. Use whatever you need."

"Thanks."

"Oh, and if I'm gone in the morning when you wake up, don't worry. I've got a few errands to run in town. I'll be back in time for breakfast."

Steven rose from the couch and walked into the kitchen, opening the refrigerator and staring absently at the contents. Inside, he was a jumble of emotions, but outside he was totally still, coiled tight like a spring. Now that Cullen was gone, his dad was all he had left. He had to make his father proud of him, even if it meant telling lies and keeping secrets. In the quiet darkness of his father's kitchen, Steven had finally achieved perfect clarity. It was a simple equation. If he lost his dad, he would lose himself. No other outcome was possible. And that thought burned into Steven's soul like acid.

8

Mary Clifford wasn't sure why she was on her hands and knees, a circle of unfamiliar faces peering down at her. Everyone wanted to know if she was okay—if she needed help. Coiling herself into a ball, her stomach churned violently and her head ached. People stomped and twirled all around her to the heavy rhythm of an electric guitar. Mary had been dancing herself a moment ago, but . . . well, now she wasn't.

Colored lights rushed at her, making her feel like she was riding a merry-go-round at warp speed. She needed an escape strategy, but she was so scared of falling that she couldn't move. Closing her eyes to shut everything out, she drifted, consumed almost immediately by a sense of pure happiness. But as the outside noise crept in, so did a picture of herself lying in a fetal position in the middle of a dance floor. It was ludicrous. She must be dreaming.

Blinking open her eyes, she felt like a newborn, stripped bare and vulnerable. The universe was pointing at her and sticking out its tongue. She had to get out, had to protect herself and her family. She saw that it was dark outside. Where on earth was she?

Crawling awkwardly through a forest of legs, Mary drew herself up on a chair. Two startled people gazed at her across a small dinner table.

"Oh. Hi," she said, straightening the neck on her gown. She scanned the crowd for her husband, finally locating him across the room at the bar. "Alden," she whispered. "I need you. Please hear me. I *need* you."

It was a familiar refrain.

Her thoughts drifted again. Many years ago, Alden had rescued her from the deep funk she'd fallen into after the death of her first husband. Her first marriage had been a disaster. She'd never really loved the man she'd married. Once the sexual attraction had worn thin, she hadn't even liked him. John Mayzer was a mean-spirited, pedantic, self-centered professor of economics, a gas bag to the core. As guilty as she felt for her lack of love during their marriage, she was even more guilt-ridden for feeling relieved when he died. But Alden had given her another chance at happiness, and this time it took.

Mary watched Alden at the bar. He looked a lot like Russel Crowe— Big and tough, but gentle too, deep inside, where it counted. He was sitting alone, nursing a drink. He was wearing the tux she'd helped him pick out. He usually dressed casually, but for Nick's wedding, she wanted him to look his best. And that's when she remembered.

"The wedding," she shouted. "Alden? We missed the wedding!" But that wasn't right. She remembered standing next to him thinking that the minister was an ass—pompous and predictable. Lauren had chosen him. If it had been up to Nick, he would have given all the wedding machinations a pass and simply eloped. Mary smiled as she thought how proud she was of her son. But then, realizing she was being stared at, she lowered her chin and retracted her head into her shoulders. She became a turtle. She hated turtles. And there it was again—that sense of dread she'd felt for weeks, a feeling of danger, of failing to see what was right in front of her eyes.

"Alden, I'm not a turtle, am I?" she called. There was too much noise in the room. He couldn't hear.

Working her way through the crowd, her feet felt light, as if they had springs attached. As soon as she reached the bar, she said, "Hop on my pogo stick, babe." What a silly thing to say.

Alden turned and stared up at her.

"What? Do I look different to you? A little reptilian?"

"No more than usual."

"I've turned into a turtle, sweetheart. But I still love you." She took his hand and pulled him toward the exit. Except, she didn't know precisely where that was. It occurred to her that perhaps Sartre was right—there wasn't one. But Alden found it in the front lobby, thus proving the existentialists wrong.

Once outside, Mary leaned against a car and breathed in the cold night air. The fog in her brain was beginning to lift. She gazed up at the trees, stripped bare by the November wind, then over to a sign on the building. "Dot's Country Bar and Grill," she said out loud. "Never heard of it."

Alden stood next to her, his arm around her shoulders. "Did Nick and Lauren leave yet? I don't know what's wrong with me—why I can't remember." He checked his watch. "My God." He jerked away from her. "It's a quarter of two in the morning."

Mary vaguely remembered following Kate and Ben Resnick outside. They'd all been eating dinner together at the head table, but Ben said there was something they absolutely had to see in the Donovans' front yard.

"We need to find the car," said Alden, scanning the parking lot. "And then we need to find our kids."

Two hours later, Alden and Mary charged through the front doors of the hospital. Alden had tanked up on coffee and felt better for it. A young guy behind the information desk on the first floor gave them Nick's room number.

Once on fifth, Alden walked ahead of Mary to the nursing station. Mary continued on to Nick's room.

Rousing a nurse behind the desk, he explained who he was. The nurse regarded him through her tiny round glasses, then in quiet, gentle tones informed him that Nick had been in surgery for almost three hours, but was now in his room. She assured Alden that his son had been given the best of care, and that he was now resting comfortably.

"But . . . what happened?" asked Alden. "All we were told was that he'd had an accident by the pool. What kind of accident?"

Alden stood stiffly and listened. Nick had jumped from the diving board into a swimming pool, filled with dead leaves. He'd sustained a broken leg, a cracked vertebra in his neck, and two broken fingers.

"None of which are life-threatening," said Alden. "Right?"

"Right."

The way she said the word made him think there might be more. "He'll be okay then."

"The reason he was in surgery was because of a skull fracture. There

56

was some internal bleeding, so the doctors had to operate to find the source and relieve the pressure."

Alden held his breath. "And?"

"He's still unconscious. He's being monitored very closely, Mr. Clifford. I'm sorry I can't tell you anything more."

"But he'll be fine, won't he? There's no brain damage."

"It's too early to tell."

"God," he whispered, closing his eyes. "What the hell happened to us?"

"You were drugged," said the nurse.

"I figured that much. But what was it? Who did it? And what happened to the rest of the wedding party?"

"Several dozen people were treated in the emergency room. A few were admitted, the rest were able to go home. The doctors think you ingested a combination of psilocin and psilocybin, compounds found in several psychedelics. From what the chief of emergency told me, the drug was most likely mixed in with the food."

"The food?" repeated Alden. That didn't make any sense. "I know the caterer. She's a friend."

"Anybody could have done it. One of her staff, perhaps? Hopefully, the police will be able to give you more concrete answers."

The police, thought Alden. The comment fired up the pain in his stomach again. "Was it LSD?"

"Possibly, but it was more likely something called shrooms or magic mushrooms. They're fairly easy to come by. Once the food is tested, I'm sure the doctors will give you more specific information. All I can tell you is that psychedelic mushrooms can cause effects similar to LSD—like loss of reality, severe anxiety, even paranoia—though it's usually not as intense and the effects don't last as long. When combined with medications a person might already be on, say antidepressants or anti-anxiety drugs, it can be dangerous. That's why several people from the wedding party were admitted for observation."

Alden felt suddenly light-headed.

"Are you all right?"

He steadied himself on the edge of the counter. "I'm fine."

"You don't look fine, Mr. Clifford. You need to be examined by a doctor."

"I want to see my son."

"Of course. But before you leave, you should be checked out."

"What about Lauren? Nick's wife?"

The nurse adjusted her glasses. "She's on another floor. I can get the room number for you if you'd like."

"What's her condition?"

"She was physically unharmed."

Once again, he sensed there was more to the story. "Then why was she admitted?"

"You'll have to speak with her doctor to get that information."

Alden waited while the nurse wrote Lauren's room number on a piece of paper. He slipped it into his billfold, thanked her, then headed off down the hall. So many of his friends had been at the wedding. He had to find out how they all were, but that would have to wait. His son came first.

Passing through the open doorway into Nick's room, Alden found him lying on his back, his head wrapped in gauze, his neck in a brace, and one leg strapped with an immobilizer. Two of his fingers had been splinted and taped. Various tubes and monitoring devices were attached here and there. Alden tried to absorb it, but it was so fundamentally incomprehensible to him that he blocked it out, focusing instead on his son's face. Nick looked ravaged, his chin and left cheek a mass of cuts and bruises.

A male nurse sat at a computer just inside the door. Alden nodded to him, then approached the bed. In a whispered voice, he relayed what the nurse had told him.

Mary was standing over Nick, stroking his arm.

"One of us should look in on Lauren," said Alden.

Mary shook her head. Her eyes said it all. She wasn't leaving her son.

"I guess I'll do it. If Nick wakes up, he'll want to know how she is." His stomach was on fire. He needed an antacid, but he'd already finished the roll of Tums he'd taken with him to the wedding.

On his way out the door, Alden fished in the back pocket of his dress slacks for his billfold. Maybe the hospital had a twenty-four-hour drugstore where he could buy himself some Maalox and another cup of coffee. His body felt like lead. He stifled a yawn with his fist, then opened the side pocket of the billfold and removed the piece of paper with Lauren's room number on it. But when he opened it, he saw that he'd removed the wrong paper. What he had in his hands was a typed note he'd received in his school mail slot earlier in the week. He'd been sent notes like it before, so it didn't exactly leave him shaking in his boots, although in the light of what had just happened, this note seemed almost prophetic.

We don't want teachers like you in our school.
Get out now before something bad happens.
You've been warned.

When Alden entered Lauren's hospital room a few minutes later, he found Gray Donovan, Nick's best man and best friend, sitting by the bed. He was holding Lauren's hand to his lips, talking to her softly. Gray was still wearing his tux, but had taken off his jacket and tie.

Looking up, Gray whispered, "I didn't think she should be alone."

Alden stepped over to the bed. "Is she asleep?"

"I don't know."

Her eyes were closed. She looked like a single white lily, slim and pale, her wispy blond hair curling delicately around her face. She was lying in what seemed to be an oversized bed wearing her once-immaculate wedding gown, one that was now stained by her husband's blood.

"What's wrong with her?" asked Alden. There were no cuts or bruises. No bandages or splints. No IV.

"They're not sure."

"What's that mean? If her doctors don't know, shouldn't they be doing tests?"

"She's been thoroughly checked over," said Gray. "There's nothing physically wrong with her." He rose from the chair and stepped over to the door, motioning Alden in close. "She hasn't said a word since the paramedics brought her to the hospital."

"Nothing?"

He shook his head. "They wanted her to remove her wedding dress, but she wouldn't do it. Several doctors have seen her, but she just won't talk."

"I suppose it could be the trauma of seeing Nick fall. That must have scared her to death."

Gray lowered his head and looked back at Lauren.

Alden wished he felt more comfortable around his new daughter-in-law, but the truth was that her personality put him off. She might be small, but she was also arrogant—and worldly in a way Nick would never be. Alden couldn't see them staying together very long because Nick was naturally easygoing, while Lauren was a perfectionist—definitely high maintenance. Alden had felt strongly that Nick needed to take more time to get to know her before they jumped into a marriage. But Nick's mind had been made up.

Alden moved back over to the bed and touched Lauren's shoulder. "Lauren, honey, it's Alden."

Her eyes fluttered open, but instead of looking at him, she stared up at the ceiling.

Alden and Gray exchanged worried glances.

"Honey, I want you to know that Nick's downstairs in another room. He's been in surgery, but it's done now. We're all praying he makes a full recovery."

She turned over on her side, putting her back to both men.

"Honey?" said Alden, baffled by her indifference. "I won't lie to you and tell you his injuries aren't serious. I thought maybe you'd like to come downstairs with me so you could see him. Your presence in the room would mean so much."

Gray placed a hand on Alden's back. "I can't allow that, Alden. Sorry."

"You can't *allow* it?"

"Think about it. If she sees Nick, it will only upset her more."

It made sense to Alden that Gray had chosen law as a profession because he liked to win almost more than anything else. Rich kids grew up with deformed mirrors and unrealistic expectations and that was Gray Donovan in a nutshell.

"Maybe it's the drugs," said Gray. "It may take a while longer before they pass out of her system."

"I hope that's all it is," said Alden. Pulling Gray aside, he whispered, "Are you telling me she hasn't said *anything*? Not one word?"

"Not even to the police," said Gray. "And believe me, they wanted her to tell them what happened."

"Did you see Nick jump into the pool?"

"No, I took off right after dinner. I needed some air. I drove around for a while, but I started feeling weird, so I crashed at a friend's apartment for a few hours. When I got back to my dad's place and discovered what had happened, I rushed to the hospital. I've been with her ever since. I plan to stay with her for what's left of the night. She shouldn't be alone."

Maybe he was right. Whatever the case, Alden didn't have the steam to argue with him. "I need to get back to ICU. I'll tell Nick you're with her. If he hears that, maybe he can rest more easily."

As Alden left the room, it struck him that Gray hadn't asked him one question about Nick's condition.

Cottonwood, Kansas
Halloween 1972

Jimmy Shore sprinted across the Van Gelders' front yard, flew over their rear fence, and raced back to his house. His dad had taken the truck to work, but the Rambler was still parked in the drive. Jimmy had only driven it a few times. He wouldn't get his permit until next March when he turned sixteen. Not that it mattered. That car was his only hope.

Creeping into the kitchen, he lifted his mother's keys from her purse. She wouldn't miss them tonight because she was in bed with the flu. Jimmy prayed she was asleep as he rushed back outside, unlocked the Rambler's front door, and hopped inside. His hands shook as he fumbled with the ignition. The plan was to chase after Frank's van and make him listen to reason. And if reason didn't work, Jimmy would do anything, even kill Frank, to get his sister back.

The engine coughed a couple of times before it finally caught. The car was eleven years old, not in the best shape. It was just the kind of crappy "family" car his father liked. To Jimmy, it made no sense. With just a little more money down, he could have bought a Mustang.

Easing the car into reverse, Jimmy backed out of the drive. He looked both ways before pulling onto the street. His instincts told him to floor it, but he couldn't risk getting caught. He didn't want his parents to find out what happened before he had a chance to set it right.

Jimmy headed for the highway. If Frank really did intend to kidnap Patsy, maybe sell her to some pervert to get his money back, he'd need to get out of Cottonwood. In Jimmy's mind, perverts only lived in big cities. Wichita was a straight shot east on 54. If the old Rambler would only hold together, and if he could keep clear of the cops, Jimmy was sure he could catch the van. And then . . . well, he'd make it up as he went along.

As soon as he reached the highway, he pressed the pedal to the metal and blasted into the night. He couldn't see the road very well and wondered if it was always this hard to drive after dark. The moon was full, but it wasn't bright enough, especially out in the country. Fiddling with the switches on the dash, it finally dawned on him that he hadn't turned on the headlights. No wonder it was so hard to see. *Dumb-ass!*

Now that he could see better, he drove even faster. The speedometer read ninety when he passed a sign that announced construction up ahead. But nobody would be doing construction after dark. The sign said to watch out for bumps. Rough road. Piece of cake, thought Jimmy. He was feeling better now that he was moving, now that he was doing something to right the wrong. Frank wouldn't drive fast because he couldn't risk getting pulled over. If the cops stopped him for speeding, he'd be dead meat. Jimmy didn't want the cops on his tail either, but he couldn't worry about it now. If they showed up, he'd just have to outrun them. Except for the fact that Patsy was in danger, Jimmy was totally grooving on the speed, the chase, the excitement. It made him feel powerful, not like some stupid kid from a hick town in the middle of nowhere.

Twenty minutes later, he was still roaring down the highway, no cops in sight. He couldn't believe he hadn't caught up to Frank. The guy didn't have that big a head start. But maybe Frank was driving faster than Jimmy thought. It was starting to drizzle, so Jimmy switched on the wipers, but the water mixed with the dust on the windshield and gunked up the glass. The rubber on the wipers was old and should have been replaced. His dad never had any money for stuff like that. He screamed about how poor they were, but he always had the bucks to buy himself a six-pack of Bud. Jimmy didn't think they were poor, he thought his dad was cheap.

And that's when Jimmy got to thinking. What if Frank stopped somewhere in town before he headed out? He could have tied Patsy up, gagged her, then stopped at a restaurant to grab a burger. That might mean he was behind Jimmy. And if that was the case, Jimmy would never catch him—unless he stopped by the side of the road and waited awhile to see if the van came past. Jimmy decided to give himself another ten minutes. If he didn't overtake Frank's van by then, he'd pull off.

Ten minutes went by and still no van, so Jimmy slowed the Rambler to a crawl and pulled onto a narrow dirt road. He nearly went in the ditch trying to turn the car around, but he finally got the front end pointed back at the highway. He figured the dirt road led back to a farmhouse, or maybe a barn. It was unlikely that anyone would be using it this time of night, so he felt safe stopping.

Flipping off the headlights, Jimmy sat in the car playing with the radio dial, trying to find a rock station. If he had to sit around and twiddle his thumbs, he might as well be entertained. But all he got was static. After his dad had repaired the aerial, the radio had turned into a piece of shit. The clock in the car didn't work either, but it didn't matter because Jimmy had a watch. Every few minutes he'd hold it next to the soft green dashboard lights. It was going on eight. He wondered what his buddies must be thinking back in town. They were probably royally pissed at him. Jimmy didn't blame them. He'd let them down. He'd have to figure out a way to make it up to them.

By ten, Jimmy was about to pack it in and drive back to Cottonwood. A few cars had come past his hiding spot, but none had been Frank's van. In the meantime, Jimmy had come up with a lie he could tell his parents to get himself off the hook. He didn't know how good it was—he wouldn't know that until he tried it on them. And that was his dilemma. Would it be good enough? Or would they see it for what it was and blame him for Patsy's kidnapping? Hell, he was to blame, but if he couldn't get her back, it made no sense to get nailed for it.

The other alternative was to just keep on driving east to Wichita, get lost in the city, and never go home again. But what was left of his money was hidden in the metal box he'd buried behind Mrs. O'Brien's pole barn. If he could just get his hands on it, he'd be in much better shape to be a kid alone, on the run. He didn't really want to leave home. Well he did, but not like this. Not yet. Then again maybe, with enough money, he could get Patsy back. He'd have to find Frank first, but nothing was impossible. No matter what happened, Jimmy would never give up on finding his sister. Never.

And that's when he saw the headlights. They were far away, just two pinpricks of yellow light in the darkness, but they were coming his way. He had a feeling about those lights. His muscles tensed in anticipation.

Jimmy kept his eyes fixed on the road until the van came into view. "I knew it, I knew it!" He rocketed up and down in his seat. "Gotcha, asshole!" He yanked the Rambler into gear, waited for the van to pass, then screeched onto the highway, blowing dirt out the back end. He floored the pedal, roared up directly behind the van, then laid on the horn, hoping Frank would stop.

The van sped up.

"Shit," screamed Jimmy. "You fucking dickhead! Stop!"

The van started to pull away from him.

Jimmy checked the speedometer and saw that they were going just under a hundred miles an hour. He also noticed for the first time that the gas tank was nearly empty. Damn his father. He had to do something fast or he'd be shit out of luck.

Pulling into the left lane, Jimmy pushed the Rambler to the max. Inch by inch he gained on the van. At this speed, even a small mistake could send him hurtling into a cornfield or worse. The highway crossed the Kettle River somewhere around here. Jimmy had seen a sign a few miles back. It was hard to keep the Rambler steady, but if it could just hold on, he had a game plan. He would pull the car in front of Frank's and slowly bring the van to a stop. He'd seen stuff like that on TV. It could work, but he had to be careful.

Jimmy kept the gas pedal on the floor, but now the van seemed to be pulling away again. "No," he screamed. "Fucking piece of shit car! Move!"

Suddenly, in his rearview mirror, flashing lights appeared. Jimmy looked up at them, trying to estimate how far back they were. And in that split second, he lost control. The car flew off the bridge and for a moment, Jimmy felt as if he were suspended in midair.

When the car hit, Jimmy blasted upward, slamming his head against the roof. At the same time, the seat heaved forward, jamming his torso into the steering wheel. An instant later, the seat flew backward, pulling Jimmy with it. He was dazed, disoriented. He held his head in his hands, feeling something dark and sticky trickle down his cheek. Searching the darkness, he realized he wasn't sure which way was up. Everything was all topsy-turvy.

As he struggled to open the door, he felt something cold seep into his sneakers. Water was rushing in fast, circling around his ankles, creeping up his legs, icy cold and black as dirt. He had to get out, but the door wouldn't budge. Instead of air, panic filled his lungs.

"Help me," he screamed, knowing in his gut that there was no help.

Sunday

9

On Sunday morning, Jane sat at her desk in her office at the Lyme House, going over the menu that had been developed for Nick and Lauren's wedding. After testing the remains of the food at the Donovan mansion as well as what was left at the catering shop, the police determined that six of the thirteen items served at the banquet contained psilocybin, the main psychedelic compound found in magic mushrooms.

The good news—if you could call it good—was that Nick was the only one who had suffered a serious physical injury as a result of ingesting the drug. He was still in a coma, still in ICU, though all his vital signs were strong. Jane wasn't allowed in to see him because she wasn't family. She'd talked with Alden and Mary several times by phone. They assured her that they knew she wasn't responsible for the food tampering. Jane also noted that they failed to extend that assurance to her catering crew.

As of this morning, no lawsuits had been filed against the Lyme House, but Jane anticipated that she'd be contacted in the next few days. She'd spoken at some length with her father yesterday. He'd put her in touch with a lawyer who specialized in food and drug law. It appeared that she could be prosecuted both criminally—for possession of an illegal substance—as well as civilly—by guests at the wedding who considered themselves in some way damaged by the experience.

So far, no criminal charges had been brought. The police were investigating the incident, primarily doing background checks on everyone in her employ. The fact that Alden and Mary hadn't pressed charges weighed heavily in her favor, but unless the police could find proof that someone apart from her catering crew had contaminated the food, Jane and her restaurant would be on the hook.

Jane was pretty sure the police saw her as a victim in much the same way as the Cliffords. They were doing their best to get to the bottom of what had really happened. Still, nobody was as directly affected by the outcome of that investigation as Jane was. It was in her best interests to do everything in her power to see that the truth came out—whatever it was and wherever it led.

While the police looked at potential suspects, Jane took a different approach. She thought it might be more productive to pursue the food angle. The first question she needed to answer was: Why was the drug present in some of the food items but not in all of them?

It was clear from examining the leftovers that the drug had been mixed *into* the menu items, not simply sprinkled on top. Unfortunately, that pointed to the catering crew, since all the food had been prepared off-site and brought to the Donovan mansion for service. Jane felt there had to be a common denominator—an element, a specific product or sauce—that had been tainted and then innocently used by her catering staff to produce those six contaminated items. If she could determine what the common link was, she might be able to figure out where it came from and who was responsible for its preparation or introduction. Speculation as to motive led her in so many different directions that she figured it was useless to consider motive until she had more specific information.

Jane poured herself a mug of coffee from the carafe on her desk, then grabbed her file folder on the wedding and moved over to the couch. Her dog, Mouse, a chocolate-colored Lab she'd found wandering the streets almost a year ago, was curled on the floor in front of the fireplace. Sensing an opportunity for affection, he jumped up next to her and placed his right paw on her arm.

"Are you going to help me with this?" she asked him, scratching down the length of his back. He closed his eyes and lifted his chin. He was smiling. She was sure of it.

Jane loved animals, but Mouse was the best dog she'd ever known. He was incredibly intuitive, sweet-natured and friendly, and yet fiercely protective. Jane had been attacked in her home several years ago. Mouse was one of the main reasons why she felt she could go back and live there again. He loved to run, so weather permitting, the two of them would take the runner's path around the lake once a day. Again, thanks to Mouse, she was in the best shape of her life.

Jane didn't think of herself as a lonely person, but down deep, she knew she was. Her partner of some ten years, Christine Kane, had died of cancer the year Jane turned thirty-five. Back then, Jane had been naive enough to believe that their life together would go on forever. Her natural optimism, and the fact that she was deeply in love, had led her to believe in happy endings. Maybe there were happy endings out there somewhere, but Jane wasn't sure she'd ever find one of her own.

She'd been in several relationships since Christine's death, one particularly important one with a woman named Julia, but in time, that had ended too. After Julia, Jane had dated a much younger woman. In many ways, Patricia Kastner had been a breath of fresh air. She wasn't like anybody Jane had ever been with before. The sexual energy between them got pretty intense at times, but the difference in their ages and Patricia's roving eye eventually led Jane to move on.

Unless she had a few too many brandies or pints of ale, Jane was able to keep her darker thoughts at bay. Being gay gave her an outsider's viewpoint, and that was something she valued. In most ways, she considered herself lucky, the success of her restaurant being chief among her good fortune. But life was complex. Nothing was black and white. Her work allowed for moments of fierce satisfaction and—though she might never say it out loud—blessed oblivion.

Mouse snuggled next to her, his head in her lap. "Okay," she said, gently tugging his ear. "This is serious business. You need to pay attention."

He yawned, then smacked his lips.

Picking up her file folder, she found the sheet with the finalized menu. "Now, Lauren was a vegetarian—not vegan, thankfully." Jane found that particular food preference almost impossible to cook for. Nick was leaning in the direction of vegetarianism, though he still ate fish. Jane and Otis had put their heads together and come up with a menu that pleased both the bride and groom.

The Lyme House served a fusion cuisine. The old English standards were always available, mainly offered in the downstairs pub—shepherd's pie, roast beef and Yorkshire pudding, ploughmen's lunches, mulligatawny soup, fish and chips. But upstairs, in the main dining room, the menu was more sophisticated and eclectic, borrowing what was interesting from all the cuisines of the world.

"Now. Lauren loves curries, Asian food, and pasta. Nick likes cheese, Greek food, and fresh shellfish, so the menu was created around their preferences."

Jane ticked off the items, tapping Mouse on the head to make sure he was listening. "Appetizers and champagne were served at six, directly after the wedding ceremony. The appetizers were: vegetarian satays with an Asian peanut sauce. Stilton cheesecake served on toast points. Cranberry coulis and Brie wrapped in puff pastry. Olive, artichoke, and rosemary crostini. Spanikopita pillows and mustard sauce. And last, oysters on the half shell topped with watercress mousse." Interestingly, the only appetizer tainted with psilocybin was the oyster dish—specifically the watercress mousse. Jane thought about that for a minute, made a couple of notes on the outside of the file folder, then went on.

"Okay. Now, dinner was buffet style. The hot food was served in standard chaffers, all the tray pans prepped back at the catering shop. Vegetarian shepherd's pie. An Indian curried shrimp and vegetables with cinnamon and raisin couscous. An herbed farfalle pasta with Parmigiano-Reggiano, roasted pine nuts, grilled portobellos, red peppers, and eggplant. A gratin of cauliflower, sweet potatoes, and Southern Comfort. Caramelized garlic, radicchio, and walnuts—that was served hot, not cold. Cold salads were a Turkish tabouli with pistachios, and a yoghurt, cucumber, and radish raita. Also, the usual breads and condiments."

Jane looked down. Mouse was asleep. He wasn't much of a gourmet.

"Now," she said, a little more softly. "The psilocybin was found in five of the buffet dishes. The curried shrimp and couscous, the shepherd's pie, the gratin, the radicchio, and the tabouli." She fished the ingredient lists out of the folder.

For the next few minutes, she studied the ingredients. It became apparent almost immediately what all of the dishes had in common.

"Vegetable stock," she said out loud. Could it be that simple? It seemed crazy—and even a little silly—to think that if she could find out who made the vegetable stock, she'd know who tampered with the food. She went over the ingredient lists one more time. Sure enough, vegetable stock was the only common denominator. That had to be it.

"Sorry, Mouse," said Jane, rising from the couch. She returned to her desk and punched in Otis's cell phone number. A few rings later he picked up.

"Otis here."

"It's Jane. I think I might have found something. I've been looking for an ingredient that was in all the contaminated foods."

"Good thinking." He sounded hungover.

"Who made the vegetable stock?"

"The vegetable stock? You think *it* was spiked?"

"That's the theory."

"Well, let me think. We rarely make stocks ourselves, it's too labor intensive. We usually order it from the restaurant. I'd have to check with Rita, but I'm sure that's where it came from. Who makes the stocks in the main kitchen?"

Jane wasn't sure, but she'd find out. "I'll get back to you on that one." Now that she had a partial answer, she needed to find the full one.

"I wish this would just fade away," grumbled Otis. "I hate answering all these stupid questions."

"Have the police been talking to you?"

"Every freakin' day. And now they're doing a background check on me."

"Well, you've got nothing to worry about."

"Yeah. Right."

"Listen, Otis, I need to get upstairs and talk to Anna."

"Good. Do that. I'm going back to sleep." He hung up.

Jane pressed a number on her phone and a moment later a man's voice answered.

"Lyme House kitchen. This is Brad."

"Brad, it's Jane. Is Anna up there?"

"She's talking to the fish vendor, but I think they're almost done."

"Fine. Thanks."

Instead of taking the back stairs, Jane headed down the hallway outside her office to the pub. The restaurant wouldn't open for another hour. It was going on ten now, but already the place was buzzing with activity. Taking the front stairs two at a time, Jane stopped for a second at the reception desk to check the day's bookings. After an article appeared on Nick Clifford in yesterday's paper, business had dropped off. She counted nineteen cancellations since yesterday morning. Not good.

Pushing through the swinging kitchen doors, Jane found Anna Carlson, her executive chef, standing next to one of the steam kettles, checking a clipboard. Anna was about the same age as Jane, but a good sixty pounds heavier.

"Have you got a minute?"

Anna tore her attention away from the clipboard. "What's up?" she asked, peering over her bifocals.

Jane nodded to Anna's office.

Once the door was closed, Jane put the question to her. "Who normally prepares our stocks? Specifically, the vegetable stock."

"Mimi Wong used to, but she quit in September. I'm training that new hire to do it. Jason Vickner. He's the really tall kid with that fuzzy business on his chin. He seems interested in learning, so I thought I'd start him on the basics. Nothing more basic than stock. We don't do much vegetable stock though. We usually need a specific prep order for it." She paged through a stack of prep orders on her desk. "Looks like the last order we got was from Otis over in catering. That was early last week. It was done on Wednesday. Otis picked it up on Thursday morning."

This was just the information Jane needed. "Is Jason here?"

Anna glanced at a chart on the wall. "Yup. Got him peeling onions again. He's getting good at it too. He came in yesterday morning wearing a diving mask and snorkel. Ripped right through those sacks without so much as shedding a tear." Her laugh was hearty and infectious. "He's got a lot of promise, that kid. Just out of curiosity, how come you want to talk to him?"

"I think our vegetable stock was tampered with."

"You're talking about the Clifford wedding?"

Jane nodded.

"You think Jason did it?"

"I don't know, but I intend to find out." She left the office and took a sharp right, passing the bakery. A long stainless prep table sat against the back wall, directly next to a row of sinks. Jason stood by himself, his back to her, using a chef's knife on a bowl of onions. Sure enough, he was wearing the mask and snorkel.

"Jason?" she said, tapping him on the shoulder.

Turning around, he removed his headgear. "Oh, hi."

"I need to talk to you."

"Ah, sure." He set the knife down.

"This is about the vegetable stock you made last week."

His eyes darted to the clock on the wall, then back at Jane. "What about it? I did it just the way Chef Carlson told me to."

"Okay. But somehow, it got tampered with. Know anything about that?"

"No."

"Ever heard of magic mushrooms?"

He gave a noncommittal shrug.

"Okay, maybe I need to be more direct. Did you add them to the broth?"

"Me? Hell, no. Why would I do that?"

"Is it possible you use them, shall we say, *recreationally,* and you just happened to drop some in the *mirepoix?*"

He stared at her.

Jane assumed he didn't like her sense of humor. Either that or he didn't know what a *mirepoix* was. So much for being interested in the basics of stock making. "Can I assume you heard what happened at the wedding we catered last Friday night?"

A muscle twitched in his cheek. "Sure, I heard. Everybody here has. It sucks."

"Yes, it does. I'm thinking that maybe we should sit down and have a talk. I just need to do some basic information gathering. You understand." She had no proof, just a theory, but Jason didn't know that. She needed to push him to see how he reacted. He wasn't much of an actor. She was sure he was lying.

"Okay. No problem. I didn't do nothing wrong."

"Why don't we use Chef Carlson's office?"

He wiped his hands on a towel.

As soon as she turned away from him, he bolted for the back door.

Jane sidestepped a woman carrying a tray pan and chased after him. When she hit the loading dock, she saw his tall, gangly form steaming across the rear parking lot. His white chef's hat had fallen off and landed on the asphalt next to a delivery truck.

Springing down the steps, she took off at a dead run. Jason couldn't be more than twenty years old and he had a head start. Not good odds. As he scrambled up a steep embankment, he slipped and fell. Jane squeezed every bit of speed she could out of her legs. But he was up quickly, rushing for the sidewalk. She knew she couldn't catch him, but she couldn't give up either. She followed him up the embankment, careful to leap around the piece of ice that had brought him down. When she reached the street, he was already halfway up Penn Avenue. She stopped and bent over, sucking in deep drafts of cold air.

"Dammit," she shouted, glancing up at his retreating figure.

She gave herself a moment to catch her breath, then straightened up, her hands rising to her hips. So much for innocence. She didn't feel completely thwarted because she had a suspect in her sights now. Unfortunately, he was her employee, which meant that if he was responsible, her restaurant was still on the hook. Unless? Maybe he'd been paid off—or coerced. There had to be more to the story. Next time they met—and there would be a next time—he wouldn't get away so easily.

10

The ancient, graffiti-filled freight elevator creaked and groaned its way up to Cordelia's fifth-floor loft. Jane had phoned before leaving the restaurant to make sure she'd be home. If Jane had to guess, she'd bet that Cordelia was in the midst of preparations for her trip to Italy. On the way over, Jane had driven past the fourplex on Dupont where Jason lived, but everything seemed quiet. There was no point in trying to kick his door down or make some other equally macho attempt to get him to talk to her. What she needed was a plan. And for that, she had to talk to Cordelia.

Jane knocked on the door, then stuffed her hands into the pockets of her new sheepskin jacket. On the phone, Cordelia hadn't sounded terribly chipper. It was probably Octavia's sudden visit that had added an unmistakable element of grimness to her voice—either that or the fact that it wasn't noon and she was already up.

When the door was finally opened, Jane was momentarily shocked. Cordelia looked positively frazzled—her makeup haphazardly applied, her auburn curls a mass of snarls on top of her head. "What's wrong?" asked Jane.

Out from behind Cordelia's skirt poked a small head.

"Hi," said a tiny toddler voice.

"Well hello, Hattie," said Jane, crouching down. "And how are you today?"

Hattie smiled. "Hi," she said again.

"Hi," said Jane.

"Hi," repeated Hattie.

"She doesn't have a particularly *vast* vocabulary," said Cordelia. "In case you were wondering."

"You look terrible."

"Thank you," she said, adding in her most portentous voice, "Hattie operates under that old Marine Corps saying, 'It's easier to ask forgiveness than permission.'"

"Feeling a little frayed around the edges, are we?"

"I feel," said Cordelia, moving to more rounded tones, "as if I've been mugged by a guinea pig."

"Hi," said Hattie.

From her six-foot height, Cordelia glowered down at the little girl. "Janey, why don't you come into our parlor?" She turned her back. "Said the spider to the fly."

"That bad?" asked Jane, following her inside.

"Oh, you cannot possibly know what I have endured since my sister and her entourage arrived on Friday night. I will spare you the details. Suffice it to say, I am *not* a born baby-sitter."

"Where's Octavia?"

"Who knows? Out spreading her Tinker dust. Getting her claws sharpened. Or maybe she's looking for husband number five."

"What about the nanny? I've forgotten her name."

Cordelia disappeared into the kitchen and returned with a cup of coffee. "Help yourself." She nodded to the coffeemaker on the counter. "You asked about the lovely Valenka, I believe. We're referring to her now simply as The Empress. She's off buying diapers and other Necessary Childhood Items."

Jane took off her coat. "And you've been left to take care of Hattie. Poor Cordelia." And poor Hattie, thought Jane.

Cordelia made a disgusted face. "Just look at this place! You wouldn't think my sister could pack *that* many toys into the six-hundred-pound stack of luggage she brought with her."

Jane had to admit, the loft was littered with an awful lot of plastic in primary colors.

"Bye bye," said Hattie, hanging on to Jane's hand for a moment, then scampering off.

"She's adorable," said Jane, watching her crawl under Cordelia's desk. "She looks a lot like Octavia."

"She's got stage presence, I'll give her that."

Jane wondered if there was a hint of pride in Cordelia's voice.

"But she's a royal pain in the ass. Never stops. She's rearranged my pot drawer three times already, and that was accomplished before seven A.M. She *never* sits down to read a book or look at a magazine."

"Why don't you try TV? I'll bet that would keep her occupied."

"I'm not having *my* niece grow up watching Bob Barker. I'll rent her something good—something with Ingrid Bergman or Barbara Stanwyck in it."

"Don't be such a curmudgeon. She's just a little kid. And she's your only niece. I'd think you'd want to spend some time with her. Besides, won't Valenka be back soon?"

"She better be," said Cordelia, dropping like a two-hundred-plus-pound sack of flour onto her favorite comfy chair. "Hey!" She pulled a plastic bunny with pokey ears out from behind the back cushion. "That hurt. See! If it hadn't been for the cushion, I'd be impaled on a rabbit!"

"An interesting image."

"Your home is a toy-free zone. You wouldn't understand."

"Are you telling me you don't like having her around at all?"

"Hattie or Octavia?"

"Either. Both."

Hattie peeked out from under the desk. "Hi," she said.

Jane waved. "Hi."

"Octavia wants something," muttered Cordelia. "I just don't know what it is yet. She's crafty. She was sweetness and light all day yesterday. It's all preparation, mark my words. When the other shoe drops, you can bet it will be on my head."

Jane was about to sit down across from Cordelia when a cat squealed.

"Lord," said Cordelia, pushing out of her chair. "She's coloring Melville again."

Melville bolted through the living room, a large blue spot on his head, an even bigger green patch on his side.

Cordelia got down on her hands and knees and poked her head under the desk. "Hattie, Auntie Cordelia wants you to stop coloring Melville. He doesn't like it. It makes him sad. It pisses him off."

Hattie crawled out the other side, a green marker grasped in her fist, a mischievous twinkle in her eye.

"Hattie, give me the marker!" called Cordelia, getting stuck as she tried to push herself through the narrow opening.

"Mine," cried Hattie, giggling.

"Hey, another word," said Jane.

Hattie ran past her. "Hi," she said.

"Hi," repeated Jane. She could see how this could get old.

Cordelia heaved herself up, took a deep cleansing breath, then rushed into the kitchen. "Hattie, dear, come to Auntie Deeya. I've got a treat for you."

Jane glanced at Hattie. She obviously knew the word "treat," but she looked uncertain.

Cordelia returned to the room with a slice of Brie.

"You think a toddler will eat *Brie?*" asked Jane.

"Who the hell knows what a toddler eats."

"You shouldn't swear in front of her."

"You think, out of the millions of words I produce in a day, that she's going to remember *one?*"

Hattie inched toward the cheese.

"Didn't Octavia bring any treats with her?" asked Jane.

"That's one of the things The Empress is out foraging for." She held the Brie to her mouth, her eyes lighting up. "Good cheese. Expensive French double-cream good cheese. Yum yum. Hattie, you give me the marker and I'll give you the treat."

The little girl might not be able to say much, but she did understand negotiations. Reluctantly, she dropped the marker and took the cheese from Cordelia's hand. But she didn't taste it. She just stood there staring at it.

"What's she doing?" asked Jane.

"She's doing exactly what I'd do if I were her age. Deciding if it passes the ick test."

Apparently it didn't. Hattie put it to her mouth, but didn't taste it. Instead, she squeezed it through her fingers. It landed on top of her shoe.

Cordelia shrieked. "Perfectly good Brie, and she treats it like Play Doo Doo. I blame Octavia for this, Janey. She hasn't given the child the benefit of *any* culinary training."

"She's only a year and a half old."

"A year and *eight* months. It's never too early to start."

Cordelia spent the next few minutes getting Hattie set up with a box of crayons and a stack of typing paper. Thrilled to see her content to doodle, Cordelia eased herself back down on the chair. "When you called, you said you'd had a breakthrough on your catering catastrophe."

Jane gave Cordelia the complete rundown on everything that had happened at the restaurant. She finished by saying that she needed Cordelia's input. How should she play it? Should she turn what she knew over to the police? Or should she try to talk to Jason first herself. But Cordelia wasn't listening. By the time Jane got to the "help" part, Hattie had tossed all the crayons over her shoulder and was digging dirt out of a planter.

Just as Cordelia got up to deal with the latest disaster, there was a knock on the door.

"Get that, will you?" asked Cordelia, dragging a now screaming toddler away from the dirt pile. "Let's hope it's The Empress."

When Jane opened the door she found Cecily Finch, one of her part-time bartenders, out in the hall. Cecily was also an aspiring actress, and one of Nick Clifford's good friends.

"Can I come in?" asked Cecily, looking tentative and, well, rather finch-like. Cecily personified her last name. She had black beady eyes and she twitched a lot. She was also delicate and small. Jane doubted she'd ever been in Cordelia's apartment before.

Cordelia was like a goddess to Cecily. If there was ever a chance for Cecily to impress Cordelia, she jumped at it. She'd secretly told Jane that she hoped lightning would strike and Cordelia would "discover her," as it were, "behind the bar at the Lyme House Pub." Sort of like Rita Hayworth being "discovered" at Schrafts drugstore. But unlike Rita Hayworth, Cecily wasn't beautiful—certainly not the leading lady type. More of a character actress, in Jane's opinion, although she was sure Cecily didn't see a little finchy person when she looked in the mirror. She probably saw Katharine Hepburn.

"I'm sorry if I'm interrupting anything," said Cecily, her eyes darting every which way. "But Anna told me you were headed over here, so I thought I'd drop by, give you both the good news."

"What good news?" asked Jane.

"Say, what a cute little girl," said Cecily, stepping inside.

Hattie was sitting on the couch sucking her thumb, tears streaming down her face. "I cwy," she said.

"Wow," said Jane. "Even more words."

"What's wrong?" asked Cecily, crouching down in front of her. "You miss your mommy, huh?"

At the word "mommy," Hattie began to wail.

"It's okay, sweetheart." Cecily picked her up and began walking her around the room, bouncing her on her hip. Magically, the child stopped wailing.

"You're a godsend," said Cordelia, flopping down on the couch. "Don't ever leave."

Cecily's expression sharpened. Jane could see the gleam in her eyes. She saw an opportunity to do a little sucking up. Okay, so Jane thought the interactions between these two theater types were generally tiresome. Cordelia enjoyed dangling raw meat in front of a lioness, or in this case, a tiny nervous bird with delusions of grandeur.

As Cecily walked around the loft showing Hattie the "pretties"—all the glittery, glitzy pieces of theatrical detritus Cordelia had scattered here and there—Valenka marched in, her arms weighed down by plastic sacks. She muttered something in Russian as she dumped the sacks on the dining-room table. Glancing at Cordelia through narrowed slits, she shook her head, then disappeared into the area of the loft that served as her bedroom.

"What did she say?" asked Jane.

"You got me," said Cordelia. "Me no speak Rooskie."

"So, Cecily," said Jane, "tell us your good news."

Cecily sat down at the dining-room table and let Hattie pull the plastic wet wipes canisters out of the sacks. "It's Nick. He regained consciousness."

"That's incredible news," said Jane. She felt like a ten-ton weight had been lifted off her back.

"Is he able to talk?" asked Cordelia.

"A little. He's disoriented. The doctors said that's to be expected. They've scheduled another surgery, this one for his leg. I guess they have to attach pins and a plate so that the break will heal properly."

"I supposed he's concerned about Lauren," said Jane.

Cecily's eyes drifted to the windows. "Yeah, I suppose."

"How's she doing?" asked Cordelia.

"Not well. She's being released this afternoon. Mary and Alden are bringing her home to stay with them—until she gets better. It would be impossible for her to live alone right now."

"What's wrong with her?" asked Cordelia.

"I don't really know. Mainly, she won't talk. Not a word since the night of the wedding."

"Must be the trauma of Nick's accident," said Jane.

"Must be," said Cecily. "Her doctors think getting her out of the hospital will do her a world of good. Gray's hardly left her side since she was admitted. He's *such* a martyr."

Jane wondered what the sarcasm was about.

As they were talking, Valenka trudged out of the back room carrying a heavy suitcase in each hand.

"*Oi, eto sestra vasha—ona sumashedshaya!* Big krazy! She say stay, stay, but *nyet, nyet, nyet. Ya ezdy na Konnetikut, ya xochy* my family. *I lubloo etoo malenkayoo, Xhattii,* no I can stay. *Nyet, nyet, nyet.* I quit. Bye, bye." She stopped for a moment, glared at Cordelia, then opened the door and left.

"I got the last part," said Cordelia. She shook her head at Hattie. "What am I going to do now? I'm supposed to attend a preliminary meeting for the gov's new arts council this afternoon. I can hardly show up with a toddler. The meeting's at the Minneapolis Art Institute. Do you know what Hattie could *do* to the Art Institute, given even a few unsupervised minutes? I might as well strap some C-4 to my leg and blow up the entire place."

"Call Octavia," said Jane. "Tell her to come home and take care of her child."

"I don't have her new cell phone number. This is *so* like my sister, to drop me in the weeds like this and not even know it. What if she doesn't come back until late tonight? That's possible, you know. She has no sense of time."

"I'd be happy to take care of her," said Cecily, playing pattycake with Hattie. "The only problem is, I already promised Mary that I'd stay with Nick while she and Alden drive Lauren back to their house."

Cordelia tapped a finger against her chin. "How long will they be gone?"

"Not more than a couple of hours. I'll come straight back here when I'm done."

Cordelia turned to Jane.

"Oh, no you don't. Don't look at me. I have a restaurant to run."

"You have an executive chef, a sous chef, an assistant manager, and oodles of eager employees. Nobody will even know you're gone."

Cecily got up and handed Hattie to Jane.

"Hi," said the little girl, touching Jane's gold hoop earring.

Jane couldn't help but laugh. "I guess it's you and me, kiddo. What should we do? Maybe we should start with lunch. You want to help me make a sandwich?"

"Hi," said Hattie again, pushing a pudgy finger into Jane's chin.

"I'll take that as a yes."

11

Lauren's eyes were closed, but Mary could tell she wasn't sleeping. It was a forty-minute drive from the hospital to Alden and Mary's home. Evergreen was a large, relatively wealthy southern suburb of the Twin Cities. Their farmhouse, or "the mother ship," as Mary liked to call it, was a few miles out of town.

Lauren was dressed and ready to go when Mary entered her hospital room just after one. It was the first time Mary had seen her wearing anything other than her wedding dress since the ceremony. Her baby fine blond hair was drawn back into a ponytail. Under normal circumstances, Lauren wouldn't be caught dead looking like that. She was always flawlessly turned out, the image of a successful professional woman. Since moving to Minnesota, she'd taken a job with Northstar Realtors, one of the hottest new companies in the state. She'd already racked up an extensive list of clients. But that had all been put on hold.

Lauren Bautel was four years older than Nick. Mary could hardly squawk about the age difference since she was five years older than Alden. But Lauren seemed old for her years. She didn't exactly exude warmth, but Mary could see where a young man might find her attractive. She had hauntingly beautiful dark brown eyes. And she was in great physical shape, worked out at a gym at least four times a week. That's where Nick had met her—at the athletic club he managed in Burnsville. Lauren was clever, though not remotely intellectual. She'd never attended college and had no interest in books or the arts—a big minus by Mary's standards.

Turning to the backseat, Mary said, "We're almost home, honey. Are you doing all right?"

Lauren's head was turned away. She stared out the window and didn't respond.

Mary and Alden had taken their cues from Dr. Parling, the specialist who'd examined Lauren yesterday morning. He felt her problems didn't rise to the level of illness. What she needed was time and the support of her family and friends to help her process what she'd been through. As of this afternoon, Lauren still hadn't spoken or looked anyone in the eye. Parling was certain that she hadn't suffered a catatonic break, she'd simply shut down. She appeared to be completely aware of her surroundings. She cared for herself—bathed, brushed her teeth, ate food when it was set in front of her. In time, he felt she would make a full recovery.

As soon as Gray learned that she was being released, he'd insisted on taking her home with him. Neither Mary nor Alden could believe he'd even suggest such a thing. How would it look to have Nick's wife staying at another man's house? Gray said he didn't give a damn how it looked. He knew Lauren better than anybody but Nick. She felt comfortable with him. But Alden refused to even consider it and Gray finally backed off.

Glancing at Alden, Mary wondered if she looked as tired as he did. It had been a terrible few days. As of 6:08 this morning, Nick had finally opened his eyes. He hadn't said much yet, and he seemed confused, but he was out of the coma, and for that she was grateful. Mary felt she had no particular standing with God, having never attended church regularly or kept to the straight and narrow, so she didn't think she qualified for heavenly favors. She hoped that Alden was praying hard. He was a good man and had a better chance to call in a few markers.

"We'll be home soon," said Alden, adjusting the heater fan. "Gray said he'd meet us at the house."

"I suppose he's just trying to be helpful," said Mary. "I'm sure Nick's grateful."

Alden kept his eyes on the road. "Yeah."

Mary leaned her head back and after a few silent minutes grew reflective. She thought about her sins. One sin in particular. She was ashamed of herself, but apparently not ashamed enough to change her behavior. She loved Alden, that was never in doubt, but during her first marriage she'd formed a pattern, one she hadn't been able to break.

During the years she'd been married to John Mayzer, she'd had dozens of affairs. Or maybe they were more like one- and two-night stands. She'd felt empty inside and unhappy with her life, and cheating on him filled a need. She was furious at him because of his distance. It was like living with a slab of concrete. She never told him about the affairs, but cheating made her feel as if she were evening the score.

Only later did it occur to her that she might have some sort of sexual addiction, or perhaps an addiction to the thrill of the chase, to sneaking around, to the pleasure of the illicit. She behaved more like men were supposed to behave. She didn't want intimacy with her paramours, she simply wanted to get laid. If the guy was any good, she might do it more than once. She liked to plan the assignations with great care. She was always careful about contraception and preventing diseases, and yet she had taken chances. A few of the men had turned out to be . . . well, unsavory, and that was putting it mildly. But it hadn't stopped her.

When she married Alden, she vowed to turn over a new leaf. The first year of their marriage was a golden time in her life. She was deeply in love and happier than she'd ever been. She stopped looking at other men and amazingly, they stopped looking at her. But it didn't last.

It was always the eyes that drew her in. She would see a tiny spark and would respond with a spark of her own. It was automatic, like smiling in response to another's smile. She never wanted to hurt Alden, but she'd grown used to the attention other men gave her. Her friends might damn her to hell for her behavior, but it had nothing to do with them, or with Alden. It *had* no particular meaning other than pleasure. Until, that is, she met Tom Moline.

Tom had begun teaching algebra and geometry at Evergreen High School in September. He'd lived all over the Midwest as a child, applied to Northwestern his senior year of high school, and graduated five years later with a degree in mathematics. He taught in Mokena, Illinois, for a while. That's where he met his wife. She was from northern Minnesota. In an effort to please her, to keep her close to her family, he applied to a number of schools in and around Grand Rapids, and finally landed a teaching position at Greenway High School in Coleraine. He was divorced in '97, but stayed on because he liked the school.

Tom wasn't handsome, but he had a chiseled "Marlboro Man" face and a drop-dead smile. She'd met him in the faculty lunchroom the first week of school. They'd stood and talked until the assistant principal reminded them that it was time to get back to class. Mary was only teaching a third-period acting class this semester. The rest of her time was spent working at the Blackburn Playhouse as a guest dramaturge for a production of Shakespeare's *Two Gentlemen of Verona*. Tom was interested in theater too—more from an historical standpoint, which was a large part of what Mary did. Most people didn't know what a dramaturge was. Tom admitted his own ignorance and said he'd like to learn more about it. They agreed to meet for coffee the following week.

And that's when the affair had begun. As Mary talked about text and story analysis, about her active collaboration with the creative director, the sound, set, costume, and lighting designers, Tom's eyes gave off the telltale sparks. He was attracted. So was she. Three days later they slept together for the first time. Oddly, Mary hadn't planned it. They'd gone off campus one afternoon to grab a quick sandwich at a local coffee shop. On the way back in the car, Tom joked that he was taking her to a motel for a "quickie."

When they pulled into the parking lot of a Fairfield Inn, Mary was not only surprised, but uncharacteristically reticent. Something inside whispered that if she allowed herself to become involved with this man, she might be getting in over her head. And yet, when he booked the room and came back out to the car to get her, she went willingly. She let him undress her. He took his time. Nothing was rushed. She could taste the adrenaline and the desire on his skin. It exactly matched her own. All the tension in her muscles seemed to liquefy when he kissed her. He cut to the core of her so quickly, her normal defenses were breached before she even knew it was happening. And when it was over, she felt changed. Not irreparably, perhaps, but profoundly.

She knew they would meet again. If it had been up to her, they would have booked the same room the very next day. But he stayed away from her for almost a week. Mary left messages in his school mailbox, even called his town house a couple of times. She assumed that they just kept missing each other, though she knew it was more than that. He'd pulled away. He simply hadn't given her the official "heave ho."

And then, one Friday afternoon as she was coming out of the theater, he was there in his car. He'd brought wildflowers. And Limoncella, her favorite liqueur. They went back to his place and made love for hours. He never mentioned the time they'd been apart. She thought he must have been torn, must have been deciding whether or not to call it off. She was married. She told him up front that she loved her husband and would never leave him. But in the end, Tom couldn't stay away from her any more than she could stay away from him. It was a total physical, chemical need to be together.

Alden had been preoccupied all summer. She assumed it was because of Cullen Hegg's suicide. It was understandable, of course, but by August, she was tired of his funk and had tried every way she could to pull him out of it. Except, whenever she broached the subject of Cullen Hegg, everything she said was wrong.

It was during those early weeks of September, when she felt more disconnected from him than she'd ever been before, that she met Tom. She knew her affair wasn't Alden's fault. She was totally to blame. She was weak. She needed to be more patient. And yet when she stepped back and looked at her life, she saw that Alden had actually been *pushing* her away. She didn't understand, and he wouldn't talk about it. Some nights, he'd come home, fix himself a drink, and then lock himself in his study. The next day, everything would be back to normal. A few days later, he'd lock himself in the study again. He'd become a Jekyll and Hyde character. Mary never knew from one moment to the next which one she was with.

Tom, on the other hand, was one of those rare men who could listen as intently as he talked. And intimacy that came from human connection was far more intoxicating to Mary than sex. When combined, the mixture was explosive.

Feeling the car hit a bump in the road, Mary fell back to earth. She was once again in the car with Alden and Lauren. She glanced over at her husband, wondering what he was thinking. It was a question she often asked herself these days.

Mary watched out the window as Alden turned off the county road into their long drive. Seeing their beautiful old farmhouse come into view, she felt suddenly lost. She didn't want to let go of Tom, but her marriage meant everything to her.

Gray's car, a green Lexus, was parked on the blacktop in front of the garage. He slid out of the front seat as they approached, took one last drag off his cigarette, then dropped it and crushed it with the heal of his shoe.

Alden cut the motor and opened his door. "Been here long?"

"A few minutes." Gray nodded to the backseat. "How's she doing?"

"The same."

Mary came around the side as Alden opened the rear door. "Lauren, we're here," she said gently.

Lauren gazed off in the distance.

"I'm here too," said Gray, leaning down so she could see him. He smiled.

She dropped her eyes to her hands.

"Come on, honey," said Mary. "Let's get you inside and warm you up. How does a cup of tea sound?"

Gray and Alden each took one of Lauren's arms and walked her into the house. Mary ran ahead to unlock the door.

As Gray helped Lauren off with her coat, Mary said, "I've got one of the upstairs bedrooms all ready for you. It's Nick's old room. I thought you'd like that. He's out of his coma now, honey, so we've all got to keep our fingers crossed. Actually, I was hoping that one day soon you'll be able to visit. Would you like that?"

"Don't push," whispered Alden. "Dr. Parling said not to—"

"Why are you whispering?" asked Gray. He didn't even try to hide his annoyance. "If I can hear you, so can she. For God's sake, she hasn't lost her *hearing*."

Alden shot him an angry look.

Ignoring them both, Mary helped Lauren to a chair by the bay window. "Honey, would you like something to eat? I could fix you a sandwich."

Lauren continued to stare at her hands.

"Just go ahead and do it," said Alden. "She's got to be hungry."

Mary crossed to the dining room and then into the kitchen. After putting the kettle on, she opened the refrigerator and took out some mayo, lettuce, and sliced turkey. While the water heated, she made the sandwich, all the while listening to the conversation in the living room.

Gray was talking. "I know you and Mary have concerns about how you're going to manage Lauren's care."

"We want her here," said Alden. "She's not a problem." He added quickly, "I mean, *you're* not a problem, honey. I don't mean to talk about you like you're not in the room."

"Right," said Gray, "but you both work full-time. I think I might have a solution for you. I met this woman at the hospital—a Ms. Cheryl Jaffery. She runs a professional home care service for psychiatric outpatients. She said she had several women who would be immediately available to come in and provide care for Lauren, should we need it. I think it's a great idea. Actually, I'd like to pay for the service myself if you'll let me."

"Not necessary, Gray. We can handle it."

"Okay. Whatever. But why don't you let me call Ms. Jaffery? I could check out a few of her service workers and then hire one of them. That would save you some time, and it would make me feel like I'm doing something to help."

"I thought we'd check out Lutheran Family Services," said Mary, returning to the room with a tray of cookies. "I know they have home care workers."

"I'm sure they do," said Gray, "but Ms. Jaffery's people are specifically trained to work with patients who have problems like Lauren's."

"Would this person want to live at the house?" asked Mary.

"I don't know," said Gray, leaning over and grabbing a ginger snap. "But I'll find out. And I'll get back to you."

Mary always kept ginger snaps around for Gray. She'd known him for almost ten years now, ever since he'd roomed with Nick their first year of college. Most of Gray's friends, including Nick, used to call him Che, as in Che Guevara. Back then, his black hair had been scruffy, and he had a full beard. He also wore a black beret to heighten the effect. Nick told her once that Gray had posters of Guevara plastered all over their dorm-room walls. Mary often wondered what kind of young man would want to cultivate the image of a Latin American revolutionary. He'd cleaned himself up after he passed the bar, but he'd retained the macho arrogance. She assumed he didn't have to work very hard to acquire that quality.

"When could she start?" asked Alden.

"If I get on it this afternoon, with luck I might be able to have someone here by tomorrow morning."

"I guess that would be okay," said Mary, hearing the teakettle whistle. Returning to the kitchen, she called, "But if it doesn't work out, there's always Lutheran Family Services."

"If you don't like the woman," called Gray, "or if Lauren doesn't, I'm sure Ms. Jaffery could send someone else."

Mary returned with the sandwich and a tray loaded with mugs and the teapot.

"There's, ah, one other thing I wanted to bring up before I go," said Gray, shaking his head when Mary offered him a steaming mug.

Mary spread an afghan over Lauren's shoulders. She was cold, so she assumed Lauren was too. She set the sandwich plate on Lauren's lap and then sat down in a rocking chair next to her.

Gray continued. "Several of the guests at the wedding banquet have contacted me about bringing a lawsuit against Jane Lawless and her restaurant. I haven't taken a retainer from anyone yet, but I'm leaning toward it. I thought perhaps you two might want to join the group. I have a feeling, as people see others suing, more will jump on board."

"Absolutely not," said Alden, pushing out of his chair.

"May I ask why?" said Gray.

Alden bent down by the woodstove and began crunching up newspapers to make a fire. "Jane's a friend. She had nothing to do with what happened at that wedding dinner."

"Nothing to do with it? Her staff prepared and served the food."

"Yes, but *she* didn't contaminate it."

"Doesn't matter. She owns the company."

"Of course it matters."

"I disagree, Alden. She bears legal responsibility and that's what the court cares about."

"Someone else put the drug in the food," said Alden, tossing strips of kindling on top of the paper. "It had nothing to do with her or her catering company."

"You know that for a fact?"

"No one has a grudge against my son—or Lauren. Who would want to wreck their wedding night? It was all aimed at me, Gray. I was the target. The fact that others were involved was just . . . what's that crass military term? Collateral damage."

Mary was completely confused. "Until the police figure out what really happened, how can you possibly know that?"

"I just do. And I don't want to talk about it." Alden struck a match and lit the newspaper. He watched the kindling catch, then stood up.

"What could you possibly have done to warrant such an attack?" asked Mary.

"Look," said Gray. "Whoever the target was, you have to face facts. Others were injured, if not physically, then psychologically. And if I take on these cases, I'll want to sue on behalf of Lauren and Nick. That goes without saying."

"Not if I have anything to say about it," said Alden, walking over to the front closet to get his coat and hat.

Gray turned to Mary. "Do you feel the same way?"

She searched her husband's face for clues to what he was thinking. She didn't understand where all these ideas were coming from. "I don't want to hurt Jane because I think she was a victim of a sick mind—just like the rest of us were. *But,* if we find out that someone on her crew was responsible for the food tampering, then I think we have to sue for damages. Nick will need a great deal of care for a very long time. Lauren may too. We need an insurance company with deep pockets to pay for it all. Nick's policy will cover some of his needs, but not all of it. And we have to think about the long-term ramifications. I'm not out for blood, Gray, just financial help with Nick and Lauren's recovery."

Alden popped a couple of Tums in his mouth, then slipped into his coat.

"Where are you going?" asked Mary. It was a simple question, but it came out more like an accusation.

"For a walk," said Alden. "I need some fresh air."

"Don't shut me out, sweetheart. *Please.*"

"I'll be back later."

After he'd gone, Mary turned to Lauren to see if she was taking any of this in. Instead of her usual faraway look, her attention was riveted on something under the dining-room table.

Gray noticed the change in her too. He followed her gaze and saw that she was looking at Dolce, Mary's new little white kitten. Dolce was hiding under a chair. "Would you like to hold her?" asked Gray.

Lauren kept her eyes on the kitten.

Picking it up, Gray carried it over to her, crouched down, and placed it in her arms. "There you go," he said, smiling at her.

The kitten sniffed Lauren's hand, then settled down to lick its paw.

Lauren stroked the kitten's fur.

"Hey, that's great," said Gray. "Maybe this is a small breakthrough."

Mary nodded, but she was lost in her own thoughts, her eyes fixed on the front door.

12

Steven's hands tightened around the steering wheel. His father had called to tell him that Doris French had finally come through with the tape of Cullen's last minutes, the conversation he had with Alden Clifford. But that was almost two hours ago.

Steven had left Minneapolis immediately. Snow had been falling since late afternoon and 35W had quickly turned into a skating rink. He was close to the Evergreen turnoff now and with luck he'd arrive at his dad's house soon, but from the sound of his father's voice, he knew he'd been drinking. Steven was afraid he wouldn't wait, that he'd listen to the tape before Steven got there. And that could be disaster.

Under his heavy coat, Steven was sweating. He couldn't turn the heater off because he needed to keep the defrost cranked up to high, otherwise the windshield would crust with ice. He hated winter. When it was time to apply to med school, he'd pick a warmer climate. Only lunatics stayed in Minnesota. Up ahead, he saw the sign that announced EVERGREEN, 2 MILES. He glanced into the rearview mirror, then pulled into the right lane. The jerk behind him laid on his horn, as if Steven had no right to change lanes. "Screw you, shithead," he snarled, giving the guy the finger.

Once he was off the freeway, the roads got even worse. Every time he accelerated, he nearly lost control of the car. If it had been colder, the driving wouldn't be so bad, but with the temperatures up near freezing, the snow was greasy—slippery beyond belief. The Corvette fishtailed down Fulbright Avenue, the windshield wipers thwacking back and forth. It was like a metronome counting out the seconds, making Steven feel even more keenly that time was passing—that he was late.

When he turned onto Bendix Lane, the car slid sideways into a ditch. "Dammit! Dammit! Dammit!" he screamed. He pressed the accelerator to the floor, hearing the unmistakable sound of spinning wheels. Realizing he was hopelessly stuck, he unhooked his seat belt and climbed out. One of the rear tires was buried in snow and the other had scoured out a deep rut. It would take him and three other guys to push the thing free. He didn't have three guys. And he didn't have an hour to round them up.

Steven cut the motor, locked the car, and left it in the ditch. Pulling the hood of his parka up over his head, he began working his way toward the house. It was less than a block, but nobody had shoveled yet, so it was slow going. With each step, his leg sunk in halfway up his knee. The wind was blowing the snow into three-foot drifts. It was a good night to stay home and watch a ball game.

As he came around a curve in the road, he saw that his dad's place was dark. But by the time he crossed the street, he noticed that a light was on in the basement. That's where his father must be.

Passing the garage, he peeked in the windows to see if his dad's SUV was still inside. There it was. At least he hadn't left in some alcohol-induced state of fury.

Trudging into the hall with boots heavily caked with snow, Steven bent over and brushed off his jeans, then kicked his boots off and headed downstairs. He found his dad sitting in a beat-up old chair, deep in the shadows near the furnace.

"The traffic was total crap," said Steven, peeling off his coat. He dropped the sodden mess over a box. "Sorry I'm late. Have you listened to it yet?"

His father didn't move.

"Dad?" said Steven, walking closer. He could see now that his father had been crying. His face was all red and puffy. "What's wrong?"

"Everything."

"Did you listen to it?"

He nodded.

"Dammit all, Dad, I thought we had a deal. You said you'd wait."

"I couldn't. I just . . . couldn't."

"Where is it?" demanded Steven.

His father pointed to the workbench.

A small tape recorder sat next to the power drill.

Steven picked it up and pressed rewind. He kicked an empty plastic pail out of his way as he carried it over to his mother's old steamer trunk, where he sat down. What he was about to hear would be raw. It would be truth. He felt like vomiting.

Pressing the play button, Steven waited through a bunch of static until he heard Cullen's voice. It sounded tinny, a little speeded up. The cartoon squirrel version of Cullen.

"It's just you and me now," said Cullen's voice.

"What are you going to do?" Clifford was farther away from the mike, but his voice was deeper and carried better than Cullen's.

"I haven't decided."

"Why did you bring the gun?"

"Why do you think?"

"To scare people. To scare *me*."

"Wrong."

"You're so young, Cullen. Don't do this. Listen to me. *Please*. Let's just talk about it."

"Why do you care so fucking much?"

"You know why."

"Do you love me, Clifford? Really love me?" Long pause. "I'm so sick of feeling alone. Nobody cares, not really. Nobody's ever going to care."

"You're depressed, Cullen. You can get help for that. We've talked about it."

"I'm *not* depressed, I'm fucking sick and tired of being galactically stupid! If anybody ever finds out what I've done . . . God, I couldn't stand it. I feel like my brain's rotted clear through."

Silence.

"I can help," said Clifford.

"Right. Like you've already helped."

"I can get you out of here, make sure nothing happens to you. You're a juvenile. You haven't hurt anyone."

"Like you'll keep my secret."

"Will you keep mine?" More silence. "What do you want from me? Just tell me what I can do."

"Nothing."

"Then give me the gun. Let's stop this right now."

"Stay there. Don't come any closer."

"Why did you bring the gun, Cullen? Really."

"You already asked me that."

"But you didn't answer."

"I went home for lunch. My dad was there, so I waited until he'd left for work and then I took it from the closet I thought . . . hell, I don't know what I thought. I just wanted to look at it. Feel it in my hand. And then, it was time to get to class."

More silence.

"You came here for a reason," said Clifford. "What was it?"

"Putting off the inevitable, I guess."

"I do care about you, Cullen. I care about you more than you know."

"You taught me a lot. I guess . . . maybe I do think you care. That's why I came. I thought maybe you could stop me. But you can't. I see that now. Nobody can."

The tape registered movement. A falling chair or desk. Something large and heavy scraping across the floor. "Give it to me."

"Sorry."

"Cullen, don't do it. There's another way."

And then the gunshot, a small sound like a cap gun. Not the huge bang you might expect, the blast that could blow away a life.

Steven pressed the stop button. "God," he whispered, lowering his head. It was worse than he'd imagined. It was all there. Everything. Except the police hadn't picked up on it. Had his Dad?

His father lifted the fifth of Seagram's. He didn't have a glass, he just swigged right from the bottle. It was that kind of moment, thought Steven. A glass would have seemed silly.

"How could my son do it? How could he be like that?"

Steven looked at his father's large, bulky body. "What are you saying?"

"Isn't it obvious?"

"Isn't what obvious?"

"My boy. He was a . . . a homo."

Steven's eyes opened wide. "You think *that's* what they were talking about?"

"What else could it be? Why the hell would Cullen ask his teacher, a man he hardly knew, if he loved him? It's sick. Perverted. I could kill that man with my bare hands."

"I don't know, Dad. I think you're reading stuff into it that's not there."

"Like hell I am. It was Clifford! He's responsible for Cullen's death. He must have seduced him and Cullen couldn't stand the guilt. Didn't he say he felt used, or words to that effect? He said if people found out what he'd done, he couldn't stand it. So he killed himself. He couldn't live with the truth of what Clifford had done to him, what he'd done with Clifford, so he *had* to take his life."

Steven was keenly aware that his father had missed the most important clues. Whether or not this homosexual theory proved to be true, it gave his dad something he'd been searching for. In his dad's mind, that was proof positive that Cullen's death hadn't been his fault. Steven could easily have pointed out that there were other ways of interpreting Cullen's words. But his father's belief that Alden Clifford had molested his son gave him back his sense of himself as a good father. Another man had corrupted his son, it hadn't been *his* personal failure. How could Steven take that away from him? In a way, it gave Steven the same thing—a way not to blame himself so much.

"Clifford has no business being a teacher," said Steven's father, his voice a low, angry rumble. "He's poison—just like all those Catholic priests. He's got to be removed."

"Are you saying you're going to try to get him fired?"

His dad took another swig of whiskey. "I'll call the principal tomorrow morning."

"And tell her what? You don't have any proof."

"Of course I do. I have the tape."

"Which you can't show to anyone because it would get Doris in trouble. It might even get her sacked. And besides, the cops already heard it. They didn't read the conversation the same way you did."

"Well, then, they're blind. Willingly blind."

"Dad, listen to me. I think you should consider the matter closed. You know the truth now. Just let it rest."

Steven's father looked over at him, his face clenched with determination. "That's not enough. Clifford is still a threat to other kids. Believe me, Stevey, I'm going to bring that man down if it's the last thing I do."

13

It was going on midnight. Jane sat in her car outside Jason Vickner's four-plex, watching for any sign that he might be inside. There were no lights on in the lower south apartment, so she assumed nobody was home, although if he was there, he might not want to advertise it. She'd driven past the fourplex earlier, after she was finished with her baby-sitting duties. She'd even buzzed Jason's apartment, but nobody answered. She'd checked the mailbox before she left. Two names were listed for Apart-ment B: Alan Vickner, and Jason Vickner.

Jane felt she'd handled her confrontation with Jason badly. She'd scared him and that had been a mistake. If he went into hiding before she got a chance to talk to him, she might never learn what he knew. She'd considered calling the police and passing on her suspicions, but decided to give him more time. Her instincts told her that, at this point, she'd get more out of him than the police would.

What she needed was a carrot, something to offer him to get him to open up. That was assuming he'd been working for someone else and wasn't just a young, budding sociopath. Jane kept going back to what Anna Carlson had said. She thought he had a lot of potential. Anna was rarely wrong about people, so Jane figured it was only right to give him the benefit of the doubt. For now.

Just after twelve-thirty, Jane saw headlights flash in her rearview mir-ror. A car made its way slowly toward her through the deep snow. At this time of night, with so many apartment buildings on the block, finding a parking space was next to impossible. Jane had been lucky, finding one almost directly across from the fourplex. The car rumbled past her and plowed into a spot up the street, one that looked more like a snowdrift. A moment later two men got out and walked back to the apartment building.

Jane felt her heart rate speed up as she slid out of the front seat. She waited until they reached the door, then approached them from behind, jingling her keys, hoping they'd think she lived in the building.

Both men were young—about the same general age as Jason. Neither seemed even slightly concerned that she might be breaching security. The shorter of the two guys even held the door open for her as she passed into the inside hall.

Jason's apartment was on the left. She hung back and fished for something in her pocket, waiting to see where the two men would go. To her surprise they stopped at Jason's door. The shorter one had a key. Recalling the names on the mailbox, she decided he had to be Alan.

"Excuse me," said Jane. "I'm looking for Jason."

The shorter guy turned around, giving her a quick once-over. "I'm his brother."

"Alan, yes. I know." She turned on her smile. It was one of her best assets. "Jason works for me."

"You own that fancy restaurant?"

"That's me. Is Jason home?"

"I don't think so," said the other guy. "I ran into him this afternoon. He seemed totally whacked out."

"How come?" asked Jason's brother.

The taller kid shrugged. "Didn't say."

"Do you all live here?" asked Jane.

"Just me," said Alan. "But Joe here is around a lot. He's our cousin."

"You want me to tell Jason you stopped by?" Alan opened the door to the apartment and switched on an overhead light.

The front room was filled with junky furniture, but it all looked perfectly neat. In the center of the room sat a huge rear projection TV.

"Nice TV," said Jane, looking over Alan's shoulder.

Alan turned around. "Yeah, it's sweet. It came with a great sound system. We watched *Lord of the Rings* on DVD last night. Awesome."

"It's Jason's," said Joe, chewing on a toothpick. He smelled of beer and clean laundry.

"He must have been saving his money a long time for that," said Jane.

"Yeah," said Alan, glancing sideways at Joe. "Guess so."

Jane smiled. "Look, I need to talk to Jason. It's important. Do you expect him back tonight?"

"Don't know," said Alan, unzipping his coat. "We don't keep tabs on each other."

"No, of course not. But if he calls, will you tell him Jane Lawless stopped by. And that I need to talk to him right away. Better yet, let me write him a note. If he calls, you can read it to him. If he comes home, you can just give it to him." She asked Alan for a piece of paper.

He took a small notebook out of his backpack and handed it to her.

"Thanks. This will just take a second." She retrieved a pen from the pocket of her jeans and pulled the pen's cap off with her teeth.

She wrote:

Jason—I need to know what happened. I can help you if you'll let me. My father is a defense attorney. He could represent you if you need a lawyer—free of charge, no strings. Please, Jason. Call me. We need to talk before this gets blown all out of proportion.

Jane

She printed her office, home, and cell number at the bottom, then folded the note and handed it to Alan. She wanted to minimize the situation so that Jason would feel less threatened. She needed to make up for scaring him so badly this morning. As soon as she left, she knew Alan and Joe would read it. Not much she could do about that. If they did know where he was, maybe the message would prompt them to track him down. Only time would tell if this was a blind alley, or if Jason Vickner would prove to be the key to unlocking the truth behind the food tampering.

Cottonwood, Kansas

November 1, 1972

When Jimmy awoke, he was lying in a hospital bed. His mom and dad were sitting on either side of him, both asleep. He touched his head and found that it was bandaged. He had a splitting headache, a bad cut on his lip, and every time he took a breath, his chest hurt like hell. He looked around for a clock, but couldn't find one. It was light out, and that meant the nightmare was over. Someone must have pulled him out of the Rambler. Fucking amazing: he hadn't died.

More than anything else, Jimmy didn't want to be hassled right now. He just wanted to stay in bed and think. After all, he'd stared death in the face and lived to tell about it. How many guys could say that? But any second his mom or his dad could wake up and demand to know what happened. Maybe they'd cut him some slack because he was all bandaged up. He might be able to use that for a while. If the questions got too tough, he could always pretend to faint. But he couldn't put it off forever. A reckoning was coming.

Jimmy's parents would not only want to know what he'd been doing out on the highway in the middle of the night, but where his sister was. He'd be jail bait if he told the truth. He had to cover for what really happened. He'd wrecked his dad's car—he couldn't lie his way out of that one. In the scheme of things, it seemed pretty small to Jimmy, compared with the mess Patsy was in, but it probably didn't seem small to his dad.

All of a sudden, tears welled up in Jimmy's eyes. His saw his sister's face inside his mind and it killed him. Where was she? Frank must have gotten away. Unless?

Maybe the police caught him! Jimmy's heart thumped faster and faster. Was Patsy okay? Did Frank spill the beans about Jimmy dealing drugs?

"Honey, are you okay?" asked his mother, touching his hand.

He stared at her wild-eyed.

"You're safe, Jimmy," she said soothingly. "Everything's going to be all right."

How could she say that when his entire life was about to blow apart?

His father cleared his throat, coughed a couple of times, and sat up. "Hey, buddy. How you feelin'?"

What did they actually know? He had to play it carefully. "What happened?" he asked, making his voice go all soft and raspy.

"Don't you remember?" asked his mother.

She looked worried, or worse—she looked as if she was about to cry too. If everybody was crying, that couldn't be good.

"What happened to Patsy?" she asked.

Her voice trembled only slightly, but Jimmy caught it. He'd never seen his mother this afraid before. "It was those guys," he said, switching his attention between his mom and dad.

"What guys?" asked his dad.

"The ones in the van."

"Jim, you have to start from the beginning," said his father. "All we know is that the police chased you for almost ten miles before the Rambler ended up in the river. If they hadn't been there to fish you out, you'd be dead."

Jimmy swallowed hard. It was one thing to lie in bed and think about last night like it was a bad dream. It was a whole different matter to have your father say the words out loud and make it real—so real you could feel the hot, sour terror ooze up in your throat all over again. Jimmy shut his eyes. The icy water tugged at his ankles. He could hear it gushing in, but he couldn't see it. Even the moonlight had been erased. He kept tugging at the door. The water was at his chest now. Then under his chin. He shut his mouth, held his breath.

"Don't cry, Jimmy," said his mother.

"I'm not crying," he said, air bursting from his lungs. "I'm not." He batted at his eyes.

"Jim," said his father, sitting down on the bed. "You have to tell us what happened. You've been through an awful experience, we understand that, but so have we. We're desperate, son. Where's Patsy? Was she"—he looked hard at Jimmy—"in the car?"

Jimmy shook his head.

"Oh, God," gasped his mother. She rocked back and forth, her arms clasped tightly around her waist. "Thank you, God. Thank you."

"We were so scared," said his father. "The police have been out all night looking for her. So have I. Where is she, son? What about these guys in a van?"

"They . . . they took Patsy."

"Who were they?" demanded his father. "Did you know them?"

Again, Jimmy shook his head. "Never seen them before. Patsy and me, we were walking down Elmhurst. I took her trick-or-treating, just like you said. She went up to the Van Gelders to get her candy, and when she came back, this van pulled up. There were two guys in it. Big guys. Mean-looking. They got out and one of them held a gun on me while the other grabbed Patsy and threw her in the back of the van. As soon as they drove off, I ran back to the house and took the car to follow them."

His father seemed shocked, unable to speak.

"Why didn't you wake me?" asked his mother. "Or call your father at the factory?"

"There wasn't time! I couldn't let them get away, don't you understand?"

Getting up, his father walked to the door and just stood there, looking out into the hall. Finally, turning around, he said, "So you took the car and chased after them."

"And I almost caught them, too, but I must have hit a bump in the road or something, because the next thing I knew, I was in the river. And then . . . I don't remember anything until I woke up here."

"Call the police," said Jimmy's mother. "Do it now. There's no time to waste."

When Jimmy turned to his mother, he saw that the skin on her face had changed color. She didn't look like herself anymore. She looked like the painted porcelain doll they kept on top of the bookshelf in the family room so nobody would break it.

"God, how could this happen to my little girl?" cried his mom.

"I did everything I could," said Jimmy. "You gotta believe me!"

"We know you did, son," said his dad. "Listen to me. The police will want to talk to you. Maybe you saw something important, something that will help them find these perverts. Don't be surprised if I bring an officer back with me, okay?" He didn't wait for a response.

Jimmy was left alone to comfort his mother. He felt tongue-tied in the presence of her flood of tears. He was a liar and a shit. It was all his fault and he knew it.

"I'm sorry, Mom. Really I am. It'll be okay. We'll find her. Please, Mom, please stop crying."

Jimmy made a vow right then and there. He would never rest until he found Frank and got his sister back. And if Frank had hurt her—even a little bit—well, he'd better say his prayers. When Jimmy got done with him, he'd be a dead man— or wish like hell he was.

Monday

14

On Monday morning, Jane was on her way out of the pub when Cordelia breezed into the foyer. She held Hattie in one arm, a bag of diapers and other childhood necessities in the other.

Jane checked the time. It was nine-fifteen. "You're up early."

"It's not *nice* to gloat, Jane." Cordelia hitched the little girl up a bit higher.

"Where's Octavia?"

"Who knows?"

"You mean . . . she didn't come home last night?"

Cordelia's eyes shot daggers.

"Hi," said Hattie.

"Hi, sweetheart," said Jane, squeezing her hand. "How are you today?"

Cordelia pivoted and steamed off toward Jane's office. She was in high dudgeon. Nobody messed with Cordelia Thorn when she was in high dudgeon.

Jane followed. The sight of Cordelia carrying a toddler in her arms reminded Jane of King Kong carrying Jessica Lange up the Empire State Building. Frightening, to be sure, but at the same time, oddly touching.

Once inside the room, Cordelia set Hattie down.

"Ooooh, Augie," said Hattie, running over to Mouse, who was lying on the rug in front of the fireplace. She flopped down, narrowly missing his head.

Mouse sniffed her from head to toe, then gave her arm a lick.

"Good boy, Mouse," said Jane. She had no idea how he'd behave around kids. He seemed to take Hattie's awkward, excessively eager attention in stride.

As Hattie alternately banged and stroked his back, Jane joined Cordelia on the couch.

"Aren't you worried about Octavia?" said Jane.

"She's smart enough to know that as long as she stays away, she'll be fine. It's when she comes back to my loft that her life will be in danger."

"She wouldn't just leave Hattie with you without calling."

An elegant eyebrow soared heavenward. "Wouldn't she?"

"Something's wrong, Cordelia. You should call the police. File a missing person's report. This isn't like her."

"This is *just* like her. She only came for a visit because she wanted something. I now know what it is. She needed a place for Hattie to stay while she went off God knows where doing God knows what."

Octavia might be unpredictable, but Jane couldn't believe she'd leave her little girl without making sure she was properly cared for. Of course, she had no way of knowing the nanny would split.

Hattie crawled into Cordelia's lap and leaned her head against Cordelia's ample bosom.

Cordelia rolled her eyes. "Do you notice anything wrong with this picture? Do I *look* like the motherly type? Do you think I *enjoy* being awakened at two, four, and seven in the morning by a screaming child? Up until last night, I had managed to escape the intense personal joy of changing a diaper. Contrary to some people's opinion, I could have lived my entire life without joining Club Mommy and still feel totally fulfilled."

"Yes, but you've got to admit, she is pretty cute."

Cordelia gazed down at Hattie. "There is that."

"And she seems to like you."

"She has taste."

"And you have the next four weeks off."

"Ah, there's the rub. Italy beckons, so I must find a nanny, Jane. And I must find one soon. I have too much to do before I leave to spend all my time taking care of *The Toddler*."

"Don't look at me."

"Actually, I was thinking about Cecily Finch. You wouldn't miss her bartending services if I snatched her for a while, right? Octavia will surface sooner or later, but until then, I need help."

If Cordelia's idea of toddler food was double cream French Brie, Jane agreed. "I think Cecily was just offered a part in a play at TRP. She's asked to have some of her hours changed to accommodate the rehearsals."

"Evening hours?"

"Mostly."

"I can work around that. She's actually quite spectacular with kids. Hattie seemed to like her. Not as much as she likes me, of course, but then, that's to be expected."

"Of course," said Jane. Even though Cordelia had blown it off, Jane was still uneasy about Octavia's disappearance.

"Does Cecily work today?"

"No, but I think she was stopping in this morning to pick up her check."

"Do you know when?"

"Let me call upstairs."

Jane stepped over to her desk and punched a button on her phone. She drummed her fingers on the desktop until Francis, her assistant manager, picked up. "Has Cecily been in yet?"

"She's here right now," said Francis.

"Will you ask her to come down to my office for a minute?"

After hanging up, Jane turned around to find Cordelia bouncing Hattie on her knee. This might be a bit of a love/hate relationship, but to Jane, it looked mostly like love.

Hattie grinned and giggled, her blue eyes sparkling.

In a deep, excessively modulated voice, Cordelia crooned:

"Higglety, pigglety pop!
The dog has eaten the mop;
The pig's in a hurry,
The cat's in a flurry,
Higglety, pigglety pop!"

Hattie was clearly delighted. She didn't understand the words, but Cordelia's voice was so full of amused ups and downs, she knew something important was being said.

"Gen," said Hattie. "Gen. Gen!"

"That means 'again,'" said Cordelia. "I'm starting to understand her gibberish. Her vocabulary is more extensive than I first thought. In my opinion, she can't be introduced to the Classics too early."

"That was a classic?"

"Don't be a snob." Lowering her voice again, Cordelia said,

> "When I am grown to man's estate
> I shall be very proud and great,
> And tell the other girls and boys
> Not to meddle with my toys."

She wiggled her eyebrows. "When I was a little girl, that was my favorite poem, Hattie. It's from *A Child's Garden of Verse* by Robert Louis Stevenson. Terrible book. It's a collection of poems English mommies and daddies used to read to their children to make them as tight-assed, sanctimonious, and bigoted as they were."

Jane laughed. "Don't hold your punches."

Cecily entered a few seconds later, looking surprised to see Cordelia and Hattie. "Hey," she said, pulling her straight brown hair behind her ears.

"I've got a job offer for you," said Cordelia, not wasting a minute.

"An offer?" repeated Cecily. Her arms went rigid and her entire body tensed. Maybe she thought her big moment had finally arrived. Cordelia was about to offer her the lead role in a forthcoming play.

So much for self-delusion, thought Jane.

"I need a full-time baby-sitter for the next few days," said Cordelia, bouncing Hattie up and down. "Possibly longer. I'd need you until my sister returns from somewhere over the rainbow, or wherever the hell she went."

Cecily's entire body drooped. "A baby-sitter," she said flatly.

"Well, a nanny, if you prefer. You're good with kids. You've got a real talent."

"Gee. Thanks."

"Hi," said Hattie, waving. She pointed at Mouse. "Augie."

"That mean's 'doggie,'" said Jane.

"Cute," said Cecily. She chewed her lower lip and twitched a little.

Jane could see that she was deciding whether this was a good move or not. It might get her closer to the prize, or it might get her nowhere.

"I'll pay you well," said Cordelia. "Don't worry about that."

"I don't know," said Cecily.

She's stalling, thought Jane. She's seeing how much she can push it.

"Hattie likes you," said Cordelia. "She already knows you. I hate the idea of having to find some stranger to take care of her. I wouldn't even know where to look."

"When would you want me to start?"

"Today. Now. I have a dentist appointment at eleven. I'm getting my teeth whitened." She smiled wide to show off her pearly whites. "This is my third and last appointment. I doubt Hattie would be content to look through magazines in the waiting room."

"No," said Jane. Sometimes she thought Cordelia lived on another planet.

"Well," said Cecily, mulling it over, "actually, I had a lunch date with Gray today. But he called me last night and canceled. He said he needed to check on Lauren. He's hired some woman to help Mary and Alden care for her. I don't know why they let Gray hire her. That's like asking the fox to repair the lock on the hen house."

"Excuse me?" said Jane.

"Don't get me started."

There had to be some major tension between Cecily and Gray, thought Jane.

"Would you need me twenty-four/seven?" asked Cecily.

"No," said Cordelia. "I'll take care of her in the evenings. Well, most evenings. We'll *negotiate*." She sighed. "All life is a negotiation, no?"

"I'd need Monday and Wednesday nights off for sure—for rehearsals. I've been cast in a play at TRP."

"So I hear," said Cordelia, prying Hattie's fist out of her auburn curls. "Congratulations. But my sister will be back soon. She has to be. I leave next week for Amsterdam, and then on to Rome."

Wishful thinking, thought Jane.

"What do you say, Cecily? How does twenty-five an hour sound?"

Cecily continued to chew her lower lip. "Is it okay with you, Jane? I'd have to bail on my hours at the restaurant."

"We'll manage," said Jane. "I think Cordelia needs you more."

"Well, okay. Why not?" said Cecily. "Of course I can help you. What are friends for?"

Cordelia sniffed inside Hattie's pants. "Hey, will you look at the time? I simply *must* fly." She handed Hattie to Cecily. "Thanks again, dearheart. Diapers are in the bag. You have my undying appreciation."

"I'm counting on that," said Cecily, hoisting Hattie into her arms. "Who knows? Someday, I might just think of a way for you to repay the favor."

Wednesday

15

Alden sat on his bed holding the cheap gold locket in his hands and thinking about his past. As a young man, he'd learned something vitally important, a truth that had served as the preface to his future. Simply put, there came a moment in everyone's life when a single defining action made you who you are. You couldn't go back and change it, no matter how much you might want to. Perhaps it was what philosophers meant when they talked about fate. The moment was a choice. And the choice was a door that locked up tight as soon as you walked through it.

Morning sunlight streamed in through the frosted windows as Alden studied the photo inside the locket one more time. He'd looked at it a thousand times since the biker had tossed it at his feet three weeks ago. The picture inside was of a little girl with a crooked smile. He didn't need a photo to remind him. The face had been burned into his memory by the fire of his own hate. The picture had been cut from an old yellowed newspaper. Though it was a poor representation of the subject, Alden would never forget those eyes. They were the color of the summer sky on a clear Kansas day.

Rubbing a hand across his forehead, he tried to massage the ache out of his mind. There were no coincidences in life. The biker had appeared because of Cullen Hegg's suicide. Alden knew he would come eventually. But why had he waited six months to deliver his message of pain and remembrance?

Clamping the locket shut, Alden let it rest for a moment in his palm. It all came down to his past, as it always did, and to the ghost he'd lived with every day of his adult life. He had no idea what would happen next. All he knew for sure was that Cullen Hegg's suicide had tied his body to the railroad tracks and that a train was barreling straight for him out of the darkness.

Rising from the bed, Alden opened the top drawer of his chest. He pushed the locket to the back, under a pile of socks. It would be safe there. He didn't want Mary to find it and demand an explanation.

Alden had taken a couple days off from teaching to be with his son at the hospital. Nick was doing somewhat better. He was still in ICU, but he was more alert, and though at times he had difficulty speaking, his doctors held out hope for a complete recovery. His leg had been operated on, the bone set so that it would heal properly. His injuries were severe, but he was alive and on the mend.

Lauren's condition hadn't improved much. She said a few words, every now and then, but mainly she stayed in her room, sitting quietly by the window or watching TV. Alden was deeply troubled by her silence and tried to engage her in conversations, but so far she'd frozen him—and everyone else—out. He sensed that she wanted to talk. Even though she kept her eyes averted, he could feel the emotion boiling inside her.

On her first night with them, Alden had brought her a couple of his favorite books—*Leaves of Grass* by Walt Whitman, and *Brideshead Revisited* by Evelyn Waugh. He thought she might like to have something good to read. She hadn't touched them. At least, that's what Kenzie Nelson, the home health aide they'd hired to look after Lauren, had said.

Kenzie was nothing like Alden had imagined she'd be—in other words, middle-aged and matronly. The morning she first arrived, Alden had stood at the front window and watched her amble up to the front porch. He'd studied her long legs covered in tight black jeans, her baggy red flannel shirt over a black tank top, and her ostrich leather cowboy boots. Her reddish-gold hair was zip cut—like a new boot camp recruit—and except for a hint of added color around the eyes, she wore little makeup. He found her attractive, in a tall, boyish sort of way. And though she was hardly beautiful, she carried herself with assurance. He figured she got stared at a lot.

And she was direct. Alden appreciated that. She explained that she would arrive by seven each day, and would leave at five—unless asked to stay later. If necessary, she would be happy to spend the night. She was there for Lauren and for them—whatever was needed. She would cook Lauren's meals, administer her medications, sit with her if she wanted, read to her, and just generally keep an eye on her.

The word "suicide" had never been mentioned, though with someone as obviously disturbed as Lauren, it wasn't far from anyone's thoughts.

Today was Wednesday. Both Mary and Alden were returning to work. Mary had already left for the Blackburn Playhouse. Alden didn't have a class until third period, but he wanted to get to school early. Substitute teachers had a way of making shambles of his classroom. He'd need some time to put things in order before his students descended.

As he emerged from the bedroom, dressed in freshly pressed chinos and a red wool sweater, ready for the day to begin, he saw Kenzie come out of Lauren's room.

"How's she doing today?" he asked, keeping his voice low.

"About the same," said Kenzie. She was carrying a breakfast tray. By the looks of it, Lauren hadn't eaten much.

Kenzie trotted down the stairs and Alden followed.

"Have you ever had a case like Lauren before?" he asked. He entered the kitchen and poured himself a cup of coffee.

"Sure," said Kenzie, dumping the remains of the breakfast into the garbage. "I've cared for people with all kinds of psychological problems."

"People who kept their feelings bottled up inside after a traumatic event?"

"Once or twice."

Alden carried his mug over to the kitchen table and sat down. "How long before they got better?"

"Every situation is different. My guess is, your daughter-in-law isn't ready to talk yet," said Kenzie. "Be patient."

"That's what my wife says. But our son, he keeps asking about her. We told him that she's just not well enough to visit, but I can tell he doesn't understand. What am I supposed to say?"

"That she'll come when she can. Pushing her to go see him wouldn't be good for either one of them."

"Yeah, yeah. I suppose."

Kenzie pulled out a chair and sat down across from him. "Mr. Donovan said you'd had kind of a bad year. One of your students committed suicide last spring. I think I remember reading about it in the papers. How well did you know the boy?"

Alden stirred some sugar into his coffee. "As well as I know any student, which is to say, not well."

"Why do you suppose he chose your classroom as the place to—"

The Maalox bottle was sitting on the kitchen counter. He reached for it and took a swig. "This is a subject that still upsets me, Kenzie. I really don't want to talk about it." His stomach was killing him again. He wondered if he was developing an ulcer.

"If you don't mind my saying so, Mr. Clifford, you use an awful lot of antacid. Maybe you should see a doctor."

"Like you said, this has been a stressful time. My stomach always caves in when I'm upset. But thanks for your concern. I think I'll run upstairs and say goodbye to Lauren before I go."

"I'll clean up down here," said Kenzie. She stood and turned to the sink. "Call if you need anything."

Once upstairs, Alden headed to Lauren's room. He found her standing with her back to the door, looking down on the side yard. A foot of snow had fallen in the past week. Stray stalks of weeds and tall grass poked up through the blanket of white. Alden wondered if she'd ever seen snow before. Amazing that this woman could be married to his son and he knew so little about her.

He knocked softly on the open door. "Lauren, I'm just about to take off. Thought I'd see how you were doing."

She didn't turn around, but continued to look out the window.

"I'm sure Mary told you, but we're both returning to work today. I'll be home around five. Mary might be a little later." He paused. "Kenzie is here for you. But, of course, you know that." He paused again, this time taking a couple of steps into the room. "I hope that . . . this evening maybe . . . that you and I can talk a little. Mary and I have tried not to bug you, but I thought . . . if I told you a little more about Nick when he was a young guy, about Mary, and even a little about me, maybe that would help break the ice. So to speak." He was handling this badly, as usual. It was just . . . he wanted her to like him. It was important that Nick's wife feel comfortable with him. He couldn't imagine a marriage starting out in a worse way.

126

The phone started to ring.

"I guess I'll see you tonight then, okay? You try to have a good day."

On his way downstairs, he nearly bumped into Kenzie.

"You've got a call, Mr. Clifford."

"Did you get a name?"

"Sorry."

"Man or woman?"

"Woman."

He glanced down at her feet. "You always wear those cowboy boots?"

"Always," she said.

"Even at night when you go to bed?"

She grinned. "Well, I make some exceptions."

He grabbed the cordless off the rolltop desk next to the stairs. "Hello?"

"Alden? This is Carla Macmillan."

Macmillan was Evergreen High's principal.

"What's up?"

"I need to see you in my office."

By the dour tone of her voice, it sounded serious. "Okay. I have classes all day. What if I stop by your office after school?"

"No. It has to be now."

He switched the phone to his other ear. "Can you tell me what this is about?"

"Not on the phone. I'll expect you within the hour."

16

Jane carried her cup of morning tea into the front hall to answer the door. Mouse raced ahead of her and stood in the center of the room, wagging his tail and growling. As usual, he was ready for anything.

"Good boy," said Jane, giving his head a scratch. They'd just come back from a morning run. Jane had showered and dressed, and fed Mouse his kibble. She had an appointment at ten, so she hoped her visitor, whoever it was, wouldn't stay long.

Cordelia nearly knocked Jane over on her way inside.

"He's after me," she said, her black cape swirling ominously around her fake cossack boots. "Close the door. Quick!"

"Who's after you?" asked Jane. At times like this, it was best to be patient. Cordelia loved a dramatic entrance.

"SpongeBob SquarePants, that's who!"

Jane wasn't sure she'd heard her correctly. "*Who?*"

Cordelia bent down and kissed Mouse on his nose. "You'll protect me from that nasty . . . *thing,* won't you, Mouse."

"I've got some fresh tea in the kitchen," said Jane, hoping to insert a little sanity into what was starting out to be another surreal Cordelia visit.

"I need something stronger than tea," said Cordelia, charging into the kitchen. "Do you have any black cherry soda?"

"In the refrigerator," said Jane. She always kept a few cans of the odious liquid around in case Cordelia had a meltdown. Black cherry soda always picked her right back up.

"God, I can hear . . . my immune system . . . crashing," she said between gulps. "I see SpongeBob SquarePants in my dreams now. I can't get away from him!"

"Who is he?"

Cordelia finished the soda, then helped herself to another. "I can tell you don't watch much Nickelodeon."

"Not a lot, no."

"Well, Hattie does. And believe it or not, so does Cecily." She took another sustaining gulp. "I kid you not, Janey. Last night I dreamt that SpongeBob SquarePants and Barney the purple Dinosaur were my *parents*."

"Aren't they, ah, both male?"

Cordelia glared. "It was a gay adoption, okay?" She surveyed the kitchen. "You got anything to eat around here?"

Jane opened the refrigerator door. "I think I have some leftover bread pudding if you're interested."

"What kind of bread?"

"German Kugel. Homemade, of course."

"Any raisins?"

"A few."

"Caramel sauce?"

"Of course."

"Bring it on." Cordelia sat down at the kitchen table as Jane removed the pan from the bottom shelf.

"It sure is quiet around here," said Cordelia, tucking a paper napkin into the top of her sweater. "You must miss Beryl and Edgar."

"I do," said Jane. Her English aunt and her aunt's husband had left a few days ago to spend the winter at Beryl's cottage on the southwestern coast of England. During the spring, summer, and early fall, Beryl and Edgar lived with Jane. "Mouse misses them too. He and Edgar really hit it off. I really do love having them here."

"And you love having them leave."

Jane grinned. "It's a great arrangement."

She glanced up at the kitchen clock. "I'm sorry to rush you, but I've got an appointment in Eagan today with a new restaurant wholesaler. I need to leave, like, now."

"But—" Cordelia looked crestfallen. She'd only taken one bite of her pudding.

"Here's a thought. If you don't have anything better to do, I wouldn't mind some company. After I'm done with my meeting, we could drive down and visit the Cliffords. See how Lauren's doing."

Cordelia gazed longingly at the bread pudding. "Do we need to leave this second?"

"You can take the bread pudding with you."

Her eyes lit up. "Deal. Don't forget to bring extra caramel sauce."

The problem was, Cordelia refused to ride in Jane's Mini. Because it was yellow, black and white, and small, she called it the "Daisy Duck-mobile." She thought it was a fine vehicle for dwarfs, leprechauns, and pygmies. Cordelia's tastes ran to the super sized. When Jane bought the Mini, Cordelia was spurred into action. She sold her ten-year-old big black Buick and went car shopping.

One summer afternoon while Jane was out cutting the grass, Cordelia rolled up in a dark green Hummer. Jane actually fell down, she was laughing so hard. It was *so* Cordelia. The interior was plush and loaded with every available option, and yet it was essentially a tank—one with a small plastic vase Cordelia had found at a car parts outlet and attached to the dashboard. If Jane recalled correctly, that day the flower of choice had been a bright red tulip. Cordelia called it her "Armageddon-mobile," suggesting she had a rather dark view of what the next century would be like.

Jane had to admit, the four-door "wagon" as it was officially called, was very comfortable, with plenty of space for half a football team. The backseat was perfect for Mouse to stretch out in. While Cordelia ate her bread pudding, Jane drove.

"So," said Cordelia, wiping a dribble of caramel off her chin, "have you heard from Jason Vickner?"

"Nothing," said Jane.

"He probably wants to stay as far away from you as he can get."

"Probably. You know," said Jane, "I sat down a few nights ago to write out all the information I'd gathered on my theory about Jason." She hit the blinker. She wanted to pass a slow-moving Chevy van. The Hummer didn't exactly have great pickup, though with its monster military look, it could easily frighten other drivers off the road. "But then I thought, why am I doing this? I mean, I'm literally giving the police a smoking gun, one that points directly at my restaurant."

"You're hoping Jason was paid to do it."

"You bet I am."

"I'm glad you've calmed down, Janey. I thought you were going to have a stroke the other night."

"I'm just glad Nick Clifford will recover. But I'm far from calm. Jason is my only lead. If I can't find him, my investigation has pretty much run into a wall."

"What do the police say? Presumably, they're still investigating the matter."

"Actually, since nobody died, I get the feeling it isn't a high priority case for them anymore."

"And if it turns out Jason is a deranged weirdo? That it was his idea, and his alone—"

"Then I guess I'll have to live with the fallout."

"And so will your insurance company. Have any lawsuits been filed?"

"The tally now stands at four. And the attorney of record for all of them is Gray Donovan. I mean, this has turned into a windfall for that guy. He's going to make a mint representing the wedding guests. If I didn't know better, I'd say he planned the whole thing. He came up with a fool-proof scheme to make himself rich and he paid Jason to carry it out."

"What makes you think you know better?" asked Cordelia.

"He's Nick Clifford's best friend. He'd hardly sabotage his best friend's wedding."

"Never liked the man," sniffed Cordelia, scraping the last bit of bread pudding off her plate. "Never trust a man who's that slick and *that* good-looking. Nick may have the better *bod,* but a bald head is harder to love."

"Nick's not bald. He just shaves his head."

"Why do you think he shaves it, Janey? Because the zip cut look is cool, but going bald isn't."

"Speaking of people who are too slick and too good-looking," said Jane, "heard anything more from your sister?"

Octavia had finally phoned Cordelia yesterday—three days after she disappeared. Cordelia had taken Hattie to Marshall Field's to buy her some new clothes, so she missed the call. All Octavia had said on the answering machine was, *"Hi, all. I'm having a great time. Hope you are too. Mamma loves you, Hattie. Do what Nanny Valenka tells you. Bye."* Apparently, Octavia hadn't gotten the word that Valenka Ivanova had quit. If Jane ever wondered if Octavia was a flake, the question had been answered. She was also a crummy mother.

"Nothing since her pathetic message last night," said Cordelia. She leaned around and set the empty plate on the floor in the backseat so that Mouse could lick it clean. "All I can say is, she better call me soon or I'll have to cancel my trip to Italy. And if *that* happens, I'll use the money I would have spent on the trip to take a contract out on her life. Don't think I'm kidding, Janey. If Octavia screws me over one more time, she's history."

Jane glanced in the backseat. Mouse was so excited to get some people food, he was chewing the plate. "What about Hattie?"

"If she doesn't call me today, I intend to talk to a lawyer and petition the court for custody."

Jane nearly drove off the road. "You're kidding."

"I don't kid when it comes to toddlers."

"You'd do that? You'd raise Hattie yourself?"

Cordelia squared her shoulders. "I shall assume the Auntie Mame role in her life. I see now that I was born for it. Hattie is my niece. And, to be fair, when she isn't emptying all my Kleenex boxes—one tissue at a time—she's kind of lovable."

"But you? Cordelia Thorn. Raising a child?"

"It doesn't fall trippingly off the tongue, does it?"

"Do you realize how it would change your life?"

"No. Of course not. But what choice do I have? I can't let Hattie be raised by wolves. She can't go live in a zoo. And I will *not* become the wicked stepmother from a Victorian novel who sends her poor innocent charge to live in a bleak boarding school where she's fed gruel and made to stand out in the rain because she forgot to curtsy to the headmaster. *And,* I refuse to pack her off to live with any of my relatives, all of whom, I might add, are far stranger than *moi.*"

The car started to beep.

"What's that?" asked Jane, afraid the Hummer was about to launch a missile.

"It's the cell phone. State of the art. Totally hands free. Just press a button and voilà!" Cordelia pressed the button. "Cordelia Thorn. Over."

"It's not a ham radio," said Jane.

"Shhhh."

"Cordelia? Are you there?"

It was Octavia.

"Well, well. The prodigal sister finally calls. Over."

"Why do you keep saying *over*?" asked Octavia.

"Where are you? Over."

"Where do you think?"

"Are we going to play twenty questions? Over."

"Didn't Vakenka tell you?"

"Tell me what? Over."

"Didn't she give you my message?"

"What message?"

"Cordelia, are you telling me that all this time you didn't know where I was?"

"If I knew where you were, don't you think I would have already sent a hit squad?"

"That's ten questions," whispered Jane.

Cordelia shot her a withering look. "Just answer my question."

"I'm in Hollywood. I'm here for a screen test. The day I left, I talked to Valenka and gave her all the information. The hotel I'm staying at. My schedule, as much as I knew it."

"Valenka quit."

Silence. "She . . . *quit*?"

"Walked out in a huff." Cordelia turned to Jane. "Wouldn't you say it was a huff?"

Jane nodded.

"Who else is there?" asked Octavia.

"Janey."

"Hi, Jane."

"Hi, Octavia."

"I had no way of knowing that Valenka quit. Why didn't you call me?"

"Because she never passed on your number—or anything else."

"Lord, what you must have thought."

"I'd be happy to tell you *exactly* what I thought."

133

"No, don't bother."

"We were very worried," said Jane.

"Not me," said Cordelia. "I knew you'd come up with some *primo* excuse."

"Is Hattie okay?"

"She's fine, no thanks to you. I've hired a temporary nanny."

"I'll pay for everything," said Octavia.

"You bet your little blue booties you will. And I expect you to book the next flight back here. I'm supposed to leave for Italy in a matter of seconds."

More silence. "Actually, that might be a problem." Her voice brightened. "I got the part."

"*Problem,*" repeated Cordelia.

"I'm going to play opposite Michael Douglas in a new psychological thriller. The title isn't set yet, but—oh, Cordelia!—it's the break I've been looking for all my life. I have to stick around here awhile longer to finalize contracts, get my schedule all nailed down, have some costume fittings. The first read-through is tomorrow. We'll be filming in Switzerland. Isn't that exciting!"

"Peachy keen. Go back to the part about when you're coming home."

"Can't you be a little happy for me?"

"You have a daughter, Octavia. What do you intend to do with her?"

"Well, I . . . we can talk about that. I mean, if your nanny is any good, and everything is working out well, maybe you'd like Hattie to stay with you awhile."

"Did you not hear me? I'm on vacation, Octavia. A well-deserved one I might add. I've been planning this trip to Italy for months."

"Yes, well—"

"Setting aside the fact that I'm a *far* more suitable parental figure than you are, what are you suggesting I do? Take Hattie with me?"

"What a wonderful idea!"

"You think I want a toddler with me and my girlfriend as we drive down the Amalfi coast?"

"Lovely idea! Hattie will have a ball."

"Octavia!"

"Sorry to interrupt, but you'll never believe who just rang my doorbell. Jack, what a wonderful surprise!"

"Jack who?"

"Nicholson."

"Oh, come *on*."

"No, no, Jack. This is a fine time. I was just about to say goodbye."

"Jack Nicholson my ass. Don't you change the subject!"

"Yes, darling, make yourself at home. A Bloody Mary would be lovely. Cordelia, I've got to go. I'll call later."

"Don't you hang up! You hear me? Don't you—"

"Over and out, Cordelia. Give Hattie a kiss from Mama."

The line clicked.

Cordelia pressed the off button. "I'm going to kill her," she said, fondling the dashboard. With a cheerfully crazed lilt to her voice, she added, "I'm going to run her over with my Hummer!"

17

When Alden walked into the school office late Wednesday morning, he saw that the principal's door was closed. He smiled at the secretary behind the reception counter. "Carla wanted to see me. Is she free?"

The secretary, Jenny Galas, a young woman who usually had a friendly smile, seemed startled by his sudden appearance.

"Something wrong?"

Before she could answer, the principal's door opened and Wesley Middendorf, a junior in Alden's fifth-period American History class, came out.

"Hey, Wes," said Alden. "I'm back. I'll see you this afternoon."

Wesley, a big blond kid who played first string tackle on the football team, kept his eyes on the floor as he shot past Alden out the door.

What's with him? thought Alden, turning to watch him go.

"I can see you now," said Carla Macmillan.

Alden swiveled around.

Carla was an imposing woman in her mid-fifties. She struck Alden as the kind of woman who'd spent her life cultivating a refined, fake genteel manner, although her choice of clothing was anything but. She wrapped her soft, bulky frame in wildly colored geometric-patterned dresses. And she wore heavy, cheap perfume. Today, the rosewater scent nearly gagged him.

After Alden had taken a chair on the other side of her desk, Carla sat down, folding her hands primly on top of the blotter. She studied him for a moment before speaking.

"I'm afraid, Mr. Clifford, that a matter has just been brought to my attention, one I consider very serious. To be honest, I've never dealt with a situation like this before, and I'm . . . at a loss."

"Something *I've* done?" said Alden.

Carla nodded to the closed door. "That student who just left. He came in to see me shortly before I called you."

"Wesley, sure. He's in one of my classes."

"Yes," said Carla, leaning forward. "He says that . . . that—" Her entire face puckered. "I see no point in beating around the bush. Wesley told me you molested him in the rehearsal room behind the stage. That it happened twice—last May, before school ended. He was a sophomore then. Fifteen years old. He didn't say anything about it before because he was ashamed—and scared of what you would do to him if he told anyone. But he couldn't stand it anymore, so he came to see me to . . . get it off his chest, as it were. And he said he's not the only student you've molested." She sat back in her chair and waited for his reaction.

Alden's mouth had dropped open. "That's a lie. Those are damn lies!"

"Yes, well. I couldn't get Wesley to open up about the other victims. He was too upset."

"You can't believe this."

"However," continued Carla, "as you may know, Wesley was one of Cullen Hegg's best friends. While we were talking, he did reluctantly admit that you'd molested Cullen too, and that's why he killed himself in your classroom."

"What?" Alden was dumbfounded. "That's ridiculous."

"Obviously, I have no way of knowing what's going on here."

"He's lying. It's all a goddamn lie!"

"Why would Wesley make this up, Mr. Clifford?"

"How should I know?"

"It's a serious accusation. Surely you must understand that I can't simply ignore what he says."

"I never molested him or anyone else."

"Wesley is a good student. He's a member of our football team, and well respected by his peers."

"He's as thick as a brick. He didn't come up with this all himself. Someone must have put him up to it."

"For what reason?"

Alden stared back at her.

"What motive would Wesley have to attack you? Have you given him a bad grade, one he feels he didn't deserve?"

"No."

"Have you humiliated him in some way?"

"Of course not."

Carla tugged the gold belt on her dress. "Let's speak in confidence for a moment. I admit, Mr. Clifford, that I don't understand this kind of perversion. From what I know of you and Mary, you appear happily married. But things aren't always what they seem."

Mary, thought Alden. God, what would this do to her?

"I've never understood homosexuality."

"I'm *not* a homosexual."

"Not that there's anything wrong with it, I'm told. In any event, my personal beliefs have nothing to do with this situation. I suppose a lawyer would make the point that this is not about homosexuality, but pedophilia."

"You're not listening to me." He wanted to climb over the desk, grab her by the throat, and squeeze until her eyes popped.

"Whether it turns out to be true or not, this is a disastrous situation for the school."

"Did Wesley offer any proof?"

"No, just his word."

"And you'd take his word over mine?"

"Of course not. But I have to deal with what he said. I can't just brush it under the rug."

"Fine, but you can't convict me without evidence."

Carla sat silently for a few seconds. "My advice to you is to find yourself a good lawyer. Under the circumstances, I can't allow you to continue to teach here after an accusation of this kind has been made. Until this matter is resolved, I'm suspending you—with pay."

Was that supposed to make him feel better? "How kind."

"Lose the sarcasm, Mr. Clifford. It's not helping your cause."

"Neither is the truth."

"I realize this is painful for you. So let me lay all the cards on the table. The fact is, Wesley said that you used pornographic videos to seduce him. He suggested a place where I might find them. Again, while this may not constitute proof in the legal sense, we're going to follow up on it. In the meantime, you are to leave the school grounds immediately."

"But . . . what about my wife? When the students hear what Wesley said—"

"This shouldn't affect Mrs. Clifford."

"Bullshit! Of course it will affect her."

Carla stiffened. "Please, Mr. Clifford. Let's keep this meeting civil."

"You want civility? After what you just accused me of?"

Once again, she leaned closer to her desk. "Mary is a valued teacher at Evergreen High."

"Who will be crucified by the student body when they learn about Wesley's accusation. Do you realize how humiliated she's going to feel?"

"You should have thought of that when—"

He shot to his feet. "I *will* hire that lawyer, Carla. And when I do, I'm going to sue you for slander. You and Wesley, and anyone else in this goddamned school who tries to promulgate this fiction."

"Good day, Mr. Clifford."

"Screw you!"

18

"Scenic vistas are so *obvious*," grumbled Cordelia, gazing out the windshield of her Hummer at the snowy fields whizzing past.

"You're in a good mood," said Jane.

"You would be too if you had a sister like mine."

Once Jane's appointment with the restaurant wholesaler was over, Cordelia, having finished her pudding, decided to drive the rest of the way to the Cliffords' farmhouse. Jane called ahead to announce their visit, but nobody answered the phone.

"Someone's got to be there," said Cordelia, adjusting the white calla lily in the dashboard vase. "I talked to Mary a couple of nights ago. They hired a woman to stay with Lauren while they're away at work."

"Have you been to the Cliffords' place before?"

"Once," said Cordelia. "Mary and Alden threw a party for Nick's twenty-fifth birthday. They had a volleyball net set up on the lawn, and a big yellow tent with lots of great food. A keg, of course. They even rented a trampoline. Nick and a bunch of his buddies spent most of the afternoon jumping off the garage roof onto it."

"Sounds dangerous."

"It was stupid. Hardly my idea of a good time. But Nick's always been a daredevil. And he was in great physical condition because he'd been working for over a year at that athletic club he manages now. He really looked fabulous and wanted to show off his muscles to all the young women."

"He's a daredevil, huh?"

"Mary told me that he was always breaking his leg or his arm when he was a kid—falling out of trees, off roofs, and generally doing stupid stunts. He even broke his back once when he was skiing."

"So, his friends would know about these . . . daredevil tendencies."

"Sure," said Cordelia. "What are you getting at?"

Jane shrugged. "Just that . . . if, say, a friend already knew Nick was prone to taking chances, if he was given a drug that altered his consciousness, removed his inhibitions, he might take a risk and—"

"End up dead?"

"Or injured. It would never be a sure bet that he'd actually die."

"You talking about Gray again?"

"Let's say you weren't out to murder someone, but just to screw up his life for a while. It would be a fair bet that the risk taker might take that risk and end up getting hurt."

"Boy, you'd like to nail Gray for everything. Maybe, if we work hard enough, we can put him on the grassy knoll back in Dallas."

"Is that your clever way of saying I'm off base?"

"Could be." Cordelia nodded to the glove compartment. "Get out the Minnesota map. I've only been down here once and I want to make sure we take the right roads."

Fifteen minutes later, Jane saw a large farmhouse come into view. It sat on a rise about half a mile away, surrounded by tall oaks, their branches stripped of leaves.

"Impressive place," said Jane.

"It's fabulous," said Cordelia, slowing down to look for the turnoff onto the property. "White clapboard siding. Big rooms filled with antiques. An old-fashioned farm kitchen with lots of modern updates. Alden and Mary have really worked on the house since they bought it in '92."

Jane noticed that up ahead on the left side of the road a cream-colored SUV had pulled off on the shoulder. "What's that car doing there?"

"No idea," said Cordelia.

As they drew closer, Jane saw a man wearing a baseball cap sitting in the driver's seat. He held a pair of binoculars up to his eyes.

"Maybe he's eating lunch," said Cordelia. "Which sounds like a good idea to me."

"Didn't you see the binoculars? He's watching the Cliffords' house."

Jane turned as they passed, trying to catch the license plate. "M-E-E, 7-8-2," she whispered. She quickly took out a pen and wrote the number on her hand. Hadn't she come across a car just recently with those first three letters. "Hey! It's the SUV from the wedding banquet," she said out loud.

"What SUV?"

"At the Donovan mansion. When I was leaving that car tore out of the driveway and nearly ran me down."

Cordelia glanced over her shoulder. "Fascinating." Her tone suggested a certain lack of enthusiasm.

"Turn around."

"Pardon me?"

"Turn around. I want to ask that guy a couple questions."

"Jane—"

"Don't argue. Just do it."

"You are *such* an autocrat sometimes." Cordelia slowed the Hummer to a stop, then backed into the Cliffords' access road. "He's leaving," said Cordelia, pulling back onto the highway.

Jane noticed now that the SUV was a Ford Explorer. And Cordelia was right. It must have seen them turn around because it was speeding away.

"Follow—"

"Don't!"

"Don't what?" asked Jane, startled by Cordelia's sudden forcefulness.

"Don't ask me to follow that car. Cordelia Thorn no longer *does* car chases."

"Since when?"

"Since I bought the Hummer. This vehicle is in pristine condition and that's the way it's going to stay. Now. Let's keep our eye on the ball, Jane." Her voice oozed patience and reason. "We've come to visit Lauren, and that's just what we're going to do."

"But that guy—finding out who he is might be important."

"One of life's little tragedies," said Cordelia, giving Jane a chuck on the chin. "We simply must suck up our disappointment and move on."

While Cordelia parked the tank, which was a long, exacting process, Jane hopped out and headed for the screened front porch. She sprinted up the steps and knocked softly on the front door. If Lauren was asleep, she didn't want to wake her. When nobody answered, she stepped over to a tall, wide window that looked in on the living room. Everything was quiet. The overhead light was on, but that was the only sign of life.

Pushing her hands deep into the pockets of her sheepskin jacket, she returned to the front steps. Cordelia had taken a roll of paper towels out of the backseat and was wiping road dirt off the rear of the Hummer. Mouse watched her from the back window.

"Cordelia? Nobody seems to be home. I'm going to check the back of the house. See what I can see."

"There's a side door and a back stairs," called Cordelia. "The stairs lead up to Alden's study. I'm almost done here."

"Don't rush. You wouldn't want to scratch the paint."

"Damn straight."

Jane followed the shoveled path around to the side door, which was locked up tight. She tried knocking again, but when nobody answered, she moved on. She stopped next to a neatly packed woodpile and surveyed the backyard. Dried cornstalks poked out of the snow about fifty yards away from the house, suggesting that the Cliffords maintained a large summer garden. Several snow shovels leaned against a metal toolshed.

The wind coming off the open fields felt raw against her exposed skin. She wished she'd thought to put on a scarf before she left home. As she chugged up the back steps to the second floor, she removed her sunglasses. Cupping her hands around her eyes to cut out the glare, she looked in the window next to the door. A woman was seated at a desk. She seemed to be singing to herself as she riffled through the contents of one of the bottom drawers. On top of the desk lay an open scrapbook or family album with a magnifying glass resting next to it.

Jane assumed this was the woman the Cliffords had hired to take care of Lauren. But if she was simply an employee—with no ties to the family and no particular interest in them—what was she doing snooping around Alden's study? Alarm bells went off.

Jane watched the woman for a few more seconds. Each folder was removed from the drawer and every document or piece of paper was checked.

"Hey, Janey," boomed Cordelia.

Jane swiveled around and saw that Cordelia had come into the backyard.

"Is anybody home?"

Jane turned back to the window. The woman had stopped her search. She was standing now, her eyes locked on Jane.

"Hi," said Jane through the glass. She spoke loudly. "We came to see Lauren."

The woman tried to cover her surprise with a smile. "I can't open this door," she called back. "No key. I'll meet you downstairs." She pointed down.

"Got it," said Jane. She trotted down the stairs, where Cordelia was waiting for her.

"Did you find the hired help?"

"And then some," said Jane.

"What's that supposed to mean?"

"Come on." She hurried around the side of the house and took the front steps two at a time.

Cordelia followed at a more leisurely pace. "I wish you'd slow down. I don't know why you have to rush around all the time. You make me feel like you're the hare and I'm the tortoise. I dislike the image for obvious reasons. I mean, *where's the fire?*" Cordelia had just crested the top of the stairs when the door opened. "Well!" she said under her breath. "There's the fire."

"Hi. I'm Kenzie Nelson." She smiled at Jane, then at Cordelia. "Come on in. You're here to see Lauren?"

"That's right," said Cordelia, her grin more of a leer.

"And you think *scenery* is obvious?" said Jane.

"Excuse me?" said Kenzie. "Scenery?"

"It's nothing," said Cordelia, looking Kenzie up and down. "Jane is just babbling. She does that a lot."

"Lauren's upstairs. Go on up if you want. But don't be surprised if she doesn't talk much. The Cliffords encourage visitors, as long as they know the score."

"We do," said Jane. "Thanks."

"Do you like the theater?" asked Cordelia, fluttering her way past Kenzie.

"Me?" The comment had come out of the blue and she clearly didn't know how to respond. "As in . . . plays?"

"Yes, plays. Actors. *Directors.* I'm the creative director for the Allen Grimby Repertory Theater in St. Paul. You've heard of that, I trust."

"Sure. I think."

"Well, you must come one evening soon." She pulled a card out of her purse. "Let me know what night works best for you and I'll make sure to leave comps at the box office."

"Comps?" repeated Kenzie.

"Complimentary tickets," explained Jane.

"Oh. Right. Thanks."

"My pleasure," said Cordelia.

Jane had some questions she wanted to ask Kenzie—specifically, why she was snooping through Alden's study—but since Cordelia was laying it on so thick, she decided to wait until they could be alone. Maybe Kenzie figured Jane hadn't seen what she was doing. If that was the case, she was in for a surprise.

On the way up the stairs, Jane whispered, "Pull your tongue back in your mouth, Cordelia. You're drooling."

Cordelia smirked. "My gay-dar is never wrong. That woman is a member of the tribe."

"Wonderful," said Jane.

"Don't you think she's a knockout? A total ten on the Richter scale?"

"She's very attractive."

"You need a hormone shot."

"My hormones are perfectly intact, thank you. I've just got a lot on my mind right now."

"Boring."

"Better boring than obvious."

Cordelia grumbled all the way to Lauren's door. Plastering on a smile, she flounced into the room. "Lauren. *Darling.* I'm sorry you've been under the weather."

That was one way to put it, thought Jane. "Hi," she said, still standing by the door. "It's good to see you again."

Lauren held a kitten in her arms. She focused her entire attention on it.

"We're here to cheer you up," said Cordelia, dragging a chair over in front of her.

Lauren stroked the kitten's fur.

Cordelia soldiered on. "Mary tells me you've been watching a lot of

TV so we don't have to bring you up-to-date on the news of the world. Besides, that wouldn't be cheerful, now would it. Are you a game show type or a soap opera maven?" She cocked an eyebrow. "I'll guess soap operas. So. Have you been keeping track of the nighttime reality shows? All that eating of worms and being covered by bees. Makes you realize life could be worse. Huh?"

Lauren stared at Cordelia.

"I can't imagine living around all those creepy bugs just to make a few bucks. And *think* of the bathing facilities." She shivered. "How did we get on that subject anyway? I guess you must have brought it up. Whatever. I don't watch much nighttime TV. I'm always at the theater." She slapped her knees. "Hey. What say we talk about a topic I do know something about. The legitimate stage. I could sing you an old Ethel Merman song. Work with me here, okay?"

Cordelia cleared her throat, coughed a few times, then broke into song. "There's NO business like SHOW business," etc. She stomped her feet, clapped her hands, and thrust out her arms. When she was finally done, she said, "Why don't I give you a list of my favorite plays? Feel free to disagree. A good argument never hurt anyone, right? Let's see." She folded her arms over her chest. "First on the list would have to be *A Lion in Winter*. Robert Preston played Henry II on Broadway and it was breathtaking. Then I'm going to throw you a curve. This next play never made it to Broadway, but it was during previews here in Minneapolis that I saw . . ."

As Cordelia rambled on, Jane had to smile. She wasn't sure what Lauren was getting out of this visit, but she'd have to admit that Cordelia was nothing if not entertaining.

19

Mary headed out the front doors of the Blackburn Playhouse around noon, thinking she'd drive over to Blumberg's Deli to grab herself a sandwich. As she approached her car, she saw Tom Moline's Subaru turn into the parking lot. He waved as he pulled his car alongside hers.

"What are you doing here?" she asked, her eyes panning across the lot to see if anyone was watching. She hadn't talked to Tom in over a week. She should have phoned him, but an attack of guilt had set in. She'd spent so much time with Alden recently that they'd reconnected in some important ways. Within a marriage, Mary had learned that there were times of intense closeness as well as periods of disconnection. Nick's accident had hurt Alden deeply. Mary couldn't understand it, but he said he felt responsible. It didn't seem fair that she had someone like Tom in her life when Alden's life was in such turmoil.

"I missed you," said Tom. "I couldn't stay away. Not today—not after what's happened."

Mary felt exposed standing outside in the open. Anyone could see them. Perhaps their relationship had moved to a different level. Not that her feelings for him had changed, but her desire to keep their relationship a secret had ratcheted up several notches.

"Get in," said Tom. "We need some time together. God, especially now. Are you okay?"

He seemed terribly concerned about her. She *had* been through a lot since the last time they'd made love. She opened the door and climbed in.

"I'm taking you to my place." His hand reached across the seat and found hers. "We need to be alone."

Thankfully, his town house wasn't far from the theater. She had to be back for a meeting at two. And Tom's Wednesday schedule allowed him a lunch break, and then a free period. It wasn't much, but it would be enough.

On the way up the steps to his front door, Tom asked how Alden was doing. She told him she didn't want to spend what little time they had together talking about her husband. He said he understood.

Once inside, Tom handed her a box from Victoria's Secret. "Open it."

"What is it?" she asked, not that she didn't get the general idea.

"You said once that I was a naughty boy. Here's proof."

He'd never given her anything like this before. She wasn't a prude, but she was a little shocked. When she opened the box, she found a skimpy black silk number—bra and panties—with a see-through rayon top. Though they'd never discussed it, she thought he understood that she found overtly sexy clothes both silly and demeaning—not the least bit sensual.

In the end, it didn't matter. Tom was so hungry for her that he didn't push her to try it on. He tossed some pillows on the floor and they undressed in front of the gas fireplace.

When their passion was finally exhausted and she was lying in his arms, she started to cry. She was overwhelmed by her physical need for him, by her love for her husband, her confusion about his current mental state, and her worry for her son. She was crying about everything and about nothing. But she couldn't stop.

"It's okay, Mary." He stroked her arm. "I can't say I know what you're feeling, but . . . I'm here for you. I'll always be here. Hey, I forgot. I bought you another present."

"Another sex-kitten outfit?"

"No, this is a dress. It's from Nordstrom's. Here." He got up and raced into the bedroom. When he returned, he'd already taken the dress out of the box. "Since I couldn't be with you, I went shopping for you. It helped me feel close even though we couldn't be together."

Mary stared at the dress. It was hideous.

"I hope you like it. I don't mean to tell you what to wear, but I thought you might want to please me. You'll look fabulous in this. And as soon as you get the divorce in the works, I want to do more shopping for you."

"Divorce?" Had she heard him correctly.

"I understand now why you dress the way you do. Alden probably likes tailored clothes. But I like a woman to look like a woman—you know what I mean? Frills. Pretty colors." He grinned.

Mary suddenly felt naked. She *was* naked, but it had seemed right before. Now it seemed grotesque. "Throw me that quilt, will you?"

Tom grabbed the one off the back of the couch and handed it to her. "Are you cold?"

She shook her head. "Did I hear you say the word 'divorce'? Tom, I leveled with you from the very beginning. I have no intention of divorcing my husband."

"But that was before." He tilted his head. "You'd stay with him? After what just happened?"

Now she was confused. "Alden had nothing to do with the food tampering."

"Food tampering? What are you talking about?"

"Nick's wedding. The hallucinogens that were mixed into the food."

"No, no." He crouched down. "After what happened this *morning*. At school. Didn't you hear? Your husband was suspended."

She laughed. "Don't be silly."

"I thought you knew. It's all over the school."

He tried to put his arm around her but she pulled back. "What is?"

"A junior in one of his classes claims your husband forced him to have sex. It happened in the rehearsal room behind the stage. The same student said your husband molested Cullen Hegg. That's why the boy committed suicide."

"Is this some kind of sick joke?"

"I can't believe Alden didn't call you."

"This is insane. I don't know what you're after here, Tom, but if it's me, it's not working." She began to pull on her clothes. And that's when she remembered. Her cell phone. She'd turned it off. Right after she got to the theater this morning, she'd been asked to sit in on the director's

149

first official meeting with the actors. If a cell phone went off during one of the sessions, the offending party was fined two hundred dollars. It was standard procedure. But she'd forgotten to turn the cell back on.

Mary scrambled over to her purse and pulled it out. When she pressed it on, the dial lit up. She had four messages. Oh, God, she prayed. Not my husband. This can't be happening. She pressed the requisite buttons, then held the cell to her ear and listened.

Message one, 11:21 A.M.
"Honey, it's me. I just got out of a meeting with Carla Macmillan. We need to talk. Call me as soon as you can."

Message two, 11:46 A.M.
"Mary, I don't know where you are, but you've got to call me. It's important. Just—*call* me."

Message three, 12:17 P.M.
"Mary, it's Alden again. I'm . . . God, I don't know where I am. I'm just driving around. Call me, okay? I need to talk to you. As soon as you get this, *call* me."

Message four, 1:04 P.M.
"Mary, where the hell are you? Something awful's happened. I don't know what to do. I need you, honey. Maybe I'll drive over to the theater, see if I can catch you there. I can't remember your schedule today, but I don't think you have a class at Evergreen until tomorrow. If you do, don't go until you've talked to me. I love you, Mary. Bye."

Mary looked at her watch. She had been making love to Tom while Alden was desperately trying to reach her. What kind of woman was she?

"Call me a cab," she said, grabbing what was left of her clothing and rushing into the bathroom.

"Why?" asked Tom. "I'll drive you back to the theater."

"No."

"Did Alden leave you a message?"

"He left me four messages." She splashed water onto her face, then dried herself off and began to reapply her makeup.

Tom came and stood in the doorway. The fact that he hadn't put on any clothes infuriated her.

"Did you call the cab?"

"Yes. They'll be here in five minutes."

"Good."

"Mary, you seem angry at me."

"Why didn't you tell me about this right away? How could you make love to me—"

"I thought you knew. Mary, you can't stay with him. Not now."

"Doesn't he at least deserve the benefit of the doubt?"

"No," said Tom flatly.

"Well, I disagree."

"When will you see him for the kind of man he really is?"

"What's that supposed to mean? You hardly know him. This student . . . he has to be lying."

"Why would he do that?"

"I can think of dozens of reasons." She pressed the lipstick to her lips with a shaky hand.

"You're not thinking clearly."

"And you are?"

"Yes. Right now, I feel I need to do the thinking for both of us."

Checking herself over in the mirror one last time, she angled past him into the living room.

"Did you hear me?" he asked.

"I heard," said Mary. She threw on her coat.

"Well?"

"Do the world a favor, Tom. Put on some goddamn clothes."

20

By ten on Wednesday night, Jane had downed her second shot of tequila. After the train wreck she'd witnessed in her restaurant kitchen earlier in the evening, she figured she might need a third. On a normal night, her staff reminded her of a team of professional dancers, each working in perfect harmony with the others to produce a work of art. Tonight, after the salamander quit working and the blower in the convection oven cut out, the usual kitchen choreography was shot to hell.

One of her line cooks broke a glass over a steam kettle full of cream soup. Jane wouldn't allow them to strain it, so the entire five gallons had to be dumped. A replacement soup had to be produced on the fly, and when one of the sous chefs dropped an entire tray pan of Yorkshire pudding as he tried to spin around one of the line cooks who had just plated a duck breast with braised fennel and was about to hand it off to a waiter, Jane knew nothing could redeem the evening. A few more nights like this and she'd be thinking about changing professions, maybe selling aluminum siding for a living.

As she leaned against the bar, tugging absently on one of her gold hoop earrings and waiting for Barnaby to pull her a lager, she tried counting the number of people in the room. She quickly gave that up. Due to the general public's short attention span, the pub was packed. Business was pretty much back to normal.

Before hitting the pub, Jane had taken Mouse outside for a walk, but after just a few minutes, the icy wind flying off the lake had driven them back inside. Mouse didn't seem disappointed. He was such a good-natured critter. And by now, he knew the ropes. He trotted ahead of her down the hall to her office and sat down while she unlocked the door. Once inside, she gave him a good scratch and then tossed the ball to him so he could get some exercise. Problem was, he never seemed to get tired. He was too young and frisky to stop chasing the ball on his own, so when Jane got bored, she dug out a dog treat from her bottom drawer and told him to hop up on the couch. "Bon appétit, my sweet Mouse," she whispered, kissing the top of his head. "Just give me another few minutes and we can head home." She closed the door on her way out.

Jane took a sip of beer as she headed for the pub's back room, but stopped when she saw Kenzie Nelson appear in the doorway. Jane had to admit that Cordelia was right. Jane's gay-dar went off like a five-alarm fire.

Kenzie was wearing a soft gray leather jacket over a red vest, a white shirt buttoned at her throat, and faded jeans. She was already tall, but the cowboy boots added a couple more inches. And Cordelia was right about something else, too. Kenzie was definitely an eye-catcher.

Pushing her way through the crowd as she surveyed the room, Kenzie smiled when she finally located Jane. Maybe it was the muted light in the bar, but Kenzie had the whitest teeth Jane had ever seen.

"Hi," said Kenzie, tucking her hands into her front pockets. "You got a couple minutes?"

"Sure." Jane didn't trust her—for good reason—and yet she found it hard not to return the smile.

"I thought we should talk. I know you saw me going through Alden's desk today. You haven't said anything to him, have you?"

"Not yet," said Jane.

Kenzie blew out some air. "Thanks."

"I didn't say I wasn't going to tell him. I said I hadn't *yet*." She'd been planning to drive down to the Cliffords' place tomorrow morning, after everyone had gone to work, and talk to Kenzie alone, face-to-face. But Kenzie had saved her the trouble.

"Can I buy you a drink?" asked Kenzie.

Jane held up her beer. "Already have one."

"Then I'll join you." She stepped up to the bar and ordered.

Jane glanced around the room looking for an empty table, but couldn't find one. She was beginning to feel the effects of the tequila. The warmth in her stomach had moved into her muscles. It felt good after the day she'd put in.

Kenzie caught up with her as Jane was loading up a basket with freshly popped popcorn. "Let's try the back room," said Jane, popping a kernel into her mouth. "It's usually less crowded."

Jane considered the kitchen the nervous system of the building. The pub's back room—with its large hearth open on two sides—was the heart. She loved the resinous smell of burning wood and the sense of warmth and intimacy it created. The only illumination in the room came from wall sconces—which glowed softly—and firelight. There weren't any bad tables, really. All had a good view of the fire, although Jane had a favorite. She was in luck. It was empty.

Kenzie set her glass down on the table. Before she sat down, she removed her coat and hung it on the back of her chair.

Jane was curious what she'd come to say. "How did you know I'd be here?" she asked, making herself comfortable.

"I called from my truck on the way." Kenzie tasted her Scotch, seemed to find it acceptable, then placed her hands on either side of the glass and looked straight at Jane. "I figured I needed an edge—because of this morning—so I did some asking around about you."

"And what did you find out?"

"That you own this restaurant. And that you're—how do I put it? An amateur sleuth? An unlicensed PI? A concerned citizen?"

"It's called being at the wrong place at the wrong time."

"Your catering company was certainly at the wrong place last Friday night. I understand you're being sued. Bad luck."

"Thanks for not assuming my catering crew was at fault."

Kenzie twisted the glass around in her hands. "I'm the one who should thank you for not talking to the Cliffords about what you saw today."

"Why were you ransacking Alden's study?"

"I think *ransacking* is a bit strong."

"Well, snooping makes you sound like nothing more than a busybody. What I saw looked thorough. Even professional. What does that make *you*?"

Kenzie shrugged, grabbing a handful of popcorn. "I was searching his office for a reason. If I tell you what it was, can I trust that you'll keep it to yourself?"

Jane laughed out loud. "Are you serious?" This woman had guts. "Look, in case you don't get it, *I'm* the one with the leverage here. Why don't you tell me what you were doing and why, and then I'll decide what to do with the information."

Kenzie's blue eyes crinkled. Her smile changed to a grin. "I like you."

"Gee. I'm bowled over."

"You're smart. I like that."

"Super. Now tell me what's going on."

"Why are you being such a hard-ass?"

"Why are you stalling?"

Kenzie pulled her drink closer. "I was also told that you're a 'prominent lesbian' in the Twin Cities."

Jane stared at her, her mouth slightly open. "And that would be important to this conversation . . . because?"

"Because . . . I, you're a beautiful woman, Jane. I'm attracted to you." She looked down, as if she was suddenly embarrassed.

"If you think coming on to me—"

Kenzie shook her head. "No, that's not my intent. I don't know why I said it. Except . . . well, it's true. Does it bother you?"

"I don't know who the hell you are, and what I do know leads me to believe you're trying to pull a fast one on a couple of friends of mine. So far, on the potential girlfriend scale, you rate about a zero."

"I'm not doing anything illegal," said Kenzie quickly. "Well, maybe *technically,* but in reality, I'm just damn good at my job."

"And that job would be?"

"I'm a reporter."

It was the last thing Jane had expected to hear. "Prove it."

Kenzie reached in her back pocket and took out a billfold. She unsnapped the card section and flashed Jane her press credentials.

Jane looked for the name of the publication. "*Wichita Prairie Sentinel.* You're from Kansas? Kind of a long way from home." Kenzie's photo was on the card. She looked younger, and her reddish-gold hair was shoulder length and curly.

Kenzie flipped the billfold shut and returned it to her back pocket. "I'm originally from a small town called Cottonwood. Southwestern part of the state."

"Never heard of it."

"Nobody has. I live in Wichita now."

"Why are you interested in Alden Clifford?"

"Everybody is. Or was. Last spring, he was the man of the hour. The hero who saved an entire roomful of schoolchildren from a crazy boy with a gun." She shook her head. "What a crock."

"Why do you say that?" asked Jane. As far as she knew, it was true.

"You mean you haven't heard?"

"Heard what?"

While she finished her Scotch, she filled Jane in on what had happened at Evergreen High earlier in the day.

Jane was bewildered. She motioned to one of the waiters and ordered another shot of tequila and another Scotch for Kenzie.

Kenzie selected a couple of popcorn kernels, then continued. "I followed Alden all this time because I knew there was a reason he was so secretive. From the very beginning, he refused to give interviews. And now I know why."

"If it's true."

"Either way, I want to interview him. An exclusive. I figure, the longer I hang around, the better we get to know each other, the easier it will be for me to talk him into cooperating. You know. The full story. The real Alden Clifford stuff."

"The *Wichita Prairie Sentinel* is interested in that?"

"Well, there was a time when every paper in the country would have run a story on Alden Clifford. But no, I've got a signed contract from *Interview Today* magazine—a very lucrative contract."

"You're doing this for money?"

"You got something against it?" She seemed insulted. "Investigative journalism has a long and proud history. Haven't you ever read about Ida Tarbell and her muckrakers? Or Nellie Bly? She feigned insanity to get into New York's insane asylum on Blackwell's Island. While she was there, she discovered that patients were fed horrible, vermin-infested food—and that some of the patients weren't mentally ill at all. Many of the women were imprisoned by husbands as a way of getting rid of them. It was a total scandal. What she wrote led to major reforms."

"You see yourself as a modern-day Nellie Bly?" asked Jane. She played absently with the thin gold chain around her neck.

"There are worse role models," said Kenzie. The grin returned.

"So you see your pursuit of Alden Clifford as something noble?"

"Maybe not noble, but necessary. People live, breathe, and eat human interest stories. That's what this is."

Jane was as perplexed by Kenzie Nelson as she was by what she'd just heard about Alden. "How *did* you get the job working for the Cliffords?"

"Long story."

"I'm not going anywhere."

"Well, I arrived in town a week or so before the wedding banquet. When Nick was hospitalized, I spent time hanging around the hospital, trying to get the lay of the land. I needed to figure out a way into Clifford's life. One Saturday afternoon, this bright idea occurred to me. You know Gray Donovan, right?"

"He's the lawyer who's suing me."

She grimaced. "That's why you may not like this next part."

"Go on."

"Well, I arranged to have a friend of mine meet him. She told him she had a company that specialized in psychiatric home care. He took the bait, called her the next day. He asked to interview one of her people and that person turned out to be me. I told him I'd lost a job about a year ago. I didn't make much money working for this home care company, but I needed work. I made it sound like I was a little desperate, that I'd take just about any job I was offered."

"And?"

"I gave him a number where he could reach me. He seemed interested, asked me some questions about my background, and then said he'd call if it turned out the Cliffords wanted my help."

"And they did."

"I got lucky. Donovan called me into his office on Sunday night. He asked me a bunch more questions, nothing very heavy. He never even asked to see a professional résumé, which I thought was weird. I'd brought one with me, something I concocted in my hotel room. I even offered it to him, but he seemed more interested in offering me a private deal. He said he'd double my salary if I'd help him."

Now she really had Jane's attention. "Help him how?"

"He said he needed information—that he was hiring me to be his eyes and ears in that house. He wanted to know everything that went on. He said that Alden worried him. Hadn't been himself recently. Gray needed to make sure Lauren was completely safe at all times. But—and here's the kinky part—he also asked me to report to him everything Alden and Mary talked about—especially with regards to what happened on Lauren's wedding night. He informed me that there was going to be litigation as a result of the injuries, and that he was the lawyer who would be handling the lawsuits."

"So . . . he's looking for information to help him nail my catering company."

"That's part of it."

"What's the other part?"

"Well, I may be wrong about this, but I think he's got a thing for Lauren. It's just a theory, but the way he looked when he talked about her was way too intense for mere friendship. He asked if I'd work for him, adding that if I didn't want to, he was sure he could find someone else. He knew he had me, but before I said yes, he offered to advance me a thousand dollars just to sweeten the deal. Took out this thick envelope and tossed it on the desk. His terms were that I keep the arrangement a secret, and that I call him at the end of every workday with a report."

"And you agreed?"

"Of course. He made sure I understood that he didn't want me to be just a passive observer. He wants me to seek out opportunities to eavesdrop on conversations. If you ask me, I would *never* want to get between him and a piece of meat."

"I agree with you."

Kenzie's wide eyes met Jane's. "I'm not doing what he asked, Jane. I'm just using the situation so that I can do my job."

"Which, if you don't mind my saying so, is also on the slimy side."

The waiter brought the shot of tequila and the Scotch.

Kenzie's eyes hardened. "Look, I grew up poor. I did a lot of stuff I'm not proud of, but find me a person who's made nothing but bulletproof decisions in their life and I'll show you a liar—or a self-deluded fool.

158

Being an investigative reporter may not make me a big-time success story, but it isn't something I'm ashamed of. I do what I do. If, in the end, Alden doesn't want to give me an interview, okay. I'll apologize for invading his privacy and back off. But I'm betting he wants to talk. That's been my experience." Her strong chin tilted up. "Go ahead. Sit there on your moral pedestal and condemn me. I don't give a damn what you think."

Except, Jane could see in her eyes that she did. She might act tough, but it wasn't who she was inside. And for some reason, that touched Jane. "I'm not judging you."

"Like hell you're not." She picked up the Scotch and took a couple of hefty swallows. "I judge myself sometimes. But I can't stop to analyze, Jane. I go for the story. This one could be my ticket out of Kansas. But I don't hurt people. If someone doesn't want to cooperate, I cut my losses and move on. That's what I've always done. It's the only way I know how to live."

"Okay," said Jane.

Doubt flickered in Kenzie's eyes. "Okay?"

"I get it. I'm not sure, given the same circumstances, I'd make the same decisions you have, but . . . I believe you when you say you won't hurt Alden or his family." She wasn't sure why she felt that way. It was just an instinct. Or maybe it was the tequila. "Just make sure you don't push him to do anything he doesn't feel comfortable with."

"I won't. I promise."

"But the thing with Gray is another matter."

She leaned into the table. "I'm not really working for him, Jane. The money will go back to him as soon as I'm done. Oh, sure, I call him every night, just like he asked me to, but I never tell him anything. There hasn't been anything to tell. Up until this morning, I would have said the Cliffords were a happily married couple with a deeply troubled daughter-in-law. Now I know there's much more."

"If it's true."

"Where there's smoke, there's usually fire."

Jane wondered if she should tell Kenzie some of her suspicions, even bring up what she'd learned about Jason Vickner and the food tampering, but she didn't really know her, even though the liquor and the firelight had crawled into the synapses in her brain and infused them with a rosy glow. It did, however, strike her that she and Kenzie had something important in common. They both had a personal stake in wanting to get to the bottom of what had happened to Alden Clifford and his family.

"Listen," said Jane, downing her third and final shot of tequila for the evening, "why don't you come back to my office? There's something I'd like you to see."

"Your office? Um, sure." Kenzie picked up her drink and followed Jane out of the pub.

As soon as Jane opened the office door, Mouse bounded over the back of the couch, wagging his tale.

"Who's this?" said Kenzie, crouching down to get a better look.

"M. Mouse, meet Kenzie Nelson."

"What's the M stand for?" asked Kenzie, scratching his ears.

"I don't know," said Jane, closing the door behind them. "It was on his tag when I found him."

"He's a stray?"

"The owner finally showed up. We mutually agreed I should keep him, but I never found out what the M stood for. Cordelia thinks we should call him Maurice."

Kenzie laughed. "She's quite a character. But Maurice? I don't think so."

"He likes you," said Jane, watching Mouse lick her hand. "He's usually got good taste."

"Maybe you should trust his judgment," said Kenzie, rising and meeting Jane's gaze. She moved in closer, running her fingertips lightly along the back of Jane's neck. "You have the most amazing eyes. They're the color of lilacs."

"I don't kiss on the first date," said Jane. At Kenzie's touch, she could feel her stomach kick and contract.

"No?"

"Never."

"Maybe you'll have to make an exception." Kenzie pressed her lips softly to Jane's. She increased the pressure, reaching under Jane's sweater and stroking the small of her back.

Jane's body shivered against Kenzie's. She felt loosened, opened up. She was afraid she was about to make one of those decisions that Kenzie talked about—the kind that wasn't bulletproof.

"How was that?"

Jane backed against the door. "Not bad."

"Maybe we should try it again."

"So we can get it perfect. Anyone ever tell you you're fast?"

"I have to be. I never know how long I'll be around. That a problem?"

Kenzie smelled of leather and Scotch—and just a hint of spice. Jane closed her eyes. "No. No problem."

Whispering into Jane's ear, Kenzie said, "We have to live in the moment, Jane. I learned that when I was a little kid and I've never changed my mind. We have to live in the moment because . . . it's all we've got."

Thursday

21

Jane was completely tangled in bedsheets and blankets, facedown on the pillow, when the phone rang on Thursday morning. As she reached out to grab the receiver, she knocked a plastic glass off the nightstand onto the rug. Mouse, who must have crawled in with her sometime during the night, vaulted over her, landed on the floor, and barked at the spilled water. Another day had begun.

"Hello," said Jane, clearing the sleep out of her voice. She flipped on her back and rubbed her eyes.

"Jane? It's Kenzie."

Who? thought Jane. Visions of last night's lovemaking jolted her back into total consciousness.

Oh. *That* Kenzie.

Jane cleared her throat again. "Hi."

"Miss me?"

She laughed. She supposed she should feel guilty for indulging in a little casual sex, which was totally out of character, but she didn't have a partner, so she wasn't cheating on anyone, and she was sick of beating herself up for being human. Maybe getting hit over the head a few years back had knocked some of the old Midwestern reticence out of her. "What time is it?"

"Nine-twenty-two. Exactly."

She groaned. She'd forgotten to set her alarm clock. "Where are you?"

"At work."

"Where?"

"At the Cliffords' place."

"Oh, ah, right." Jane ran a hand through her tangled hair. Mouse hopped back in bed and snuggled down next to her. She stroked his head.

"I'm in the basement to be exact. Mary asked if I'd do a load of wash."

"How's everything there? Did Alden tell Mary why he was suspended?"

"He swears up and down that there's no truth to it."

"Mary must be pretty upset."

"An understatement. They both are."

Jane could hear the washing machine sloshing in the background.

"Alden left about an hour ago to go talk to a lawyer," continued Kenzie. "Mary left shortly after he did. She had a meeting at the theater. Guess what?"

"What?" said Jane, propping another pillow behind her back.

"I think Mary may be having an affair."

Jane opened her eyes even wider. "Why do you say that?"

"This guy—his name is Tom, that's all I know—has called twice this morning. I answered both times. The first time Mary was here so she talked to him."

"And you eavesdropped on the conversation."

"Is eavesdropping a mortal sin, or just a venial one?"

"Continue."

"She was angry at him for calling her at the house—she made that *real* clear. And then she told him she couldn't talk. She had to go. She cut the conversation off after less than a minute. When I walked into the room, she had that guilty look on her face. You know, the one that says, oh . . . him? He isn't anybody important. Don't give it another thought. And then she plastered on a fake smile, all innocence and light—another telltale sign. She left a few minutes later."

"And he called back."

"As she was pulling out of the drive. I talked to him briefly. He sounded really pissed off. He told me that if I talked to Mary, to tell her to call him. And then he said something like, 'Oh, hell. I'll see her at school. Just forget it.' And then he hung up."

"At school? I wonder if he's a teacher?"

166

"That's my guess. Boy, people can really fool you. Mary doesn't seem like the kind of woman to have a guy on the side. She seems too—I don't know—nice."

"Minnesota Nice," said Jane. "It's a terminal condition, but you don't need to worry. You have to be Scandinavian and Lutheran to catch it. I suppose this guy could just be a friend."

"Oh, yeah. Sure."

"Did Alden say anything more specific about the charges that boy brought against him? By the way, what's the boy's name?"

"Wesley Middendorf. No, nothing. At least, not while I was around. I imagine he and Mary talked about it last night. They seemed pretty normal together this morning, but she's got to be wondering what kind of horror show she married."

Jane caught something in Kenzie's voice that surprised her. It was just a flavor. Something hard, angry, even bitter. "You sound like you think he's guilty."

"What if I do? Maybe that's what the fairy dust in the wedding food was all about. Nick and Lauren weren't the target. He was. One of his victims was trying to get back at him."

"Do you know something I don't?"

She laughed. "I would imagine I know lots of things you don't."

"You know what I mean."

"When can I see you again?"

"You're changing the subject."

"You *are* the subject. I called because I wanted to hear your voice. I really liked being with you last night, Jane. I was hoping it might happen again."

"Before you saddle up and ride out of Dodge."

"Just because I wear cowboy boots doesn't mean I like cowboy metaphors."

"Sorry."

"So what about tonight?"

"Actually, you caught me at a time when my social calendar is fairly open."

Another laugh. "I'll stop by the restaurant around nine. You can buy me dinner. I assume your place serves a decent steak."

"I think we could rustle one up. How do you like it cooked?"

"Doesn't need to moo, but I like it rare. Baked potato. Nice green salad. I'm not a gourmet, Jane."

"You don't have to be."

"Figured. See you tonight."

Jane showered and dressed while Mouse ran up and down the second-floor hallway with a stuffed dragon in his mouth. It was his favorite toy. After tucking a cranberry-colored silk shirt into a pair of soft gray cords, she strapped on a belt. Before she left the bedroom, she did her hair up into a French braid and removed her gold hoop earrings, replacing them with a pair of silver studs.

Once out in the hallway, she tugged the dragon away from Mouse and raced downstairs. As usual, by the time she reached the foyer, he was already there, leaping into the air, trying to bite the toy back.

"Let's get us some breakfast," she said, holding the toy above her head as she walked into the kitchen. She tossed the dragon in the air and Mouse caught it before it hit the floor. "You're a real athlete, you know that? I wish I could bottle your energy, take sips of it all day long."

She got him his kibble and some fresh water, then cranked up the espresso machine. She'd planned on working from home this morning, so getting a late start wasn't a complete tragedy. After making herself a double espresso, she carried the tiny white cup into her office. First thing on the agenda was a call to Norm Toscalia, her father's paralegal. Norm had twenty-five years' worth of legal connections in the Twin Cities. She always called him when she needed some help. He was great about providing whatever he could—and not asking a lot of questions. She'd tried calling him yesterday afternoon, when she got back from the Cliffords' place, but he'd already left for the day.

A secretary answered the phone and then passed the call on to Norm. "Toscalia," said a deep voice.

"Norm, it's Jane."

"Hi! Hey, sorry to hear about your legal troubles. Your father told me all about what happened at that wedding. The police come up with any new leads?"

"I haven't heard a word from them in days. But individual lawsuits are being filed against my restaurant. It's a total and complete mess."

"I wish I could help."

"You can," said Jane. She gave him the license number of the SUV she'd seen yesterday—the same one that had roared out of the driveway at the Donovan mansion. "Can you get me the driver's name and address?"

"No problem."

"And something else. I hired a young man in September." She had Jason's personnel file in front of her, opened to the personal history form he'd filled out. "His name is Jason Vickner. He's twenty—graduated from Washburn High School in Minneapolis. No college." She passed on as much information as she had. His parents' address. His employment history. His birth date and social security number. "What I'd like to know is, does he have any kind of criminal record?"

"If I get lucky, I can have it all for you by the end of the day."

"Great. I'll be at the restaurant."

"I'll catch you there. Keep your chin up, Jane. You'll get through this."

"Thanks. I appreciate the help."

As she hung up, she heard the doorbell chime.

Mouse leaped off the floor and charged into the front foyer. Jane grabbed her coffee and followed. She glanced through the peephole before opening the door.

"Good morning, Jane dear," said Cordelia, using her most rounded tones. She held Hattie in her arms. The little girl seemed totally entranced by Cordelia's wavy auburn hair. She held the curls in her closed fists, tugging on them and then giggling when Cordelia winced.

"Another early morning," said Jane.

"Hi," said Hattie.

"Hi, sweetheart," said Jane. She poked a finger inside Hattie's coat, gave her tummy a little tickle.

Mouse bounced up and down until Cordelia acknowledged him.

"Augie!" cried Hattie, clearly delighted to see Mouse again.

As soon as Cordelia set her down, she and Mouse were off.

"You look—"

"I look," said Cordelia, carrying a paper sack into the kitchen, "like someone's taken a wrecking ball to my life."

"You mean Hattie?"

"I mean my *sister*." She set the bag down on the counter. "Hattie, come to Auntie Deeya. Come on, bunny. Come see Deeya."

Hattie and Mouse chugged into the kitchen, both looking like they'd been up to something.

"What's in the sack?" asked Jane.

"Hattie's breakfast. And some other . . . necessities."

"Where's Cecily?"

Cordelia glanced at her watch. "She's supposed to meet me in a few minutes. I knew you were working from home this morning, so I figured we'd do the pass off here. I have a lunch date with Marion at eleven-thirty. I'm going to break the news to her that I may not be able to make our trip to Italy."

"Is that for sure?"

"Nothing is for sure."

"Will Marion be upset?"

"If you hear a loud bang, say, something on the order of a hydrogen bomb exploding, that will be Marion."

"I'm really sorry, Cordelia. I know how much you've both been looking forward to it."

Hattie plunked down on the floor next to Mouse. She appeared to be fascinated by his collar.

Cordelia dug a foil-wrapped package out of the bag. "I brought her breakfast. It's a Fluffernutter sandwich."

"A what?"

Cordelia's hand rose to her hip. "Don't tell me the big-shot gourmet has never heard of a Fluffernutter."

Jane shrugged.

"Peanut butter and marshmallow fluff? It's to die for." She unloaded several more sandwiches.

"You packed enough for a small army."

"When I get nervous, I like to cook."

"*That's* cooking?"

"Don't be annoying." She unwrapped one of the sandwiches and sat down at the kitchen table. "You got any milk?"

Jane poured Cordelia a glass, then joined her at the table. "So, you've heard nothing more from Octavia?"

"She left the phone number of her agent on my answering machine. And she gave me a whole bunch of medical information, in case anything happened to Hattie. But she conveniently failed to give me the name and phone number of her hotel. She probably figures I'd call and yell at her."

"Which you would."

"Damn right."

Hattie crawled up into Cordelia's lap. "I tight," she said.

Cordelia hugged her close. "I'm learning what things mean. 'I tight' means she wants me to hold her tight."

"She's so sweet."

"Yeah. She's a peach all right."

Hattie leaned back. "I weed, Deeya? I *weed!*"

Cordelia pointed to the sack. "Jane, get that book for me, will you? Hattie wants to read."

"Isn't she a little young to be reading?" asked Jane.

"Just get it."

Jane found a plastic book at the bottom of the sack. "Ah, I see. It's like her personal photograph album."

"I put it together last night. She just adores it. Wants to look at it all the time." Cordelia opened up the front page and pointed to the first picture. Of course, it was a photo of Cordelia. "Who's that?" she asked the little girl.

"Auntie Deeya," said Hattie, clapping her hands together.

The next page was a photo of Octavia. Jane found it interesting that Mommy came second.

Cordelia turned the page. Jane glanced over and saw an old picture of Roland Lester, taken when the famous movie director was in his mid-forties. Lester was Hattie's father.

Next came Cordelia and Octavia's father, Hiram Thorn.

"And who's that?" asked Cordelia, pointing to the next page.

Hattie snuck a peek at Jane. "Gainy," she said, dropping her eyes shyly.

"You put my picture in there," said Jane. She was touched.

"Of course I did. And who are they?" She turned the page.

"Ooofer."

It was a photo of Cordelia's three cats.

"That's how she says Lucifer. She can't pronounce Blanche or Melville for some reason. Okay, Hattie. Who's this a picture of?" She flipped another page.

"Augie!" said Hattie with a squeal of delight.

Mouse raised his head.

"All the important personages in Hattie's life are in this book," said Cordelia, spreading open the two last pages. "And who are these two women?"

Hattie pointed to a picture of Bette Davis and said, "Beggy."

"That's right," said Cordelia, beaming with pride. "Bette. And this woman?"

"Ba-ba."

"Barbara Stanwyck. Excellent." Turning to Jane, she said, "Helen Hayes and Tallulah Bankhead will be next. We can't leave out stars of the legitimate theater. Then we'll move on to Katharine Hepburn, Betty Bacall, Joan Crawford—"

"A well-rounded education."

"That's the ticket, Jane. She'll cut her teeth on film noir and Tennessee Williams. We'll have to wait awhile before we can introduce Shakespeare."

"We?"

"We in the royal sense," sniffed Cordelia. "Meaning *me*."

Mouse pricked up his ears.

"Why's he doing that?" asked Cordelia, feeding Hattie a bite of her Fluffernutter sandwich.

"He must have heard a car door slam outside."

"Cecily's here. Time to do the handoff. You know, Janey," said Cordelia, rising from the table and hoisting Hattie into her arms, "I'm beginning to feel like I'm part of a relay race. I think we should write the Olympic Committee and suggest they make toddler-passing an official event."

22

After Cordelia left, Jane invited Cecily into the living room. She'd been wanting to talk to her about Gray Donovan and now seemed the perfect opportunity. While Hattie sat in Cecily's lap sucking her thumb and fighting sleep, Jane lowered herself into the rocking chair next to the fireplace. She began the conversation by asking how Nick was doing.

"He's . . . okay," said Cecily, brushing Hattie's blond hair away from her forehead. She didn't make Nick's recovery sound quite as miraculous as Mary had.

"Mary said he was doing great."

"Physically, he's making progress. But between you and me, Jane, Mary doesn't know the whole story. If she did, Lauren wouldn't be staying at her house."

"Sounds like you're not a big fan of Nick's new wife."

Cecily rocked Hattie in her arms. "At first I thought she was just kind of snobbish, but now I realize she's trouble—big trouble. I wish I'd gotten to know her better before the wedding."

Jane had the impression that Cecily was dying to unload what she knew. All she needed was a little prompting. "Why do you say that?" asked Jane.

"Don't get me started."

"No, really. I'm interested."

Cecily hesitated, but only for a second. "I can't talk to anyone in Nick's family about this. I mean, it's way the hell too explosive. And honestly, I trust you, Jane. Cordelia thinks the world of you. She says she'd trust you with her life."

"It's mutual."

Cecily turned, careful not to wake the sleeping toddler, and set Hattie on the couch next to her, covering her with a fuzzy yellow blanket. Mouse sniffed the little girl for a few seconds, then curled up on the floor beneath her.

"Does it have something to do with Gray?" asked Jane.

"That's amazing. How could you possibly guess that? Cordelia thinks you're very intuitive. Not as intuitive as she is, of course—"

"Of course."

"But, yes. Gray's a big part of it. See, Gray and I . . . we dated for a while. I'm afraid I got serious real fast. I thought he was serious too. He made it clear right off that he thought marriage was a useless institution. I suppose, as a lawyer, he's handled his share of nasty divorces and it took a toll." She seemed to drift for a minute. "But I didn't care about marriage. I figured we'd live together. But when Lauren entered the picture, I knew right off that Gray was attracted to her. We broke up shortly after they met and I knew she was the reason. I don't think Nick ever realized Gray was attracted to his girlfriend. But then guys can be so thick sometimes, don't you agree? Nick was totally out of his mind about her. He acted like a heat-seeking missile the night she strolled into the athletic club for the first time. I was there. I mean, *come on*. She's not *that* good-looking."

"No," said Jane, "but she's sexy. She dresses for maximum impact."

Cecily grunted. "I guess. I don't think she'll age well."

Jane laughed. It was clear Cecily didn't like her.

"And speaking of Nick . . . if I didn't know him personally and happened to bump into him in, say, a grocery store or something, I'd think he was just another steroid case. Body beautiful and brainless. But the muscles are all natural, you know. And he's really smart. Gray, on the other hand, isn't so pumped, which is more my type. Not that he isn't good-looking. You think he's handsome, don't you?"

Jane nodded. She wasn't sure why it was necessary to acknowledge it, but apparently, to Cecily, it was still important. Jane was getting the impression that she wasn't over him yet.

"So, yeah, I admit—it hurt me pretty bad that Gray was so totally blown away by Lauren. But Nick was the one who asked her out first. They got hot and heavy right away, so as it turned out, Gray gave me up for no good reason. That's why I figured he'd be back. Man, you should have seen Nick and Lauren when they danced together. They were so hot they almost melted the dance floor. Nick was absolutely ga-ga about her. Gray watched it all from the sidelines—at least, that's what I thought."

Jane pulled an ottoman between them and they both put their feet up. She could tell it was going to be an ottoman kind of conversation.

Cecily twisted her sleek brown hair around her finger as she talked. "Because Gray was the best man and I was the maid of honor, we were each other's date for the wedding. We both worked like mad to make sure the wedding came off without a hitch." She shook her head. "As wedding planners, we suck, right? Anyway, while people were gathering in the music room—that's where the wedding was supposed to take place—I went to find Gray. He'd promised to help me organize the gifts table. He was normally so responsible I figured he'd just forgotten. When I walked into the back hallway, the one that led to the rooms where the brides-maids and groomsmen were getting dressed, I heard Gray's voice. I don't know why, but I just knew he was talking to Lauren. They were in the media room. I snuck up next to the door and listened."

Cecily coughed a couple of times. "You wouldn't have a Coke or a Pepsi would you? My throat's kind of dry."

"Sure," said Jane, anxious for her to continue. She hurried into the kitchen, grabbed a Coke from the refrigerator, and returned to the living room.

"Thanks," said Cecily, cracking the can open and then taking a long drink. "I need a sugar and caffeine fix to get through this."

"Look, if you don't want to——"

She held up her hand, still drinking from the can. "No, I want to. It's good to finally tell someone the truth." Resting the Coke on her leg, she continued. "To make a long story short, that afternoon, before the wed-ding, I heard Gray demand that Lauren dump Nick and run away with *him*. He said his father's private jet was waiting at the airport. He wanted to take her to Ireland, to a small fishing village where his dad's parents had lived before coming to America. There was still a family house there, or whatever. He said he'd find a priest in the village. He knew about a small church where they could get married. He said stuff like, 'You love me, you don't love Nick. Just admit it.' I mean, I was . . . speechless."

"How did Lauren respond?"

"She denied it. She told him to leave her alone. Somewhere in the conversation it came out that they'd been sleeping together—before *and* after she got engaged. Lauren said she was sorry she'd cheated on Nick. That Gray should back off and not make a scene."

"Meaning Gray had threatened to talk to Nick?"

"I didn't hear him say it, but I assumed from what Lauren said that, yes, he wanted to take Nick aside and tell him. Love makes people do crazy things. I think Gray thought that if he told Nick the truth, that Lauren would come to her senses and see that *he* was the man of her dreams. And yada yada yada."

"You're not very sympathetic."

"Why should I be? I wish both of them would fall off a cliff—anything that would keep them out of Nick's life. They're jerks, Jane. Nick deserves so much better. I was about to read them the riot act when I saw Nick swing around the corner into the back hallway. I wish now that I'd done it differently, but at the time, my first thought was to protect him. So I rushed past the media-room door and grabbed Nick's arm. He looked so nervous I thought he was going to puke. He had a bad case of wedding jitters. I told him I sympathized, but that he couldn't be in the hallway— if he stuck around he might catch a glimpse of his bride before the wedding, and that was bad luck." She chugged the rest of her Coke.

"Do you think Gray and Lauren heard you and Nick out in the hallway?"

"They might be jerks, but they aren't deaf."

"And so the wedding took place."

"Yup. And I was too big a coward to stop it." She lifted her feet off the ottoman and sat forward. "It was after the wedding dinner that all hell broke loose."

"You mean the drugs in the food."

"Well, there was that, yes. I mean, the drugs added to the chaos, but . . . it was just before we started feeling the effects—right after Nick and Lauren had cut the cake. That's when it happened. Waiters were passing cake around. Nick started moving through the tables, shaking hands accepting congratulations. I was sitting at the head table talking to one of the bridesmaids when I saw Gray walk up to Nick and put a hand on his shoulder. He whispered something in his ear and a second later Nick followed him out. That made me real nervous."

"You thought Gray was planning to tell Nick about his relationship with Lauren."

"You bet I did. I remember feeling this horrible panic, like the ceiling was about to fall in. I got up, but before I'd moved two feet from my chair, my dress caught on a chair leg and I fell down. One of the groomsmen helped me up and yanked my dress free, but I knew I'd lost precious time. When I finally got to the back stairway where Nick and Gray had gone to talk, I could tell I was too late. Nick's face—you know what fair skin he has—had turned this deep red. He'd grabbed Gray by the lapels and pushed him into a wall. Right then, Lauren walked in. She'd been standing by the wedding cake when Gray and Nick left the room. I assumed she must have seen them leave and knew what was about to go down. It was awful." She closed her eyes.

Jane gave her a moment.

Wiping a hand over her eyes, Cecily looked up. "Gray told Nick about the affair. Nick was furious. For a minute, I thought he was going to kill Gray. He had him by the throat, but Lauren begged him to let him go. Right about then was the first time I noticed the effects of the drug. I felt light-headed. My concentration became sort of scrambled. I saw Nick leave the room and Lauren followed him. Gray just sank to the floor. I thought maybe I should follow Nick just to make sure he was okay, but then I decided I'd just be in the way. He and Lauren needed time to talk. And so . . . I floated back to the music room. I don't know how to explain what happened after that. All I can say is . . . everything was just so fascinating. I followed a glowing ball upstairs and sat in one of the bedrooms watching TV for a while. It was weird. I knew I was at the wedding, but then, it was like I was somewhere else."

"What happened to Gray?"

"No idea. A policeman found me down by the lake. They took me to the hospital. By then, I was kind of coming out of it. As I was waiting around in the emergency room, Nick was wheeled in on a gurney. And Lauren was there too. She was gulping and screaming, and then she got real quiet. That night is such a mixed-up confused blur."

"I'm sorry," said Jane. "Really. So very sorry."

"Mary and Alden think it's strange that Lauren hasn't gone to see Nick. I imagine they find it equally strange that Nick isn't talking about her much either. This mental patient act she's pulling is convenient for both of them."

"You think it's an act?"

"Of course it is. She can't face Nick—and he can't face her. And yet they're married. By keeping quiet, she doesn't have to talk to anyone about what really happened that night. She's just biding her time, letting the people around her take care of her until she figures out what to do."

Cecily's explanation was plausible, but something still seemed to be missing.

"Nobody knows what really happened that night except the four of us," said Cecily. "I may be wrong, but I think Gray still thinks he's got a chance with Lauren. If you ask me, it's sick."

"You don't suppose Gray had anything to do with slipping the drugs into the food."

"No," she said, shaking her head. "Not Gray. He's too—" But she stopped before completing her thought, appearing to reconsider the question. "On the other hand—" An icy realization billowed in Cecily's eyes. "God, do you think he could be *that* twisted?"

"Somebody was," said Jane. "As far as I'm concerned, Gray's as good a candidate as any."

23

Steven had always thought of Wesley Middendorf and Lukas Pouli as the Beavis and Butt-Head of his world. They'd been Cullen's friends, so it was only natural that Steven got to know them. Wesley was so pale and his hair was so light that he looked like an albino. He also had the social skills of a tree frog. But he was loyal and good at math—and that's all that was required. Behind his sixteen-year-old baby fat beat the heart of a brute. Lukas was dark-haired, good-looking, and crude. He had a calculating mind that while not precisely cunning was nevertheless clever. Steven suspected Lukas of being a certified whack job—crazy and cruel, though Lukas kept that part of himself tightly zipped. Girls seemed to like his dramatic excesses and his rancid sense of humor. Steven had no idea why.

Lukas and Wesley were juniors this year. Lukas had his sights set on a good eastern college. Wesley was headed for a military career. They both seemed like normal, average, middle-class teenagers. They were reasonable students with good families and promising futures. But the trick was, they were really thugs in training. And Steven had been their trainer.

When Steven bounded down the stairs on Thursday morning, he wasn't exactly thrilled to find the two of them sitting in his dad's living room. After Cullen's death, Steven had cut them off. He told them he was through with them. He was angry that they hadn't leveled with him about how depressed his brother was. But the real reason for turning his back on them was that they reminded Steven that he'd been a worthless brother. He couldn't stand the sight of them.

"What's up?" asked Steven, looking directly at Lukas. Of the two, he was the leader. Scum always rose to the top.

"Sit down, Steven," said his father. "Something's happened—something you need to know about."

Steven looked from face to face. They all seemed so dead serious it scared him. "What? Tell me."

Wesley squirmed in his seat.

"Tell him," said Lukas. He was smoking a cigarette, watching the ash drop into an ashtray.

"I, ah—" said Wesley, his hands flopping in his lap like dying fish in the bottom of a boat. "I, well—"

"Carla Macmillan called me this morning," said Steven's father, starting the ball rolling. "It seems that Wesley went to see her yesterday." He stopped, glancing at Wesley to continue.

"It's . . . Alden Clifford," mumbled Wesley.

"Yeah," said Steven. "What about him?"

"I told Ms. Macmillan that he'd . . . messed with me. Twice."

"*Messed* with you?"

His eyes dipped. "You know. Like . . . sexually."

"You're shitting me," said Steven.

Wesley seemed to shrink into himself. He shook his head.

"And tell him what else," said Steven's father.

Lowering his chin to his chest, he mumbled, "I think he messed with Cullen too."

Lukas blew smoke out of the side of his mouth. "I had this really weird conversation with Clifford the first week of school this year. All I know is, he gives me the creeps. Probably because he's a fag."

Steven was hardly a PC sort of guy, but he had a lot of gay friends at the U, and he hated the term "fag." Besides, if anybody in the room needed a security check on his sexual preferences, it was Lukas.

"Don't you see what this means?" said Steven's father. He hoisted himself out of his chair and began pacing back and forth in front of the picture window. "I was right. That tape we listened to—it's proof. It's the goddamn smoking gun. That tape is going to nail Clifford's hide to the wall."

"Have you already played it for Macmillan?" asked Steven.

His father shook his head. "I took your advice. I didn't want to get Doris in trouble. But I made an appointment with Carla for this afternoon. I wanted to talk to Wesley first, so I asked him to stop by."

Lukas raised a finger. "But you know what, Mr. Hegg? We should probably get back to school. Study hall is almost over."

"Oh. Okay. I wouldn't want to get you boys in trouble. Thanks for coming by. Wesley, you know how much your help means to me. We'll fix that teacher. We'll make sure he never bothers another kid as long as he lives."

Wesley kept his eyes on the floor. "Yeah."

"Give my best to your parents."

Steven followed them outside. He had a few questions of his own. "Wait up," he said as they made a beeline for Lukas's Camaro.

Wesley turned around. "We gotta go, Steven."

Steven pressed the garage-door opener, then motioned them inside.

Neither looked very interested in having a private chat, but Steven didn't give a rat's ass what they wanted. They'd do what he told them to do.

"Make it fast, okay?" said Lukas. He dropped his cigarette butt onto the cold cement.

The inside of the garage was dark and dank—and even colder than the outside air. Once they were all gathered next to the Explorer, Steven lowered his voice and said, "Tell me the truth. Did my father put you up to this?"

"What?" said Wesley, squinting at Steven. "Why would he do that?"

"Did he?"

"He told us his theory," said Lukas, acting as if it was nothing. "That's all. But then Wes up and tells me that it's true. So I, like, tell him he should go talk to Macmillan."

"It really happened? Clifford and you . . . you know?"

"Yeah," said Wesley. "It happened."

Steven switched his gaze to Lukas. "And you think maybe he was trying to hit on you?"

Lukas shrugged. "Could be. He said if I had a problem like Cullen's, he could help me."

"That could have more than one meaning."

"He was talkin' about sex, man. Flirting with me like crazy. I'm not an idiot. Your dad's right, you know. If he's going to pull shit like that, he shouldn't be a teacher. He shouldn't be *alive*."

Steven didn't know whether to believe them or not. He turned to Wesley. "Why didn't you tell somebody before now?"

Wesley looked at Lukas. "I was ashamed?"

"Is that a question or an answer?" asked Steven.

"Ah, like, an answer," said Wesley, nodding his head.

"Why didn't you stop him?"

Wesley's face flushed. He tore his eyes away from Steven and looked pleadingly at Lukas. "Do I have to talk about this?"

"No, dumbass. You don't." He glared at Steven. "Leave him the fuck alone."

"What did my brother tell you? You said Clifford tried to molest Cullen."

"Before Cullen died," said Lukas, "he and Clifford were together a lot."

"Being together doesn't mean shit."

"Cullen told me it happened," mumbled Wesley.

"Told you what?" demanded Steven. "Exactly."

"That they were . . . doing it. Doesn't matter that Cullen liked it. He was underage."

The words burned Steven. Not because his brother might have been gay, but because he hadn't felt as if he could tell Steven the truth.

"It's true," said Lukas.

Behind the sincerity, Steven could see a wisp of amusement flicker in Lukas's eyes. The shithead was enjoying this. "Let me get this straight, *dude*. My brother told you that he and Clifford were having sex."

"Yeah," said Wesley.

"Two nights before Cullen died," said Lukas, firing up another cigarette, "he and Clifford were together for hours."

"We saw them together," said Wesley. "They were sitting on a bench near the baseball diamond in Water Tower Park."

"What the hell were you doing following them?"

"We weren't following them," said Lukas, sounding hurt. "Wes and me, we were, like, smoking a little weed back in the bushes when we saw Cullen and Alden trot down the hill and sit on a bench by the baseball diamond."

182

"We watched them," said Wesley. "They talked for a while, and then Clifford took Cullen's hand and led him back to his car."

"Took his hand?"

"Yeah," said Wesley, puffing out his chest.

"Did you *see* them have sex?"

Wesley looked at Lukas before answering. "Well, yeah."

Steven grabbed Wesley by his coat and slammed him against the car. "You're lying."

"Don't hit me," said Wesley, ducking his head.

"He won't hurt you," said Lukas. "He can't 'cause he knows how easy it would be for us to hurt him back."

In an instant, Steven's switchblade was in his hand. He pressed the blade to Lukas's throat. "Are you threatening me?"

Lukas's eyes bulged. "No way."

"Good. Because you don't want to provoke me, Lukas. I'll cut your dick off and stuff it down your throat."

"Stop it," whined Wesley. "He didn't mean anything. It's true what he said about Cullen and Clifford. Don't shoot the messengers."

Steven felt like cutting Lukas just because he didn't like his attitude. Just because it was Thursday morning and he didn't like Thursday mornings. "You think it's funny that my brother was gay? *If* it's true."

"Hey, man," said Lukas, all soberness and respect now, "I don't care if he screwed a moose. That was his business."

"You disgust me, you know that? I should never have given either of you the time of day." Steven held on to Lukas for a moment, then shoved him away. "Get out of here. Both of you."

Wesley bolted for the Camaro. Lukas eased more slowly past Steven's knife, but then took off at a dead run.

24

Once rumors started to fly at Evergreen High School, Mary's mere appearance in the teachers' lounge cleared the room. As she hung her purse over the side of a chair, both of the teachers who were seated at the long, scuffed table got up, nodded to her, and made a hasty exit.

Fine, thought Mary. If that's the way the faculty wanted to deal with a student's unsupported accusations, to hell with them. And yet the furtive looks and the whispered comments were starting to get to her. In the hall, on her way to class, she could feel the momentum building. It was Salem, Massachusetts. 1692. Alden had been accused of witchcraft. He would be tried in people's minds, condemned without proof, and hanged on Gallows Hill.

Mary knew that pedophilia was serious business, that it was an unspeakable crime against an innocent child, and yet she believed firmly that her husband was innocent. Alden was a truthful man. He insisted he was being set up. What Mary couldn't figure out was why.

As she poured herself a cup of coffee, Tom Moline entered the lounge, shutting the door behind him.

"Mary?" he said, his voice tentative, his hand still on the doorknob.

She turned her back to him and looked out the window at the athletic field. "How did you know I was here?"

"I saw you come in. I was standing in the hallway talking to Gillian Campbell."

"Ah. One of the members of the jury."

"Huh?"

"There's a witch trial going on at Evergreen High. Didn't you know?"

She'd tried her best to avoid Tom, and yet she knew running into him was inevitable. After teaching today's class on Jacobean Drama to a room full of curiously somber students, all she wanted was a few quiet minutes to relax before she headed to the hospital to visit her son. Obviously, she wasn't going to get it.

After stirring some sugar into her coffee, she sat down. "You might as well say what you want to say."

He stayed near the door. "Look, Mary, I'm sorry. I never should have come on so strong this morning."

Over the rim of her coffee cup, she saw that he seemed tired. There was something about the mixture of his craggy face with his soft, vulnerable eyes that melted her. If she could manage to stay angry at him things would be a lot easier. She knew she'd never sleep with him again, but seeing him now, all the bluster and arrogance gone, she felt sorry for him. "I'm partly to blame."

He took another step into the room, but maintained his distance. "Let me help you."

She wasn't sure what he meant.

"You'll need a place to stay."

"Why? Where am I going?"

He looked at her hard. "After what's happened, you can't stay at the farmhouse. It's too dangerous. Alden could be violent. I can see it in him, Mary. He's like a coil ready to snap."

"That's ridiculous." A laugh just slipped out. She couldn't help it.

Tom acted as if she'd slapped him. His expression darkened. "It's not, Mary. You think you know him, but you don't. He's dangerous. You're not safe as long as you're in the same house with him."

"What gives you the right to make that kind of pronouncement? You barely know my husband."

"I know him well enough."

"To convict him without a trial?"

"What I see in Alden is something you apparently can't. He's a frightened man, Mary, a man who's hiding something. How can I convince you of that?" The muscles in his jaw tensed with frustration. "Look what he just did!"

"You should have told me you were part of the jury."

"Please, Mary, be reasonable."

"Is it reasonable to convict and condemn a man on the word of a student—with no other proof?"

"But they found proof."

Her eyes narrowed. "What?"

"Wesley Middendorf said that Alden seduced boys by showing them pornographic videos. They found a bunch in the rehearsal room behind the stage, right where Wesley said they'd be. The police took them away last night." He watched her for a moment. "Do you hear me? I don't know this for a fact, but I'll wager they find Alden's prints all over them. Why would this kid lie, Mary? Why?"

"I—"

"Let me help you. You can move in with me. I'll take care of you, Mary. If Alden comes anywhere near you I'll beat the bloody crap out of him."

"This makes no sense." She could hear the tremor in her voice and it sickened her.

"If not my place, then go somewhere else. A hotel. Or how about your son's apartment? He's not using it. Go there, Mary. Lock your door and don't let Alden in. When he finds out you know the score, who knows what he'll do?"

Mary couldn't even begin to understand what was happening. There had to be an explanation. Alden couldn't have done those things. He couldn't. "I've got to go, Tom," she said, rising and lifting her purse off the edge of the chair.

Passing him on the way to the door, he took hold of her arm. "I love you, Mary. Don't push me away. I only want to help."

She looked him square in the eyes, then continued on out of the room.

Cottonwood, Kansas
November 10, 1972

Jimmy left the hospital two days later. By then, the streets of Cottonwood had been plastered with posters of his sister, offering a reward to anyone who could give the police a tip that would help them track her down.

Jimmy's parents didn't have a dime, so their friends got together and collected five thousand dollars. A fortune, in Jimmy's opinion. Only problem was, Jimmy was the only person who could give the police the tip they needed. But if he 'fessed up, he'd end up in jail.

That five thousand dollars called loudly to him, though he knew he'd never get his hands on it. He had a little money—less than a thousand—that he'd buried in a metal box, money he'd skimmed from drug sales, but before he used it, he needed to give the whole situation some real thought, not just go off half cocked like he usually did.

Jimmy's right knee was wrapped in an Ace bandage, but his first thought after being released was to steal a car and head for Wichita. He knew it wasn't exactly a great idea, but it was the only thing he could think of. Except his mom wouldn't let him out of her sight. She seemed to need to touch him, to make sure he was in the same room with her. His father pulled him aside the day after he got out of the hospital and told him he needed to humor his mother, do what she asked, even if it seemed strange. Jimmy promised he would. He felt intensely guilty, knowing he was the cause of all her pain. And the guilt that dogged him made him even more determined to find Frank and get his sister back.

While his mother seemed to stop moving entirely, spending most of the day lying on the couch in the living room, alternately crying and watching TV, his father was a blur of activity. He'd been plastering signs up all over the county. When that produced no results, he and a few of his buddies decided to drive to Wichita, and then on to Kansas City. TV shows were covering Patsy's disappearance and they wanted to interview the parents. His mom refused to go. She said she was afraid all she'd do was cry. But his dad was eager to get the word out.

Jimmy had begged his father to take him along, but his dad said he had to stay home with his mother—see that she ate three meals a day, and that she went to bed at a decent hour. His father had taken him out of school for a few weeks, so he had no excuse not to stick around the house—the house that now felt like a prison.

Before his dad left, he showed Jimmy where his mother had hidden a bottle of vodka. He told him that she probably had other bottles stashed around the house, but he didn't have time to search for them. He asked Jimmy to watch the bottle. If another one appeared, he was to empty it partway, then fill it back up with water to dilute it. His dad explained that his mom was using booze to dull the pain, and that Jimmy had to make sure that if she drank too much, she didn't hurt herself.

While his dad was gone, Jimmy felt sick watching his mother slip into the bedroom and then lurch her way back to the couch. As the days wore on, her crying grew worse. During her blackest moments, she'd demand that he come sit next to her. She'd rub his hair or the skin on his arm, and once she fell asleep with her head on his shoulder. Her voice would slur when she talked about Patsy, how much she loved her and missed her, and what she'd like to do to the man who took her little girl. But it was when she started talking to Jimmy about private stuff between her and his dad that Jimmy felt totally grossed out.

His father was only supposed to be gone three days, but on the third day he called and said he had a chance to be on a TV show in Omaha, so he was headed there. He asked if everything was okay at home. Jimmy lied. He said everything was fine. He'd spent most of one day trying to find the liquor bottles his mother had hidden around the house, but she was better at hiding than he was at finding. He couldn't quite figure it out. After Patsy was taken, did she just go out and buy dozens of bottles of booze? His father brought his six-packs of beer home and put them in the basement. Why didn't his mother do the same thing?

By the time his dad got home, his mother was a total wreck. The day before, Jimmy had tried to get her to take a shower. She promised she would, but she never seemed to get around to it. She hadn't combed her hair since the day his dad had left. Jimmy could see the shock in his father's eyes when he carried his suitcase into the living room and saw her there all bleary-eyed and groady on the couch. Jimmy wanted to tell him that he'd tried his best to keep her fed and covered up at night so she wouldn't get cold. But it wasn't enough. They both knew it.

It was exactly ten days after Patsy had been taken that the police finally called with news. It was late afternoon. Jimmy was in his bedroom when he heard the phone ring. Stepping into the hallway, he listened as his father picked up the extension in the kitchen. He could tell right away that it was a serious call. His father listened for a long time without saying a word. Jimmy moved to the kitchen door. From there, he could see his mother lying on the living-room couch. She wasn't hiding her bottle anymore. His father had given up trying to get her to stop.

His father sat down at the kitchen table. His head drooped. All he said was, "Yeah. I'd like to see it. Thanks." And he hung up.

He sat there for a long time. Jimmy wanted to ask what the phone call had been about, but the look on his father's face made him keep silent.

After a few seconds, his mother called, "Who was on the phone?"

His father closed his eyes.

"John? Are you there?"

"I'm here," he said, his eyes still closed.

Jimmy's mom appeared at the door on the other side of the room. "Oh, God," she said, and she slid straight to the floor. "No!"

His dad didn't even try to help her. He put his head in his hands. His entire body heaved. Jimmy had never seen his dad cry before. He hoped he'd never see anything that awful again.

"It's Patsy," he said, pressing a fist to his lips. "The police found her fairy costume." He grasped the edge of the table to steady himself, but it didn't help. Tears streamed from his eyes. Jimmy felt tears streaming down his own face. His mother was wailing, crawling across the floor.

"The costume was soaked in blood."

Jimmy's mom screamed.

"They're doing a test on the blood to see if it's Patsy's type. They didn't find her, but . . . they think she's probably——" He couldn't say the word.

But Jimmy could. "Dead," he whispered.

And that's when the lights went out for Jimmy. Forever.

25

"Three words," said Cordelia.

Jane held the cell phone next to her ear, waiting for Cordelia's three pearls of wisdom to drip from her lips. "And they are?"

"*Follow the money.*"

It was Thursday evening. While waiting for Kenzie to arrive at the restaurant, Jane had taken a steno notebook into the pub to do some work. Sometimes it was easier to concentrate with the buzz of a crowd all around her. Cordelia had called just to check in. It had turned into a lengthy conversation. "What money would that be?"

"If Jason was paid off, Sherlock, you've got to find the person who paid him. Hey, why don't you stop by later. We could make some popcorn and watch a movie. I rented *Double Indemnity* for Hattie."

"She won't be interested in that. She isn't even two years old."

"*One* word this time, Jane."

"And that is?"

"*Osmosis.* The noir beauty will seep into her little childish brain cells even if she's chasing Melville with a Magic Marker or doing her best to dent my copper pots. It will help her to grow up with a true appreciation of all things dark and dramatic."

"Noir *rules.*"

"Amen, *sister.* It's certainly better than a constant stream of Cartoon Network."

Jane couldn't argue with that.

"So how about it? You want to come over later?"

"Can't."

"Why not?"

"I've got a date." Jane could almost feel Cordelia's arm plunge through the phone line and grab her by her shirt.

"A date? With whom?"

"Kenzie Nelson."

A gasp. "That major babe we met at the Cliffords'?"

"I doubt she'd appreciate being described as a *major babe*."

Silence. "You work pretty fast for a date-challenged dweeb."

"I beg your pardon."

"You know I'm only saying it because it's true. Have you two . . . you know?"

"None of your business what we do or don't do. And now, although this has been a pleasure, really it has, I've got to go."

"Call me in the morning with the play by play."

"Good night, Cordelia." Jane cut the line. But before she could stuff the phone back into her pocket, it rang again.

Jane steeled herself for round two with Cordelia. "This is Jane."

"Hi, it's Norm."

"Hey!"

"I tried calling you on your private line at the restaurant, but when I got your voice mail, I decided to give your cell phone a shot. I've got most of the information you asked for."

"Great." She flipped the notebook to a new page. "I'm ready."

"The owner of the SUV is a man named Burt Hegg."

"Hegg?" she repeated. There couldn't be that many Heggs in the world. "He doesn't by any chance live in Evergreen."

"Yup. 17893 Bendix Lane. In case you're wondering, I checked. He's Cullen Hegg's father."

"No kidding." Why had Cullen's dad been at the Donovan mansion on Nick and Lauren's wedding night? And what was he doing parked on the highway, watching the Cliffords' house yesterday afternoon? Both good questions with no obvious answers. "Any info on Jason?"

"He's got a juvie record, which means it's sealed. I asked around to see if I could determine what he was into. From what I learned, it was all petty stuff. He burgled a car. Got caught smoking marijuana. Tried to cash a check that didn't belong to him. Nothing hard-core. He graduated from Washburn High School three years ago. But here's an interesting detail. He grew up in Evergreen, went to Evergreen High until his parents moved to Minneapolis the summer before his senior year. It may prove to be a significant connection."

"Thanks so much, Norm. I really appreciate it."

"Let me know if I can do anything else."

"I will. Thanks."

Jane spent the next few minutes drawing doodles on the steno pad. So Jason had gone to Evergreen. Could he have been part of some twisted revenge plot to get back at Alden? But that meant Jason had to have known about the supposed molestation before Wesley Middendorf came forward. It was pretty apparent that Jason had recently come into some serious money, though it was unlikely that he'd received that money from a teenager. Follow the money, Cordelia had said. Maybe she was right.

"You look deep in thought," said a voice from behind her.

Jane turned to find Kenzie smiling down at her. Tonight, the gray leather coat had been replaced by a jeans jacket with a Harley-Davidson Eagle patch on the sleeve. Underneath she wore a navy blue V-neck sweater over a white T-shirt, a pair of skintight jeans, and her usual cowboy boots. She looked hot enough to melt frozen asphalt.

"Hi," said Jane. "You're early."

"Where's my steak?"

"At home in my refrigerator." She stood, grabbing the notebook off the table.

"We're not eating here?"

"I thought I'd make dinner for us tonight at my house. Prove to you I can really cook."

"As if I had any doubt." She touched Jane's arm.

Jane blushed. Cordelia was right. She was a dating dweeb. "Kind of warm in here, isn't it?"

"And it's cold outside. You sure you want to leave? You could have one of your chefs make us something simple and we could eat it in your *very* comfortable office."

Jane's house was only a few blocks away, but right at the moment it felt like it was on the other side of the moon. Mouse would get the wrong idea about her if she didn't watch it. She'd never been the kind of woman who'd jump in the sack with someone she barely knew. Her behavior was an aberration. It had to be the full moon. Or the anti-anxiety drugs she was on. Maybe they'd reduced her anxiety too much. But—hell if she cared. "It's all because of that knock I took on the head," she said to no one in particular.

"What knock on the head?" asked Kenzie, looking at her quizzically.

"Nothing. How about we have dessert first?"

"And the steaks at your place later?" She grinned. "Sounds like a plan."

By nine, they were back at Jane's house. Kenzie leaned against the counter as Jane pan-fried two thick filet mignons encrusted with sea salt and cracked black peppercorns. She'd brought home some prebaked bakers and popped them in the oven, so they wouldn't take long. When the steaks were seared, she stuck the pan in the oven to finish them, then started on the asparagus.

"This is a feast," said Kenzie, trailing her fingers lazily up Jane's arm.

"Don't do that or we won't be eating anytime soon."

Kenzie laughed.

After cleaning the asparagus spears, she tossed them with a little olive oil, some sea salt and pepper, and fresh rosemary, her current favorite herb, then dumped them in a pan and put it in the oven so they could roast while she and Kenzie were otherwise occupied.

When the tenderloins were medium rare, she took the pan out of the oven and removed them to a warm platter.

"Time to eat?" asked Kenzie, pouring them each a glass of pinot grigio.

"Almost. I want to make a simple sauce. It adds a lot." Jane sautéed some chopped shallots for a few seconds, then deglazed the pan with cognac and beef stock, reduced it slightly, tasted it for seasoning, and at the last minute tossed in a pat of butter and some fresh chopped parsley, whisking it briskly so that the sauce didn't break.

They carried their loaded plates into the dining room. Kenzie had already lit the candles in the center of the table. While Mouse hunkered down next to Jane, Kenzie took her first taste of the steak. "This is fabulous. You can make this for me every night."

"I'd hate to think what your cholesterol would be like if I did. Besides, when you've got your story in the bag, you'll be on your way back to Kansas, right?"

Kenzie didn't answer. She pretended to be too interested in her food.

"Speaking of Alden Clifford," continued Jane, "are you getting to know him better? Gaining his confidence?"

"It's been slow," she admitted, digging into her potato, to which she'd added a mountain of sour cream. "He's so upset about that student's accusation, he pretty much keeps to himself. Spends a lot of time in his study. But we've talked a couple of times. At this point, I'm curious what he has to say about his background."

"Educational? Personal?"

"All of it. Our history forms who we are."

"And who are *you*?" asked Jane, taking a sip of wine.

Kenzie smiled. "Just a good ol' country gal who likes to have a good time. You know me. Easygoing. Live and let live."

Somehow, Jane doubted it. "Got any brothers and sisters?"

"Nope, I'm an only child." She took another bite of steak. "You?"

"A brother. Younger. Works at a local TV station as a cameraman."

"Are you close?"

"Next to Cordelia, he's my best friend."

Kenzie pressed her hands against the top of the table and sat back in her chair.

"Something wrong?"

"I don't know. I guess . . . I just wish we had more time."

"Well, you're not rushing back to Kansas tomorrow, are you?"

"No, but . . . I will be leaving one of these days."

"Love 'em and leave 'em. Maybe you really are a cowboy at heart."

Kenzie's eyes lingered on Jane's. "That's not how I feel about you. You said I was fast, but really, I've only had one decent relationship in my entire life, and it was a long time ago. I spend all of my time working, Jane. That way I don't have to analyze. I'm way the hell too busy, even for friends. I come home at night, eat a bowl of cereal or whatever's in the fridge, maybe pour myself a drink, watch a little TV, and then hit the sack. But when things quiet down, like tonight, like right now, I realize how much I miss having someone to come home to. Someone to care about."

Kenzie's eyes seemed stripped of all pretense and full of tenderness. "I know what you mean," said Jane.

"Am I crazy to think we might have a chance together?"

Jane didn't know what to say. At this moment, Kenzie seemed so honest and real, but at other times, she seemed wary, her emotions buttoned up, like she might be hiding something. Jane wanted to enjoy what was happening between them, but she couldn't. Not yet. Not until she understood what was really going on.

Out of the blue, Kenzie leaned into the table and said, "You know, don't you, Jane."

The words caught her off guard. "Know what?"

"That I've lied to you."

Looking down, she said, "I don't know the details, but . . . yes, I know."

"There are things I simply can't tell you. Not now. Maybe not ever."

The phone rang.

"Let it ring," said Kenzie. She held out her hand to Jane.

"I've got to take it. But I'll only be a minute. I promise. We're not done talking." She pushed away from the table and hurried back to the kitchen. She checked caller ID before she answered. The name on the screen said, *Unknown Caller*. "Hello?"

A thin, high voice said, "Is this Jane Lawless?"

"Yes?"

"You own the restaurant on Lake Harriet?"

"That's me. Who's calling please?"

"My name is . . . Brittany. I'm a friend of Jason Vickner's."

Jane's pulse quickened. "Is Jason there? Can I talk to him?"

No response.

"Are you still there?" asked Jane.

"Yes." Silence. "Jason doesn't know I'm calling you. I found the note you left him. You said you wanted to help him."

"That's right. But first he needs to tell me the truth."

"About what he did. At your restaurant."

"Exactly. So, can I talk to him?"

"He's not here right now. It's just me."

Jane tried to hide her disappointment. "Do you two live together?"

"We have for the last few days. Jason had to leave his apartment. He went back to get some of his stuff, and that's when Alan gave him your note."

"How come you're calling me instead of Jason?"

More silence. "Because . . . he's not ready to talk to you. He's scared. We both are."

"Scared of what?"

"Of, uh . . . well, of—" Her voice trailed off.

"Of the person who paid Jason to plant the drug?"

"Yeah."

"Does this person know where Jason is staying?"

"No. I don't see how."

"So this person . . . this man . . . doesn't know about your relationship with Jason?" Jane made some logical leaps and hoped she wasn't wrong.

"I . . . don't think so. But it wouldn't matter. We're not staying at my place."

"You're in a motel."

"Something like that. Jason's got money, so it's not a problem. But this guy . . . he's been looking for Jason. We heard about it from . . . different people."

"Looking for him why?"

"Because he's afraid too."

"Of what?"

"Of what Jason knows."

Jane felt her heart pump faster.

"If he thinks Jason might talk, there's no telling what he'd do."

"You mean, you think this guy could be violent?"

"Why else would I risk calling you? You're maybe the only one who can get us out of this mess. You said your dad was a lawyer. That's what Jason needs. Somebody in the legal system to be on his side when he talks to the police."

"Do you think he'll agree to do that?"

"He has to. He just . . . has to. We can't go on living like this. When he's gone, I don't even want to get out of bed. I'm at a pay phone right outside the door and I'm scared to death!"

Jane had to think fast. "Is it possible for you to convince Jason to call me soon? Like tonight?"

"Does the offer still hold? About your dad?"

"Absolutely."

"Have you gone to the police already about Jason?"

"No."

"Thank God. That will help tons. Jason probably never said anything to you, but he admired you. He talked about you a lot—like, he'd say he thinks it would be cool to own his own restaurant someday."

"Tell him I'll do anything I can—as long as he comes clean." If someone paid him to tamper with the food, Jane assumed she might be able to escape the worst of her legal problems.

"I'll talk to him."

"When will he be back?"

"In a couple hours."

"I'll meet him whenever he wants. Tonight, if possible. Just call me, okay? I know I can help you if you'll let me."

"Thanks, Ms. Lawless. We'll be in touch."

Jane clicked the phone off, then stood for a moment allowing what just happened to sink in. "Yes!" she said, socking the air with her fist.

She hurried out of the kitchen, eager to pick up her conversation with Kenzie where they'd left off. But when she entered the dining room she found that it was empty.

Kenzie had gone.

26

Jane stayed up late thinking Jason might call. She also tried phoning Kenzie at her motel, but nobody answered. Either Kenzie wasn't there, or she was ducking Jane's calls. All in all, a fairly great day that had tanked in the last couple of hours.

Jane finally fell asleep on the living-room couch in front of the fire. She awoke around three to the ring of her phone. Struggling out of a heavy quilt, she grabbed the cordless off the floor.

"This is Jane," she said, assuming it was Jason, but wishing it were Kenzie.

"This is Jason Vickner." He sounded very formal and very young.

"Hi," she said, sitting up. "I was hoping I'd hear from you."

"I understand you and Brittany connected. She shouldn't have called—except I'm kinda glad she did."

"I think we need to talk."

"Yeah. Me too. You gotta know how sorry I am, Ms. Lawless. I never meant to hurt anyone. I thought, hell, it was good money, and kind of, you know, funny. Getting everyone high as a kite at some stuffed-shirt affair." He stopped for a second. "I mean, what did I care if someone wanted to do a number on Alden Clifford and his family? But it was more than that. I should have known. Clifford should watch his back is all I can say."

"Why?"

Silence.

"Why don't we just talk on the phone right now. I've got so many questions."

"No, I'd rather meet in person because . . . there's something I need to show you. Proof that mixing the dope in with the stock wasn't my idea."

"Okay. Just tell me where."

"I've been thinking about that. I sent Brit to spend the night with her parents, so I'm alone at the motel. No use her getting mixed up in my mess." Another pause. "Do you know where the Varsity East is?"

"Over by the U?"

"I'm in room 215. Park in the lot and come up the south stairs. You enter all the rooms from an outside balcony, so you don't have to check in with anybody at the reception desk. Knock twice, okay? *Twice.* That way I'll know it's you."

"I'll be there in half an hour," said Jane.

"I'll be waiting."

The Varsity East was considered a dump twenty years ago when Jane had been a student at the U. Nothing much had changed. Over the years, she'd witnessed various attempts to spruce it up. New exterior paint. New shrubs. A larger VACANCY sign. She'd been in one of the rooms a few years back. It had smelled of unwashed bodies, centuries of mildew, and a cloying lemon-scented disinfectant. All the place had going for it was its location and the price of admission.

Sailing down Washington Avenue, Jane took a left at Seven Corners and then another left onto the Tenth Avenue bridge. At this hour of the morning, even the University quieted down. Once she'd crossed Second, she began searching for a parking spot. She didn't want to park in the motel's lot because it seemed too open, too visible. She finally found one half a block away. After cutting the motor, she sat for a moment and gazed at the old motel in the distance. Most of the rooms were dark, although a few lights burned here and there. The last paint job had been the color of peanut butter. In the glow of the streetlights, the two-story concrete block structure looked more like a sick pink. The NO VACANCY light flashed on and off, so the place was full-up. If she'd been Jason, she would have picked a motel farther out of town. But for a kid who'd grown up in Evergreen, the big city probably seemed like a better place to hide.

Locking her car, Jane half walked, half sprinted toward the motel. She was dressed in dark clothes, with a black stocking cap pulled over her head, mostly for warmth, but also because an inner voice told her this meeting might be dangerous. She was about twenty yards from the south stairs when a squad car, lights flashing but the siren silent, whizzed past her and turned into the motel's lot.

It might be nothing more than a bunch of drunk college kids making a ruckus. She continued on toward the south stairs, but this time she approached more cautiously. When an EMT van rounded the corner behind her, she ducked into the open hallway that led to the first-floor rooms. She heard a low, deep guttural moan. A woman screamed. Police officers shouted orders.

Jane hid by the stairs, not sure what to do. The focus of attention seemed to be the center of the second-floor balcony. She peered around the edge of the stairway, her eyes sweeping across the second floor. As she did, a dark form clanged down the metal stairs and pitched forward right in front of her.

"God, shit," said a young man's voice, holding out a hand to steady himself on the railing.

He looked dazed, disoriented.

"I'm gonna puke," he said. And he did. Right there on the concrete walkway.

As he lurched away from the stairs, Jane took hold of his arm. "Are you okay?"

"God, this is freakin' nuts. Some guy just got knifed up there."

"Can I get you something? Anything. Water?"

He shook his head. "I just got back from seeing my girlfriend and found this guy lying on the balcony. When I turned him over, he had a knife sticking out of his chest." He pressed the back of his forearm to his mouth. "I think I'm going to hurl again."

Jane stepped back. When he was finished, she helped him over to the hood of a car, where he sat down to catch his breath. "Did you know the guy?"

"Never seen him before."

"Did you see what room he was in?"

"Yeah. I used his phone to call 911. It was 215. It was a switchblade," he went on. "Six-inch. Just like my brother's. God, who would do that to another human being? There was blood coming out of his mouth. The sweatshirt was soaked. I never seen anything like that before."

"Did he say anything?"

"Just asked for help. But when I came back after I made the phone call, he wasn't talking anymore."

"Was he breathing?"

"Pretty shallow. I told him to hold on, and he opened his eyes and looked at me. But then—" He hunched forward, started to rock. "Then, it was like his eyes went dead. I tried to get him to talk to me, but he wouldn't."

"It's not your fault."

"Don't you get it? He's *dead*. The guy died right in front of me." He gave himself a minute, then stood up. "I gotta talk to the police."

"Sure," said Jane. "But . . . just one more question."

"Yeah?"

"Did you see anyone around? Anybody leave the room? Anybody on the balcony?"

He shook his head, then gave her a wary look. "How come you're so interested?"

"I think I may know him."

"The guy who died? Oh, Jesus. I'm sorry."

She nodded.

"But I still gotta go talk to the police."

As he hustled back up the stairs, Jane returned to her car. She felt both sickened and defeated. Talking to Jason had been the break she'd been praying for. But whatever it was that he knew, someone out there was willing to kill to prevent him from giving it up. And that led her to an inescapable conclusion. This whole mess was far more dangerous than she'd ever suspected. Jason was dead. And lucky her. She was knee-deep in the same quicksand and sinking fast.

Friday

27

Mary walked into the kitchen holding the gold locket in her hand. "What is this thing?" she demanded.

Alden turned his head away slowly from the morning paper. He'd drunk one too many vodka shots last night and had a banging hangover. The locket brought him up cold. "Where did you get that?" he said, trying to grab it away.

She stepped back, refusing to let go. "Where do you think? You hid it in your sock drawer." She opened it up. "Who *is* the little girl in the picture?"

"Give it to me."

"Not until you tell who she is."

He pushed back from the table, but didn't get up. "You have no right to snoop through my things."

She gave him a look that was as bewildered as it was defiant. "You're an only child, Alden, so who is this little girl to you? How can you keep secrets from me after what's just happened?" And then, a sudden comprehension dawned in her eyes. "Is this what that man on the motorcycle tossed at you? Is it? You refused to show me what it was, said it was nothing. But you were lying then and you're lying now. The little girl, she's important, isn't she? Why, Alden? Who is she to you?"

"She's *nobody*."

"Then why did you keep it? Why did you hide it from me?"

"Look, Mary, the girl's face reminded me of someone I knew when I was a kid. That's all. If you're looking for a deep dark secret, there isn't one."

She studied him for a few seconds, then shook her head. "I don't believe you. In fact, I don't know what to believe anymore."

"We talked it through. I thought you understood. Wesley Middendorf's accusation is a complete fabrication. You're my wife, Mary. You know me."

"Do I?"

"I'd never do something like that."

She dropped the locket on the kitchen table next to his coffee cup. "You said someone's out to get you, to ruin your life. But you won't tell me why."

He stood, moved toward her, but she backed away. "I can't because I don't know why."

"You must have some idea."

"Mary, please God, let's not argue. All we do is go in circles."

She looked like she was about to say something, but thought better of it. "I have to go. I've got a meeting at the theater."

"What about your class? You don't know how much it sickens me that you're the one who has to bare the brunt of that malicious accusation."

"I'm calling Carla Macmillan this morning, telling her to get a sub to teach the class until this . . . situation . . . gets resolved."

"Good. That's good." He desperately wanted to touch her, to hold her in his arms and tell her how much he loved her, how much her belief in his innocence meant to him. And yet he could tell she wasn't sure of him anymore. "Mary, I may be guilty of many things, but I have *never* molested an adolescent boy. Wesley Middendorf is lying. I don't know why, but he is."

"I want to believe you," she said. But then her eyes dropped to the locket.

As she left the room, Alden turned and saw that Kenzie had been standing in the dining room, listening to their conversation. It wasn't as if he could keep any of this from her. And yet it seemed deeply wrong to have a stranger in his house watching his life crack apart.

Wesley's accusation had made the front page of the *Evergreen Morning Herald,* complete with a photo of Alden taken last year after Cullen's suicide. This time, he wasn't the hero of Evergreen High. He was the monster. He hadn't deserved the hero status, but he didn't deserve the title of pedophile either. After all the pain he'd caused in his life, the irony of the situation—getting nailed for something he *didn't* do—hardly escaped him.

"Mr. Clifford?"

Alden stared at her cowboy boots.

"For what it's worth, I don't think you did it."

He laughed and shook his head. "And how did you reach that conclusion?"

She leaned a shoulder against the door frame, hands in her pockets. "I've had a lot of experience with different sorts of people in my life. Maybe I'm wrong, but I figure I'm a pretty good judge of character."

"And you think I'm innocent."

"Nobody's innocent, Mr. Clifford. But I don't believe you molested those kids." As she entered the kitchen, she stopped to look at the locket. "Cute kid."

Alden studied the photo, then looked up at Kenzie, scrutinizing her face for a few seconds, then back down at the photo.

"Something wrong?"

He shrugged. "Must be a stress reaction."

"What is?"

He looked up into her face again, noting the wide blue eyes, the faded freckles.

"That little girl," said Kenzie. "She was important to you. You don't have to spell it out. I know what I see."

He picked up his coffee mug. "I wish I did."

"Can I warm that for you?" She stepped over to the kitchen counter, picked up the coffeepot.

"Why not."

"I've been up in Lauren's room. I actually think she might be feeling a little better today. She seems more focused. I found some photo albums in the living room yesterday. I thought she might like to see pictures of Nick when he was a kid."

He held the cup while she poured. "And did she?"

"She looked at the photos as I turned the pages." Kenzie filled a mug for herself. "I was wondering. Do you have any other albums around? Maybe some of you and Mary when you were kids?"

Alden swept the locket off the table, pressing it into the pocket of his chinos. "Nope. Just what's in the living room."

"No pictures of you when you were younger?"

"My parents' house burned down when I was in college. Everything went up in smoke."

"Too bad," she said, sitting down at the table. "Where are you from?"

He took a sip of coffee before answering. "Florida, Missouri, Texas, Georgia, Virginia, Oklahoma—everywhere there's an army base."

"You were an army brat, huh?"

He looked at her over the rim of his mug. "How about you?"

"Me? I'm a Midwesterner, born and bred. Grew up in a small town."

"Close family?"

"You'd think so, to hear everyone talk about small towns and family values. But no, we weren't close. My dad was the original ice man, and my mother, well, she never wanted kids. I always felt like I was in the way. Couldn't wait to get out on my own. When I left, I never looked back."

It sounded so familiar it made Alden shiver. "I'm glad Mary and I could give Nick a better start in life."

"You must love children."

"I do. Maybe I'm kidding myself, but I feel like I communicate well with them—teenagers, especially."

"That's a rare gift."

"I suppose." He tapped his fingers on the table.

"You ever think about telling your story?"

"What story?"

"About your life as a teacher, what really happened with Cullen Hegg? I'm sure you were deluged by requests last spring."

He laughed. "Even had a guy want to 'do' a movie deal with me. Some independent film company wanted to make a film about what happened."

"Not interested?"

"No way. Nobody's going to put my life under a microscope."

"You're afraid it wouldn't measure up?"

"I know it wouldn't."

Kenzie's eyes stayed on his. "Do you believe in redemption, Mr. Clifford?"

He found it an oddly prescient question. It was an issue he'd struggled with his entire life. "I used to think I did."

"But you've changed your mind?"

"I believe," he said, pushing a hand into his pocket and touching the locket, "that what goes around, comes around."

"Karma."

"Exactly. What you put out there into the universe comes back at you like a karmic boomerang. I'd hoped I could get around that little universal detail by changing my ways. I put some pretty bad stuff out there when I was young." Alden didn't know why he was telling her all this. Maybe it was because, in the scheme of things, she was nobody. She couldn't hurt him and she didn't really care. "The ghosts of your past never leave you alone."

"Any ghost in particular?"

Before he could answer, the doorbell chimed.

"I better get that," he said, glad to extricate himself from a conversation he really didn't want to have.

When he opened the front door, he found Gray standing outside.

"This was on your porch," said Gray, handing Alden a videotape.

Alden's name had been written on the outside in red ink. It wasn't wrapped and there was no postage, so it couldn't have been mailed. "Where'd you find it?"

Gray pointed to a wooden bench next to the door. "Are you going to make me stand out here and freeze?"

"No, no. Come in."

Gray stepped into the foyer in his cashmere topcoat, his gray linen trousers, and his Gucci loafers.

Alden felt like a *shlump* wearing chinos and a T-shirt. Not that he cared. He could hear Kenzie cleaning up breakfast dishes in the kitchen. A moment later she appeared in the dining room, her coat slung over her shoulder and car keys in her hand.

"Hi, Kenzie," said Gray. "Nice to see you again."

Her eyes lingered on him. "Hi."

"So, how's our patient doing?"

Alden found the "our patient" thing just short of barfworthy.

"Better today," said Kenzie.

"You going somewhere?" asked Alden.

"I need to run to the grocery store. Would now be an okay time?"

"Sure. There's a partial grocery list on the fridge. You might want to take that with you." As she left the room, Alden returned his attention to Gray. "I assume you didn't come to see me. Lauren's up in her room."

"Actually, I need to talk to you first."

"What about?"

The back door clicked shut. Looking out the dining-room window, Alden watched Kenzie cross to her truck.

"I didn't come here to judge you, Alden, but I heard what happened on Wednesday. You were accused of molesting one of your students."

"None of it's true," said Alden. He turned his back on Gray and walked into the living room, wishing Gray would leave him alone.

Gray remained in the front hall. "Have you hired an attorney?"

"Why? You looking for another client? I'd think you'd have plenty to do now that you're helping half of my friends sue Jane Lawless."

Gray unbuttoned his coat. "Just some friendly advice, okay? You better get yourself some representation. Otherwise, you don't have a prayer of keeping your job."

Alden had talked to several lawyers yesterday. The attorney for the school had contacted him first, telling him not to talk to Wesley Middendorf's lawyer under any circumstances. Alden had also spoken with a defense attorney, a man who'd given him the same spiel as Gray. He insisted that the school lawyer would not be working on Alden's behalf.

As Alden sat in the man's office, he was sickened by what he heard. The lawyer assured him that if the matter went to trial, he'd make Wesley's life hell under cross-examination. He would put *Wesley* on trial. Alden left the office with a headache the size of Mount Rushmore and a stomach that felt like he'd swallowed ground glass.

"I've already hired a lawyer, Gray, so you can get some sleep now. I know my problems must be keeping you up at night."

Inspecting the videocassette, Alden said, "If there's nothing else——" He was curious about the tape. He wanted to see what was on it, but he didn't need an audience.

"One more thing. I think it's time Lauren came home with me."

Alden's shoulders tensed. He looked up at the wall in front of him. "We've already had this conversation."

"That was before you were accused of—"

"I told you, it's not true."

Gray stepped under the archway. He looked like he was posing for a *GQ* ad. "But I don't know that for a fact, now do I. What I do know is that this isn't a good environment for Lauren. You're under a great deal of strain, Alden, and she'll pick up on it. Even if it turns out you *are* innocent—"

"Thanks for the vote of confidence."

"Lauren shouldn't be subjected to your chaos."

Alden bowed his head. Maybe he was right. "Let me think about it."

"No. I'm here to take her now."

"You arrogant sonofabitch. Get out of my house."

"Not without Lauren."

Bumping past him, Alden threw open the closet door and grabbed the box off the top shelf. Gray was halfway up the stairs when he pulled the gun free and thumbed off the safety. "Stop. I mean it, Gray."

With his back to Alden, Gray said, "I'm not arguing about this anymore." When he turned around and saw the gun, he froze.

"I repeat. Get out of my house."

"Have you lost your mind?"

"Possibly."

Gray walked back down the stairs. "You don't want to pull a gun on me, old man."

"I just did. Bummer, huh?"

"Does Nick know you have a firearm in this house?"

Still holding the gun, Alden opened the front door. "You're a lech, Donovan. You're after your best friend's wife. I've known it for months. You should be ashamed of yourself."

Gray's eyes widened slightly, then turned righteous. "You're full of it."

"Probably, but I'm also right." As soon as Gray stepped across the threshold, Alden slammed the door and locked it. That small act immediately eased the tension he'd been holding all morning in his stomach. He lowered the gun, feeling oddly energized. There weren't any witnesses to prove he'd pulled it, so he wasn't worried that Gray would be back with the sheriff anytime soon.

After returning the .38 to the front closet, his thoughts turned to the video. All of a sudden, he had this overwhelming urge to make himself a bowl of popcorn. A videotape turning up on his porch couldn't be good news. But he always ate popcorn when he watched a movie. Why stop now?

While the microwave did its number on the popcorn bag, Alden melted butter in a pan on the stove. He felt unreasonably lighthearted, even going so far as to do a little whistling. Maybe he should pull a gun on an asshole more often. It was better than Maalox.

Once the video was in the VCR, Alden sat down on the couch and switched on the TV. The bowl rested in his lap as he crunched away contentedly through the first minute of what was obviously a home movie. The camera bounced up and down as the amateur cameraman lurched his way up the front walk of what appeared to be a town house. The camera zoomed in on the number above the front door. 2123. Nobody Alden knew.

The screen went black. Then a new image appeared. It was the same building, but it was dark out now. Alden guessed the cameraman had moved around to the side or the back. The lens floated in on a first-floor window, zoomed through a crack in the curtains. It took a moment for the camera to focus properly in the dim light. When it did, Alden could make out a bed with a tangle of sheets on top of it.

"Shit," he said under his breath. "It's a porn video. Shot by a Peeping Tom. Why do I have all the luck?" He continued to watch, continued to eat his popcorn. There was no sound on the tape except for an occasional street noise—and the breathing of the smart-ass holding the camera. As the two people on the bed mauled each other, the cameraman's breathing became deeper, louder, faster. "My God, he's jerking off," said Alden. This was too much. He was about to switch off the TV when a face appeared out of the tangle of sheets.

Alden set the popcorn bowl down on the coffee table and moved up closer to the TV. A second face appeared. He watched in stunned silence as his wife and a math teacher from Evergreen High threw off the covers and made it there right in front of him.

It was like watching a car crash in slow motion. He couldn't pull his eyes away. At the very end, before the picture went dark, he heard laughter. Soft at first, then louder and meaner until it echoed through every part of his brain. His wife was cheating on him with a man who looked like he should be rustling cattle for a living. The horror and sheer aesthetic insanity of it was almost too huge to wrap his mind around.

Alden switched off the TV, then dropped down on the floor. He hadn't cried in years, but he cried now. Cried until there was nothing left inside him but a raw, roiling bitterness.

When he'd finally pulled himself together enough to look up, he saw that Lauren was standing under the living-room arch, watching him.

"Oh, God," he said, twisting away from her. "How long have you been standing there? What did you see?"

There was no pity in her eyes. No concern, only that flat, cold stare of hers.

"I have to make some phone calls," he lied as he got up. He wanted to lock himself in his study and never come out.

But before he could make his exit, Lauren said, "Gray's a bad man."

"What?" Her voice was so soft, he wasn't sure he'd heard her correctly. "Say that again?"

"I refuse to go with him. I want to stay here."

She wasn't interested in his response. She'd come downstairs to make her demand, and when that was done, she turned and with her ramrod-straight back, walked slowly back up the stairs.

28

When Jane and Mouse returned home from their morning run, Cordelia was in the kitchen brewing a pot of tea. She'd arrived while they were out, bringing with her a sack of cinnamon sugar bagels and a tin of cream cheese.

"I didn't think you'd be here for another hour," said Jane, unhooking the leash from Mouse's collar.

Jane had called Cordelia around eight, knowing that with Hattie there, she wouldn't be asleep. Jane explained briefly about what had happened to Jason. Cordelia was aghast, not only because a young man had been murdered, but because Jane had been so close to it. She pointed out that if Jane had arrived a few minutes earlier, she could easily have walked in on the murderer. Nothing Jane hadn't already considered.

Cordelia insisted on coming over, which was fine with Jane. After last night, she didn't really feel like being alone.

"Shhh," said Cordelia. She stood in the kitchen with her arms folded, listening to a small nine-inch TV Jane had recently installed under an upper cupboard. "You missed it."

"Missed what?" Jane tossed Mouse a Milk-Bone.

"The local news just reported on Jason's murder. The police don't have a suspect, but they're saying it was drug-related."

"I suppose Jason's girlfriend may be the only one who knows what really happened."

Narrowing an eye and pointing a finger at Jane, Cordelia said, "What you need is an official mega-sized bulletin board."

"I do?"

"Every cop has one. It helps arrange the players, keep track of clues. And it creates the right professional . . . idiom."

"I'm not a professional, Cordelia."

"So? *Look* the part. That's half the battle. After you called, I ran out and bought you the biggest badass bulletin board I could find. And I've already started filling it up."

"Gee."

"I know. I'm awesome."

Cordelia darted into the hallway and dragged a large, three-foot-wide by five-foot-high bulletin board into the kitchen. She leaned it against the counter, then raced back into the hallway, returning with an official-looking pointer stick.

Jane was amazed at the work she'd already done. "Where did you get the photos?"

"Old newspapers. I save the front section and the arts section, toss the dreck out."

She turned back to the board. "Now. I've got eight players here, two rows of four—no photo of Jason, so I used an old picture I had lying around."

Jane squinted at the photo. "That's John Malkovitch."

"Exactly. I thought we should take each individual and, you know, discuss them. See what conclusions we can draw. I'll point to the picture, you say what you think might be relevant. Okay?" She placed the pointer first on Nick Clifford. It was an old picture, back when he was less beefy and had hair.

"I didn't mention this to you before," said Jane, "but it seems that on his wedding night, he learned that his new wife had been sleeping with the best man."

Cordelia's eyes popped. "You're kidding."

Jane shook her head. "Put your pointer on Gray Donovan."

Cordelia moved it.

"From what I understand, he thought Lauren should have married him. Who knows? Maybe he wanted to ruin the wedding just out of spite because she chose Nick."

"He certainly has enough money to pay Jason to do his dirty work."

"And he finessed the situation so that he became the lawyer representing the guests who are currently suing me."

"Profit motive, Janey. Like I said, follow the money."

"I've never been clear on one major point. At the wedding—was someone after Nick and Lauren, the entire Clifford family, or just Alden?"

"No idea," said Cordelia.

"I probably shouldn't be telling you this, but Gray hired Kenzie to, well, to infiltrate the Clifford household."

Cordelia did a slow one-eighty. "You're telling me Kenzie's a *mole?*"

"Well, not really. She took the job because she has an agenda of her own."

"And that is?"

"She's an investigative reporter. She's got a contract from *Interview Today* to do a feature article on Alden. Because of the Cullen Hegg thing."

Cordelia stared at her for a second, then burst out laughing. "Hel-*lo!* That's the lame-est thing I've ever heard. You believe that load of bull?"

Jane was somewhat taken aback. "Yes. I do. She showed me her press credentials. She works for a newspaper in Wichita."

Cordelia shook her head. "Jane, wake up. She's snowing you. She's probably just what she told you she was. A mole. Hired by Gray Donovan to spy on the Cliffords. And to that I say"—she scrunched up her face—"*yuck.*"

"Yes, but—"

"Face it, Janey. You've hooked up with another winner."

Now Jane was angry. "People in glass houses—"

"Shouldn't throw stones. Yeah, yeah, yeah. I haven't always picked the best women either. I can understand why you got sucked in. Kenzie's very attractive—and then some."

"I'm not that shallow. I like her, Cordelia. A lot."

"Well, caveat emptor is all I can say."

"I'm not *buying* her."

"No, but you bought her load of bull."

"Let's move on, shall we?"

Cordelia gave a smoky chuckle. "Never let it be said that Cordelia Thorn cannot *move on.*" Placing the pointer on Lauren's photo, she continued. "Lauren Bautel Clifford. Real estate agent and part-time floozy. She probably clammed up after Nick took that nosedive into the empty pool because of guilt."

"Cecily thinks that too."

"I doubt Lauren had anything to do with the magic mushroom extravaganza. She had no motive. In my opinion, she falls under the category of 'guilty bystander.'" Cordelia moved the pointer to Mary Clifford. "Another bystander."

"Agreed," said Jane.

"Next we have John Malkovitch, otherwise known as Jason Vickner. Your turn, Janey."

"Okay. Jason was paid to lace the wedding food with hallucinogens. We know that because he admitted it to me on the phone last night. He said he was sorry, but that he didn't think it would be a big deal. He actually thought it was kind of funny, which makes me believe that whoever talked him into it either felt the same way or tried to sell him on the notion that it wasn't dangerous. But we also know that he was running from that same person."

"Because?"

"The guy was afraid Jason would tell the police he paid him, thus getting him in trouble. But is that a strong enough motive for murder? Actually, I've been thinking all morning that I should probably talk to the police, tell them everything I've learned."

"Dumb idea."

"Why's that?"

"Because you know very little and can prove even less. *And,* you'll just get your restaurant in deeper with the lawsuits because Jason was your employee."

"I'm not sure lawsuits are the point anymore." Jane pinched the bridge of her nose. "I doubt it's a coincidence that Jason grew up in Evergreen. He graduated from Washburn, but before that, he went to Evergreen High."

"So that means he probably knew Cullen Hegg." Cordelia's reading glasses hung from a chain around her neck. She put the glasses on and looked more closely at the photo of Cullen. "This is a family shot. He apparently has an older brother named Steven. Really tall guy. Dark hair.

Looks kind of geeky. My guess is that Steven and Jason are about the same age, so it's possible they knew each other too." She turned around. "Is that significant?"

"Only if Steven Hegg is the one who paid Jason to tamper with the food."

"No motive, then," said Cordelia, dismissing it. "And no money. It says here he's a college student."

"Unless . . . what if he thought Alden was responsible for his brother's death?"

"That means he had to know about it long before this Middendorf kid came forward."

"True." Jane rested her head on her hand. "Nothing in this moves in a straight line. Oh, I forgot to tell you. Burt Hegg, Cullen's dad, was the guy who nearly ran me down at the wedding. I doubt he was an invited guest. I figure he was doing the same surveillance thing there that he was doing the other day out on the road by the Cliffords' place."

"We're talking about the guy with the binoculars parked on the side of the road?"

"Right."

"What do we know about Burt Hegg?"

"Zip."

Cordelia thought for a few seconds, looking at the pictures on the bulletin board, then let out a loud, hopeless sigh. Grasping the lapels of her sweater, she turned and fixed Jane with a hard look. "It's official now. I am *totally* confused."

After Cordelia left, Jane dragged the bulletin board into her study. It wasn't a bad idea, just a little big. She propped it against a bookcase, then sat down behind her desk and studied it. The more she considered Cordelia's comments about Kenzie, the more she felt they might be true.

Picking up the phone, Jane punched in 4 1 1 and waited for the operator to come on the line. She asked for the number of the *Wichita Prairie Sentinel,* the paper Kenzie worked for.

"Sorry," said the operator, "but there's no listing for a *Prairie Sentinel* in Wichita."

"Are you sure?" said Jane. "It's the main daily newspaper."

"I can give you the number for *The Wichita Eagle.*"

"No other daily newspapers?"

"Nothing listed here."

Jane took down the number. After thanking the woman, she punched it in. A switchboard operator answered.

"*Wichita Eagle.* May I help you?"

"I'd like to speak with Kenzie Nelson."

"Is this an employee of the paper?"

"Yes," said Jane.

"Ah . . . I don't show a Kenzie Nelson. I do have a Catherine Nelson, or a Kurt T. Nelson."

"You're positive? No *Kenzie* Nelson? She's a reporter."

"Not for us. Sorry."

"Have you ever heard of a newspaper called the *Prairie Sentinel?*"

"Not in Wichita."

Jane couldn't think of any other questions to ask. "Thanks," she said, hanging up.

As the shock wore off and the realization that Kenzie had played her took hold, Jane wrote Kenzie's name on a piece of paper, got up, and added it to the group of pictures on the bulletin board. She didn't believe for a second that Kenzie's reason for taking care of Lauren was as simple as the money Gray had offered. But if she wasn't a reporter, who was she?

Sitting back down behind her desk, Jane flipped through her address book until she came to Alden's home number. Kenzie had taken off last night and then refused to return her phone calls, but Jane intended to talk to her today—even if she had to drive down to Evergreen to do it.

After a couple of rings, Alden picked up. "Hello?"

"Hi. It's Jane Lawless."

"Oh, hi."

She thought she detected something odd in his voice. A certain hoarseness. Maybe he had a cold. "I wonder if I could talk to Kenzie."

"She's not here."

"When do you expect her back?"

"Well, actually, I told her to go home."

"Is she feeling okay?"

"Yes, I just didn't need her help today."

"You doing all right, Alden?"

"Just dandy."

She caught the sarcasm.

"You know, Jane, I was just about to step into the shower."

He didn't want to talk. "Okay. Give my best to Lauren, and to Mary."

"I'll do that. Bye."

"Bye," she said, but he'd already hung up.

Glancing down at Mouse, Jane shook her head. "Something's up."

He wagged his tail.

"Listen, kiddo, I have to leave for a while. I'll be back later to pick you up and take you over to the restaurant. That okay with you?"

He sat up and put his paw on her knee.

"I love you, Mouse." She crouched down, wrapped her arms around his neck, and burrowed her head in his fur.

29

Half an hour later, Jane entered the front doors of the Ramada Inn. As she climbed the stairs and hurried down the long hallway to Kenzie's room, she bit back the urge to let fly with the anger she was feeling. If she lost it, she'd never find out what was really going on. And she needed to know. Badly needed to know.

Jane's feelings for Kenzie had developed way too fast. It didn't take Dr. Phil to tell her that. But those feelings had somehow crawled deep inside and gripped her hard. She'd long ago given up trying to understand the physics of human attraction. It was what it was. What she felt for Kenzie was serious.

Knocking on the door, Jane scanned the hall. The hotel had been built less than a year ago. It still smelled of new carpeting and fresh paint. Kenzie's room was right next to the back stairs. Jane didn't know what Kenzie's plans were for the rest of the day, but it was a given that she would have to return to her hotel room sooner or later. Jane knocked again. When there was no answer, she sat down on the carpet, pulled her knees up to her chest, rested her arms on top of them, and waited.

Jane had almost fallen asleep with her head resting against the wall when she heard footfalls on the back stairs. She opened her eyes just as Kenzie came through the stairwell door.

"Jane," said Kenzie, coming to a full stop.

"Miss me?" Jane repeated what Kenzie had said to her yesterday morning.

"Well, I—"

Jane stood. "You're coming in, yes?"

"What are you doing here?"

"You wouldn't answer my phone calls. Don't you think we should talk?"

"About last night."

"Among other things."

A wisp of doubt flickered across Kenzie's face. "Okay. Come in." She pressed her card into the slot, pulled it back out as she turned the door handle. "I don't remember how I left the room. You're kind of a neatnik."

"I am?"

She laughed softly. "No one would ever accuse me of that." Opening the door, she said, "It's a suite, not that it's very fancy."

The suite, like the hallway, was done in salmon and olive tones. Generic furniture filled the long narrow living room. Double doors opened onto the bedroom with its king-sized bed.

Kenzie was right. Clothes were strewn everywhere. So were file folders and books. A laptop sat open on the desk next to a snarl of papers and magazines.

"Like I said, it's a mess." Kenzie smiled with her mouth, but it didn't reach her eyes.

"Surely you can't think I'm bothered by it?" Jane stepped up to her and was about to put her arms around her when Kenzie backed up.

"Okay," said Jane. "No touching. I can deal with that. But at least take your jacket off."

"Sure," said Kenzie. But she didn't move.

Jane couldn't figure out what was going on. "What's wrong?"

"Nothing's wrong."

"Are you going to throw me out?"

Kenzie's eyes softened. "No, of course not."

"Then, can I sit down? Can we both sit down?"

Jane sat on one end of the couch, Kenzie on the other. It wasn't a big couch, so they weren't very far apart, although the separation between them felt like a chasm.

"Seen any good movies lately?" asked Jane.

"Okay," said Kenzie, shaking her head with a smile. "You've made your point."

"Why did you leave last night?"

"It's complicated."

"Isn't everything. Why don't I take a stab at it? You up for that?"

Kenzie looked down at her cowboy boots. "Jane, I didn't mean to hurt you. Really. I just couldn't stay."

"I figure it was for one of two reasons. Sometimes, when I let someone into my life, let them see the part of me that's vulnerable, the part I usually keep hidden, I get scared. I've entered the unknown with a person I may not know all that well. It's tough to take a chance on somebody new, especially when you've been hurt before. Sometimes, when I realize what I've done, I sort of . . . disappear. Until I can figure out what to do next."

Kenzie's eyes remained on Jane. "Is that what you think happened?"

"Well," said Jane, "either that, or you felt guilty because you lied to me."

Kenzie opened her mouth, but nothing came out.

"You're not a reporter. There is no *Wichita Prairie Sentinel*."

"You checked?"

Jane shrugged. "It's pretty obvious I'm gullible, but eventually even I wise up. Who are you really? And what are you doing messing around in Alden and Mary's life?"

Kenzie got up. Instead of taking off her jacket, she began to pace, her hands stuffed into her front pockets. And that's when Jane saw it. The slight bulge on the waistband at the back of her jeans.

"Is that a cell phone, or—" Her eyes locked on Kenzie's. "It's a gun. You're wearing a holster. That's why you wouldn't let me near you, why you can't take off your jacket."

Kenzie stopped in the middle of the floor. She passed a weary hand over her eyes, deciding how much she could afford to tell. Finally, taking off her jacket and tossing it over a chair, she unsnapped the holster and removed the gun. Then she sat down on the couch, closer to Jane this time. "There's something you need to understand. What I tell you absolutely must remain between us—for now. I'm taking a chance here, Jane. Don't make me sorry."

"You're a cop?"

"No. I'm private."

"You're a PI."

She nodded.

"Licensed?"

"By the state of Kansas, yes." She took out her billfold and pulled the license from under the back flap.

Jane examined it. It looked real, although the press credentials had too. "If you're a private investigator, that means someone hired you."

"That's right."

"Who?"

"I can't tell you."

"Okay. Why were you hired?"

Kenzie leaned her shoulder into the couch. "In 1972, an eight-year-old girl named Patsy Shore was abducted from her hometown of Cottonwood, Kansas."

"Same place you're from."

"Yes. It was Halloween and she was out with her brother, trick-or-treating. The brother, James Shore—or Jimmy, as he was called—said that two men in a van stopped and grabbed her. They held a gun to Jimmy's throat while they stuffed the little girl in the back of the van. There was some talk at the time that Jimmy might have been lying, that he had something to do with her disappearance, but nobody could ever prove it."

"Did they find the little girl?"

Kenzie shook her head. "The police did find part of the costume she was wearing the night she was grabbed. It was covered in blood. The theory was that she'd been murdered shortly after she was abducted. If that's true, it's probably a godsend. You don't want to be a kid who falls into the hands of some pervert. Believe me." Her eyes dropped to her hands. "Jimmy Shore was fifteen when all this happened. Shortly after he turned sixteen, he skipped town. After that, he simply disappeared. In 1974, the remains of a child were found on a hillside just outside Cheyenne, Wyoming. Forensics weren't as good back then, so no DNA matching was ever done, but they found the jacket Patsy was wearing on Halloween night buried with the remains. One way or the other, I think we can assume that Patsy Shore is dead."

"So why are you here?"

"Because someone thinks Alden Clifford is Jimmy Shore. And if that's true, they want to talk to him."

"Just talk? Nothing more?"

Kenzie gazed quietly at Jane for a moment, then got up again. "Here. Let me show you something." She stepped over to the desk and picked up a file folder. Returning to the couch, she paged through some papers until she found the one she wanted. She handed it to Jane.

Jane read through it. "It's a birth certificate for Alden Clifford."

"And this." She handed Jane another page.

"This is his SAT grade." She glanced at the date. "June, 1974. He was a smart young man."

"One more," said Kenzie.

The next page was a copy of the grades Alden had earned at Clemson University in South Carolina. He'd graduated with a masters in American Studies. "So what's wrong with this picture?" said Jane. "What am I supposed to see?"

Kenzie handed Jane the last page from the file.

It was a death certificate. Jane stared at it a moment, then the light finally dawned. "Alden Clifford died in a car accident in August of 1974."

"And he entered Clemson one month later. You see the problem."

Jane handed the paper back to Kenzie. "I assume Alden must look like Jimmy Shore."

"He's aged, but yes. He's the spitting image. It's possible he could have stayed lost forever if it hadn't been for Cullen Hegg's suicide. Because of that one event, his picture was plastered on the front pages of newspapers and on TV shows all over the country."

Jane leaned back against the couch cushions. "Are you one hundred percent certain Alden Clifford is Jimmy Shore?"

"I'm one hundred percent sure he's not Alden Clifford. I'm still trying to prove his connection to Jimmy Shore. Let's say, at this point, I'm ninety-eight percent sure."

"Is that good enough for your client?"

"Probably. But it's not good enough for me."

"So what's it going to take?"

"Well, a personal admission would be nice. Barring that, I'm not sure there's any way I can be absolutely certain. The thing is, someone seems to be after Alden Clifford. I don't know who or why, but I'm trying to find out. This morning, something major occurred. I'd gone out to get groceries and when I came back, he looked like he'd been hit by a truck."

Jane recalled how odd he'd sounded on the phone. "Do you think Wesley Middendorf's accusation is true?"

Kenzie's eyes drifted over to the TV. "I think that Wesley Middendorf has it in for Alden. But I believe he's lying. At first I thought someone was just playing with Alden, trying to make his life miserable. But now I think it's more than that. I think someone wants him gone from Evergreen High."

"Wesley?"

"He's got to be part of it. Have you ever met him?"

Jane shook her head.

"I have. I stopped him outside of the school a few days ago, said I was a reporter and that I wanted to get his take on what had happened to him. Believe me, Jane, Wesley Middendorf will never be asked to join Mensa. I can't believe he's behind what's happening to Alden. I think he's being used, but I also get the feeling he's involved. He's built like a Bradley fighting vehicle, so it's possible he's the brawn of the operation. But someone else is definitely the brains."

"Another high school kid?"

"Possible, but unlikely. If I had to guess, I'd say this all goes back to Cullen Hegg. That's where I've been concentrating my efforts for the last couple of days."

It was a lot of information for Jane to process. "This Jimmy Shore. You said he might have had something to do with his sister's disappearance?"

"Yeah. That was one theory. It's all conjecture, though. Nobody knows for sure."

"Are Jimmy's parents still alive?"

"Nope. Both dead."

So they couldn't have hired Kenzie. Who else would have an interest in the case all these years later? "Did Jimmy have any other brothers or sisters?"

"Just Patsy."

"What kind of a kid was he?"

"Wild. Some people thought he was a sociopath in training."

"But Alden isn't like that."

"He doesn't appear to be. It's odd. People don't outgrow personality disorders."

"So maybe he isn't Jimmy Shore."

Kenzie studied Jane before answering. "You like him, don't you?"

"I've always thought he was a great guy, yes. I know Mary thinks he's been a terrific father to Nick. Nick isn't his natural child. But that never seemed to matter to Alden. It would to some guys."

"So what am I missing?" said Kenzie, a faraway look in her eyes.

If Kenzie would only tell her who'd hired her, a lot of Jane's questions would be answered. But there was little chance of that. "Where did you get that press credential?"

"Huh? Oh, that's easy. You can get anything you want on the street. That's how Jimmy became Alden. He bought the identity, and probably the real Alden Clifford's SAT scores right along with it. You can get anything you want for the right price."

"How do I know your PI license isn't fake?"

Kenzie slipped her hand over Jane's. "I guess you don't."

"I suppose you think I should trust you."

"I'd never hurt you, Jane. You have to believe, that."

Funny thing was, Jane did.

30

Steven sat sprawled on the couch, sipping a beer and watching a soccer game on ESPN when he heard his phone give two quick rings. It was the security system in his building telling him someone was buzzing his apartment. He leaned over and grabbed the cordless from the end table. "Hello?"

"Steven? It's Lukas. Wesley's with me. We gotta talk."

"Shit, man. You need anything, you talk to Sean. I've got nothing to say to you."

"Don't hang up," pleaded Lukas. "This is important."

"I'm busy."

"It's about your father."

Steven sat forward, switched off the TV. "What about him?"

"Let us come up and we'll tell you."

He took a last slug of beer, then crushed the can in his fist. "Oh, hell. Get up here." He buzzed them in.

By the time he got back to the living room with another beer, they were outside knocking. "Yeah yeah yeah," he said. When he drew the door back, he smiled. "If it isn't Beavis and Butt-Head."

Wesley looked hurt. "Is that how you see us?"

"Nah. You're more like Laurel and Hardy."

"Who?" asked Wesley.

"Just come in." Steven returned to the couch. "Shouldn't you boys be in school?"

"School ends at two," said Lukas. "Wes and me, we're model citizens these days. Gotta keep our eyes on the prize, man. Just like you."

"Sure," said Steven. He stretched his arms along the back of the couch. Since the last time he'd seen Lukas, Lukas had had a haircut. With his hair short and neatly combed, he looked almost clean-cut. Almost. He still looked greasy around the edges. "You still after the big Ivy League experience, Lukas?"

"That's the plan."

"Well, that just friggin' makes my day, Luke. Whatever you've got to say, make it fast."

"Mind if I smoke?" asked Lukas. With one quick glance, his sharp eyes took in the entire room.

Steven shrugged. "It's your lungs." He pushed an ashtray across the end table to him.

Wesley watched Lukas light up. He seemed fascinated by the flame. As soon as Lukas blew out the match, Wesley dropped into a chair across from Steven. His face puckered. "You gotta call your dad off, man. He's driving me nuts."

"Meaning?"

Lukas took a deep drag, blew smoke out of the side of his mouth. "Your dad's been on the horn to Wes at least half a dozen times since we were at his house the other day. He keeps pressing Wes to tell him everything he remembers about Cullen."

Steven narrowed his eyes at Wesley.

Wesley looked away. "I should never have said that Clifford messed with Cullen before he died. Your dad's, like, *freakin' out,* man. He wants to know, like, every detail. I need him to leave me alone. Tell him to stop calling me, okay?"

Steven studied Wesley over the rim of his beer can. "You know, guys, I been thinking about it and here's what I've concluded: I don't believe your story about being molested, Wes. I think you lied about Clifford and about my brother, and I want to know why. Did my father put you up to it?"

Wesley's eyes rose to Lukas.

"Don't look at him," ordered Steven. "Look at me."

Wesley's body snapped to attention. "Okay. Geez."

"It's all a lie, right?"

What color there was in Wesley's face—and there wasn't much to begin with—disappeared. "No. No, it's God's honest truth."

"Screw this," said Steven, slamming the beer can down on an end table. "Get out."

Wesley stood up. "But, will you talk to your dad?"

"I don't know what game you fucks are playing—"

"I don't play games," said Lukas, leaning over and stubbing out his cigarette on a dirty plate. When he straightened up, the edges of his mouth twitched.

"How come you're always so goddamn amused?" asked Steven.

Lukas shrugged. "Life's a kick, you know? Like that old saying goes, 'If you will the end, you must will the means.' That's kind of, like, my motto."

Wesley had already crossed to the door.

Lukas stood his ground. "Wesley's parents hired a lawyer. They're trying to get charges filed against Clifford. Your dad's been over at Wesley's house. He stays for hours. He's totally driving Wesley's parents nuts too, man. We're trying to warn you."

"And I should care why?"

"Because Wesley wasn't kidding. Your dad is freakin' out."

Steven sat forward on the couch. "Okay. I hear you. Now leave."

Lukas turned, but stopped before he got all the way to the door. "I suppose you heard about Jason Vickner. Got knifed last night. Not three blocks from here."

"Yeah," said Steven. "I heard."

"Life's a bitch, ain't it?" said Lukas. He smiled, giving Steven his best thug stare.

"Why did you really come here?"

"To tell you about your old man," said Wesley.

"You don't give a damn about my dad."

"No," said Lukas, "but he's making Wes's life, shall we say, *difficult*."

"And you care about Wes. How touching."

Wesley's white face turned pink. "Your dad's pushing too hard, man. You know that if he digs too deep, he could totally come up with stuff that could screw us all."

"So call him off," said Lukas.

"Get the hell out of my apartment," demanded Steven. He was about to get up and physically throw them out when the phone gave another double ring.

"Later, dude," said Lukas. He shut the door behind him on his way out.

"Yeah?" said Steven into the cordless.

"Is that you, son?"

"Dad?" Steven was shocked to hear his father's voice. He'd never come to his apartment before. When Steven moved out of the house, he and his father had formed an unwritten pact. His dad allowed him complete privacy as long as Steven kept in regular touch. His father had never broken the contract before. Not until this moment.

"Can I come up?"

Steven's eyes spun around the living room. "Well, I, ah—"

"I need to talk to you."

Steven's jaw tightened. "Hey, how about I buy you a cup of coffee? Just let me throw on a coat and I'll be down in a sec."

Steven carried two tall lattes over to the table. The Starbucks close to his apartment building was usually filled with students at this time of day, books spread out on the table in front of them. Today was no different. "Here you go," he said, setting one latte down in front of his father.

"Plain coffee would have been just fine."

"This is better. I had them put vanilla syrup in yours. You like your coffee sweet."

His father took a taste. "It's good. Thanks."

"So, how come you drove all the way up here?" Steven dropped his jacket over the back of the chair and sat down.

"I talked to the police this morning—finally got one of them to promise he'd listen to the tape they made of Cullen and Clifford. Their next step is to call Clifford in for questioning."

"Dad—"

"This is great news, Steven." His eyes burned with an unhealthy glow. "I told you we'd nail that bastard. God, if it hadn't been for Wesley, none of this would ever have come out." He took another sip of coffee. "I understand now why my son was so distant the last few months of his life."

"He was clinically depressed, Dad."

"It was more than that." He ran a hand over his unshaven face, rubbed his bloodshot eyes.

"Did you get off work early?"

"Huh? Work?" He laughed. "Didn't go today. I called in sick. Called in sick yesterday too. Hell, I *am* sick. Sick to death of thinking about what happened to my son. And here I figured it was all my fault. I was putting in so much overtime last spring. I felt so guilty, coming home late the way I did, night after night. How could I know there was a predator at Evergreen High, a man who was busy corrupting my son?" He took out a handkerchief and wiped the sweat off his face.

"You feeling okay, Dad?"

"Me? Aces. Never better."

"You know, I think it might be a good idea for you to take it a little easier. Obsessing about Alden Clifford won't bring Cullen back."

"I gotta keep the pressure on, Steven. We can't let this monster get away with what he did."

Steven blew on his latte. "I hear you've been spending a lot of time at the Middendorfs."

"Who'd you hear that from? Wesley? He's a good kid. So's that Lukas Pouli. They were Cullen's best buddies, you know?"

"I wouldn't go that far."

"I like the Middendorfs' place. It's warm. Comfortable. With so many kids coming in and out, there's always something going on. I like that. Makes me remember what it was like when you guys were young. We had a great time, didn't we?"

"We did," said Steven. This was harder than he'd expected. His father was so desperately lonely. "You know, Dad, you should invite your friend Doris over for dinner sometime soon. You could make Mom's meat loaf."

He shook his head. "No time."

"Sure there is."

"If I ask you something, you'd tell me the truth, wouldn't you?"

"Of course I would."

"Steven," he said, staring hard into his son's eyes, "do you use drugs? You know what I mean. Not an occasional beer, but the hard stuff. Crack. Ecstasy. Street drugs."

"No," said Steven firmly. "And I'm not bullshitting you. You taught

Cullen and me that they were for stupid people, bored people, and that if you weren't stupid before you took them, they made you that way."

"Truthfully?"

"Absolutely. I smoked marijuana a few times when I was in high school, but that was it."

His dad nodded. "And so you think Cullen didn't do drugs either?"

"I not only think, I know he was clean. He drank some, and I was always after him to watch it. The police did a drug test on him after he died, Dad. He was way over the legal limit for alcohol, but they didn't find any drugs present."

"I know," said his father. "I just needed to hear you say it out loud."

"Look, I'm not a saint. Neither was Cullen. But you taught me something important about how to live your life—how to manage people. Never keep someone you love on a short chain. Give them the space they need. If you act like you trust them, they'll return that trust. That's the kind of relationship you had with me, and it's how I tried to be with my brother."

"Did I teach you that? Really?"

"Damn right." Steven grinned.

"Huh. Amazing."

Steven glanced at his watch. "Hey, you got any dinner plans?"

"Me? No."

"You hungry?"

"I could eat."

"Let's hoof it over to Maxwell's and grab a sandwich. And when we're done, why don't we take in a movie?"

His dad looked at him quizzically. "You don't have to study tonight?"

Good point, thought Steven. He did have a paper he needed to write. But he could always pull an all-nighter. He did it all the time. His dad was here, and he needed not to be alone tonight. "Nope, I'm all up-to-date on my studies. So what do you say?"

His dad high-fived him. "I say I've got myself a great son. You're on."

Cottonwood, Kansas

March 28, 1973

Jimmy's sixteenth birthday wasn't a celebration, it was an afterthought. For days he'd been wondering if his parents even remembered. His mother was drinking all the time now. She never seemed exactly drunk, but she sat in the living room with the TV on and sipped from a glass of Coke and ice. She snuck the vodka from a bottle she hid behind a chair. Jimmy's father knew about it too, but Jimmy figured he'd made a decision. He couldn't save both his wife and his daughter, so he'd chosen his daughter. Jimmy wasn't even on his radar screen anymore.

His father didn't believe the bloody fairy costume the police had found three months ago was absolute proof that Patsy was dead. He spent all his free time tacking up posters and talking to radio shows and community meetings all over the state. Jimmy wanted to believe that his sister was still alive too, but his emotions were all over the place. He could accept that she was gone in his head, but it was much harder to believe it in his heart. Maybe his dad was having the same problem.

But the truth was, Jimmy had let go. He saw what refusing to let go was doing to his parents and he didn't want that to happen to him. His frantic desire to find Patsy, to bring her home safely, had been replaced by an equally frantic desire for vengeance. When he saw Frank again, he'd make him pay. Jimmy had bought himself a gun with part of the money he'd skimmed from selling drugs, and he kept it loaded. If his parents had thought about him long enough to ask him what he wanted for his birthday, he would have told them more ammunition. He didn't care what anybody thought. He'd get Frank one day, make him sorry he'd ever been born.

Two days after Jimmy turned sixteen, his father took him aside and apologized for forgetting such an important day. Jimmy said it was okay. He was a big kid now. People didn't need to make a fuss about his birthday anymore. But his dad wouldn't let it drop. He hugged Jimmy and cried. Jimmy stood stiff as a board and endured it. Then his dad clapped his hands and said they were all going out to dinner. Only his mother said she wasn't feeling well, that they should go on without her.

So Jimmy and his father sat at a back booth at the Happy Rooster and silently ate their burgers. After dinner, his dad presented him with a multifunction watch. Jimmy loved it instantly. He was so ridiculously happy to have it, he felt his eyes begin to fill. The watch was a regular watch, and a stopwatch, and it had a timer function and a compass. He thanked his dad, and he also thanked his mother when he got home, but he could tell by the spacey look on her face that she had no idea what he was talking about.

Jimmy kept his eyes peeled for Frank. There were many times he wanted to blow off school, hijack a car, and head for Wichita, or Kansas City, or anywhere just to feel as if he was actively doing something to find him. But Jimmy already felt like he was in major trouble. He suspected that the police didn't buy his story about what had happened to Patsy. And if he pulled anything new, there was one cop for sure who would gladly slam a cell door on him and throw away the key.

On a warm Saturday afternoon in late March, Jimmy's mom asked him to run to the grocery store and pick up some Velveeta and bread so they could have grilled cheese sandwiches for dinner. What she really wanted was to get him out of the house. The vodka bottle behind the chair was empty. She needed to replace it with a full one, but part of her game was to act like it was always the same bottle. She was going nuts because Jimmy just kept hanging around the living room. She made lots of suggestions about things he could go do, but it was more fun watching her have a meltdown. He hated her for the human wreck she'd become.

When he couldn't stand being in the same room with her another minute, he took the money she offered him and left on his bike, heading for Langer's Food Mart. As he turned onto Main, he saw a white van pull into Picket's Standard Oil at the other end of the block. It looked like Frank's van, but he couldn't be sure unless he got closer.

Changing gears on his ten-speed, he shot through the intersection and pedaled hard, skidding to a stop about thirty yards behind the pumps. A kid he knew from school, Ryan Mullroy, was standing next to the driver's side door, talking to whoever was in the front seat. Ryan worked at Picket's on the weekends, so he was pumping gas into the side of the van while he talked. He smiled a lot, even laughed a couple of times, so Jimmy had the feeling he knew the person he was talking to.

Leaning his bike against a post, Jimmy crept up behind the van. He crouched next to the rear bumper and listened. Sure enough, it was Frank's voice coming from the front seat. He and Ryan were discussing the ins and outs of growing marijuana. Jimmy couldn't believe his good luck at finding Frank again, but without his gun, there was little he could do. By the time the van pulled out of the station, he'd returned to his bike. He followed the van to the edge of town, but when Main became a highway, he was left in the dust. Frank didn't live in Cottonwood, which meant he was in town for a reason. And the only reason Jimmy could think of was drugs. Maybe he'd found someone new to deal for him.

Jimmy kept his eye on Ryan for the next few days. Ryan and Frank had seemed so friendly, it made Jimmy wonder if Ryan wasn't his new dealer. Ryan Mullroy lived on the west side of town. He was a year ahead of Jimmy. He'd never been a friend, run with any of the same crowd, but from what Jimmy was able to observe, he was well liked by most of the jocks, some of the fringers, and all of the girls.

Jimmy started asking around to see if anyone knew where he could buy a lid. Ever since he'd lost his status as the school's resident pharmacist, friends took pity on him and passed him a joint when they could. But nobody seemed to know where he could get his hands on anything larger than a dime bag. And nobody was passing out names. Things had tightened up since his sister had gone missing. There'd been too many cops around the school for guys to take the chances they'd been taking before.

Jimmy decided that the only way he'd ever know for sure if Ryan was dealing for Frank was to ask Ryan outright. But for that conversation, Jimmy needed privacy and an advantage. His size provided a slight edge. From age fifteen to age sixteen, Jimmy had shot up five full inches. He was now five feet eleven, and he was big. But he'd need more than size. For a real advantage, he'd bring the gun.

At ten to eight on a Saturday night, Jimmy left his house, his gun inside the pocket of his coat, and headed to Picket's gas station. His mother, as usual, was passed out in the living room. His father was up in Leavenworth, speaking to a Kiwannis Club about child kidnappings, and the need for better resources from the federal and state governments. Nobody cared what Jimmy was up to, and that was fine with him.

He'd been watching and knew that Ryan got off at eight. Jimmy was on foot this time because Ryan always walked home after his shift. Jimmy felt so light on his feet, he nearly floated all the way to the gas station. All his senses were sharpened. He felt stronger, faster, keener-eyed—ready for anything.

Seeing Ryan standing next to the cash register talking to Mr. Picket, he bided his time in the shadows next to the Wash 'n Save Laundromat. Ryan kept up his conversation with Mr. Picket until a little after eight, then came out the door into the crisp night air, gazed up at the starry sky for a moment, put on his baseball cap, and headed for home.

If he took the same route he'd taken last night, Jimmy figured he could cut through the end property and intercept Ryan just as he passed Mason's Thicket. The thicket was a small wooded area just north of the high school.

Jimmy kept his distance behind Ryan for half a block. When he turned off Main and headed the same direction he had last night, Jimmy knew he had him. Feeling for the gun in his pocket, Jimmy tore off down the alley between Main and Willow. His eyes panned across the backyards. The farther he got from the central area of town, the darker it became. He ran flat out to the end of the block, then hopped a fence. When he reached the thicket, he ducked behind a low pine. A minute or two later, Ryan came along. He was singing softly to himself.

Jimmy waited until Ryan had crossed the street, then he straightened up and called, "Hey, Mullroy. Over here."

Ryan stopped and squinted into the darkness. "Who's there?"

"Jimmy Shore."

"Geez, man, you scared me."

"Sorry." Jimmy stepped away from the pine. "I need to talk to you."

"What about?"

A full moon lit their faces.

"Frank Gand."

"Who?"

"The guy you were talking to the other day at the gas station. Drives a white van. You know, Frank."

Ryan shook his head. "I don't know who you're talking about."

Jimmy felt he was laying the dumb act on a little too thick. "Frank Gand. You working for him now?"

"I don't know what your deal is, Shore, but I gotta get home."

Jimmy moved in closer, grabbed Ryan's arm. "Not so fast."

"Hey, what's wrong with you?" said Ryan, pulling his arm away. "You on something?"

"What's that supposed to mean?"

"Drop the innocent act. Everybody knows you're a major pipe head. I heard you even sell the stuff."

"Not anymore."

"Well, boo hoo. Now leave me alone." He backed up.

That's when Jimmy pulled the gun.

Ryan's eyes dropped to the muzzle. He froze.

"When's the next time you meet up with Frank?"

Ryan didn't say anything for a few seconds. Finally, his eyes rose to Jimmy's. "That thing real?"

Jimmy cocked the trigger. "Very real. Answer the question."

"Look, Shore . . . I don't know what you're talking about. Frank Gand? Who is he?"

"You're pissing me off."

Ryan backed up another step. "Just, calm down, okay?"

"I've gotta talk to him. You can take me to him."

"I can't. You've got the wrong guy."

"You're afraid of him. I get it. But I suggest you be more afraid of me."

"What's wrong with you, man? I told you. I don't know him. I can't help you."

Jimmy was getting more frustrated by the second. The gun felt heavy in his hand. He was sick of getting nowhere, of hitting blind alleys. Here was the only one who could help him, and he was sticking to his bullshit story.

"Put the gun down, okay?"

"Don't fucking tell me what to do!" His arm trembled. Suddenly the gun jumped in his hand. He felt the recoil, saw the bright blast. It was all over in less than a second. Ryan lay at his feet, bleeding from a wound in his chest.

Jimmy dropped to his knees. "Mullroy? Are you okay? Say something, man. I'll go get help. Just hold on." Ryan's eyes were open and there was a stunned look on his face, but he didn't say a word.

"Come on, man." Jimmy bent over, put his ear next to Ryan's mouth. "You're not breathing. Breathe, goddammit!" He shook Ryan's shoulders, felt for the pulse in his neck. But there wasn't one.

"I didn't mean it! You gotta believe me. I just wanted your help!"

Jimmy stood up and stumbled backward. The gun dropped from his hand. The night swung crazily in front of his eyes.

Pull yourself together, he told himself. All he could focus on was his need to get away before the police found out what he'd done. He glanced down at his watch, the one his father had given him. It steadied him somehow.

He pulled Ryan's body into the bushes, then tore off across town to the O'Brien's place, where what was left of his money was buried in a metal box behind their pole barn.

The last thing he did before he split town was to return to his house. He entered the living room and, for a few minutes, watched his mother sleeping. Tears rolled down his cheeks. Finally, unable to take the pain any longer, he kissed her on the forehead, whispered that he loved her, and left Cottonwood forever.

31

"**W**hy are you sitting in the dark?" asked Mary. She stepped cautiously into the living room. She'd just arrived home from work, not knowing what her husband's mood would be. She hadn't heard from him all day, but then she hadn't called either. The good news, if there was any good news, was that she hadn't received any calls from Tom Moline. She wanted him out of her life, *yesterday,* and hoped he'd gotten the message.

"Can I turn on a light?" she asked.

Alden didn't answer.

"Are you okay?"

"Not even in the same hemisphere as okay." His voice was thick and hoarse.

Mary switched on the light next to the TV. The sight that met her eyes shocked her into silence. Alden's face was twisted in pain. His cheeks streamed with tears. In his right hand he held a vodka bottle, bouncing it on his knee.

"I've turned into my mother," he said, a mirthless chuckle coming from deep inside his chest.

"What happened?" It couldn't be Nick. She'd spent several hours with him earlier in the afternoon and knew he was doing well. "What's wrong?"

"Everything's wrong, Mary."

She moved toward him.

"Don't," he said, raising his hand as if to ward off a blow.

"Alden, please!"

He pointed the remote at the TV and switched it on.

"Oh, honey, not now," she said, her tone full of frustration. "We need to talk."

"This first."

She half turned toward the set. "What is it?"

"Gray came to the house this morning shortly after you left. He found a videotape on our porch."

"Gray?"

"He didn't bring it, he just found it. Someone else must have dropped it off."

"Who?"

"Oh, I suspect some helpful little gnome hoping to start my day off with a bang."

As the video progressed, Mary lowered herself into a chair. When she saw that the photographer had captured the front of Tom's town house, her hand flew to her mouth. "Turn it off."

"Yeah, I suppose it's redundant. I mean, you were there."

"Alden, *please*."

He let it run to the end. "It's a shame there's no real audio. Just the photographer . . . enjoying himself. Were you and Tom laughing at me, Mary?"

"Laughing?"

"You do this often?"

"You have to let me explain."

"What? It's a body double? That's not really you in the picture?"

As soon as he turned off the TV, the silence in the room engulfed them both.

Alden took a swig from the vodka bottle. "I'm curious, Mary. Why Tom Moline? Is he a great lover? Better than me?"

"Don't do this."

"You're leaning more toward hardened Clint Eastwood types these days, is that it?"

"Stop it." She kneaded the arms of the chair. "He's not like that."

"Ah, defending the paramour. Not good." He paused. "Do you love him?"

"No," she said, wiping her eyes with the backs of her hands. "It's over. I never meant to hurt you."

"You mean you never expected to get caught."

"Okay. Yes. But it meant nothing."

He held up the vodka bottle to see how much was left. "Do you realize what a timeworn old stereotype this conversation is? It's pathetic. I've always thought of us as the kind of people who don't swim with the commonplace, run-of-the-mill fishes. I guess this is my wake-up call."

"How can I explain what I don't understand myself?"

"Another wonderfully clichéd nugget, Mary. Isn't it about time you tell me that I drove you into his arms because I was cold and uncaring?"

She looked away.

"No? I suppose you can't say that precisely because it isn't true. Well, we'll pass over that part of the banalities."

"Why are you doing this?"

"Doing what? Having a conversation with my wife? Communication, that's what it's all about. Right? That's what keeps a marriage strong."

"This isn't a conversation."

"Golly. And here I thought it was. I guess maybe I'm insensitive. There you have it! I'm not cold and uncaring, but I *am* insensitive. That makes this partly my fault. I knew we'd get there eventually."

"I didn't say that."

He erupted off the couch. "What *are* you saying, Mary? Because I'm not hearing anything but a lot of crap. How could you *sleep* with that creep? I've been sitting here all day—*all day*—wondering how I could have possibly hurt you so badly that you felt the need to get involved with another man. How long has it been going on?"

She looked up at him helplessly.

"How long!" He came at her with his fist.

She turned her face away. "A couple of months," she said. She couldn't believe this was happening. "But it's over. It has been for—" She hesitated.

"For what? Days? Hours? Five minutes?"

"I told him from the very beginning that I loved you. That I'd never leave you."

He punched the air. "Brilliant, Mary. Clear ground rules. Bravo. But what if I don't agree to them?" His eyes shimmered with anger.

"You're in no condition to talk about this right now."

He bent over her. With his mouth next to her ear, he whispered, "Get out of this house. Now, Mary. Before I do something I'll regret."

She pulled her head away, then squeezed past him out of the chair. "You don't mean that."

He stumbled backward. "I don't know what the hell I mean anymore."

"Maybe you're right. Maybe I should go. I can spend a night or two at Nick's apartment. I think we need some space."

"Hah!" he said, hooting as he spun around. "The clichés are still flyin' fast and furious. Space! The mighty Yuppie cure-all. All God's chillin' need *space*." Coming to a stop near the piano, he said, "Spend the rest of your life at Nick's apartment for all I care." He dropped back down on the couch, took a long pull on the bottle, then tilted his head back against the cushion and closed his eyes.

Mary turned to the stairs, startled to find Lauren sitting about halfway up. Alden's sarcasm must have rubbed off because for the first time since Lauren had arrived, Mary didn't feel sorry for her. "Did you enjoy the show?" she asked.

Without saying a word, Lauren got up and walked back up the stairs to her bedroom.

After tossing some things in an overnight bag, Mary returned downstairs. She slipped into her coat, then walked back into the living room. Alden had turned off the light. "Will you be okay?" she asked, no longer able to see his face.

"Right as rain," he said.

"Lauren heard our conversation."

"Oh, goody."

"Alden?"

"Hmm?"

"I love you. I never stopped loving you. And that's not a cliché."

Alden had no idea how long he sat in the dark after Mary left. It could have been ten minutes or five hours. His mind was swimming in a lethal mixture of alcohol and self-pity. He wished his wife would come back and sit next to him, tell him that everything would be all right. He wanted comfort and he knew he wouldn't find it in a bottle. He hated people who got sloppy drunk as a way of dealing with the blows life sent their way. And that meant he hated himself. Which wasn't new. As hard as he tried to act the part of the successful teacher and loving husband, he'd never felt anything but contempt for himself. What good had come to him was all due to the life Mary had shared with him. A beautiful son. A family life that filled every corner of his soul. It was her love and kindness he'd fed off of to stanch his insatiable desire for forgiveness and redemption. It had been hers to give, and hers to take away.

But he never thought she would.

As a way of coping with the guilt left over from his childhood, Alden had become a kind of split personality. He believed that he was corrupt to the core, could even be called evil if you wanted to get all metaphysical about it. At the same time, he thought he was special. The exception to every rule. A cut above. Smarter than the average guy. How could this . . . this dichotomy, these two disparate views of himself, live in the same mind?

Staring into the darkness, Alden knew with total certainty that he was insane.

After setting the vodka bottle down, he got up and half walked, half lurched outside. Standing on the front porch, the world swaying in front of him, he had the urge to walk away from the house and never look back. Without a coat, he probably wouldn't last long. Not that it mattered much. He examined the sky to locate the moon, but the heavens were nearly starless, full of the same blackness as his soul. He breathed deeply as he walked out to the garage, but the dizziness wouldn't go away.

And that's when he heard it. The scrunch of boots on snow. Before he could turn around, he felt a hand like a vise grip his arm and slam him hard against the garage. He lunged forward, trying to ward off the attacker, but the booze had made him slow and awkward. The next instant, he was on the ground with a ten-ton weight perched on his chest.

"I should kill you," said a deep voice.

"Go ahead," said Alden, bucking hard to fight the man off. Something cold suddenly pressed against his throat. He couldn't see what it was, but he knew enough to stop struggling.

"You *molested* my son," whispered the voice.

"What? Who—"

"Burt Hegg. Cullen's dad."

Alden tried to focus his thoughts. "That's a lie. I never touched him." The thick metal pressed harder against his windpipe.

"I've been following you for months, Clifford. I always suspected you had something to do with Cullen's death. And now I know for sure. Perverts like you deserve to die."

Alden's mind slid sideways.

"I got this tape. The cops recorded what you and Cullen said in your classroom the day he killed himself. What did my son mean when he asked you if you loved him?"

"If I can't talk," Alden choked out, "I can't answer."

Hegg eased up on the pressure. "What did he mean?"

Alden sucked air deep into his lungs. "He was just repeating to me what I'd said to him a couple nights before."

"You told him you loved him?"

"Yeah."

"What kind of sicko are you?" He pushed hard again with the crowbar.

Struggling to speak, Alden said, "Kids with problems like his . . . they get to me. I care about them."

"What do you mean *problems?*"

"Cullen was doing drugs. Major drugs."

"You're crazy. He tested clean."

"It's true. I helped him get off them. I worked with him for months. Remember, his last report card—how much better his grades were?"

The crowbar lifted slightly. "Yeah? So?"

"It was because he'd been getting straight. At least I thought he was. But he was clinically depressed. I didn't realize it until too late. He used drugs to self-medicate. I've seen it before—I just didn't realize—"

"Drugs aren't free," snarled Hegg. "If it's true my son did drugs, where did he get the money?"

"I don't know. He wouldn't tell me. Listen to me, okay? I know what I'm talking about. I did drugs myself when I was a teenager so I recognize the signs. I've helped lots of kids over the years. That's why I was so concerned. Cullen and I . . . we talked a lot. I did love him, but not the way you're thinking. I could tell there was some secret he was keeping from me, something that ate away at him, but I never found out what it was. Maybe you know."

"Are you saying his depression was my fault? That I wasn't a good enough father?"

"Depression's a chemical imbalance, it's nobody's *fault*. A guy starts thinking drugs and alcohol make him feel better, but in reality it just makes everything worse."

"My son didn't do drugs."

"Believe what you want," said Alden, sensing that no matter what he said, Cullen's father wouldn't buy it.

Hegg didn't move.

"Look, just *try* to hear what I'm saying, okay? Your son and I talked a lot last year. By spring, I saw the depression for what it was. I encouraged him to see a doctor so he could get on antidepressants. He resisted because he was terrified that you'd find out he'd been using crack. He didn't want to disappoint you. He looked up to you, loved you *so* much. He felt he'd let you down and that killed him. I tried to help him see that you'd want him to get whatever help he needed. That if he was in trouble, you'd be there for him."

"I would have been," said Hegg, easing up even more with the crowbar.

"The day Cullen came to my class with the gun, he was drunk and deeply, deeply depressed. I have a feeling that he regretted ever talking to me. He thought it gave me power over him and that if I told anyone about the drugs, he'd not only get in trouble with the law, but he'd lose your respect. I always assumed that when I told kids what I'd done when I was young, that it would make them trust me, because now they had something on me too. But Cullen had a hard time with trust."

Hegg lifted the crowbar off Alden's neck.

"I'm sorry, Hegg. I do feel partly responsible for what happened to Cullen. I should have talked to you, told you the truth. But if kids think you're going to run to their parents with everything they tell you, they'll never tell you anything worth knowing."

"What about Wesley? What he told the principal? Did you molest him?"

"No," said Alden. "I never touched him. I swear."

"Why would he lie?"

"I don't know."

Hegg stared at him for almost a full minute, then climbed off him.

Alden waited for a few seconds to make sure he wasn't going to get attacked again, then sat up and rubbed his throat.

"I'm gonna check this out, Clifford. I'm not sure you're leveling with me, but . . . I can't be sure you're not."

"Don't worry," said Alden, pulling his knees up to his chest. "I'll be here if you want to come back and finish the job."

Hegg tossed the crowbar into the snow and walked off toward the highway.

Alden closed his eyes and sucked in deep drafts of air. One more broken promise in a long line of broken promises. After Cullen had committed suicide, the last thing his grieving father needed to hear was that his son was an addict. That's why Alden had kept silent about it.

Taking one last deep breath, Alden got up. Every joint in his body ached, but his left knee was the worst. He limped back to the porch. When he reached the steps, pain stopped him. Sure enough, the knee was swollen. Mary kept an ice pack in the freezer. That and a little more vodka and he'd be a new man.

As he looked up at the door, wondering if he could make the stairs, a searing pain exploded at the back of his head. He felt himself falling.

Even before he hit the ground, Alden's world went dark.

32

"Let your reptilian brain work on it, Janey," said Cordelia.

"I beg your pardon?" Jane had been working the dinner meal in the dining room when her cell phone rumbled. It was just after nine. She took the call because she needed a break. While Cordelia gave her the scoop on Octavia and her imminent return to Minneapolis, Jane trotted down the back stairs to her office. Mouse was lying on the couch, so she sat down next to him and kicked off her shoes.

"Your reptilian brain," repeated Cordelia. "The part of your mind that works on instinct. Didn't you ever read Carl Sagan's *The Dragrons of Eden?*"

"Yes, but apparently my reptilian brain has memory lapses."

"It's no joke. Instinct rules, Janey, in case you forgot."

"In your life, maybe. I like to think mine operates on a little higher level."

While Jane was at Kenzie's hotel, a homicide detective had stopped by the Lyme House asking questions about Jason's connection to the restaurant. Jane was glad she hadn't been around. She didn't want to lie to the police, but she didn't want to talk to them right now either.

Before she headed upstairs to work the evening meal, she spent some time on the phone talking to various people in the archives section of *The Wichita Eagle* and the *Cottonwood Herald*. She was looking for copies of newspaper articles on Patsy Shore's abduction. She asked to have the information faxed to her home as soon as possible. She paid a small fee at each newspaper with her credit card, making sure the individual she spoke to understood that time was an issue.

"So," continued Jane, smoothing the fur on Mouse's head, "how long will it take for my reptilian brain to kick in and come up with a solution to Jason's murder?"

"Hard to say." Cordelia was chewing something.

"What are you eating?"

"Hattie's dinner. I made her my famous lemon currant scones and my equally famous potato leek soup. I pureed the potatoes and the leeks with cream and butter. It was fabulous if I do say so myself, but Hattie turned up her nose, as usual. Do you think it's my cooking?"

"No, Cordelia. I think it's Hattie's age."

"That's nice of you. But I'm beginning to wonder." She sighed. "We settled on thin slices of cheddar cheese slathered with Western dressing—her favorite—and a quarter of a Fluffernutter sandwich."

Jane felt momentarily nauseous. "Is she in bed now?"

"Fast asleep. I sing her songs when I put her down. She loves it. Her favorites are 'Desolation Row' and 'Comfortably Numb.'"

"What happened to 'Twinkle Twinkle Little Star'?"

"Heavens, Janey. Hattie needs more intellectual stimulation than that."

"Look, can we get back to Jason?"

"I'm settled in my easy chair with my feet up and my loft looking like it's a Toys R Us outlet. But enough about me. Why don't *you* talk about me for a while."

"Cordelia!"

"You have my complete attention."

"Good." Jane quickly filled Cordelia in on what she'd learned about Alan—and Patsy Shore—at Kenzie's hotel room earlier in the day. Once Cordelia had sputtered about Kenzie and her "lying ways" for a few minutes, Jane moved on to Jason's murder. "Now. Here's the issue in a nutshell. Jason and Brittany were hiding at that hotel. They were scared someone was going to find them, so they were being extremely careful. If that's true, how did someone get to him before I got there last night?"

Mouse lifted his head and looked at her.

"I see the problem," said Cordelia.

"Is it possible I led someone there? If so, who could possibly know I was even in communication with him?" Jane didn't want to give voice to her suspicions because it would only make them seem more real. But she had no choice. "As far as I can see, Cordelia, there's only one person who could have known."

"Kenzie."

"Exactly. She was at my house having dinner with me when I got that call from Brittany. She was in the dining room, so it wouldn't have been hard for her to overhear what I said. I repeated Jason's name more than once. I think I asked if they were staying at a motel. I definitely said that I wanted to talk to him asap. When I got back to the dining room, she was gone. I thought it was because our conversation had turned a bit heavy, but now I'm wondering if it wasn't something else. What if Kenzie took it all in, then left and waited in her car for me to leave so she could follow me."

"That wouldn't get her to the motel before you, Janey. No, if she's any kind of PI at all, she probably had your phone tapped. That's pretty easy to do these days. My guess is, she went and listened to the tape and, bingo, she knew where he was and how to get in."

Jane hadn't even considered the possibility of a phone tap.

"Which means she could be listening to us right now," said Cordelia. "Yoo-hoo, Kenzie!" she shouted. "You sleazebag whack job, you . . . you disgusting hussy. Stay away from my friend. You don't want to mess with Cordelia *M.* Thorn!"

"Cordelia, stop it. There might be other ways it could have happened."

"Name one."

"Kenzie's not a murderer."

"Don't be too sure."

"I'm very sure, and you can't convince me otherwise But she might have wanted to talk to him. And if she used me to find him—" Jane heard a knock on the door. Turning around, she called, "Come in."

Kenzie stuck her head inside the room. "Got a sec?"

"Cordelia, I've got to go," said Jane, her mind slipping into overdrive.

"Why?"

"Someone just stopped by."

"Is it Kenzie? Janey, you be careful!"

"I'll use my reptilian brain."

"No you don't! I'm going to lock you in a trunk and throw away the key. I know I've threatened it before, but this time I'm actually going to *do* it. You hear me? I'm going out to buy the trunk right now!"

"Wonderful," said Jane, smiling at Kenzie. "I'll look forward to it."

"Don't you hang up on me!"

"Bye." Jane clicked off the phone as she stood up.

"Come here," said Kenzie, motioning Jane over.

"Why?"

"Closer," she whispered. "Come on. This is important."

Jane wasn't quite sure what to do.

"I won't bite," said Kenzie.

She stopped about a foot away, but Kenzie pulled her nearer, easing her arms around Jane's waist.

"What is it?" asked Jane.

"Just . . . this," said Kenzie. She leaned in and kissed Jane softly. After a long moment, she backed up and smiled. "That's all I came to say."

Jane touched Kenzie's cheek with the tips of her fingers. "Succinct. To the point."

"That's me." She kissed Jane's nose. "Gotta run."

"But—"

"I'll call you tomorrow."

For the next hour, Jane tried to push everything out of her mind and just concentrate on work. By ten, she realized she was getting nowhere. She'd been staring at the same page for half an hour. She kept fighting the notion that Kenzie had used her to find Jason. She thought about running back to her house to check her phones, see if she could find a bug, but instead, refusing to give in to Cordelia's paranoia, she and Mouse hopped in her Mini and drove over to Jason's apartment. It was late, but she hoped his brother would still be up.

Seeing a light on in the ground floor south apartment, Jane told Mouse she'd be right back, then jumped out of the front seat and headed for the door.

Once inside the front foyer, a man's voice answered her buzz.

"Is this Alan?" she said into the speaker.

"Who's there?"

"It's Jane Lawless. I don't know if you remember me, but—"

"The restaurant owner?"

"Yes. I was hoping you might have a minute to talk."

Silence. "Well, uh . . . okay, I guess."

When the door buzzed open, Jane pushed through into the building and headed up the steps to the apartment. Alan met her at the door, holding it open as she walked into the living room. The big-screen TV was on. Next to the couch was a half-eaten sandwich and a bottle of Coors.

"I'm sorry if I'm interrupting your dinner," she said, turning around.

Alan shut the door. "No problem." He was dressed in gray sweatpants and a black T-shirt.

"First, let me say how sorry I am about your brother."

He moved around her, over to the couch, and sat down. "Thanks."

"I know this must be a tough time for you."

"Yeah. My parents are taking it pretty hard." He sat forward, arms resting on his knees. "I am too."

Jane wasn't sure if she should sit or stand. "Have the police learned anything new?"

He shook his head.

"Listen, Alan, I assume the police have talked to you about your brother."

"Yeah." He looked up at her. "Did you ever find him? I gave him the note you left."

"I talked to him on the phone. I know he was hiding from someone. Do you have any idea who that someone might be?"

"No." He locked eyes with her. "Why did you come here that night? Did Jason do something wrong at your restaurant? Something illegal? You said your father was a lawyer. Why would he need a lawyer?"

"Did you tell the police about the note I left?"

"Sure. I had to."

So that's why the cop had showed up at her restaurant this afternoon.

"Answer my question," said Alan.

Jane sat down on a director's chair. "Jason admitted to me that someone paid him to mix illegal drugs into food that was used by my catering company."

"You mean that business with Nick Clifford's wedding?"

"That's right."

"Jason did it?"

She nodded. "Your brother and I were supposed to meet so he could give me the details, as well as proof of who put him up to it, but it never happened."

"So you don't know who paid him?"

"I don't. Alan, other than me, has anyone come around here looking for Jason?"

"Nobody. The police asked me the same question, but Jason didn't have a lot of friends. Except for his family, he was kind of a loner."

"But he had a girlfriend."

"You know Brittany?"

"I talked to her on the phone too. You don't by any chance know her last name, do you?"

"Sorry. Jason may have told me, but I don't remember. God, I knew he'd done something bad when he showed up here with all that money. I just knew it."

"How much was it?"

"Five thousand dollars."

"Where did he say he got it?"

"From a guy he did a favor for."

"A guy?"

Alan shrugged. "A rich guy. That's what he said."

"Did you know he was staying at the motel?"

"Yeah. But he made me promise I wouldn't tell anyone where he was living. I knew something bad was about to go down. I told him maybe he should leave the state. I wish he had." He ran his palms down the fronts of his thighs. "God but this sucks."

"So you didn't tell *anybody* where he was staying?"

"Nobody asked."

Jane had hoped for more, but at least she'd learned something important. The person who'd paid Jason was a "rich guy." That let Kenzie off the hook.

Rising from her chair, Jane thanked Alan for his time. "I'll let you get back to your dinner."

He walked her to the door.

"You said you had a large family," she said, more for conversation than anything else.

"Jason was my only brother. No sisters. But we got lots of cousins."

"All of them live around here?"

"Most of them have moved away. But a few still do. Wesley took it the hardest. I suppose because of what's going on in his own life."

Jane's ears pricked up. "Wesley?"

"Wesley Middendorf. His mom is my dad's sister. Wesley's kind of a goof, but he's a good guy."

Jane buttoned up her jacket. "Did Wesley ever ask where Jason was living?"

Alan looked away, giving it some thought. "Yeah, come to think of it, he did. He and Jason were always pretty tight."

"Did you tell him?"

"Sure. Wesley wouldn't hurt Jason. I'm sure I told him to keep his yap shut about it. He's not the brightest bulb in the socket, but he understands English."

"Did you tell the police Wesley knew where Jason was?"

Alan shrugged. "Never thought about it until just now. It doesn't mean anything, does it?"

"Probably not."

Jane thanked him again, then walked out into the cold winter night. Alan might be certain Wesley was a good guy, but Jane wasn't. She'd just stumbled across a potentially significant connection, one that might very well lead her straight to a killer.

33

Instead of going home, Jane drove back to the Lyme House. It was late, so the dining room and the main kitchen were dark, but the pub was still open.

Before going inside, Jane and Mouse walked a quarter of the way around Lake Harriet and back, just to get some fresh air and a little exercise. Jane took Mouse back to her office and gave him a beef bone to chew on while she checked her messages. There were three from Cordelia, one from her brother, Peter, and one from a homicide detective named Wedeman. None from Kenzie.

After pulling herself a pint of ale in the pub, she stood and talked to Barnaby, her head bartender, for a few minutes. He said it had been a slow night. The usuals had been in to play their games of cribbage or darts, but not many outside the neighborhood had stopped by.

Jane glanced around the room while they talked. She recognized a few of the locals, but nobody she knew well. It was close to midnight. She considered grabbing a basket of popcorn and spending a few minutes relaxing in the back room, but decided instead to run upstairs. She loved the dining room at night after everyone had gone, loved the hushed quality of a place normally buzzing with activity. Moonlight streamed in through the windows as she sat down at a table overlooking the lake.

She sat like that, sipping her ale, lost in thought, until a soft voice called her name and brought her back to the moment. She turned and peered into the darkness. "Can I help you?"

"Are you Jane Lawless?" asked a young female voice.

"Yes?"

The woman hesitated for a few seconds, then stepped closer. She was small and thin, wearing an old corduroy jacket that looked three sizes too big for her. "I need to talk to you. I'm Brittany—Jason's girlfriend?"

Jane stood and turned. "I had no idea how to get in touch with you because I didn't know your last name. I'm so glad you came."

"You heard what happened to Jason?"

Jane nodded. "He called me and we agreed to meet at the motel."

"Did you talk to him?"

"By the time I got there, he was gone."

Brittany put a hand up to her face, covered her eyes.

"Maybe you should sit down."

"Yeah. Maybe."

Jane helped her over to the table by the window. "Would you like a glass of water?"

"No, I'm okay. It's just, it happened so fast. I should have been there. Maybe if I had, I could have stopped it." She looked down at the table-cloth, bit her trembling lower lip.

"I'm so sorry," said Jane, sitting down across from her. "I didn't know Jason, but my executive chef really liked him. Were you two together long?"

"Yesterday was our five-month anniversary." She removed her small round glasses and scraped tears away from her eyes. "He was the best guy I've ever known. Really sweet and caring. I never thought I'd get so lucky."

Jane gave Brittany a moment, then said, "Jason was about to tell me who paid him to tamper with the food. Do you know who did it?"

Her nod was stiff.

"Will you tell me?"

"I'm afraid," she said in a tiny voice.

"Because of what happened to Jason."

In the moonlight, her eyes glistened with tears. "Yeah. But if I don't do something, I'm afraid what happened to him will happen to me. If I tell you the truth, will you get your father to help me—the way he was going to help Jason?"

"Sure."

"You absolutely promise?"

Jane reached across the table and covered her hand. "I promise."

Brittany sat quietly for a few seconds, bundling the coat more tightly around her shoulders. Finally, she said, "A guy named Lukas Pouli paid him. Jason had a note Lukas had written to him, but it was at the motel. I can't get in there now because the police taped it off."

"Just tell me what you know," said Jane. "We'll worry about the note later."

"Well," she said, frowning in thought, "Jason knew Lukas because Lukas sold pot, among other things. Jason liked to relax with a little grass every now and then. That's, like, not a big deal with you, is it?"

"It's not a problem. Who's Lukas Pouli?"

"He's just this guy—a junior at Evergreen High School."

"He deals drugs and he's in high school?"

"That surprises you?"

Jane sighed. "No, I suppose not. What else can you tell me about him?"

"He's a good friend of Wesley Middendorf's. Wesley was Jason's cousin. From what Jason told me, both Wes and Lukas did some dealing, but Lukas was the ringleader. The first week of school, Mr. Clifford talked to Lukas, told him that he was watching him—or words to that effect. Lukas was afraid that Mr. Clifford would eventually figure out he was dealing. So he developed this scheme to get rid of Mr. Clifford. First he tried dumb stuff like leaving threatening notes in his mailbox. When that didn't work, he got the bright idea to mess with the food at Mr. Clifford's son's wedding. With all the nasty notes he'd been leaving, he thought Mr. Clifford would get the message and quit his job—go find a teaching position somewhere else."

"And because Jason worked at the restaurant, Lukas came to him and offered to pay him to tamper with the food."

"Yeah. That about covers it."

"How did he find out we were catering Nick and Lauren's wedding?"

"I imagine Jason told him, or maybe he told Wesley. Jason knew Mr. Clifford because he was in his American History class his junior year.

Lukas made it sound like it was just a prank—no big deal. When he offered Jason five thousand dollars, Jason just couldn't say no."

"Tell me more about Lukas Pouli."

"Well, I've only been around him a couple times, but he struck me like the kind of guy who'd, you know, enjoy squashing bugs in his spare time just to watch their guts explode. He was funny, and sort of nice-looking, I guess, but also sneaky. Like he'd be talking to someone else, but you knew he was looking at you out of the corner of his eye. And then he'd say something sweet, a compliment or whatever, but you knew what he said could be taken more than one way—and one of the ways wasn't so nice—so you weren't sure if it was a compliment or not. He was totally playing with you, like he thought he was better than you. A couple times I caught him just staring at me. Just being in the same room with him gave me the creeps."

"Was he the one who got Wesley to accuse Alden Clifford of molesting him?"

"I'm sure he was. Lukas no doubt saw it as the perfect solution to their problems—a foolproof way to get Mr. Clifford fired."

"So, it was all about Lukas and Wesley selling drugs—and not wanting Alden Clifford to find out."

"Pretty much, yeah. But Jason told me some other stuff too. See, Cullen, Lukas, and Wesley used to call themselves the Three Stooges. They were a team. It was supposed to be funny, but it was also kinda true. The three of them ran this drug ring at Evergreen. Only problem was, Cullen had a major drug problem. Mr. Clifford tried to help him with it, talked to him a lot and actually did get him to stop, although I don't think he ever knew Cullen was not only a user, but a dealer."

"And Jason learned all this because he was Wesley's cousin?"

"They were good buddies, yeah. Jason had done some bad stuff when he was younger, but he'd straightened himself out by the time I met him. Well, except sometimes he had bad judgment. He should never have taken Lukas's money."

"Five thousand dollars seems like an awful lot."

"Lukas and Wesley probably make that in a week."

"So Jason knew why Lukas and Wesley wanted to get Mr. Clifford fired."

"Sure. But after Nick Clifford ended up in the hospital, Jason got real nervous. For days he went around screaming that Lukas Pouli was a worthless psycho, that he didn't want anything to do with him ever again. He moved in with me last Monday. After high school I got a job at a nursing home. It pays okay, so I rented a small efficiency apartment and that's where I've been living for the past couple of years. But then we heard that Lukas was looking for Jason. Jason got scared. So we moved to the Varsity East and dropped out of sight. I think it was when Jason stopped answering Lukas's phone calls that things really went downhill fast. Lukas put word out on the street that Jason was a dead man if he said anything to the police."

"Did you know that Alan told Wesley where you and Jason were staying?"

Brittany's eyes grew wide and frightened. "How could you possibly know that?"

"Because I just came from Alan's apartment. Apparently Wesley had been asking about Jason and Alan didn't figure Jason would care if he told him where he was staying because Wesley was family."

Brittany stared at Jane for a moment, then bowed her head. "*That's* how Lukas got to him. I never even considered it. Not once."

"You're saying Lukas murdered Jason?"

"Of course he did. He *is* a psycho, Jane. He meant it about Jason being a dead man if he went to the police."

"But how would he know Jason was about to do that?"

"I don't think it mattered anymore. Jason was a loose end. One word to the cops and Lukas and Wesley could kiss their promising futures good-bye. Nobody was gonna rat them out. If I were Alden Clifford, I'd watch my back."

Jane rested her elbows on the table. "Do you have *any* proof that would tie Lukas to Jason's murder?"

"Just the note in the motel room. But I'll bet by the time the police got there, it was gone."

"Nothing else?"

Brittany slipped her glasses back on. "Well, there is one thing. See, Alan has this computer in his bedroom. Sometimes, when he was gone, Jason and I would go on-line and look around. You know, drop in on chat rooms, or we'd look at stuff to buy. Jason even got his own E-mail address through Yahoo. It's free and private. He didn't tell Alan about it. When Jason found out Wesley was on-line, he got his address and would send him E-mails, oh, maybe a couple times a week. Just silly stuff. Rude pictures. Funny Web sites. That's how Lukas first contacted him. I have no idea if Jason saved that E-mail. Probably not."

"What did the E-mail say?"

"Just that Lukas had a highly lucrative offer for Jason. Lukas sent him a Web address where you could buy shrooms—magic mushrooms. He told him to buy them, even told him how much to get. But I'm sure Jason deleted the message."

Jane felt sure this was the key. "There are computer experts who can retrieve information from computer hard drives, even if the information's been deleted. Look, Brittany, I don't want to push you, but the only way out of this is for you to go to the police and tell them what you know. I don't see any point in waiting. The sooner Lukas and Wesley are put in jail, the better for everyone."

"Are you saying we should talk to the police *now?*"

Jane nodded.

Brittany folded her arms protectively over her chest. "I think . . . maybe that's one of the reasons I came. I know what you're saying makes sense, but I needed to hear it from another person." She hesitated. "If I do go now, will you come with me?"

"Sure. I'll even drive."

"And you'll call your father? I might need a lawyer."

"I'll call him right away. You're doing the right thing, Brittany. If Lukas and Wesley were really behind all this, your testimony will clear up a lot of questions, and put two murderers behind bars."

34

Alden woke to darkness, and a deep, throbbing pain at the back of his head. "What the hell?" he muttered. Nausea roiled in his stomach. He sat very still, hoping the pain would go away. As he grew more fully conscious, every muscle and tendon in his body screamed at him. It was like the old days, when he'd wake up after a night of drinking and drugging, knowing he'd been in a fight, but never quite sure if he'd won or lost.

And then he remembered. He'd been arguing with Burt Hegg out in the yard. But Hegg had left, walked off toward the highway. Alden recalled turning back toward the porch and then . . . he was here. It felt like a second between then and now.

He tried to get up, but found that he couldn't move. He'd not only been tied to a chair, but blindfolded. Panic exploded inside him. His chest tightened as he struggled to breathe. He tugged and bucked to free himself, but nothing he tried worked.

"Help!" he called out. "Mary? Help me." But that was all wrong. Mary was gone. He was alone. Except for—"Lauren? Are you there? Dammit, answer me!" He didn't even know if he was still at his house. He could be anywhere.

From a short distance away, the floor creaked.

Wood floors, he thought, his mind seizing on the clue. He must still be home. He tilted his head in the direction of the sound. "Who's there? Lauren, is that you?"

More creaking.

He didn't know if he should talk or remain silent. He didn't know if it was day or night. He didn't know jack shit.

"Listen," he said, hearing the quiver in his voice. The fatalism he'd wrapped himself in for months dissolved instantly. "I don't know who you are or what you think I've done, but I'll do anything to make it right. Just name it. If you want money, I'll give you everything I've got. It's not much, but it's yours. Just take off the blindfold, okay?" He knew better than to make big demands. "Just the blindfold, that's all. So we can talk."

The creaking came nearer.

"I don't feel well. Could I . . . could you get me a glass of water?" Something soft, like the brush of a bird's wing, touched the side of his head.

Feeling warm breath on his ear, a voice whispered, "Don't worry about Lauren. She won't bother us. We've got all the time in the world, just you and me."

Alden jerked his head away. "Who are you? What did you do to Lauren? Tell me what the hell is going on!"

More movement, more creaking floors. Inside his shirt, sweat trickled down his chest. He tried to anticipate what would happen next, tried to catch the light at the edge of his blindfold, but the futility of it overwhelmed him.

He jumped as the voice whispered in his other ear, "I want you to think about what you did, Jimmy. You know why?"

He stopped breathing.

"Because, all my life, I've been waiting for this day. You know why it's so special, Jim?"

He closed his eyes.

"Because this is the day you die."

Saturday

35

Jane turned over in bed when she heard Mouse's tail begin to whack against the pillow.

"What's wrong with this picture?" asked Cordelia, her voice amused.

Jane raised her head. For a moment she thought she was looking at a large, round, brightly colored marble. But then the marble coalesced into human form.

Cordelia shook her head. "Oh, how the mighty have fallen. You're usually the one who wakes me up."

"What are you doing here?" asked Jane, running a hand through her hair. "What time is it?"

"Just after eleven on Saturday morning. Hattie's been up for hours. So have I. And so have all the birdies and the bees. Well, maybe not the bees. They're probably frozen solid. But everything else is up and all atwitter."

"Well I'm not," said Jane, letting her head drop back on the pillow. "You shouldn't sneak up on a person when they're asleep."

"You do it all the time."

Jane and Cordelia had keys to each other's homes. It occurred to Jane now that it was a mistake. "What if I hadn't been alone?"

"I knocked. Well, knocked softly to be precise, but I did knock."

"When? Where?"

"On the front door before I let myself in."

"For your information, Kenzie's not here."

"I can see that."

Jane swung her legs out of bed and sat up.

"You look terrible."

"Thanks. I didn't get to sleep until after four."

"Heavens. You two are really burning up the sheets."

"Not because of Kenzie, Cordelia."

"No?"

"Do me a favor and wipe that prurient look off your face. In case you're interested, I was down at City Hall."

Cordelia stepped into the room, a frown forming. "And pray tell, why would that be?"

Jane explained briefly about Brittany's visit to the Lyme House last night. She finished with what she'd learned about Wesley Middendorf and a kid named Lukas Pouli. "From what I understand, the police got a partial print off the knife that killed Jason. If it matches either of those two, they're probably already in jail."

"What happened to Brittany?"

"I took her to a hotel. The police want her back today for more questioning, but she'll be safe for now."

Cordelia sniffed the air. "I think the coffee's done."

"You made coffee?"

"Before I came up. When on vacation, Cordelia Thorn knows how to live it up."

"That's a joke, right?"

"What was your first clue?"

After showering and dressing, Jane met Cordelia downstairs in the kitchen. "When does Octavia get back?" she asked, digging through a white pastry sack and selecting a prune kolachi.

"Not sure. All I hear is 'soon.'"

"What about Hattie—and your trip to Italy?"

"I'm predicting it's off. Unless I decide to take Hattie with me."

"I thought you refused to do that."

"Well, I got to thinking, what would Auntie Mame do? Being the beneficent person that I am, I'm thinking now that exposing Hattie to a little Italian culture might be a good thing. We could do the Vatican—"

"Only you would *do* the Vatican."

Cordelia plunked down on a chair, her bracelets clanging together like an iron wind chime on a windy day. "Speaking of Kenzie."

Jane had just about had it. "Don't you need the pretext of at least *some* segue when you change the subject to my personal life?"

"It's the subject du jour, Janey. No segue necessary. Besides, with the exception of your first and one true love, Christine, you seem to be attracted to the loose cannons of the world."

"And you're my protector?"

"If I have to be, yes." She unwrapped a knob of bubble gum and popped it into her mouth. "What did Kenzie want when she stopped by the restaurant yesterday?"

Jane smiled when she recalled the kiss. "Nothing much. She just came to say hi."

Cordelia tutted her disgust. "How you can be attracted to such a *personage* is beyond comprehension. All that sneaking around behind Alden's back. I have half a mind to call him and tell him what she's up to."

"Don't," said Jane, taking a bite of the kolachi. "Just . . . *don't*." As she sipped her coffee, the phone gave a double ring.

"That's your fax line, right?" said Cordelia.

Jane grabbed her coffee and pastry and hurried down the hallway to her study. When she turned to see if Cordelia was following, she saw her slip Mouse a piece of a cherry Danish. "I saw that."

"Saw what?" said Cordelia, innocence incarnate.

"I don't feed him junk food."

"I agree with you totally, Janey. I would never feed him junk food."

It was an old argument, one Jane never seemed able to win.

"We're still on for dinner tonight, yes?" called Cordelia.

"At the restaurant, if that's okay with you. You can try out some of the new fall dishes. They're really spectacular." She sat down behind her desk, hoping to find that the fax was from one of the newspapers she'd called yesterday. Sure enough, the *Cottonwood Herald* had come through. By the time the fax machine was done rolling, Jane had six pages in her hand.

Cordelia sauntered into the room, swinging her long beaded belt and chewing her gum. "Whatcha got?"

Jane glanced up. "You look like the second banana in a thirties comedy."

"*Never* say second banana in reference to me, Jane. I am always the primo banana. On the other hand, you've captured the essence of my idiom this morning."

"Good for me." Jane started sorting through the articles.

Cordelia lowered herself onto the couch. After crossing her legs, she adjusted her skirt over her knees and said, "Shoot."

"Shoot what?"

"Read me what you just got. I can tell you're dying to *share*."

Jane arranged them in order by date, starting with the earliest. "Okay, these are newspaper articles about Patsy Shore's abduction. Here's the first one."

She read out loud:

Cottonwood Herald
November 1, 1972

REAL-LIFE HALLOWEEN HORROR: COTTONWOOD GIRL KIDNAPPED

Patsy Eileen Shore, eight-year-old daughter of John and Maureen Shore, was abducted last night by two men in a white van near the intersection of Elmhurst Avenue and Brady Road. At the time of the kidnapping, Patsy was trick-or-treating with her brother, Jimmy, age fifteen. Jimmy gave chase in a family car, but lost control of the vehicle when it drove off the highway bridge over the Kettle River.

Thanks to quick police work, Jimmy was rescued from the submerged car and rushed to Stansfield Hospital, where he is listed in good condition.

No ransom note has been delivered to the Shore family, but the police are watching the situation closely.

Jane moved to the next page.

Cottonwood Herald

November 4, 1972

JOHN SHORE GIVES
PRESS CONFERENCE

On Thursday afternoon, John Shore, father of Patsy Shore, the child who was abducted from Cottonwood on Halloween night while trick-or-treating with her brother, appeared before the press today in Wichita, pleading for the man or men who kidnapped his daughter to return her unharmed.

Shore, 41, a factory foreman at the Ingle's Meat Processing plant in neighboring Willburn, Kansas, offered a five-thousand-dollar reward to anyone who could provide information that would lead to the recovery of his daughter. During the final moments of the TV interview, Mr. Shore said, "We are desperate to find Patsy. If she can hear my voice, I want her to know that we're doing everything we can to find her and bring her back home. We love you, Patsy." Mr. Shore then broke down and had to be led away.

"Boy," said Cordelia. "That must have been grim. Don't you wonder what happened to that little girl?"

"I do," said Jane.

"Do you think she could still be alive?"

"I don't know. But when you think of what she must have gone through—" She shuddered.

"If she is alive," said Cordelia, "she's got to be terribly damaged."

Jane flipped to the next newspaper article. "Listen to this."

Cottonwood Herald

November 11, 1972

NEW LEAD IN PATSY SHORE
ABDUCTION: POLICE FIND BLOODY FAIRY COSTUME

In a startling revelation, Wichita police today announced that the fairy costume believed to have been worn by Patsy Shore on the night she was abducted was found partially buried in a ditch along Hwy. 59, near Connersville, nineteen miles north of Wichita. Shortly after the announcement, John Shore, the father of Patsy Shore, identified it as belonging to his daughter.

In a statement released by the Cottonwood Sheriff's Office this morning, Deputy Sheriff Terrance Tuchman said that the costume was covered with blood. Experts with the Wichita PD are running tests to determine if the blood type on the costume is the same as that of the missing girl.

In a personal interview, Deputy Sheriff Tuchman said: "The fact that no body was found is significant. It could mean that Patsy is still alive. Then again, with the amount of blood on the clothing, it may be a long shot. But nobody's giving up hope. You can count on that."

"There sure are some sick people in this world," said Cordelia. Jane continued:

Cottonwood Herald
November 24, 1972

BLOOD ON HALLOWEEN
COSTUME A MATCH

Police released information yesterday confirming their suspicion that the blood found on Patsy Shore's fairy costume, the one dumped on the side of the road near Connersville, Kansas, is the same type as that belonging to Patsy Shore.

Asked for a comment, John Shore, Patsy's father, said, "I urge the public to continue to help my family search for Patsy. This is a setback, but I believe with all my heart and soul that Patsy is still alive and that one day soon, we will bring her home."

Jane examined the next page, reading through it silently. "Oh, my God."

"What?" said Cordelia.

She read a moment more. "Here's something Kenzie failed to tell me about." She read out loud:

Cottonwood Herald

March 30, 1973

COTTONWOOD BOY FOUND
MURDERED

Two children playing near Mason's Thicket early Sunday morning discovered the body of a young man who had been shot in the chest. Ryan Mullroy, the seventeen-year-old son of Leon and Bliss Mullroy, was a senior at Cottonwood High School. According to classmates, he was well liked by everyone. "Nobody can understand why this happened," said Hannah Matticchio, a friend of Ryan's who worked with him on the school newspaper.

Ryan is survived by his parents and three younger siblings. The County Sheriff's Office released a statement saying that a handgun had been found at the scene. Deputy Sheriff Terrance Tuchman told a reporter for the *Herald* that a forensic team had been called in from Wichita and had put time of death at between eight and midnight on Saturday night. So far, the police have no suspects in the crime, and no motive has been given.

Jane quickly moved on to the final article. "Listen to this."

Cottonwood Herald

April 3, 1973

BROTHER OF ABDUCTED
PATSY SHORE PRIMARY SUSPECT IN MURDER OF
RYAN MULLROY

Police officials today announced that James Shore, the sixteen-year-old brother of kidnap victim Patsy Shore, has been named the primary suspect in the murder of Ryan Mullroy.

Shore, a junior at Cottonwood High School, disappeared from his home the same night Mullroy was shot. A comparison of fingerprints taken from the gun used to kill Mullroy with prints found in the Shore home confirms James Shore was the shooter.

In an interview Deputy Sheriff Terrance Tuchman said: "We believe that there is a direct connection between Jimmy Shore's sudden disappearance, Ryan Mullroy's murder, and the abduction of Patsy Shore. Beyond that, I have nothing more to say at

277

this time. However, let me assure the public that we hope to have answers soon." John and Maureen Shore, the parents of Patsy and James, were unavailable for comment.

Jane let the last page fall to her desk. "He killed a boy."

"If," said Cordelia, "and I underline that word, Alden really is this Jimmy Shore."

They exchanged glances.

"I think he must be," said Jane.

"Then how come Kenzie left that part out? It's kind of an important point, wouldn't you say?"

"Maybe she doesn't know," said Jane.

"Yeah, right," snorted Cordelia. "And maybe I'll wake up tomorrow morning on the planet Mars."

Jane stared down at the fax pages. "If he murdered Ryan Mullroy, he'd still be wanted for the crime. Murder charges don't go away."

"I'll bet that's who hired Kenzie. Somebody who wants to put Mullroy's murderer in jail."

"It's possible." But Jane saw other possibilities too.

"On the other hand, wouldn't it be something if Pasty Shore did survive and she was the one who hired Kenzie." Cordelia tapped a long red nail against her chin. "Or, how about this? What if Kenzie *is* Patsy Shore. Wouldn't that be a kicker? Who knows what Jimmy Shore was up to all those years ago? Maybe she holds him responsible for what happened to her."

"Kenzie isn't Patsy Shore," said Jane firmly.

"Why not? She's about the right age."

Jane simply couldn't believe it. "She lied to me once. I don't think she'd do it again."

"Janey, think about it. If she did even a small amount of research on you, she would have learned that you've had some experience solving crimes. You're the wild card in all this, Janey. If she came here for, say, vengeance, she'd have to keep an eye on you. You've been pulled into Alden Clifford's life because of what happened at his son's wedding. You're smart, easily capable of foiling whatever plan she has going, so getting involved with you would be a good way to keep you off balance—and also a way to keep track of what information you might be uncovering.

You know what they say? Keep your friends close, but your enemies closer."

"I'm not her enemy."

"No, but you could be."

"You're building a house of cards, Cordelia."

"It's called a *theory*. And a very respectable one at that."

"You're saying that the only reason she's been with me is because she needs to keep an eye on me?"

"Give that lady a cigar."

Jane shook her head. "No. I don't believe it."

"You think it's true love."

"Of course not. But whatever it is, it's real. Something I haven't had in my life in a long time."

"Okay," said Cordelia. "I'm just saying I think you need to be careful."

Jane picked up her phone and tapped in the Cliffords' number.

"Who are you calling?"

"Kenzie."

The line rang and rang, and finally the answering machine picked up. "Kenzie," said Jane. "If you're there, I need to talk to you." She waited, checking the clock on her desk. It was almost noon. "Kenzie, please pick up the phone. This is important." Another few seconds went by. "Okay, I guess . . . I'll try later." As she hung up, she glanced over at Cordelia. "Where could she be? If she had to go out for some reason, either Alden or Mary has to be at the house for Lauren. So why isn't anybody answering?"

Cordelia shrugged her padded shoulders.

Jane had a bad feeling about it. As she sat back and looked at the faxes, the feeling only grew worse.

36

Late Saturday morning, Steven sat in a jail cell in downtown Minneapolis, feeling like he'd been hit by a truck. Just a few hours before, the police had broken down the door of his apartment and arrested him with a swiftness and force that had left him virtually speechless. They'd transferred him handcuffed in a squad car to an interrogation room, where a heavyset cop in a cheap suit had informed him that two of his dealers had just rolled over on him. Lukas and Wesley were in custody and were singing like a choir of fallen angels. They had Steven on multiple counts of drug trafficking and possession of illegal substances, and were attempting to prove he'd been in on the murder of Jason Vickner as well. They'd ID'd Lukas's prints on the murder weapon, so the assumption wasn't a huge leap. But it was a leap in the wrong direction and Steven went ballistic. He demanded to see his attorney.

Steven knew he was about to do some major time; the only question was how much. Speaking privately to the slime bag that took care of his legal affairs, Steven insisted that he knew nothing about Jason's murder. He wanted the lawyer to get those charges dropped, no matter what it took. Steven had information he figured the cops would want. His lawyer could broker the deal. Steven might be a criminal, but he wasn't a killer.

With his head sunk in his hands, he regretted the day he ever got involved with Lukas and Wesley. They'd been Cullen's friends, not his, but he'd reluctantly agreed to include them in because it was what his brother wanted. Steven had dealt drugs himself while he was a student at Evergreen. He didn't see any reason why somebody else shouldn't take over his trade when he left for college. Cullen was the obvious choice. Wesley and Lukas promised to bring in new customers, so Steven okayed it, on the condition that Cullen was top dog. Wesley and Lukas did what Cullen told them to do, no questions asked.

By the time Steven was a freshman at the U of M, he'd moved from dealer to small-time supplier, but even at a small-time level, he'd become a wealthy young man. He had to hide it from his dad, but that wasn't a big deal. His career in crime was going to pay for his future career as a doctor. It was the perfect plan, allowed him plenty of time to study without the necessity of finding a part-time job. And it would have worked, too, if it hadn't been for Cullen's two idiot buddies.

"Hegg?" called one of the guards, stepping up to the cell door and unlocking it. "You got a visitor."

"Who is it?"

"Don't know. Get up and turn around."

The guard cuffed him, then led him to the same room where he'd been interrogated. When the door was opened and Steven saw his father seated at the table, he felt like a needle had been shoved into the center of his heart.

His father stood, his face an agonized question mark.

"Dad. What—who called you?"

"Some police officer. I don't understand any of this, Steven. I don't understand why you're here, why this is happening." He kept shaking his head. "You told me yesterday you had nothing to do with drugs."

"I told you I didn't *do* drugs, Dad. And I don't."

"But you sell them?"

Steven nodded.

"What the hell kind of double-talk is that?" His father sank back down on his chair. "God in heaven," he said, staring at Steven as if he didn't recognize him.

Steven stepped farther into the room.

"How long?"

"Have I sold drugs? A long time."

"How long!"

Steven cringed at the anger in his dad's voice. "I was a sophomore in high school when I was first approached. I told you I'd smoked some marijuana when I was younger. That's how I got connected. First I sold pot, then other stuff."

"And . . . you . . . gave drugs . . . to your brother?"

The words hammered into Steven's body like bullets.

"Tell me!"

"No, I didn't give him drugs to *use*. He sold them. Just like me. I was his supplier. That's all."

"That's all? That's *all*!"

"Dad, you've got to calm down."

"You gave your brother drugs, Steven!"

"To sell."

"But he *took* them, don't you get it? He used them himself."

"No," said Steven. "Never. He promised me. He drank too much, sure. If I'd been around more, maybe I could have stopped that. And he was depressed. I see that now. But drugs, no. No way."

"Don't lie to me!"

"I'm not!"

"I talked to Alden Clifford last night. He said he'd helped Cullen get off crack. That's cocaine, right?"

"Yeah, but—"

"He said that Cullen was ashamed of himself. He made Clifford promise not to tell me that he used. He was clean when he died, but he was still fighting it. I can see that now. I should have seen it then, but I wanted to believe everything was all right, even in the face of all evidence to the contrary. I was willingly blind, Steven. I wanted the fairy tale. Good kids, good lives, everybody loves everybody. And when that didn't happen, I wanted to blame someone else for my own failures. You're doing the exact same thing."

"Dad, you've got to believe me—"

"Shut up!" His fist slammed into the table. "If you gave him drugs to *sell*, how do you know he didn't *use* some of them?"

"Because he promised," said Steven. His voice had disintegrated to a whine. Could it be true? Steven had asked him point-blank once if he used, but Cullen had insisted he didn't. Said he agreed with Steven. Drugs were for suckers. Steven held on to that because it gave him permission to go on doing what he wanted to do. "I should have spent more time with him, Dad. That's all. He didn't kill himself because of the drugs. He was depressed. Drinking too much. It wasn't drugs. It wasn't!" His body was shaking so hard it was an effort just to stand upright. "I trusted him. I told you that. It's what you taught me. To trust others. Don't hover over them. That way they can live up to their true potential."

"Steven, listen to yourself!" His dad twisted away from him, put his head down, almost between his knees. In a softer voice, he said, "That's total garbage and you know it. You're a drug dealer. A goddamn criminal. My *son* is a criminal! And you turned Cullen into one while you were at it. Maybe you can live with what you did—what you *are*—but he couldn't."

"It's not my fault! Dad, please! It was just a way to make some money. That's all. If people want to use, that's their problem. Right?"

His father's hands clenched into fists. "I could kill you for what you've done."

Steven backed up, then backed up more. "You don't mean that."

"I *should* kill you."

"I'm sorry. Dad, please. Listen to me." He hit the wall, then crumpled to the floor. "I'm so so sorry."

"My sons," whispered his father, closing his eyes. "I loved you both so much. You were my little guys. My whole life. I only wanted what was good for you. How on earth did we get here?"

Steven couldn't stand the pain in his father's voice. Tears streamed down his face. "I never meant to hurt you or Cullen. I never meant for any of this to happen."

When his father got up, Steven turned his head away. He drew his knees up against his chest, steeling himself for whatever his father was about to do. His father had never hit him before, but if he did now, Steven wouldn't blame him. He'd take it. He'd take it all and be a man.

But when the door closed and Steven looked up and found the room empty, the cushion of bravado he'd been hanging on to for dear life popped, dropping him to earth with a violent thud.

His father hadn't hit him. He'd done something far worse.

He'd left Steven alone.

37

Alden was startled awake by the sound of a ringing phone. He jerked his head toward the sound, but the blindfold blocked his vision. As he waited for the answering machine to pick up, his sluggish brain focused on the throbbing in his knee and the even worse throbbing in the back of his head. He had no idea what time it was. He assumed that while he was unconscious, his captor had rolled him into a blanket, then wrapped something tight around his body—maybe a rope, maybe duct tape. He could move his fingers, his elbows, and his feet, but as hard as he tried, he couldn't seem to leverage himself off the chair. Or maybe it was the couch.

He'd been sitting in the same position for what felt like days, although it was probably more like hours. Every time he heard a creak or a groan in the old house, he yelled at his captor to show himself, to get it over with.

Alden had spent his life hiding in a hole and now that hiding place had been found. He'd considered running, but realized he simply couldn't do it anymore. This was where he'd built his life. This was where he would make his last stand.

When the biker arrived on his doorstep a month ago and tossed that locket at his feet, he knew the jig was up. But whoever had tracked him was taking their old sweet time about finishing him off. So much so that Alden had become weary of waiting. He was standing on a trapdoor with an unseen hand holding the lever. Was it Patsy's hand? Everywhere he looked these days, he saw her face. He'd lived with her ghost for so long that she'd become part of his everyday life, like breath or food or water. He desperately didn't want to die, but if it came to that, he needed to know the truth.

The answering machine beeped.

"Kenzie, it's Jane. If you're there, I need to talk to you." Silence. "Kenzie, please pick up the phone. This is important." Another few seconds passed. "Okay, I guess . . . I'll try later." The answering machine gave the time: 11:51 A.M.

"Goodbye, Jane," called Alden. Apparently she didn't know that he'd fired Kenzie yesterday. He wanted to be alone, and figured he could take care of Lauren himself. He wished Lauren had gone with Gray yesterday. It would have made his life—and now perhaps his death—so much easier.

Alden was wide awake now, listening for any sound that might alert him to what was happening in the house. He'd heard footsteps on the stairs a while ago. Then the back door closing. He cursed himself when he thought of what his captor might have done to Lauren. Not that he had any real love in his heart for her. And that was sad. Just one more sad comment on a deeply sad life.

Alden drifted off again. He woke to the sound of the phone ringing again. This time it was Mary, calling to say she knew they needed to talk, but she wanted to give him some time to cool off.

He laughed to himself. He was anything but cool. Inside the blanket, he was sweating like a pig.

Mary went on to assure him that her affair with Tom Moline was over.

Yippee, thought Alden. "You might as well stay with him," he shouted. "I doubt I'll be around to care what you do."

She begged his forgiveness, told him she loved him with all her heart.

Alden gritted his teeth, wondering if he'd ever see her again. The machine gave the time: 6:42 P.M. Awhile later, the back door opened and then shut. Soft footsteps approached from the dining room.

"Who's there?" he called, twisting his head back and forth, trying once again to see out the edges of the blindfold. The room was dark now. Dark and quiet. "Dammit! Tell me who the hell you are!" He had to face the truth. Unless a miracle happened, he was going to die.

Across the room, the rocking chair creaked with the weight of a body settling into it. He could feel his captor's eyes on him, watching him, hating him, condemning him to death. "You're a coward, you know that? If you're going to kill me, at least show me your face."

A hammer cocked.

Alden's body tightened. "Do it! Just . . . do it! Get it over with!"

But nothing happened. No explosion. Just the suffocating weight of possibility that any moment could be his last.

"Is this it? I'm supposed to sit here and wait for the bullet? Sweat it out? Hell, I've been sweating out this day all my life. If you're expecting me to beg, you can forget it. I don't give a damn what you do. I deserve it." Only thing was, he did want to live. And he wanted to see her face.

"I figure I must know you, right? You crept into my life when I wasn't looking. You saw my picture in a paper somewhere, thought you recognized me. I tried to convince myself you were dead, you know, that it didn't make any sense to look for you anymore because you were gone. But you're not gone. You hate me for what you think I did to you. But don't you want to hear it from me? What really happened the night you were kidnapped? Aren't you even a little curious?"

More silence.

He waited this time, hoping his words would sink in. "I admit it. I have no idea what you've gone through. I thought about it millions of times, imagined millions of different scenarios. That's why I hoped you *did* die, that you weren't twisted into a creature that wasn't even human." He shook his head. "My intimate ghost has turned into a very real, very alive ghoul. A fine distinction, I suppose. But you know what I mean. Maybe I'm sitting here talking to someone else. I hope I am. I hope you're dead. If you are, the little girl I loved so much gets to stay young and innocent forever."

He heard the rocking chair creak again. She was up now, standing over him. He could feel the heat from her body, smell the stale coffee on her breath. He was so thirsty, his mouth so terribly dry, it was hard to talk. And he wanted to keep on talking because he still needed answers. "If you're not going to shoot me right away, could I have a glass of water?"

He felt her body press close to his, heard a cap being unscrewed, smelled the stink of alcohol as the neck of the bottle was shoved at his mouth. She must have seen the vodka behind the couch. He pulled his head away. "I don't want booze, I want water."

"This or nothing," whispered the voice.

He was so parched, he drank it down until it was all gone. Almost immediately, ripples of mellow warmth began to seep into his muscles.

"You don't have to whisper, you know. I know who you are."

"Do you, Jim?"

This time, she didn't move away.

"I've been sitting here, thinking about that ghost story I used to tell you when you were little. Remember? The one about the little girl who got lost in the big woods after dark. She spent the whole night there, met some ghosts that scared her half to death, but she crawled out of the forest the next morning and somehow found her way home. Only problem was, the legend of the big woods said that if a little girl spent the night there, she'd become a ghost herself. And that's what happened. The only person who could still see her was her brother. But he couldn't help her because she was dead. Do you remember what you always asked me when I finished that story?"

No response.

"You said, why didn't the brother use some magic to bring her back to life? I always explained that he wanted to, but he didn't have the power. And then you'd say, well, maybe the little girl had special powers now because she was a ghost. I figured that made sense." He paused for a moment, wishing he could see her face. "I've wondered many times if you'd spent the night in the big woods, Patsy. You might have been there for years before you got out. But when you did, even though you thought you were alive, were you dead? Did that part come true? I'm in no position to ask a favor, I realize that, but if you'd grant me one, that's what I most want to know. I need to understand if that's how you feel inside, because ever since you were taken away from me, it's how I feel. All that should be sacred and mysterious in my life died when I lost you." His chin began to quiver. "Did somebody kill that in you too? Is that what you're here to tell me?"

With a sudden jerk, the blindfold was ripped off and he was staring up into her face.

"My God," he said, his mouth dropping open. "But . . . it can't be. Your eyes. They're brown."

Lauren stared down at him.

"Are you Patsy? Are you!"

She raised the gun and pointed it at his forehead.

"Are you wearing colored contacts? Sure, that's it. God, it *is* you. All this time and I didn't know." Beads of sweat trickled down his face. The booze surged through his bloodstream, blasting away his inhibitions. "But . . . you married my son. Why would you do that?"

"He's not your son," she said, her voice full of disdain. "He's nothing like you."

"Patsy. God, Patsy!"

"When I finally found you, I needed a way into your life. Nick was the door. I didn't care if I hurt him. But I'm sorry now that I did. He didn't deserve it."

"Did you put the drugs in the wedding food?"

"Of course not. That's not what I'm talking about." Slowly, she released the hammer on the .32, then switched on a light next to the couch. "I'd say you've made yourself some enemies in your new life, Jimmy. In my experience, if somebody wants to hurt you, they hurt you. Whoever's after you wants to scare you, play with your head. But that just made it easier for me to slip into your life. Chaos is a great cover."

He had so many questions. "What happened to you? Where did Frank take you?"

"Who's Frank?"

"The man who abducted you. Don't you remember?"

She backed up, pulled a chair closer to the couch, and sat down. "You first. Tell me what you were up to back in Cottonwood, Jim. I've waited a long time to hear that."

He tried to see the little girl in the grown woman, but she wasn't there. He felt that something was wrong, something didn't add up, but maybe his expectations were the problem. After all this time, all this agonizing over her fate, did he actually expect to find some remnant of the little girl he'd once loved? "Just tell me the truth, okay? Are you my sister?"

"What do you think?"

"I don't know!"

"Would you like me to be?"

This *was* torture. "Yes."

"Then I'm Patsy."

"How do I know for sure?"

"You don't deserve 'for sure,' Jim."

"But your face. The bone structure—"

"The last time you saw me I was eight years old. You've changed too."

"But you must have recognized me."

"Believe me, Jim, I'd know you anywhere. After what you did to me, I made sure I'd never forget what you looked like. I knew one day I'd find you."

"You hate me."

"What I feel for you goes way beyond hate."

He could see it in her eyes. "Were you the one on the motorcycle? The one who threw the gold locket with your picture at me?"

She smiled. "Nice touch, don't you think? You deserved a warning."

"But . . . you met Nick last June. Why did it take you so long to make your move?"

"Time was never the issue. At first, I needed to make sure you were who I thought you were. And then, after I had that nailed down, I wanted to get to know you, see what kind of man you turned into. You surprised me there, Jimmy. I thought for a while that maybe you'd changed. But then, true to form, I find out you've been seducing your students. You're damaged goods. You were from the day you were born. Who knows? Maybe you're evil, but I suspect you're basically just stupid."

He hated what she was saying. He wanted to hurt her. If his hands were free, he would have. "I never touched those boys."

"No? Well, what the hey. Doesn't matter much now."

"Because you're going to kill me."

"That's the idea. But unlike you, I'm not stupid. I'm going to make it look like a suicide—and I'll get away with it too. I wrapped you in that blanket so you wouldn't have any marks on your ankles or wrists. When I stuff *your* gun in your mouth and pull the trigger, people are going to think, Gosh, poor Alden. His wife had just left him for another man. The community where he lived and worked realized he was a pedophile. It was just too much for him, so he ended it. Boo hoo."

"Sounds like it could work."

She leaned back in her chair, settled into herself with a satisfied look on her face.

"Hey, what about Mom and Dad! Don't you want to know what happened to them?" The alcohol was making him giddy.

Her expression darkened.

"Well, see, Mom drank herself to death. I wasn't around, so I got this thirdhand, but by the time she died, everyone in Cottonwood knew she was an alki. I guess she'd wander all over town after dark looking for her lost children. Kind of tragic and kind of predictable, huh? And Dad, well, after Mom died, seems he took the car out for a spin one night and drove it into a tree. Some people thought it was an accident. I knew better. I guess maybe you're right about the stupidity thing. I ruined four lives because of what I did. That's quite an accomplishment for one stupid guy."

"You ruined more lives than just four," said Lauren. "Many more lives."

Alden turned to the front hall as a key slipped into the front door lock. A moment later, Kenzie walked in.

"What's going on?" she said, coming to a full stop just inside the living-room arch. Her eyes fell to the gun in Lauren's hand, then rose to take in the entire scene. "Lauren, what are you doing? You said you'd wait for me. And why's he all tied up like that?"

"Shut up," said Lauren, rising from her chair.

"I thought we had this worked out."

"Change of plans."

"What change?" Kenzie's gaze zeroed in on the gun again.

"Don't try to stop me. It ends right here. In this room."

"Wait a minute. This wasn't what I signed on for."

"You do what I tell you."

"Or else what? We've got all the proof we need. It's time to call the police."

Alden's eyes ping-ponged between the two women.

"No police," said Lauren, moving away from the chair. "From here on out, we handle it my way."

"You never said anything about hurting him, about—"

"You think he deserves to live?"

"I think it's a police matter."

Lauren shook her head. "You know what the justice system is like. I'm not letting him get off on some idiotic technicality."

Kenzie unzipped her coat, her eyes shifting warily between Lauren and Alden. "Did you ask him about Ryan? Did you even *ask*?"

"Ryan," repeated Alden, suddenly confused.

"Ryan Mullroy," said Lauren. "Remember him? The young guy you gunned down before you left Cottonwood."

"Sure, but . . . who was Ryan to you?" The mellow rush from the vodka was all gone now. In its place, Alden was gripped by a sudden feeling of panic.

"He was our brother," said Kenzie.

He looked at Lauren, searched her face. "You mean, you're not Patsy? You're not my sister?"

"What did you tell him?" demanded Kenzie.

Lauren shrugged. "I was just playing with him, seeing what he'd say." She turned to him, her eyes as cold and hard as two ball bearings. "Who knows what hell Patsy lived through? Couldn't have been too much worse than the one you condemned me and my sister to."

He couldn't get his mind around it. He started to shake. "She's got to be here. I have to talk to her. Don't you get it? I deserve to die. Okay, I accept that. But not yet. Not until I know what happened to her!"

Lauren raised both her eyebrows at him. "Well then, Jim, in that case, I'd say you're in for one helluva disappointment."

38

Jane pulled her Mini over to the side of the road and flipped open her cell phone. She'd just pulled out of the Ramada Inn's parking lot. Pressing Cordelia's number on her speed dial, she waited through several rings until the phone picked up.

"This is Cordelia. I am floating on a cosmic high, doing research into the psyche of my inner toddler. Whoever this is, make it quick."

"Cordelia, it's Jane."

"Janey, hi! Wassup?"

"It's Kenzie. I can't find her."

"Well, hot damn. The age of miracles is not past. Let's hope she stays lost."

"Cordelia!"

"Kenzie is *not*—praise the Lord and pass the ammunition—my problem."

"Just listen. I left a message for her on the answering machine at the Cliffords' this morning, and another one on her motel phone and cell phone this afternoon. I asked her to call me back, but she hasn't."

"Where are you now?"

"I drove over to her motel and banged on her door. The desk clerk said he hadn't seen her all day. I'm just about to head down to Evergreen, to the Cliffords' place. I don't know what else to do."

"Janey, you listen to me. You stay out of this."

"But what if she's in trouble?"

"She probably went shopping at the *Über* Mall of America and got lost in Camp Snoopy. Or she's off getting a seaweed wrap."

"Cordelia, she doesn't do things like that."

"How do you know? All civilized people get seaweed wraps, Jane. Is she civilized?"

"Generally."

"Well, there you have it."

"Look, I thought I should let you know that I might not make it back in time for our dinner date tonight."

"Janey, it's dark out. Let Kenzie take care of herself."

"I'll call you when I get back."

"You hang up on me one more time, Jane Lawless, and I won't be responsible for what I do!"

"Later, babe."

"Stop! Don't touch that button! I mean it, Jane. Don't you hang up!"

She clicked the phone off.

Jane took 35W south. Just as she passed the Cliff Road exit, she ran into a traffic tie-up. By the time she passed the two-car crash, both vehicles had been moved off the freeway and traffic was beginning to thin out. She'd lost nearly half an hour, but she wasn't in a race, merely in a hurry.

It was going on eight when Jane finally drove into Evergreen. She hung a left on Willow and headed west out of town on county road 71. She slowed as she neared the Cliffords' place. Her headlights caught Kenzie's Dodge Ram truck parked on the opposite side of the highway. That's odd, she thought to herself. Why hadn't she parked on the property?

Jane pulled her car to a stop opposite the truck and got out. Her eyes swept across the road, but everything seemed quiet. Pulling the collar of her sheepskin jacket up around her neck, she walked up the long drive to the Cliffords' farmhouse. There was a light on in Lauren's bedroom, and one in the living room. The rest of the place was dark.

Alden's car was parked in the drive, exactly where Kenzie's truck had been the day Jane and Cordelia had stopped by to see Lauren.

Instead of ringing the front doorbell, Jane decided to walk around the outside of the house and see what she could see. Most of the blinds were up, so it was pretty easy to look in. A low-watt bulb burned over the stove in the kitchen, but otherwise, the room was dark and quiet. She examined the backyard, tiptoed up the steps, and peered into Alden's study. Again, everything was quiet.

When she came around the far side of the house, she saw that the living-room window was too high for her to get a good look inside. She glanced around for something to stand on, but finding nothing suitable, she returned to the backyard and grabbed a thick piece of firewood. When she placed it under the window, it raised her up a good six inches. She squinted through the screen and the dusty glass, into the dim light.

"Jesus," she whispered.

Alden was tied up on the couch. Lauren stood a few feet away, holding a gun on Kenzie. Jane ducked so they couldn't see her, not that it probably mattered since nobody seemed to be looking at the window.

Crouching down, Jane was seized by a moment of doubt. What was going on in there? Someone had to get inside and stop Lauren before she used the gun, but who was doing what to whom? She inched her head up again and watched as Kenzie and Lauren talked to each other. They were clearly angry, though Jane couldn't hear what they were saying. As she examined the living room and then the dining room, her eyes caught sight of movement in the window on the opposite side of the house. Someone was standing outside the dining-room window waving at her.

"What the—" Jane jumped down off the log and rushed around to the front yard, nearly bumping into Cordelia who was rushing around from the other side of the house.

"What are you doing here?" Jane meant to whisper, but it came out as more of a muffled hiss.

"I told you. If you hung up on me, there was no telling what I'd do. I asked Cecily to stick around and put Hattie to bed, then I hopped in the Hummer and motored my way down here to save your ass, *as usual*. What the hell's going on in there?"

"I don't know," said Jane. She looked up at the porch. "But we've got to stop it before it gets out of hand."

"You don't call *that*"—Cordelia swung her thumb at the house—"out of hand?"

"Keep your voice down." Jane could hear shouting coming from the living room. If they were shouting, that meant the tension was escalating. "I need to get inside."

"You *need* a lobotomy."

"Do you have your cell phone with you?"

"Why?"

"Here's my idea. I ring the doorbell. They let me in. You call 911. You tell the cops to get here on the double. Then you create a diversion. The diversion gives me just enough time to get the drop on Lauren."

"Or get your head blown off."

"Think positive."

"Right. You're a believer in the Norman Vincent Peale school of hostage negotiation."

"Cordelia! Just do what I asked, okay?"

"What do you mean by 'a diversion'?"

Jane was already up on the porch. Over her shoulder, she whispered, "You're the creative director. You come up with something."

"This is dangerous, Janey. Guns kill people! Maniacs kill people too!"

"Just . . . run up the back steps, okay? Make a racket upstairs. Pound on the door. Break a window. Anything that's loud." She stood by the front door and pressed the bell.

The shouting stopped.

A second later, Kenzie appeared. When she drew the door back and saw who'd come to call, she stepped outside. "Jane, hi." Her eyes darted over Jane's shoulder. "Are you alone?"

"Yes. Can I come in?"

"I, ah—" She smiled. "This isn't a good time."

"Why not?" asked Jane, shoving past her into the front hall.

"Jane, stop," said Kenzie, twisting around.

But it was too late. Lauren walked out of the living room holding the gun. "This is just great," she said, her eyes locking on Kenzie. "Now what are we going to do?"

"*We?*" repeated Jane. She'd been right to have doubts. Obviously, she'd misunderstood what was going on.

Lauren motioned for Jane to walk in front of her into the living room.

"Alden? Are you okay?" asked Jane.

"You shouldn't have come," he said, his voice a deadened, dull rasp. His face looked badly bruised.

"Just listen to me for a second," said Kenzie, turning to Lauren. As she talked, she stepped in front of Jane. "I'm leaving and I'm taking Jane with me. No problems. No questions. All you have to do is let us go."

"I can't."

"Sure you can."

"Why did you have to get chummy with her?" demanded Lauren. "You've ruined everything."

Jane touched the back of Kenzie's jacket. She was wearing her holster. The jacket was short, but it covered the gun. Jane couldn't lift it without Lauren noticing.

Kenzie raised her hands to her hips, pushing the jacket back, allowing Jane easier access to the holster. "What did you think I'd do? I'm not with you on this one, Lauren. You can't kill all three of us. It's not in you."

"Says who?"

Jane kept her eyes on Lauren, but her hand found the gun.

"Says me. Your sister."

Jane's eyes widened. "Her *what?*"

In the next instant, the world exploded. Glass shattered. Plaster and lath blasted inward as the Hummer crashed through the dining-room wall.

Jane pushed Kenzie out of the way and lunged at Lauren, slamming her to the ground. The gun flew out of Lauren's hand. "Grab it," yelled Jane, but Kenzie didn't need directions. She'd already pulled her own gun.

Lauren grabbed Jane by the throat and they tumbled together on the floor.

"Stop it!" yelled Kenzie. "Lauren, let her go."

Lauren pressed her thumbs hard into Jane's neck. Suddenly Jane couldn't breathe.

Kenzie fired off a shot. "I said let her go! *Now.*" She moved around so she could look into her sister's eyes. "It's over, Lauren. We got what we came for. It's time to stop fighting."

Lauren stared up at Kenzie's face.

"Jane's not your enemy. Let her go."

Lauren released her grip and sank down on the carpet.

As the dust settled around them, Cordelia climbed out of the front seat. She watched calmly as the dining-room light fixture crashed on top of the collapsed dining-room table. Turning to Jane, she shrugged. "Was that diverting enough for you?"

Two Nights Later

39

"Mine," said Hattie.

Jane and Hattie sat at Cordelia's dining-room table drawing monsters. Jane wanted to use the blue crayon, but Hattie refused to give it up. She was into owning things right now. According to Cordelia, Hattie owned nearly everything in the apartment.

"Learning a new word, like *mine,* is very good, Hattie. But could I use the blue crayon for just a second? I need to draw some ears on my monster and I thought blue would look best."

Hattie scribbled for a few seconds more, then looked up at Jane and smiled. "Hi."

"Hi," said Jane.

She dropped the blue crayon on Jane's piece of paper.

"Thank you, Hattie."

Out from the back of the loft came Cecily, dragging a trunk stuffed with clothes and other essentials. She looked hot and sweaty, and about ready to drop. Cordelia flitted about the room, issuing orders to the men she'd hired to haul all their luggage to the airport. Two vans had been enlisted. It wasn't only Cordelia's and Cecily's "necessities" that were flying with them to Switzerland, but Octavia's and Hattie's too. Marion, Cordelia's girlfriend, would meet them in Geneva.

Octavia popped her head out of the kitchen. "Fifteen minutes, ladies.

If we're not out the door by seven, the plane will leave without us and my Hollywood career will tank before it even gets off the ground."

Cecily walked by Jane and winked. She was, as she so aptly put it, "totally psyched" that she was getting to go along on the location shoot. Cecily might have been hired merely to take care of one of the actor's kids, but people, she pointed out, got discovered in all sorts of ways.

Cordelia materialized next to Jane with a list. "Here you go, Janey. This is everything I need you to do while I'm away. Water the plants. Feed the cats. Make sure my Humvee gets all buffed out after the garage is done repairing the dent. Oh, and Melville. Remember to drag him around the bathtub every day or so. He loves it. And then, I have some cleaning you need to pick up. Some library books that need to go back to the library. Oh, and—"

Jane grabbed the list. "I can read. I'll figure it out."

Octavia called for Cordelia to come help her, so Cordelia flitted off.

Jane was glad Cordelia's vacation, although altered beyond recognition, would still happen. Even though Cordelia was being blasé about it, Jane knew she was secretly ecstatic to be able to watch a movie being filmed. Apparently, she and Octavia had buried the hatchet, although they both knew where it was interred, so they would doubtless live to fight another day.

At two minutes to seven, Octavia stood by the door and clapped her hands. "Everyone out. Our chariots await."

Cordelia floated regally past the dining-room table in her new fake fur-trimmed coat and hat. Hattie had on her pajamas with the feet in them. Cecily had stuffed her feet into a pair of red sneakers, but the shoes kept falling off. Hattie was also wearing her favorite coat—the purple one. She hated pink. Hated all pastels. Already, she had the makings of an unusual child.

"Come on, baby," said Octavia, motioning her to the door. "We're flying in a *big* plane tonight."

Hattie wobbled over, looked up at her mother for a second, and suddenly started to cry.

"What's wrong, honey?" Octavia crouched down and tried to hug her, but Hattie pulled away.

She ran straight to Cordelia. "Mine," she said, yanking on Cordelia's hand. "Tight." She held up her arms.

Cordelia's face flushed with pleasure. "Of course I'll hold you tight. I'll hold you tight all the way to Switzerland if you want."

Octavia looked a little put out by the interaction, but she was too busy to let something so insignificant bother her.

Jane and Cordelia glanced at each other. They both had tears in their eyes. Hattie had made a conquest since coming to Minnesota. She had something better in her life than an Auntie Mame. She had an Auntie Cordelia.

As everyone filed out, Jane kissed Hattie on the cheek, then gave Cordelia a bear hug, holding on a little longer than normal. "I love you, kiddo. You be safe—and have a great time."

"I will," said Cordelia, still wiping tears from her eyes. "I don't know what's come over me. I've turned into a water faucet in my old age." She smiled at Jane, squeezed her hand, and then she was gone.

Jane closed the door and switched off all the lights. She loved the loft at night with the panorama of downtown Minneapolis spread out in front of her like a magic carpet, thousands of twinkling stars embedded in the fabric. She had one more event on her social calendar tonight. One more person she had to say goodbye to.

At seven-thirty, there was a knock on the door.

When Jane opened it, she found Kenzie standing outside in the hallway. "Everybody gone?" she asked, looking around.

"We're alone," said Jane.

Kenzie stepped inside. "Wow, this is some view. I can see why you asked me to meet you here."

"I've opened a bottle of Frascati," said Jane.

"Sounds good." Kenzie took off her coat and tossed it over a chair.

"You're not wearing the holster anymore," said Jane, pouring the wine.

"Don't need it."

"You really thought Alden could be that dangerous?"

"He killed my brother. I figured I'd better be prepared."

Jane had only seen Kenzie once since Saturday night, the night all hell broke loose at the Cliffords'. Alden had been arrested and taken to jail. Lauren had been arrested too, as had Kenzie. They were charged with attempted murder, but the charges against Kenzie had been dropped by Sunday morning because it became apparent that she had no knowledge of her sister's plan to murder Alden.

After Kenzie was processed out, Jane drove her back to the Ramada. Kenzie was exhausted by the all-night interrogation and deeply worried about her sister, but she tried to answer as many of Jane's questions as she could. Mainly she wanted Jane to understand that she felt horribly guilty for all the lies she'd told, but that she figured she hadn't had a choice. She and Lauren were afraid that if Alden got wind of what they were up to, he might run. And if he did, they'd be right back to square one. They'd have to start their search for him all over again. There was too much at stake for Kenzie to let that happen.

Kenzie explained that Lauren had been searching for Jimmy Shore all of her adult life. When she saw Alden's picture in a San Antonio paper, she quit her job the next day and flew to Minneapolis—she was that sure she'd found her man. Kenzie said she saw now what she'd failed to see earlier—that her sister's desire to put the man who murdered their brother behind bars was no longer just a search, it had become an obsession.

Right before she left to go up to her motel room, Kenzie said that meeting someone like Jane was the last thing she ever expected to happen to her while she was in Minnesota. But it had, and even if Jane never wanted to see her again, she wasn't sorry.

There were so many things left to say, but Kenzie was too tired to continue, so they'd made a date for tonight.

Jane spent most of the morning helping Cordelia get ready for her trip. Mary Clifford had called Cordelia around one, saying she needed to hear a friendly voice. She explained that, in the next few days, Alden would be transferred back to Kansas, where he would stand trial for the murder of Ryan Mullroy. She also said that Nick was in a great rehab unit now, and that he was getting speech and physical therapy every day. Since he was in such competent hands, Mary didn't feel guilty leaving him. She planned to follow Alden to Kansas, to be there to support him during the trial. She said she'd made a lot of mistakes. So had Alden. She didn't know what the future held for either of them, but she still loved him and had to see this through to the end.

Jane handed Kenzie a glass of wine. "I don't even know your last name. Is it Nelson? Or Mullroy?"

"Mullroy," said Kenzie. "I bought those fake IDs from a friend of Lauren's. I figured they might come in handy. Jane, you have to understand. We didn't have any kind of hard and fast plan, we just knew we needed proof that Alden was Jimmy Shore. Our idea was to somehow embed ourselves in his life. We never expected to actually get into his house. But once we were sure we had him, we planned to take the information to the police and let them handle it from there."

"But Lauren had her own ideas about what to do with him."

"Yeah. Unfortunately, she did. But I found out this morning that Alden flatly denied that Lauren tried to kill him. He wants her released. Says he'll cooperate with the police, but only if they let her go. Apparently, he feels she was entitled to some payback, but that she's no murderer. You don't know how relieved I am. She could be out as early as tomorrow morning."

"What will she do?"

"Probably go see Nick. She's so sorry for what happened to him. I may be wrong, but I think she's actually in love with him. She didn't realize it until she nearly lost him. But with everything that's happened, I don't really think they have much of a chance."

They stood in front of the windows looking down on the city lights.

"That day I first saw you up in Alden's study," said Jane. "I thought you were singing to yourself, but you weren't, were you. You were talking to Lauren."

Kenzie sighed. "Yeah, I was. I was afraid maybe you'd seen her standing in the doorway. If you'd arrived just a few minutes earlier, you would have seen us together in the study. That would have blown everything."

"You were playing a dangerous game."

"We had to if we were going to bring our brother's murderer to justice."

"Your brother. What was he like?"

"I don't remember him as well as Lauren does. I was six when he died, Lauren was ten. We have another brother too. Gavin. But he was already off in college when Ryan died. Lauren and I have never been particularly close to him. But Ryan, he was great. More like a father to us than a brother. Our dad was always gone, either at work, or golfing, or whatever the hell he did with his free time. And our mother, well, she never really wanted kids. I always felt like we were in her way, that she had more important things to do. Ryan not only played with us, he took care of us. Lauren adored him. When he died, she didn't speak for almost a year. Actually, when Nick was injured, it made sense to me that Lauren stopped talking. Sure, it was a way into Alden's house, but she did shut down for a day or two. It's the way she copes with stress."

"I know so little about you," said Jane.

Kenzie turned to look at her. "You know what's important."

"But where do you live? What do you do for a living?"

"Well," she said, taking a sip of wine, "I've lived in Chadwick, Nebraska, for the past eight years. I'm a professor of cultural anthropology at Chadwick State College."

"A teacher?"

"Afraid so. Not as sexy as a PI huh?"

"Forget the PI. You mean to tell me you're not really a cowboy?"

Kenzie laughed and looked down at her boots. "Well, now that gets a little tricky. Depends on what you mean by cowboy. I own a house on about thirty acres of land. And I've got two horses and a bunch of chickens. The chickens I tolerate because I like fresh eggs, but the horses, well, they're probably my two best friends."

Jane liked the sound of that. "You like your life."

"Yeah, I do. But it can get lonely."

"I wish you didn't have to go back. I suppose you've got tenure."

"Matter of fact, I don't. But I should have it by this time next year." She moved a few inches closer to Jane. "I don't suppose there's any chance you'd sell your restaurant and open up a hamburger shack in Chadwick."

Jane's smile had some sadness in it. "My life is here. All my friends and family are here."

"Got it." Kenzie stared straight ahead.

"We both know that long-distance romances never work."

"Never," said Kenzie. She took another sip of wine, then curled her fingers around Jane's hand. "But, hey, I'd give it a shot if you would."

"Deal."

"You'll have to come down and meet my horses. If they like you, you're in."

Jane laughed. "Same goes for my family."

"This is beginning to sound serious."

"Could be. It just could be."

Standing here, looking down on the city she loved, with Kenzie standing next to her, Jane couldn't remember a time when she'd felt happier. Life had a way of tossing curve balls at you, but sometimes those curves were really gifts in disguise. Maybe, just maybe, Kenzie would turn out to be one of those gifts.